*Praise for*

"An outstanding series. The American Patriot books are the most complete, complex, and textured retelling of the Revolutionary War I've found in historical fiction. Hochstetler is not only a masterful storyteller, but a genuine historian. These are timeless classics, destined to be read—and relished—more than once."

—JOCELYN GREEN, AWARD-WINNING AUTHOR OF THE HEROINES
BEHIND THE LINES CIVIL WAR SERIES

"Reading J. M. Hochstetler's The American Patriot Series is like watching a thrilling historical television mini-series. With each new season, something new enthralls the reader and keeps her coming back for more. In the long-awaited Book Five, *Valley of the Shadow,* Hochstetler maintains her gripping action, suspense, and star-crossed romance. Once I started reading, I couldn't put it down. I highly recommend this latest installment in a very fine, meticulously researched American Revolution series."

—LOUISE M. GOUGE, AUTHOR OF *Then Came Love*

"In *Valley of the Shadow,* master wordsmith J. M. Hochstetler has woven together an enthralling page turner brimming with authentic history, thrilling suspense, breathtaking description, and memorable characters. The love letters written between Jonathan and Elizabeth are among the most beautiful and emotive I've ever read. The golden thread running throughout this intricate tapestry depicts a loving God who will bring about the best for those who love and trust Him no matter the circumstances. I eagerly await Book Six in this amazing series, The American Patriot."

—SUSAN F. CRAFT, SIBA AWARD-WINNING AUTHOR
OF *The Chamomile* AND *Laurel*

"This series about the American Revolution should be in every high school and library in the U.S. and Canada. It brings history alive with complete accuracy."

—Bonnie Toews, author of *The Consummate Traitor* and *Treason and Triumph*

"I adore the way you portray the emotions of your characters while keeping the historical aspect pure. I love the delicate balance of the romance, and how you managed to keep the tension going without it driving the reader (me) over the edge. This is really a powerful book and I can hardly wait to read the next installment."

— Patricia Riddle Gaddis author of *Battered but not Broken* and *Dangerous Dating,* and editor of Angels column, Bauer Publishing

"The author's detailed building of the plot, and the skill of detailed creation of characters, makes this series the best one ever! In today's world, atheists will object to the author's references of God in the lives of the characters. As a Christian, I found it fascinating!"

—Jim Barham *(Amazon)*

"These books have it all—romance, suspense, and adventure—against the backdrop of the American Revolution. Through these books I have learned so much about the real life historical characters and the battles that were won and lost in the Sons and Daughters of Liberty's pursuit of freedom."

—Sher *(Amazon)*

# Valley of the Shadow

## THE AMERICAN PATRIOT SERIES
### ~Book 5~

# J. M. HOCHSTETLER

ELKHART, IN
46514 USA

Published by Sheaf House. Requests for information should be addressed to:

Editorial Director
Sheaf House Publishers
1703 Atlantic Avenue
Elkhart, IN 46514

*jmshoup@gmail.com*
*www.sheafhouse.com*

Library of Congress Control Number: 2015903718

ISBN: 978-1-936438-26-6 (softcover)

All scripture quotations are from the King James Version of the Bible. The verses quoted are: p. 37, 2 Kings 6:16; p. 127, Isaiah 42:7; p. 161, Psalm 23:4; p. 262, John 15:13.

The hymn quoted on pp. 428–429 is "Jesus, Lover of My Soul," by Charles Wesley, originally titled "Temptation."

Cover design by Marisa Jackson.

Cover image: *Combat d'Ouessant, 23 juillet 1778*
      Théodore Gudin
      1839
      © Musée national de la Marine/P. Dantec

Maps by Jim Brown of Jim Brown Illustration.

MANUFACTURED IN THE UNITED STATES OF AMERICA

This book is dedicated to the men and women who suffered and died aboard British prison ships in New York Harbor during the Revolution. May their sacrifice for the cause of liberty never be forgotten.

*Yea, though I walk through the valley of the shadow of death, I will fear no evil: for Thou art with me.*

—PSALM 23:4

*By faith Abraham, when he was called to go out into a place which he should after receive for an inheritance, obeyed; and he went out, not knowing whither he went. By faith he sojourned in the land of promise, as in a strange country . . . for he looked for a city which hath foundations, whose builder and maker is God . . .*

*These all died in faith, not having received the promises, but having seen them afar off, and were persuaded of them, and embraced them, and confessed that they were strangers and pilgrims on the earth. For they that say such things declare plainly that they seek a country. And truly if they had been mindful of that country from whence they came out, they might have had opportunity to have returned. But now they desire a better country, that is an heavenly: wherefore God is not ashamed to be their God: for He hath prepared for them a city.*

—HEBREWS 11:9*a*, 10; 13-16

An award-winning author and editor, J. M. Hochstetler is the daughter of Mennonite farmers, a graduate of Indiana University, a professional editor, and a lifelong student of history. With Bob Hostetler, she authored *Northkill*, Book 1 of the Northkill Amish Series, closely based on the inspiring true story of their Hochstetler ancestors. *Northkill* won the 2014 INDIEFAB Book of the Year Bronze Award for Adult Historical Fiction. Her contemporary novel *One Holy Night* was the Christian Small Publishers 2009 Book of the Year and finalist for the American Christian Fiction Writers 2009 Carol Award.

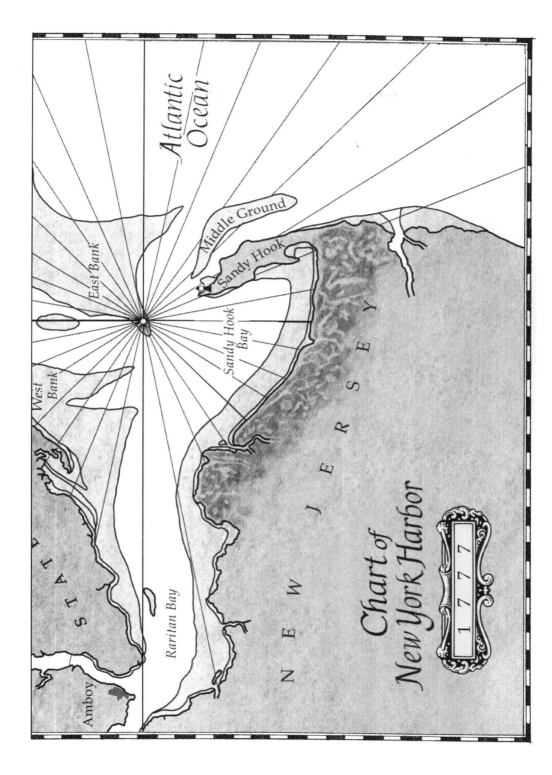

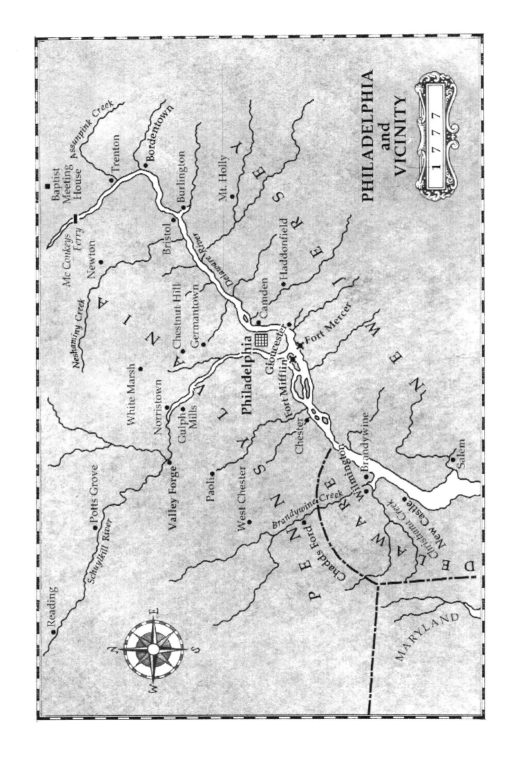

PHILADELPHIA and VICINITY

1777

*In previous volumes...*

## BOOK 1, DAUGHTER OF LIBERTY

EASTERTIDE, APRIL 1775. In the blockaded port of Boston, Elizabeth Howard, the beautiful daughter of Tories, plays a dangerous game as the infamous courier Oriole. Hunted by the British for smuggling intelligence and munitions to the Sons of Liberty by night, she flirts with British officers by day to gain access to intelligence the rebels so desperately need.

But she hasn't counted on the arrival of Jonathan Carleton, an officer in the Seventeenth Light Dragoons. To her dismay, the attraction between them is immediate, powerful—and fought on both sides in a war of wits and words. As the first blood is spilled at Lexington and Concord, Carleton fights his own private battle of faith. And the headstrong Elizabeth must learn to follow God's leading as her dangerous role thrusts her ever closer to the carnage of Bunker Hill.

## BOOK 2, NATIVE SON

BRIGADIER GENERAL JONATHAN CARLETON has pledged his allegiance to the cause of liberty, his service to General George Washington, and his heart to fiery Elizabeth Howard. But when Washington takes command of the American forces, he orders Carleton to undertake a perilous journey deep into Indian country and persuades Elizabeth to continue her work as a spy.

Captured and enslaved by the Seneca, Carleton is stripped of everything but his faith in God. At last rescued by the Shawnee, he is taken into deep Ohio Territory and adopted as the warrior White Eagle. When he rises to become war chief, he is drawn unwillingly into a bitter war against the white settlers who threaten to overrun the Shawnee's ancestral lands.

Meanwhile, as General William Howe gathers his forces to attack the outmatched Continental Army at New York City, Elizabeth despairs of ever learning Carleton's fate. But as the western frontier erupts into flame, the name of White Eagle begins to spread beyond the borders of Ohio Territory.

## BOOK 3, WIND OF THE SPIRIT

ELIZABETH HOWARD SCRAMBLES for crucial intelligence—and her life— as the fateful confrontation between the Americans and the British explodes at the Battle of Brooklyn. Her assignment leads her into the very maw of war, where disaster threatens to end the American rebellion. Yet all the while her heart is fixed on Brigadier General Jonathan Carleton, whose whereabouts remain unknown more than a year after he disappeared into the wilderness.

With Washington's army driven out of New York and the patriots' cause on the verge of extinction, Elizabeth is reunited with Colonel Charles Andrews. She joins him on a desperate journey to find Carleton before the British can capture and execute him for treason.

Far out on the western borders, Carleton, now the Shawnee war chief White Eagle, is caught in a bitter war of his own. As he leads raids against the white settlers who encroach on Shawnee lands, he must also walk a treacherous tightrope between the alluring widow Blue Sky, the vengeful shaman Wolfslayer . . . and the longing for Elizabeth that will not give him peace.

## CRUCIBLE OF WAR, BOOK 4

RETURNING FROM THE SHAWNEE, Brigadier General Jonathan Carleton rejoins General George Washington's army to find the patriot cause faltering. In a daring gamble, the American force twice crosses the Delaware amid raging nor'easters to defeat Hessian outposts at Trenton and Princeton, and then vanishes into the impregnable mountain bastions at Morristown.

Back in New York, Elizabeth Howard is drawn ever deeper into the intrigues that swirl around British General William Howe and his brother, Admiral Richard Howe. She and her Aunt Tess move to Philadelphia in summer 1777 to gather intelligence about a rumored British attack on the city.

When Carleton is ambushed and almost captured while the Americans dig in at Brandywine Creek, Washington transfers him to General Horatio Gates's army in the upper Hudson Valley, where Carleton's old nemesis, British General John Burgoyne, closes in on Saratoga. With decisive battles looming on both fronts, Elizabeth and Carleton face a crucible of war that will test their mettle, faith, and love to the very limits—and beyond.

## Chapter One

*Thursday, 30 October, 1777*
*11:05 p.m.*

IN THE FLICKERING CANDLELIGHT the words swam and blurred before his eyes. Clenched in his hand, the paper shook.

Brigadier General Jonathan Carleton stared at the letter, his mind gone blank. A wave of terror and rage squeezed the air from his lungs and brought bile into his throat.

By degrees he became aware of the gusting wind that beat against the inn, the sudden bursts of freezing rain flailing the window panes, his own ragged breath. Despite the heat radiating from the hearth's blaze, chill sweat trickled down his brow and beneath his worn buckskins, darkly rain-slicked from the downpour his Rangers had ridden through. He swallowed with difficulty and forced himself to focus on the letter's signature.

*William Howe.*

Knight of the Bath. Commander in Chief of His Majesty's forces on the North American Station.

"Jon, what is it?"

Behind him, Colonel Charles Andrews's voice sounded hollow and far away. Ignoring his friend, Carleton studied the words scrawled boldly above Howe's name as though, if he willed it, they would say something else.

That the American cause was entirely lost. That Washington had surrendered to the British. That Howe's entire army waited outside the door to escort Carleton to the scaffold, there to hang for treason.

Anything.

Not this.

*Tuesday 28 October, 1777*

*Brigadier General Jonathan Carleton*

*Sir,*

*This is to inform you that I hold Elizabeth Howard prisoner. If you wish her to live, present yourself to me, alone and unarmed, at my headquarters no later than two days following your receipt of this letter. The guard that bears it has orders to conduct you directly to me with all courtesy due a general officer.*

*Be advised that if you do not appear or if anyone accompanies or attempts to follow you, Miss Howard will die in that hour.*

*I am, sir,*
*Your most humble servant . . .*

*Humble servant.* If he did not loathe Howe so intensely at that moment, he would laugh.

"Jon, please—"

His expression masked, Carleton thrust the letter at Andrews. The colonel threw an alarmed glance at the brigade's chief physician, Major Pieter Vander Groot, before bringing it close to the candle to scan its contents. When he looked up, his face had gone chalk white.

"Dear God! He has Beth!"

Vander Groot strode across the cramped chamber of the modest inn on the edge of the small village of Baptist Meeting House, where they were staying the night on their journey across New Jersey. He tore the letter from Andrews's hand and after reading it dropped the page on the table and slumped into one of the chairs drawn up to it, groaning, his face buried in his hands.

"It's my fault. My rashness caused this." Taking a shaky breath, Carleton moved woodenly past the two men.

Andrews grabbed him by the arm and spun him around. "What do you mean?"

"When they ambushed me at Gray's Hill," Carleton reminded him hoarsely. "I taunted Howe to his face. You warned me he'd move heaven and earth to capture me. Obviously he has." Again he stepped toward the door.

"You can't mean to go to him!"

Carleton tried to wrest his arm free, but Andrews gripped him by the other as well and forced Carleton to face him. "This is insane! Think, Jon. He'll arrest you—hang you."

For a suspended moment Carleton regarded the colonel blankly, unable to make sense of his plea or to come up with a coherent response. "I know," he rasped at last.

"Do you truly think he'll release Beth in exchange for you?"

"No."

"You're right. You'll accomplish nothing but to hand him your head on a silver platter—one of our best officers, the very one who so magnificently fleeced the British of every scrap of intelligence the patriots needed! What you suffered when General Gage arrested you back in Boston will be nothing to what Howe will do now. Didn't he say in Beth's hearing that he wanted to personally hand your scalp to George the Third? He'll make you the prime example of what happens to those who dare defy the king, then execute you both."

Carleton tore out of his hold, but before he could reach the door, Vander Groot sprang to block him. "What Charles says is true. I know Howe well enough to be certain of it."

"I—cannot—allow her—to die—alone," Carleton said, his voice thick, each word an effort. *"I will not."*

Andrews's expression hardened, and he grasped Carleton by the shoulder. "Do you honestly think Howe hasn't thought of that, that he'd allow you to catch even one glimpse of each other, or that he'd give either of you the comfort of being hanged together? He'll never allow her to know that you gave yourself up for her, never allow you to see her one last time and assure her of your love!"

His voice broke. "After he hangs you, he'll simply let her rot away in misery in some stinking hellhole, knowing full well what would happen if you came, but wondering still whether you ever learned of her fate—or whether your love failed."

Staggered, Carleton tried blindly to turn away. Vander Groot shoved a chair toward him, and he collapsed into it. Leaning forward, hands gripped between his knees, shoulders heaving, Carleton fought to ride out the tide of agony that bore over him. But it rose all the higher until he feared he must either drown or be swept away to some unspeakable act of violence.

"Lord, what am I to do?" he whispered.

Vander Groot pulled up a chair and bent over him, his hand resting on Carleton's back. "First we have to verify that Howe's not lying, that indeed he does hold Beth. I'd not put any deception beyond him."

Carleton wrenched upright. "I have two days to present myself at Philadelphia before he executes her, Pieter! A detachment waits outside to take me to him—"

"They're under guard and will wait as long as we deem fit," Andrews countered. "Howe will do nothing unless he's certain you'll not come."

"But Beth—"

"Jon, you know I love Beth as much as you do," Vander Groot broke in, his face contorted with anguish. "To think of her suffering or—" Breaking off, he made a painful gesture before continuing, "If Howe hangs her, he'll lose the only hold he has over you and gain your undying enmity. Even a commanding officer can't completely secure himself from attack by a determined assailant, and if he doesn't know by now that there's no one more determined and capable than you, he's more thick-headed than even I give him credit for. Despite his threats, he dare not take that course and risk losing everything while there's yet hope you might be persuaded to give yourself up."

"You have the right to ask for proof of his claims," Andrews approved, "and that'll give us time to come up with a plan to rescue Beth."

Carleton gave a short laugh. Shoving out of his chair, he began to pace the room.

"If that were even possible, how could we rescue her when we've no idea where she's held?"

"His headquarters are in Philadelphia—"

Carleton rounded on Andrews. "It's certain he'd not hold her there, Charles, not with us on the way to join Washington, near at hand with his entire corps. There'd be too much opportunity for our spies to discover her location—"

"Then where?" Vander Groot's eyes narrowed. "New York?"

Carleton stared at him for a taut moment, then let out his breath in a groan. "When we left Albany, I sent her and Caleb downriver to Dobbs Ferry to take the post road to Boston. Her parents' ship was due in at any time from England, and I believed that route the easiest and fastest. My most trusted informants confirmed that after capturing the forts on the upper Hudson General Clinton withdrew his force to New York and that the militia had regained control south beyond Dobbs Ferry. I had every confidence they'd be entirely safe."

"Don't blame yourself. Beth knew the risks she was taking and took them freely." Andrews raked his fingers through his hair and released a sigh. "I wouldn't be surprised if Howe had her and Caleb followed from the time they left Philadelphia and was only waiting for his suspicions to be confirmed in order to take them."

"Howe's detachment found us here so it's likely we've been followed as well. Or someone's betrayed us as Jeffreys did." At thought of his former aide's treachery, which had too nearly resulted in his own capture by the British, Carleton ground his teeth.

"It's easy enough to track as large a force as ours," Vander Groot reminded him. "The Jersey militias may control this region, but there are still many loyalists all too willing to pass intelligence along to the British."

"You set patrols?" Carleton said sharply to Andrews.

The colonel made a dismissive gesture. "Two troops along with native scouts ranging two miles out, as usual. But neither Howe nor Clinton is foolish enough to risk sending a force against us and provoking a general engagement. He'd have not only us, but also the Jersey militia on him like a hound on a badger."

"Then how did this detachment get through?"

"They didn't," Andrews pointed out. "Even though there are only ten of them, which would make it easier to find cover, Lieutenant Matheson's patrol intercepted them crossing the fields west of here despite the storm and darkness. He told me they made no show of resistance, but immediately showed a flag of truce and demanded to be brought to you."

Pulling a map out of Carleton's rawhide pouch on the table, he bent over it. "If Beth and Caleb were captured around Dobbs Ferry or even farther east along the post road, then New York's where they'd logically be taken. Howe would believe them fully secured from rescue or escape there."

Vander Groot snatched the letter from the table and studied it for a moment. "This letter is in Howe's hand, but judging by their uniforms, the detachment that delivered it belongs to one of Clinton's regiments."

Andrews's eyebrows rose. "Oh ho! Then Howe must have been in New York when he wrote it—which means he had a very urgent reason to leave off trying to smash through our puny defenses on the Delaware and travel all that way. I'll wager everything that Beth's in New York and Howe's headed back to his headquarters on the double. He wants you to come to Philadelphia in order to throw you off the scent and keep you as far from her as possible."

Carleton nodded, grim-faced, feeling that they grasped at straws. In the absence of any alternative, however, what choice did they have?

He arrested his steps abruptly. Covering his face with his hands, he thought, *No. We have another choice. We are not alone. The One for whom nothing is impossible is with us.*

He steadied and turned to his companions. "Pieter, you're familiar with British dispositions in the city. Where are their prisons located?"

"The North Dutch Church and a number of other churches have been turned into prisons. And there's the Provost's gaol at—" Blanching, Vander Groot broke off, horror coming into his eyes.

Carleton came to his side. "What is it? Tell me!"

Sweat beaded the doctor's brow. When Carleton shook him, Vander Groot met his alarmed gaze with a hopeless one.

"There's only one place on the continent where he'd be confident we could never get at her. Aboard one of the prison ships in New York Harbor. Guarded by the Royal Navy."

A wave of nausea twisted in Carleton's gut. "The devil himself wouldn't treat a woman so!"

"Perhaps not the devil," Vander Groot returned, his voice echoing the despair that gripped Carleton's breast. "But I wouldn't put it past Howe."

Cursing, Andrews slammed his fist on the table, toppling the guttering candle. It cast dizzying shadows as it fell, then abruptly extinguished, deepening the chamber's gloom.

Vander Groot went to the fireplace, brought a candlestick from the mantel, and placed it on the table where it faintly brightened a circle around them. "If that's the case, how are we to reach her, much less get her safely off one of those rotting hulks—if we can even determine which one she's aboard? Or to begin with, verify that she's indeed held on one of them?"

Carleton's shoulders slumped, and he let out a harsh laugh. "We'd need a navy to even get into the harbor, much less to overcome the British fleet."

Light dawned at the same instant comprehension came into his companions' eyes.

"You have a navy!" the two officers exclaimed in unison.

"With the merchantmen you outfitted as privateers this past summer, that gives you how many ready for combat—a dozen?"

Staring at Andrews, Carleton shook his head, hope plummeting to despair. "Even if every one of them were at hand—and they aren't— what's a tiny squadron of privateers compared to Lord Howe's entire fleet? He'd swat them like a handful of fleas, send them to the bottom of the ocean."

Andrews gave him a calculating look. "But we won't be going against Black Dick's entire fleet, Jon," he said, referring to Admiral Lord Richard Howe, General William Howe's elder brother. "A large number of his warships are in the Delaware, trying to blow through Washington's defenses and open the sea roads to Philadelphia. Others are at Newport Harbor, still more prowling along our southern coast or in the Caribbean."

For some moments the three men regarded one another soberly, each calculating the odds.

"He'd never leave New York without sufficient guard," Carleton pointed out. "There's no doubt that enough warships are stationed there to tilt the odds decisively against us. And don't forget that Newport's just outside Long Island Sound, and British ships are constantly prowling those waters."

"Do your ships not fly the French flag?" Andrews demanded.

"When they're not flying the Union Jack or the Spanish ensign," Carleton conceded with a shrug. "My uncle, le comte, had their lines altered so that with a little paint and other adjustments by the ships' carpenters they can appear as French, Spanish, or British."

"The French and Spanish aren't party to this war—yet. A small, harmless convoy of French merchantmen, say, blown off course during a gale at sea and seeking a port to make repairs and resupply should expect to be accommodated even by the British."

"Brilliant!" Vander Groot exulted, rubbing his hands together.

"How many of your privateers are at hand?" Andrews demanded.

Carleton mentally reviewed the latest reports from Louis Teissèdre, his French agent. "Only three could be in port at Boston now or due within the next week: *Liberty, Destiny,* and *Invictus.*"

"Three ships will arouse less suspicion than a larger number. *Destiny* carries 100 guns, equal to the largest warship in Howe's command, and *Liberty* and *Invictus* are 74s. That's firepower enough for a bold stroke."

Carleton resumed his pacing. "They'll all have to be refitted and take on supplies before they can sail again. It'll take too much time."

"That can be delayed, can't it? They'll not be going far."

"Perhaps, but what difference will it make if we don't know which ship Beth's aboard?"

"The prison ships are clustered in Wallabout Bay," Vander Groot noted thoughtfully. "There are only three, including the hospital ship, and she's not likely to be held on that one. That leaves two. I was aboard one of them last spring and am known to the captain."

"That will make our task easier." Andrews turned to Carleton. "Send Stowe on his way to Boston tonight, and Briggs with him. Then wait until mid morning to send the detachment back to Howe so they can't reach him before nightfall."

Carleton stopped in front of the window and stared hopelessly out into the stormy night. "Even riding the fastest post horses, with a minimum of rest and no interference from the British, it isn't possible to reach Boston any earlier than six days from now, Charles. And then the ships will have to be stripped and readied for action. I'm ordered to surrender myself at Howe's headquarters *the day after tomorrow!*"

Vander Groot joined him at the window. "Then we have to stall. You have the right to demand proof that he has Beth, that this isn't simply a lie meant to trap you. Write a letter assuring Howe that you will turn yourself in—but only after receiving verification that she is indeed his prisoner."

Andrews moved to the fireplace to warm his hands at its blaze. "What proof will you demand?"

"That Howe send Caleb to me with a letter from Beth—written in her own hand."

"Perfect!" the doctor exclaimed. "Caleb may be held aboard the same ship as Beth or at least have some idea where she is."

Carleton let out an oath. "If Caleb knows where she is, Howe will never send him."

Arms folded, the doctor gnawed his lip while regarding Carleton with apprehension.

"I highly doubt Howe would hold them in the same place. I wouldn't." Andrews laid another log on the fire and prodded the seething embers with the poker. "In any case, as Pieter said, New York Harbor is the one place on the continent he'd believe Beth to be beyond our reach. He'd never credit you with the temerity to take on the Royal Navy right under Clinton's nose even if you knew exactly where she was held."

Vander Groot resumed his seat at the table. "And Howe won't risk losing you by refusing to negotiate terms for your surrender. He's no choice but to agree, and that'll give us just the time we need."

Leaning back in his chair, he studied the shadowed ceiling thoughtfully. "Let's see . . . it'll be tomorrow evening before Howe's detachment can deliver your letter. Then at least four more days until Howe's messenger can reach Clinton—who then must summon Beth and force her to write a letter. And another couple of days for Caleb to deliver it. Approximately a week in total."

Andrews joined Vander Groot at the table, his expression exultant. "You'll have a couple days more before you're expected at Howe's headquarters, Jon. By then your ships should have arrived at the rendezvous. And when you don't show at Philadelphia, it'll take another four days for Howe's commands to get to Clinton—more if our forts along the Delaware keep him busily enough engaged—"

Eyes narrowed, Carleton rounded on the two men and jabbed his finger in the direction of the window. "You hear that out there? What do you think that's like at sea? I've experienced it, and so have you, Charles. The fall storms are already on us. My ships are likely to encounter dirty weather and high seas on the way. If another storm hits before they leave port, it could be as long as a week until they can sail!"

"What other choice do we have but to take the risk?" Vander Groot demanded.

Carleton felt as though he had to fight for every breath. He swallowed with an effort and said gruffly, "Even with all my privateers, and even if the weather cooperates, there's no certainty of success against a large portion of Lord Howe's fleet. To attempt such madness will only extend Beth's suffering and might well endanger her life even more."

"Whether we attempt to rescue her and fail or you turn yourself over to Howe, Beth will certainly die," the colonel said forcefully. "Pieter's right—we have to risk it if there's to be any hope at all of saving her."

"She's strong," Vander Groot agreed, his tone sounding to Carleton as though he was trying to reassure himself. "She'll not give up without a fight. We've nothing to lose, and everything to gain. And if all goes well, we might free not only Beth, but the prisoners with her."

"Inform your French and Spanish captains of the stakes," Andrews added, "and they'll converge on New York Harbor like sharks scenting blood."

Carleton could not suppress a smile. For the first time on that dark night, a measure of hope filtered through the anguish that held his heart in its iron grip. Rubbing his burning eyes, he stopped at the table, rifled through his pack, and pulled out a map of New Jersey.

He sank into a chair and unrolled it. While Andrews and Vander Groot leaned over him, he ran his finger slowly along the coastline, then stopped.

"Barnegat Bay. The draught should be deep enough for ships at New Inlet, there, at the end of Squan Beach. It's less than two day's ride from here, and if the winds are fair, less than two days from Boston by sea as well and only hours from New York Harbor."

He looked up. "It's been a dozen years since I rode through there, but then it was sparsely settled. Pirates and smugglers have been very active along that coast for a hundred years or more, and I'll wager the inhabitants are more than a little sympathetic to our cause. The main concern is the treacherous tides."

"I'll talk to our local guides right away to make sure it's sufficiently isolated," Andrews noted with approval. "We'll set the rendezvous point by their recommendation."

"Tell them no more than they have to know, and make haste. I yet need to write orders to *Destiny's* captain, and I want Stowe and Briggs off to Boston within the hour—with a small guard to accompany them, all in common dress but well armed, Charles. Warn them to remain on exceptional alert every moment and be prepared to take any measures that become necessary should they encounter the enemy."

Andrews gave him a meaningful look. "Stowe will get through."

"If I know him, he will." Head drooping, Carleton pressed his fingers against his temples. "Once that's done, we all need rest if we're to think clearly on the morrow. It's been a very long day, and we can do no more tonight. My head's pounding, and I need at least to lie down and close my eyes for a few hours, though I doubt I'll sleep."

Vander Groot clasped Carleton's shoulder and for a long moment regarded him earnestly. "Remember, we're not alone."

"Thank you," Carleton said huskily, returning his look with a grateful one. "It's certain we'll need God's help to carry off this mad plan."

Vander Groot conceded a faint smile, then bade him and Andrews good night and quietly moved to the door. There he hesitated and swung back to see Carleton and Andrews bending over the map with their heads close together.

For a long moment the doctor fixed them both in an assessing look. At last he set his shoulders and eased the door open. Nodding to the guards posted outside, he stepped past them into the dark passage.

*Friday, 31 October*
*12:50 a.m.*

VANDER GROOT LOOKED UP from the letter he was writing to meet the hard gaze of the powerfully built black officer seated opposite him at the table. The tap of sleet and buffet of the storm's assault on the building filled the small chamber off the kitchen at the inn's rear.

"It's going to be a cold, wet ride."

"That be the least o' your worries," Major Isaiah Moghrab objected with a scowl. "You tryin' to get back into New York be foolhardy. You ride with us when the army parade through Philadelphia, and maybe some Tory reco'nize you and tell the British."

The doctor laid down his pen and stretched back in his chair. "That's unlikely. General Carleton gave me permission to ride with the corps only because my parents assured me that all their Tory friends had joined the exodus out of the city. There was no one left who might recognize me. At any rate, the loyalists who'd stayed were cowering in their homes that day for fear of reprisals from the patriots if they showed their faces."

"Gen'l Carleton don't give you leave to go."

"That's why I'm not telling him. If you wait to deliver this letter until my absence is discovered, no one will be able to catch up with me."

Isaiah snorted. "And I take the blame."

"He won't fault you once he reads this."

"How you get into New York?" Isaiah countered.

Pulling a paper from the capacious leather pocketbook lying beside him, Vander Groot tossed it across the table to Isaiah. The major scrutinized it, his expression doubtful.

"You forget my parents were close friends of the brothers Howe— still are for all they know. The night you arrested me at Montcoeur, I'd just come from trying to meet with the admiral about these very prison ships where we suspect Beth's being held. Lord Howe was otherwise engaged, but his aide was more than happy to provide me a pass so I could visit my family in Philadelphia whenever I chose. I held onto it in case it might prove useful someday."

Although the strain on Isaiah's face eased, he stared into space, drumming his fingers on the arm of his chair. "We got to get to Miss 'Lizabeth somehow and soon, that's sure," he muttered, before returning his attention to the doctor. "I guess you find out whether you been betrayed when you reach New York."

Vander Groot dipped his pen in the inkwell and bent over his letter. "If we're to have any hope of success, we need someone inside the city who can locate Miss Howard, keep General Carleton informed, and have arrangements in place by the time his ships arrive. I'm the only one who can manage that, but I can't overpower a ship's crew alone. I want you with me and as many men as you can spirit across the Hudson. Can you leave one of your captains in charge of your troops while you're gone?"

When Isaiah nodded, Vander Groot finished writing, wiped his pen on an ink-stained cloth, and set it down. "You remember where you crossed the Hudson to reach Montcoeur the night you arrested me?"

Isaiah nodded. "One o' our brigades still in control o' the Jersey side o' the river there. But I need orders from the gen'l if they goin' to help us get 'cross since we don't have Pete to fetch us," he added. His younger son, who had secretly transported Elizabeth between the

Hudson estate she and her aunt had leased and the islands of New York Harbor aboard a small sailboat, now served aboard *Destiny*.

"Good."

Frowning, Isaiah cocked one eye at the doctor. "You intend to stay at Montcoeur?"

Vander Groot scattered sand across the page. "My home's not only right in the city, but is also being used as a hospital for the wives and children of British soldiers. Trying to explain the comings and goings of a party of black men to the staff would be difficult, to say the least. The caretaker and his wife at Montcoeur are a black couple named Stebbins that Sarah engaged," he added, referring to Isaiah's wife, who served as housekeeper for Elizabeth and her Aunt Tess. "I'm known to them, and the hospital occupying my house should provide sufficient pretext for them to allow me to stay there temporarily."

Isaiah rubbed his jaw. "If Sarah hire them, then they likely be sympathetic to our cause. And know things we don't."

Vander Groot's eyes narrowed. "As soon as I get there, I'll feel them out. If they are sympathetic, they might be useful in recruiting a party to help us take control of the prison ship—or find out if Miss Howard's being held somewhere else. There's an old carriage house at the back of the property used for storage where you and your men should be able to lie in concealment until we determine the lay of the land. I'll meet you there Sunday morning."

He shook the sand off the letter. Folding the page, he handed it to the major.

"I guarantee General Carleton won't deny you anything for the journey, and I'll supply what's needed at New York." Frowning, he watched Isaiah tuck the letter into the pouch on his belt with every sign of reluctance. "Bring at least half a dozen of your best men. They'll serve you well should you run afoul of any British patrols along the way."

Isaiah waved his hand in a dismissive gesture. "After all the troubles they suffer from us Continentals and the Jersey militia last winter and spring, they pull all their troops back 'round New York. All we got to worry about is loyalist spies."

"Wear common dress for the journey. Luckily you and your men can pass as servants, which will allow you much greater liberty to come and go unremarked."

"You know if soldiers be caught behind enemy lines in civilian dress, they be counted spies and hanged."

"Is that going to stop you?" When Isaiah grinned and shook his head, Vander Groot said, "Nor me."

He pulled out his watch, studied it, then got to his feet. "It's already past one o'clock. I better get on the road. As long as this storm doesn't delay me overmuch, I should reach King's Bridge tomorrow afternoon and be in the city around nightfall. Be prepared to leave with your men as soon as you talk to the general. That'll put you half a day behind me."

Isaiah rose, shaking his head, brow creased with worry. "All this take too long, while Miss 'Lisabeth be sufferin'. A woman can't last as long as a man in such conditions."

Vander Groot swallowed around the lump in his throat, feeling as though a cruel hand squeezed the breath from his lungs. Images of the misery he had witnessed aboard one of the prison ships the past spring rose up to haunt him. To think of Elizabeth being forced to endure such horror filled him with inexpressible rage—and a sickening fear.

Controlling his emotions with an effort, he muttered, more to himself than to Isaiah, "If we rush ahead pell-mell, we'll only guarantee our failure. We have to trust God to watch over her and guide us to her. He's never failed us yet, and I've every confidence that He won't now."

He spoke bravely. Yet his heart was deeply torn.

## Chapter Two

*3:10 a.m.*

HAD HE ONCE NAIVELY THOUGHT that mere separation from Elizabeth was the greatest torment he could endure? This was greater far. There could be no torture worse than this: that his actions had placed into danger his dearest love save God alone, and that she now suffered and faced an agonizing, protracted death because of him.

He cared nothing for himself. All that mattered in the universe was to save her. Let the British capture and execute him afterward. Let them crush the rebellion into dust and cast every person on the continent into slavery. It was a matter of completest indifference to him. For the thought of what Elizabeth must be enduring at that very moment while he lay safe in bed, powerless to give her succor, drove him mad.

The storm raging outside was but a weak reflection of the one that battered his soul. Every fiber of his being ached to act, to get to her by any means, no matter what violence he must wreak to do so. He would welcome it, in fact. Could he but save her, he would regret nothing.

Sleepless, in bitterness of soul, he contemplated every form of wreckage he could think of. With his brigade of Rangers, a large body of native warriors, and a dozen well-armed privateers at his command, there was much.

Yet not enough. The odds against reaching her at all were so high; the chances of accomplishing a rescue even if he did, so heartbreakingly small; and the possibility that she might die before he found her so great that black despair consumed him.

He felt physically ill. Nauseated, shaking, his entire body drenched in cold sweat, he lay on his back, staring into darkness, fallen into a void more fearful than any he had ever yet experienced.

The clock on the mantle chimed thrice. He had tossed and turned to no purpose for what seemed an eternity. In reality it had been but two hours. Lightheaded with fatigue and anguish, he threw off the bedcovers and stumbled to his feet.

His threadbare linen shirt and drawers offered scant protection against the icy drafts that seeped around the closed shutters and crept across the floor. Inured to cold and other discomforts while a slave of the Seneca, he pulled on stockings, breeches, and boots only by habit and in preparation to do . . . something.

Leaving the collar of his shirt unbuttoned, he absently raked his fingers through his hair and pulled the tangled locks back, tying them with a black ribbon at the nape of his neck. He splashed his face with icy water from the basin and vigorously scrubbed dry on the towel. It availed little.

Bleary-eyed, he took a candlestick from the mantel, stooped at the hearth, and raked a glowing ember from beneath the ashes of the banked fire. With the tongs he held it to the candle until the wick flared to life.

The dim, wavering light drove the night's shadows into the corners but could not dispel them from his soul. He built up the fire and lighted the other candles in the chamber with no more effect, then sprawled in a chair at the hearthside, listening to the storm that still beat against the inn, though its force had noticeably diminished.

In his desperation he contemplated extinguishing his life by his own hands. That doing so would be to abandon Elizabeth to an unthinkable fate was all that stayed him.

He tried to pray, but all that came to his mind was an anguished, wordless plea for deliverance. For her. For him.

At length, seeking distraction, he willed his mind to focus on the matters at hand. Their New Jersey guides had enthusiastically endorsed Barnegat Bay as perfect for the vague purpose Andrew had outlined to them, nor, experienced in such matters, had they asked for any details. One who had connections in the region would leave at daybreak to meet with local patriot leaders in the vicinity of Squan Beach to ensure that the inhabitants avoided the rendezvous point and turned a blind eye to activity along the coast.

Along with the coded orders Stowe carried to *Destiny's* captain, Carleton had also sent a brief letter, written in invisible ink, to Elizabeth's aunt, Tess Howard, at her home in Roxbury on the mainland outside Boston. Alerting her to Elizabeth and Caleb's capture, he had warned that she and Elizabeth's parents must under no circumstances obey any demand from Howe to come to him and for their safety must not leave Massachusetts. To do so would only endanger Elizabeth further, he had emphasized, adding that he coveted their prayers.

More than that he had not committed to paper. Stowe would advise Tess—and Elizabeth's parents if they had by then returned from England—of the efforts Carleton meant to make toward Elizabeth's rescue.

His thoughts skittered away from the letter he must write to Howe. Instead he pondered the need to alert Washington as soon as possible and enlist what aid the General could—and would—give them.

The clock struck the half hour, echoed by a soft rap at the door, muted by the rain drumming on the roof. "Come," Carleton growled, his throat feeling raw.

His chaplain, Captain James McLeod, entered, his normally good-humored face creased with concern. He sketched a salute.

"I couldna sleep and figured ye'd be awake as well, sir. Seein' the light under yer door . . . " He let the words trail off.

"You're fortuitously come. I was about to summon you. Charles explained our situation?"

"He did," McLeod affirmed in his thick Scottish burr. "We'd crossed paths right after he interrogated the British captain, and from his manner I'd already guessed somethin' was sore amiss. What can I do?"

Carleton motioned him to the table. When they were seated he explained, "I need you to carry an encoded letter to Washington. The corps was in Montgomery County outside Philadelphia at last report, but be careful whom you ask for direction to the camp."

Cocking his head, Carleton listened for a moment. "The wind's dropping and the rain's lessened. If you leave at daybreak, you should be able to reach headquarters by nightfall even over muddy roads. Make the General aware of anything not included in my letter and answer any questions he may have. I need him to keep us supplied with intelligence about Howe's movements, particularly if he suddenly disappears from sight."

"The brigade'll stay here then?"

"For the time being. Charles will take command while I rendezvous with my ships. He'll do everything possible to ensure that my absence remains undetected by the enemy and will forward any communications from Washington or Howe to me."

McLeod leaned back in his chair and gave him a worried look. "I should return by nightfall tomorrow. Ye'll be needin' a courier to carry other messages to and fro as well. I'll be verra happy to serve in that capacity."

Gingerly Carleton massaged his brow. It felt as though a particularly industrious blacksmith had taken residence in his brain, there to pound ceaselessly on his anvil.

He forced a smile. "As a country parson riding about to tend to his congregation, you should arouse no suspicions. Take along a couple of officers from the local militia to serve as guides. They can pose as your companions in transacting church business."

He glanced over his shoulder when another muffled knock sounded at the door. "Come."

The door creaked open and Andrews stepped inside, bleary-eyed, hair tousled and clothing rumpled. "I couldn't sleep either," he said, looking from Carleton to McLeod. "I went to find Pieter, but he doesn't seem to be anywhere about. When I saw the light under your door, I assumed he was with you."

Carleton got to his feet, followed by the chaplain. "I haven't seen him since he headed off to bed."

"Neither have I." Slowly, as though its absence had just then dawned on him, Andrews added, "His pack wasn't in his room, though his uniform lay folded on the bed. Surely he wouldn't have gone anywhere in this storm."

Carleton stiffened, the hammering in his head increasing its tempo. "If he has, I'll wager I know where." At the two men's questioning looks, he rasped, "To alert Howe to our plans. We're only a day's ride from the general's headquarters."

Andrews's mouth fell open. "You can't believe that Pieter'd betray us."

"Wouldn't he? Lest you forget, his parents are close friends of the Howes."

"Were," Andrews corrected him, "an allegiance they had occasion to repent of last summer."

Carleton dismissed Andrews's protest with a wave of his hand. "I arrested him, forced him to join us against his will. Not to mention that he loves Beth. Despite his protests to the contrary, I wouldn't be surprised if he still bears a grudge."

"He was on his way to join the army when you arrested him. He wanted to fight. And he was naturally shocked to discover Beth's relationship with you and her role as Washington's spy in such a manner."

"You prove my point. He threatened both Beth and me. You were witness to it. We've only his word for his change of allegiance."

"His word and his actions." Andrews cast McLeod a troubled glance.

The chaplain shook his head, brow creased. "Ye canna' give this credit, sir. I've had many an occasion to talk wi' our good doctor, and he's always impressed me wi' his sincerity and lack o' guile, his commitment to the way o' Christ."

"Besides, he does love Beth. He must know that if Howe gets wind of our plans, he'll execute her immediately."

Carleton regarded Andrews coldly. "Perhaps he thinks he can strike a deal to exchange me for her. Then he'd have her to himself."

Andrews reached for the doorknob. "I'll go see if his horse is here. Perhaps he went for a walk to clear his head."

"If you don't find him, send Red Fox to track him. He surely wouldn't have left before the storm let up, so he can't have gotten too much of a head start." His tone mocking, Carleton added, "Tell Red Fox that if he finds the *good doctor* on the road to Philadelphia, there's no need to bring him back."

Andrews stared at Carleton, the color draining from his face. "If he has gone, someone had to have seen him, talked to him before he left. I'll find out what I can." He turned abruptly and went out the door.

CARLETON DROPPED Vander Groot's letter onto the writing table and rubbed his hand over his face. After three cups of the inn's tarry coffee, strong enough to wake the dead, his headache had eased to the point that he felt reasonably alert and coherent.

He glanced up at Isaiah, then transferred his gaze to Red Fox. Along with his younger brother Spotted Pony, the tall, imposing Shawnee warrior had been Carleton's most trusted ally in the war against white settlers filtering into Ohio Territory the previous year.

"Were you able to track him?" Carleton asked in the Shawnee tongue.

Red Fox nodded curtly. "The rain washed much away, White Eagle, but my dogs picked up his spore. I found his horse's track before I had gone far toward the sun's rising. He travels east toward New York."

Releasing a sigh, Carleton dismissed the warrior and slumped against the back of his chair as Red Fox went out the door. "You were right, of course, Charles. I judged Pieter unjustly, and I'm sorry for it."

"The affair with Jeffreys soured you," Andrews responded, referring to Carleton's former aide, who had betrayed him to the British. "No one can blame you for that."

"I blame myself for jumping to unwarranted conclusions. Pieter's been nothing but faithful in his duties and loyal to me personally. I've served him ill."

Carleton stared out the window, where night was giving way to the first faint streamers of dawn. Suddenly he brought his fist down hard on the table, causing every object on its surface to jump and the other officers to start involuntarily. He sprang to his feet.

"But what's he thinking? Does he truly believe he can stroll back into New York unchallenged? He's an officer of the Continental Army in civilian dress, and if he's been identified to the British, they'll arrest him and hang him for a spy! First, however, they'll torture him, and if he breaks and tells them what we're about, the game's up for us as well."

"I tell him it be foolhardy to try it, but he don't listen."

Arms folded, Carleton glared at Isaiah. "He knew I'd forbid him to go." At Isaiah's reluctant nod, he snapped, "It would have been a considerable help it you'd not delayed in alerting me to his plans."

Isaiah's eyes narrowed. "But he be right, gen'l. Somebody needed in the city. If we can find Miss 'Lisabeth and—"

Carleton held up his hand to stay his protest. "I know, I know. At any rate, considering how early he left, he's gone too far for any of us to stop him. Which means we've not only Miss Howard and Captain Stern to worry about, but now Major Vander Groot too."

Isaiah shifted impatiently from one foot to the other. "Me and my men got to leave right away if we to meet him tomorrow morning at Montcoeur. As soon as I know what be going on, I send word back."

Resuming his seat, Carleton tore a scrap from a sheet of paper, then from the pack on the floor beside him pulled one of two vials of invisible ink he carried. He dipped his pen into the fluid and wrote rapidly in a small hand on the scrap. The words slowly faded away as the ink dried.

Finished, he rolled the paper, which now appeared to be blank, into a tight cylinder. He retrieved his cartouche box from the corner by his weapons. Removing a cartridge, he untwisted the end and emptied the gunpowder into the fire, where it sparked and popped, throwing up a small grey cloud. After stuffing the paper into the cartridge, he tightly twisted the end and presented it to Isaiah.

"Since the British have withdrawn from most of Jersey, you shouldn't run into any trouble as long as you take a northern course. But in case Clinton decides on another of his excursions, we'll take no chances. Whatever happens, however, don't use this cartridge," he added dryly. "When you reach the camp at Bergen, give it to the commander. To read my orders, he must heat the paper over a flame, but warn him to first make sure no gunpowder adheres to it."

Isaiah smothered a guffaw as he took the cartridge. "I be sure to tell him."

"He should provide you and your men safe transport across the Hudson to Montcoeur. Once there, exercise all caution. As soon as you join Major Vander Groot and determine what he's about, send one of your men to report to me here before we leave for the rendezvous. I'll send him directly back with instructions."

Isaiah saluted and turned to leave, then glanced back when Carleton said abruptly, "Isaiah . . . tell the major I sorely misjudged him, and I ask his pardon."

Isaiah gave a curt nod. Again he began to turn away, but stopped when Carleton again spoke softly.

"Tell him I love him. And I thank him." Carleton let out his breath and massaged the back of his neck. "But if he's not to be found when you get there, then God help us all."

He had avoided the task as long as he could. The trouble was that every time he thought about writing the necessary letter to Howe, the image of Elizabeth confined amid the horrors of a British prison ship rose stark before his eyes, and he lost all reason. He wanted nothing more than to curse Howe to his face, tell him in bald terms his personal opinion of George the Third, his ministers, General and Lord Howe, and everyone connected to them. But that would only make things worse.

*We are not alone. The One for whom nothing is impossible is with us.*

Remembering the assurance given him earlier, a measure of peace returned, and a sense of the Almighty's presence. He returned to his seat at the table, buried his face in his hands, and for some time sat motionless, intently listening for a voice in the silence.

*"Fear not: for they that be with us are more than they that be with them."*

He straightened with an effort and pulled forward a sheet of paper. Feeling entirely unequal to the task, he dipped his pen into the inkpot and began to write.

*Friday, 31 October, 1777*

*General William Howe*
*Philadelphia*

*Sir,*

*You consider me a fool if you believe I would turn myself over for execution without absolute proof that you indeed hold Miss Howard captive.*

*If your claim is true, then you hold Captain Caleb Stern under arrest as well. I require that he bring me a letter written by Miss Howard, in her own hand and witnessed by him, assuring me that she is in good health and has been well treated. You must include your personal warrant on your honor as a gentleman that you will release her directly upon my arrest. Captain Stern must travel alone, with no escort, and he must not be followed.*

*On receipt of these proofs, I will deliver myself to you at your headquarters, alone and unarmed, at the earliest instant.*

Not bothering to add the customary niceties, grimly certain that any guarantee Howe might feel moved to make would be as trustworthy as the devil's, he scrawled his signature at the bottom.

## Chapter Three

"Just a sip. It'll soothe your throat," coaxed Elizabeth Howard.

She cradled the soldier's emaciated form against her breast and pressed the battered cup to his cracked lips, struggling to maintain balance against the ship's heave and sway. She dearly wished she had better comfort to offer the dying youth. He could not have been as old as she, for his form was slight and he showed little evidence of a beard. Perhaps eighteen years marked his mortal span, although it was hard to tell in one who had wasted to skin and bones.

His eyes remained closed as though he had no strength to open them, but his lips fell slack. Wrinkling her nose, she dribbled the brackish water into his mouth, afraid it might do more harm than good.

Mercifully, it was clear that he would soon leave the misery amply shared by all those tightly packed into the bowels of the aging hulk, their discomfort multiplied by the ship's violent movements in the storm and the cold drafts and seawater that seeped through cracks in the hull. She could not wish him to linger longer in that evil place.

"Ain't more ye can do fer him, Miss Howard. Might as well lay him down." Pressing against her shoulder, tall, gaunt Captain Josiah Hutchinson knelt beside her, a darker form against the stygian gloom.

"Please call me Beth," she urged, as she had numerous times since her arrival. Shaking her head, she added, "If I hold him, at least he'll know that he's not alone and that someone cares for him."

"Truly ye're an angel."

Elizabeth looked up from her charge, barely able to make out the captain's craggy, bearded face by the flickering shafts of lightning that from time to time glimmered through the grate in the deck close overhead. Guessing it to be near morning, she prayed that the storm would cease with the dawn.

"You're surely my angel, Josiah," she whispered, again bending her head over the boy.

"Aw, Miss Howard, no man'd do any less. A pox on Howe and Clinton! It's a pure outrage that a lady like ye is condemned to share the fate of such as us."

"You heard the guard say that I'm a spy, a traitor to the king and deserving of hanging. To share your extremity is not punishment enough in their eyes."

Awkwardly he placed his arm around her shoulders, and they swayed together as the seething waves beat against the hull's exterior. "All o' us here are counted traitors 'gainst the one who calls hisself our sovereign. But only God's our Sovereign and worthy of our allegiance. I've no regrets, nor, I think, do ye, Miss . . . Beth . . . though it's sure hangin'd be better than this," he ended, his voice dropping to a mutter.

She leaned into him, grateful for the faint heat of her protector's body against the hold's damp chill. His touch offered comfort otherwise lacking, and she sensed that he drew the same from her.

It had been two days since she had been dragged from her prison cell on shore and cast like so much refuse among the American prisoners on the rotting, dismasted ship's main gun deck. While she had been imprisoned alone at the back of a decaying, rat-infested warehouse, her mind had conjured up innumerable horrors that awaited her, and she had prayed with desperation that Howe would relent in assigning her to the prison ships. The reality of her present situation and her new companions' plight, however, was worse by far than her most fearful imaginings.

Already she could not recall a time when a deep chill did not painfully stiffen her limbs nor the reek of human excrement, vomit, sickness, and death clog her senses. Every breath she dragged into her lungs caused her to gag.

She quailed to think of what yet lay ahead. Yet the firmness of Josiah's spirit hardened hers, and resolutely she tilted her chin to a defiant angle.

"Our cause is just. I'll not regret any suffering for freedom's sake." By force of will she kept the tremor from her voice and fought back the fear that threatened to belie her brave words.

Even as she spoke, the last sight of her cousin Caleb Stern's dazed and bloodied face as the British marched him away at Dobb's Ferry and the thought of Carleton's anguish when he learned of their fate rose up to accuse her. Her words sounded glib to her ears, and the knowledge that the results of her decisions affected not only herself, but also them and her immediate family, bore heavily upon her.

*Surely Jonathan has received Howe's message by now. What must he feel? What will he do? He can have no idea of where Caleb and I have been taken, no way to find us. And even if he could, he'd never make it through Admiral Howe's fleet to get to us. Oh, Lord, don't let him even try! If I must die, only keep Jonathan from harm and let him live. Let him forget me.*

"Ye've a . . . a family?"

She forced a smile, grateful for Josiah's delicacy in asking few questions, and then only general ones. Indeed, she deemed it safer for these men to know only a minimum of details about her.

"Yes—in Boston."

Softly he said, "They're safe then."

She nodded, throat knotting. *If Howe keeps his threat to summon them, please, Lord, don't let them go!*

"It'll be time for the guard to come fetch the dead afore too long, so take a count of the ones around you as didn't make it through the night."

The quiet admonition reached them from the rickety companion-way leading to the upper deck. Elizabeth identified Tom Spencer, one of several subordinates Josiah had enlisted to exercise informal command over the American prisoners aboard the ship.

"Then mebby some o' us'll get a turn topside," complained the older man Elizabeth had come to know as Sergeant Jim. As usual, he fiercely guarded his position under one of the grates in the overhead planks, from which occasional drafts stirred the stagnant air.

"How come they throwed a girl in here 'mongst men? Ain't decent." It was one of the new prisoners from the previous day who spoke, his whine high pitched.

"Ain't nothin' 'bout this place decent, Jack," a sarcastic voice snapped.

A low chorus of despairing moans and hacking coughs sounded all around Elizabeth in the dim hold, and, muffled by the planks underfoot, from captured French, Dutch, and Spanish sailors on the berth deck below them, and black sailors and soldiers suffering the worst conditions of all in the hold, the lowest part of the hulk. The faint reflection of light through the hatch had strengthened slightly, and overhead the footfalls of sailors began moving back and forth, pursuing their morning duties despite the buffeting wind and waves.

"No need for holystonin' the decks this mornin', boys, but they got plenty to keep 'em busy after that storm," Tom called cheerfully.

Hearing the muted rasp of breath, Elizabeth started and looked down at the youth in her arms to see that his blank gaze was fixed on a distant vision. Josiah reached over to briefly hold his hand above the boy's mouth, then fumbled for his wrist. After a moment, he gently closed the boy's eyes.

"Lay him down now. He's gone on to a better place."

Her throat painfully constricted, tears burning her eyes, she eased the still form back onto the greasy deck. "If only we could let his family know what became of him."

She could see the muscles tense in Josiah's jaw as he shook his head. She looked up when red-haired Billy Finnegan, the other of Josiah's volunteer subordinates, squeezed in beside them. "Even knew we who they was, Miss 'oward, them British devils won't let us send nobody word."

His Irish lilt brought a sad smile to her lips. Before she could respond, Tom crawled around in front of them.

"Here, let me carry 'im over by the companionway. Once they got things under control on deck, the guards'll be down to make us carry off them as has passed overnight." His spare face brightened. "And maybe they'll bring us some grub today."

Billy's mouth twisted into a cynical smile. "No reason to get excited, Tom. 'T won't be fit to eat no ways even if they do."

"Wouldn't mind a piece o' hardtack with a nice mess o' weevils er maggots," one of the men nearby broke in. " 'Least not if we had us a fire so's we could cook 'em down 'ere. I'd relish a bit o' meat for a change, but I ain't eatin' what they bile in seawater in the galley up top even if'n I starve."

The thought of eating meat boiled in water drawn from the bay polluted with refuse of all sorts, dead bodies included, increased Elizabeth's nausea.

"Fer vegetables we can have some of that tasty green mold on the side."

Josiah's words were tinged with what sounded suspiciously like amusement. That any of these men could find humor in their bleak situation astounded her.

Her stomach lurched as the ancient tub wallowed clumsily in the swells of Wallabout Bay. At least nausea relieved her of any desire to satisfy the hunger gnawing ceaselessly at her vitals.

Tom gathered up the youth's limp form. He staggered even under that light burden as he pushed to his feet, his gaunt shoulders hunched to keep from cracking his skull on the beams overhead.

Before he could move toward the companionway, they heard rough footfalls approaching from above and the cry, "Turn out the dead!" A ray of firelight illuminated the stairwell as a small detail of red-coated soldiers descended into the gloom, none much cleaner than their prisoners, though better fed and clothed. A small contingent broke off to thump on down to the berth deck, and then the hold.

Their sergeant's torch cast flickering rays across the men huddled on the filth-laden planks. Squinting against the sudden light, Elizabeth eased off her knees to sit on the floor. She drew farther back into the shadows, grateful for Josiah's protective form between her and the marines.

The sergeant's glance took in Tom and his burden. Exposing teeth as rotten as the moldering frigate, he rubbed his jaw.

"I see we got us another meal for the fishes. Since you got 'im already, I'll let you carry 'im up topside."

Abruptly he motioned the soldier up the stairs. Cringing away from him and his comrades as though fearing a blow, Tom scuttled up the stairs and out of sight.

"Any more?" While designated prisoners carried away the bodies of comrades who had given up their struggle overnight and contingents of French and black sailors carried up even more from below, the sergeant gloated, "A fresh lot o' your fellows'll be joining ye later today. Wouldn't want ye to get overly comfortable with all this room."

His harsh laugh echoed in the constricted space. Then his roving gaze settled on Elizabeth, and his grin broadened.

" 'ow's our pretty little spy 'oldin' out?"

She felt Josiah's arm tighten around her shoulders. The torchlight's glare rippled across the twitch of jaw muscles beneath his beard, and her chest constricted.

The sergeant saw it too. "I should'a known ye'd take that little piece o' trash fer yer doxy, Hutchinson," he mocked. "Been a long time since ye had any female flesh, ain't it? Bet she's a real lusty piece too. I should'a sampled me some afore I threw her to ye."

When Josiah tensed, Elizabeth clutched his knee. "Don't!" she hissed. Feeling the hardness of his muscles ease a fraction, she let out her breath.

The sergeant directed a meaningful look at the rest of the men. "Don't let 'im keep 'er all to hisself, now. A strumpet like 'er needs more'n one man to satisfy 'er."

Some of the men darted surreptitious glances at Josiah, while others stared, stony-faced, into the air. No one spoke. Cackling, the sergeant stamped back up the stairs, his detail following, and torchlight gave way to the former gloom.

Elizabeth swallowed past the dryness of her throat. The sergeant's rude jests, coupled with her surroundings, reawakened suffocating memories from an earlier entrapment: the motion and cloying odors of the fishing sloop that had regularly spirited her from Boston to the mainland on her clandestine missions; Captain Dalton's leering visage when he threatened to expose her and her Aunt Tess to the British commander; his dark eyes boring into hers, bony fingers painfully digging into her flesh while he pressed his lustful demands. Only God's grace had spared her from utter ruin.

As the fearful images spun through her mind, a sickening surge of fear threatened to overwhelm her as it had then. If not for Josiah's implacable presence, she would have broken down in tears.

"Don't you pay no attention to 'em, Miss Beth. I'll give my own life up afore I let anybody do ye harm."

Josiah's tone left no doubt that he meant what he said. Tom had rejoined them, and he and Billy reiterated the captain's assurances.

Elizabeth bit her lip hard, clawing her way back to a measure of calmness. "You mustn't give them any reason to punish you. What would I do if ill befell you?"

Josiah scanned the hold and gave a short laugh. "It's only the British ye need fear, not these men. Most are too grateful for the service ye've done our country to do ye harm. And as to the rest—well, none have strength to treat ye in any ways unkind anyhow."

Elizabeth gave him a grateful smile. When first brought here, she had been terrified of what the desperate men confined aboard the ship might do to her, a lone woman. That the British sailors and guards would not touch her, she knew, for General Clinton had passed on Howe's explicit orders that she was under his personal protection and not to be harmed. But when she had been thrown, helpless, among the prisoners, she had been overcome by a depth of fear and hopelessness she had never before known.

Instead of either taking advantage of her vulnerability or leaving her to suffer alone, however, the majority of her fellow prisoners had exhibited a nobleness of spirit she had not expected, offering a nod and smile, an encouraging word or a pat to her shoulder in passing. Josiah especially had delegated himself her protector.

As she had countless times over the past day, she breathed, *If I must endure this degradation, Father, thank you for placing me in the care of these good men. Thank you for allowing me to share their suffering—and yours.*

Another enormous blessing had been that the British guards who delivered her to the ship did not strip her of her heavy coat and boots. Indeed, when one of the prisoners had tried to wrest her coat away, Josiah and his allies had immediately imposed severe consequences for the attempt.

Without the captain's leadership in enforcing military order and discipline, she was certain, none of the prisoners could have long survived under the harsh conditions they were forced to endure. She had watched him constantly minister to, encourage, exhort, and command the men under his informal authority to behavior conforming to the highest ideals, and it was clear they loved him for it. Surely he had been placed there by a supernatural power, for he brought hope to a very dark place.

Indeed, only God's hand could have spared from death the few men such as Josiah, who had endured the previous winter with no fire or covering and only scant, rotten food and foul water to sustain them.

How any of them were to survive the coming winter was beyond her comprehension.

Lacking their protection and the masculine dress that provided her reasonable covering against the cold, she knew she would certainly perish. And she thanked God for these sustaining mercies, even while she agonized over Carleton's anguish and Caleb's unknown fate and wondered how long any of them would be able to endure.

# Chapter Four

TAKING IN THE DISGRUNTLED SOLDIERS slouching behind their muscular commander in the muddy yard outside the stable door, Andrews restrained a laugh.

"The tack room would at least have been reasonably clean . . . colonel." His lip curling in a sneer, the captain fastidiously flicked dust, chaff, and bits of hay off his brilliant red coat.

"And full of potential weapons, as I'm sure you're aware, Captain Baxter. Your accommodations might have been worse. At least the feed room offered hay for bedding as well as warmth and shelter against the storm. I trust you received breakfast this morning as I ordered."

"Such as it was."

Clearly it had not been to the captain's taste. Unimpressed, Andrews assessed the heavy cloud cover that seethed across the shrouded sky and the bite of the wind before returning his attention to the captain.

"Luckily we're unable to entertain you longer. Your horses have been fed and watered. Now that the storm's abated, a guard will escort you to the Delaware and ensure that you get safely across." He proffered Carleton's letter. "Be so good as to present this to General Howe, with General Carleton's compliments."

For a moment Baxter stared at the letter as though it were a snake. "We were told we'd be escorting a prisoner," he said haughtily, eyes narrowing.

"Assure your commander that the man he seeks will turn himself over the moment he receives the proofs he requires. In the meantime, until we receive General Howe's response we'll camp here so his messengers will be at no bother to find us."

To every side, scores of Rangers, native warriors, and their women and children came and went, busily employed setting up a wet camp after a night spent crowded together as best they could in hastily thrown up tents and the inn's barn, stables, and outbuildings. Carleton's intention had been to move out that morning, ford the Delaware, and locate Washington's corps somewhere outside of Philadelphia, plans that had now to be placed indefinitely on hold.

Baxter received the letter with a furious frown. "The General will not be pleased."

Andrews lifted an eyebrow. Before he could come up with a reasonably politic response, he spied Blue Sky coming toward them, their bundled infant son in her arms, his small head bobbing over her shoulder.

She was garbed in supple, beaded doeskin that clung to the curves of her shapely form far too seductively, and Andrews's heart contracted. As always on first sight of this woman he loved so dearly, he reflected that everything about her seemed to glow.

The soldiers took note of her too. When Blue Sky came to a halt in front of him, her gaze full of tender concern, they exchanged meaningful glances that immediately set Andrews out of temper.

"You did not come to me last night, my husband," she began in the Shawnee tongue.

"Is that your squaw, colonel?" a British sergeant drawled. "My, my, my. She's right purty. Got a purty baby too. Now ain't that fine."

Blue Sky directed a guarded glance from the sergeant to the rest of the soldiers, who were assessing her hungrily as though she were a particularly tempting haunch of meat. When He Leads the Way fussed and began to squirm, she tucked the edge of the baby's wrappings over his head, and met Andrews's warning gaze with a troubled one.

"This morning Laughing Otter said Red Fox told her Healer Woman has been captured," she said, using Elizabeth's Shawnee name. "I'm very worried about my sister."

"I sure wish I had me an Injin squaw," one of the soldiers put in, leering at her. "I'll wager she keeps you real cozy at night."

"You'll do well to remember you're my prisoners and mind what you say," Andrews reproved sharply, rage sizzling through his veins.

Turning back to Blue Sky, his voice hard, he said in Shawnee, "Howe has her, and we'll have to stay here for a few days. Go back to the women—"

"But, Golden Elk—"

"I'll come shortly and explain everything."

He turned to see that Baxter regarded Blue Sky and the infant in her arms with an interest that caused Andrews's gut to tighten. "Speak Indian, do you?" the captain said, his smile baring small, sharp teeth.

Teeth gritted, Andrews suppressed the impulse to smash them with his fist. "That's none of your affair," he growled.

Undaunted, Baxter surveyed Andrews with a smug look. "General Howe might just make it his. Come to think of it, seems I recall a nice reward's been posted for your arrest too."

His oily tone and the malice in his eyes sent a shaft of fear through Andrews. With a gentle touch, he urged Blue Sky in the direction of the warriors' camp. Giving the British detachment a last, apprehensive glance, she retreated around the end of the stable and out of their sight.

"I'd take real good care of that pretty squaw if I were you, or someone might take her away."

They were interrupted by a detachment of warriors who rode up fully accoutered for war, with Red Fox and Spotted Pony at the van.

Returning his gaze to Baxter, Andrews hissed, "Get out of my sight before I change my mind about letting you . . . live. My warriors know what to do with the likes of you."

The captain flushed and stiffened. "You wouldn't dare do harm to us or else your precious Miss Howard will get what she's got coming to her—in the worst possible way."

Andrews considered Baxter, his eyes clouded by a film of bloody red. Despite the captain's protestations during his interrogation the previous night, it was clear that he had indeed been made privy to the contents of Howe's letter and knew much more than he admitted.

The British detail hastily mounted, more than one regarding their native escort with considerable trepidation, Andrews noted in dark satisfaction. Deliberately he took a step that placed him toe to toe with Baxter, over whom Andrews towered.

"My concern for Miss Howard is the only thing that stays my hand," he murmured in a voice too low for the others to hear. "But should harm come to her or to my wife and son, I swear not even the devil and all his demons will stand between you and me."

The thick menace in his tone caused Baxter to blanch and flinch back.

Andrews allowed a cold smile. "And tell Howe the same applies to him."

Baxter's mouth tightened. He swung on his heel and mounted without another word. Urged forward without ceremony by Red Fox, Howe's messengers rode off in the warriors' midst.

Andrews looked after them until they disappeared from sight. Then he turned to stare in the direction Blue Sky had taken their son, fury giving way to a bone-deep chill.

THE CRACK OF A PISTOL FIRING at measured intervals drew Andrews to the large garden behind the inn. He found Carleton, pistol in hand, facing a weathered fence almost 200 yards distant. His carbine lay beside him on a rickety wooden table, along with a powder horn and leather bullet bag.

He watched as Carleton raised the pistol with a casual movement and fired without appearing to aim. Splinters flew from a fence post on which was pinned a rude paper target. All that remained of the scrap was the outer edge; its center had been entirely torn away.

Deliberately Carleton cast the pistol onto the table and took up the carbine. With practiced skill he loaded it, aimed, and pulled the trigger without pausing. Flame and smoke spit from the barrel, and the top of the riddled post disintegrated. He stood motionless, staring at his handiwork.

A deadly, nerveless coldness Andrews had not sensed in his friend before impressed itself on his mind. It occurred to him that it was the same emotion he had felt confronting Captain Baxter a few minutes earlier.

Without looking toward him, Carleton said, "I'm running low on ammunition, Charles. Be so good as to fetch me a supply."

Andrews glanced from the carbine in Carleton's hand to the ruined post. "What do you expect to gain by more practice, Jon?" he enquired politely. "Simply obliterating that post would seem to be a waste of powder and lead that could more profitably be spent elsewhere."

For a moment longer Carleton stared at his target, his visage hard as marble. At last he swung around to meet Andrews's gaze with an assessing one.

"What now? Another disaster to deal with?"

Andrews looked away, heat rising to his face. "You might say so. At least it is as far as I'm concerned."

At the emotion in his tone, Carleton put down his carbine and strode to him. Andrews tersely relayed the scene with the British patrol.

Carleton laid his hand on Andrews's shoulder. "I'm sorry. But it was bound to happen. I've known from the beginning that you wouldn't be able to safely keep Blue Sky and the baby with you, but . . . " He lifted his shoulders and let them drop.

"But you thought I wouldn't listen, so you let me learn the hard way."

Regarding him kindly, Carleton murmured, "Something like that."

"Well, it's sure they can't stay any longer. I'll have to send them back to Grey Cloud," Andrews said, referring to the Shawnee sachem who was his adoptive father.

The words choked in Andrews's throat. Carleton gave him a concerned look, then went to retrieve his carbine and pistol. Andrews followed, hoping to bury his misery in action, but failing.

"Why is Stowe never around when I need him?"

Andrews grabbed the powder horn and bag. "Because you always send him off on some errand."

Carleton grimaced. "That's no excuse."

He led the way through the inn's rear door and up the back stairs to his chamber. "It's not just me Howe wants," he said as he laid the weapons on his pack and straightened. "He'll never forget that you were involved in treason too. And you're all the more vulnerable if you're forced to worry about Blue Sky's safety as well as your own."

Andrews relinquished the powder horn and bag. "He wants me so he can use me as a weapon against you, more than for anything I've done. What happens to my wife and son in the process is of no account to him."

Not meeting his gaze, Carleton pulled off his gloves and threw them on the table. "Charles, I'm sorry."

"It's hardly your fault."

"It's because of me that the three of you are in danger."

"It isn't your responsibility. It's mine." Andrews raked his fingers through his hair.

"I think it wise for you to send Blue Sky and He Leads the Way back to our people, and keep a strong guard with you at all times as well. No use taking unnecessary risks."

Andrews waved Carleton's words away. "Howe won't make a move until you're either in his hands or nowhere to be found."

He wandered to the window and stared bleakly outside, his hands jammed in his pockets, his gaze fixed on the troops completing the camp's dispositions in the pasture behind the inn. He could feel Carleton's sober gaze on his back.

Carleton came to join him. "Spotted Pony told me that many of our warriors are eager to take their women and children home before the winter storms blow in and stay until spring. They meant to leave as soon as we returned to the corps, but now they might as well be on their way as soon as possible."

Seeing Andrews flinch, he added softly, "I promise you'll be able to go to them each winter."

Misery tightened its hold on Andrews's chest. "The problem is all those months between."

He shook off Carleton's hand with a quick shrug and strode to the door, not glancing back. "I'll go break the news to Blue Sky. If the party leaves on the morrow, they'll have to begin preparing for the journey right away."

"I WISH TO STAY WITH YOU, White Eagle," Red Fox said, a frown creasing his brow.

"As much as I want you with me, my brother," Carleton countered, "I need both of you to report to the council on Burgoyne's defeat and tell them that Howe's squandered every opportunity to overcome the Long Knives by a decisive stroke."

Spotted Pony snorted. "If what we've seen is an example of how the British fathers fight, then they have neither determination nor ability to win."

Red Fox exchanged a meaningful glance with his younger brother. "Spotted Pony can make as persuasive an argument as I."

"Indeed he can," Carleton agreed. "But your word holds the greatest sway with the matrons who influence the elders, and as they vote, so will the rest."

When Red Fox made a dismissive gesture, Spotted Pony said, "White Eagle is right, Red Fox. Our people must walk a prudent path between the Long Knives and the British, and if you press this matter privately with the matrons and elders, we have stronger medicine before the council."

As Carleton looked from one to the other, he thought, as he did often, that he was doubly blessed in his adoptive cousins. The two brothers were as tall, lithe, and muscular as he, strikingly handsome and so similar that they could have been twins despite the two years that separated their births. Their coppery complexions, flowing black hair, and dark eyes provided an arresting counterpoint to Carleton's sun-bronzed skin, blond locks, and deep blue-grey eyes.

"I know that many of our people support allying with the British. But it is the worst course we can possibly choose," he said, his voice hard.

"Come with us then, White Eagle," Red Fox pressed. "Your medicine is still the strongest."

Carleton released a sigh. "I cannot think of this now. First I must rescue Healer Woman, if that is even possible. But I will send Golden Elk to you as soon as I can spare him. He can speak to the council for me and consult with Black Fish, and also with Blue Jacket."

"I know how our people hate the Long Knives, but if they defeat the British and we have warred against them, they'll destroy us when the British are driven out," Andrews pointed out. "We must make peace with them now, before that happens."

Spotted Pony shifted restlessly from one foot to the other. "Whatever we decide, we cannot delay longer if we're to leave by the sun's rising. *Kini kiishthwa,* the Long Moon, approaches, and the sun will set many times before we reach Grey Cloud's town."

Carleton locked his gaze with Red Fox's. "The decision is made."

The Shawnee warrior's jaw tensed, but he conceded a reluctant nod.

Carleton handed him a sealed letter. "These are my orders that as scouts for my brigade you're to be given safe passage by any Long Knives you meet. Considering all the bad blood between us, however, I cannot warrant that they'll regard even this. It'll be wise for you to avoid white settlements altogether."

Red Fox considered for a moment, then turned to his brother. "The Nescopec Path is the shortest route to the Susquehanna. There we will cross into Delaware lands."

Spotted Pony nodded his agreement. "Our Delaware and Mingo scouts know the shortest path from there."

Carleton went to his pack, from it took his small New Testament. Returning to the warrior, he said, "I have another reason for sending you, Red Fox. You've made great strides in learning to read this book. Long have I yearned to read passages from it to those of our people who believe in Jesus' teachings and encourage them to remain faithful. I cannot do it now, but you can."

He extended the book. "I make this gift to you. Will you take it and speak to all our people of Moneto's love?"

Red Fox's stern visage softened. He looked from Carleton to the Testament, then took it in his hands. Gazing down at it, he caressed the soft leather cover. When he raised his eyes to Carleton's, there was moisture shining in them.

"I thank you, my brother. And I accept this charge from Moneto."

They gripped hands, both smiling. In spite of the fears that oppressed Carleton, it felt as though one burden, at least, had been lifted from his shoulders.

## Chapter Five

F INISHED HELPING JOSIAH and his companions distribute the day's
rations, Elizabeth settled back into her place, grateful she could help
in some way. This small task also provided opportunity for her to examine
the sick to determine whether any should be sent to the hospital ship—
if the *Erebus's* captain could be persuaded to authorize their removal. In
the short time she had been aboard, she had learned that the man's rule
was tyrannical and that he resisted improving his charges' lot in any way.

"Thank you, Tom." Meekly she accepted the stale biscuit and portion of salt pork the young soldier held out to her with a stern look.

For once the meat had been boiled over a small galley fire built
beneath the deck's central grate on a rude brick hearth packed with sand.
In spite of the heavy charcoal vapors that filled the gun deck as a result,
every man who could find space pressed close to the meager warmth
the coals radiated.

"Ain't often we're favored with such luxuries, so enjoy 'em while we
got 'em," Tom urged at her hesitation. Noting her shudder, he added,
"It's foul, I know, Miss Beth, and I'm sorry we've nothing better. But ye
got to eat and drink what ye can to keep yer strength and spirits up."

"If it doesn't kill me first." She forced a smile though she knew it
was hard for him to see in the gloom. "But please don't apologize. I
know it's all we're given, and I must bear it, as you and the others do.
Your courage is my example."

The last thing she wanted was to eat. Since her arrival unrelenting nausea had kept her from touching the scant, rotten food that was their only sustenance. Only when thirst became intolerable could she force down a sip of the stagnant water drawn from moldering barrels.

Increasingly, however, she was overtaken by faintness and the cramping pains of hunger. Earlier she had overheard Josiah ordering Tom to make sure she ate something that day. She forced down the gall that swelled into the back of her throat and considered her weevil-infested biscuit with apprehension.

"Truth is, weevils add some nourishment—a bit of meat, if you will." Billy lowered himself to sit cross-legged beside her. "It makes swallowin' 'em easier if you don't look."

Keeping her tone cheerful, she said, "Thankfully it's dark enough that I can't see them."

Josiah appeared out of the gloom and resumed his seat on her other side. The small supply of biscuit and pork would be all the prisoners would receive that day and perhaps for several more, and he and his lieutenants enforced strict equality in its distribution.

"Ye get used to it," he said, his tone dry.

She gave a strained laugh. "Somehow I doubt that."

"Soak it in yer water like this." He demonstrated by plunging his biscuit into his cup, holding it up so she could make out his movements. "Once it's soft ye can break it up and make a kind of soup. We generally soak the meat in it, too, when we get some—which ain't often, but today's a good day. Even when we got to eat it raw, it goes down easier that way, and after a while it seems real tasty."

She could make out that he smiled as he said, "But first let's thank God for His provision."

Blinking back tears, Elizabeth bent her head with the others while Josiah led them in a short prayer of thanksgiving as he did each day. Echoing his amen, she bravely submerged the biscuit in her cup as her companions did and held it beneath the surface of the slimy water. She wrinkled her nose at the feel of its tiny inhabitants wriggling under her finger.

"I hate taking from the little provision you're given," she said hopefully.

Josiah, however, was having none of it. "Well, don't! When I first come here, seemed like all the men did wahr t' fight for their part, and some ended up with more, an' others with none. So Billy and Tom and me set laws to keep us from barbarity. The first is that we all share equally any rations we're given, 'ceptin' only those so ill they can't swallow no more and there's no hope of 'em gettin' better."

Elizabeth suppressed another shudder. Her biscuit had dissolved into a mush, and she dropped in her fragment of pork and stirred the mixture. Steeling herself, she forced down a sip of the noxious fluid, trying desperately not to imagine the weevils floating on its surface.

She gagged, and her cup sloshed. Tom grabbed it as the mouthful threatened to come back up, while Josiah and Billy bent over her.

"I will get used to it," she gasped, fighting to swallow the vile taste that coated the inside of her mouth.

She got little more down. Within minutes, cramps twisted her bowels, and she bent over, groaning.

Billy helped her to her feet and supported her as she stumbled aft over the sprawled limbs of their fellow prisoners to where the overflowing necessary tubs sat in the deeper shadows of the deck's far end, enveloped in an overpowering stench. Several others shuffled after them.

By dint of sheer willpower she might learn to keep rotted food down, she reflected. But her heart sank at the realization that there was no way to prevent everything she ate from passing through her so rapidly that it left her even more debilitated. And if she developed the bloody flux or any of the numerous diseases common to such conditions . . .

She knew the hazards all too well due to her training as a doctor. Her friend and colleague, Dr. Pieter Vander Groot, had seen the graphic

evidence the previous spring aboard these very ships: smallpox, yellow
fever, typhus, dysentery, scurvy—infections and fevers of all kinds.

No, to think of what might happen would be to give in to despair.
She had to focus her energies on dealing with immediate needs.

Billy stood in front of her, back turned, shielding her from view of
the men. She grasped the ragged waistband of his breeches with one
hand to maintain her balance against the deck's pitch and sway, while
relieving herself as best she could without allowing her clothing to dip
into the stinking waste. There was nothing with which to cleanse herself,
and as she clung to Billy's arm on the way back, her cheeks burned with
humiliation.

"Don't they ever empty the waste?"

Billy snorted. "Oh, every week or so they order some of us to carry
the tubs up and dump 'em out in the bay. Gets pretty nasty 'tween
times."

She grimaced. Waste dumped into the bay from the ships anchored
in New York Harbor was undoubtedly a substantial source of the heavy
miasma that overlay the city, too well remembered from her sojourn
there with her aunt the previous winter and spring. That and the decaying bodies of the dead dropped into the water like so much debris.

And this water was what the scraps of meat they received was
cooked in unless they insisted on eating it raw or—on the rare occasions
when they received charcoal—cooked over their own fire, as Josiah and
his men did. No wonder so many died.

When she resumed her seat between the others, a sudden piercing
awareness cleared her mind: The shock of arrest, coupled with the
degradation of her imprisonment had paralyzed her. But she had found
herself in desperate situations before and had never given up hope as
she had now.

A surge of defiance and determination drew her erect. *Help us, Lord!*
she pleaded silently. *Have you not promised to succor your people?*

"Ye have to keep on eatin' no matter how bad it seems," Josiah warned, his tone severe but kind. "Ye can't survive without nourishment, and yer body'll get used to it over time."

Elizabeth dismissed his words with a weak wave of her hand. "I'd rather get off this hulk."

Her companions exchanged glances. "Good luck to ye, then," Billy scoffed.

Tom rubbed his bearded jaw. "Ain't no way. Everybody thinks that at first, but it don't last long."

She gritted her teeth. "I've overcome more than one supposedly unmovable obstacle. I refuse to believe this is any different."

"I understand how ye feel. Truly I do. But Billy's right—"

"There's always a way, and we've but to find it, Josiah—or make one! How many of us are there?"

She felt him shrug. "Varies day by day. Men die and others come aboard. When the *Kitty* burnt a couple weeks or so afore ye arrived, her prisoners as survived wahr shifted over here to us. At the moment we've 150 or thereabouts alive on this deck. How many foreign and black prisoners are below I can't say. More'n likely 200 or more."

"Then we well outnumber the sailors aboard this ship!"

"Their weapons outnumber ours," Tom put in with dry humor.

"In case ye haven't noticed, we've no weapons at all and nothing at hand to make any. All we'll accomplish is t' hasten our deaths." Josiah's look and tone were grim.

"Then so be it!" She glanced around to make sure none of their immediate neighbors paid attention. Reassured, she added vehemently in a low voice, "I'd rather die than live in such horror! And the truth is that if we do nothing we'll die anyway."

He let out a sigh. "When I first come here, I considered ever' possibility, Miss Beth. Now and again we're let up on deck, and I put my mind to studyin' the crew, the ship, and those anchored nearby." He stopped and shook his head.

"We all done the same," Tom noted. "Didn't take us long to figure out that all's we can do is take care of one another as best we can and try to stay alive till the war ends."

"Or somebody breaks through to rescue us," Billy offered, his tone hopeful. "That's what keeps us goin'. Those as give up hope is the first to die."

Elizabeth sank back against the curve of the hull, eyes closed. *I'll never give up,* she vowed. *They can't be right. Lord, help us to find a way of escape! With You all things are possible—even this.*

## Chapter Six

HIS FACE SET IN TAUT LINES, Andrews carried Blue Sky's packs to her horse and secured them behind the saddle, fumbling with the straps in the predawn darkness. The first glimmer had just begun to brighten the sky above the eastern treetops, promising a pristine day, and the air's cold mantle, hushed of wind, lay heavy and unmoving upon the earth.

"If I go, I will not learn whether Healer Woman lives," Blue Sky said plaintively. "I may lose my sister and never know it."

Frowning Andrews fixed his gaze on the riders clustered several yards away, Red Fox and Spotted Pony in the van. Carleton stood beside them, with Red Fox leaning down from the saddle to speak to him.

The line of mounted warriors, women, and children extended for some distance along the western road, all bundled in blanket coats, buffalo robes, or bear hides, many leading loaded pack horses. Slightly back from the center, Mary Douglas, the widowed young mother Blue Sky had befriended while both were with child, settled the straps of her infant son's cradleboard around her shoulders. When her anxious gaze met Andrews's, he allowed a tight smile. She returned it with a fleeting one, then mounted awkwardly with the help of Sweetgrass, Stowe's Shawnee wife.

"Of course you'll know," Andrews said to Blue Sky in the Shawnee tongue, turning back to her abruptly. "Will I not myself bring you news as soon as I come? Can you doubt that Moneto will keep us all safely?" he added, using the Shawnee name for the Creator.

She bent her head over the baby tightly wrapped and secured on the cradleboard clutched in her arms. Her lips quivered, and the tear that trickled down her cheek caused his heart to melt.

"But when will you come to me, my husband?" Her voice was barely audible, and in spite of the heavy blanket coat that wrapped her against the cold, she noticeably trembled.

"I promise I'll come as soon as I can—hopefully by *Shkipiye kwiitha,* the Sap Moon."

He spoke gruffly, not moving to close the short distance between them. He feared that if he touched her or the babe, his tears would join hers. Instead he scowled and looked again to the east, where dawn's faint blush now sparkled on the frost edging the trees' bare branches.

"It is too long! Do not send us away, Golden Elk! How can I bear it? If my sister were to die or something were to happen to you, my husband—if I never see you again—"

"If something happens to me, then I want you with our people," he cut her off, his voice harsh. "You know it's not safe for either of you to stay with the army. It was hard enough for me to care for you last winter, and now we have a child to consider. I cannot worry about providing food and shelter for the two of you and keeping you safe from harm on top of all my duties and being away when there's a battle—"

"But you do not need to worry for us! I am able to—"

"Blue Sky, don't make this harder for me than it already is!"

Her shoulders drooped, and she stared at the ground, tears spilling unchecked down her cheeks. His own eyes burning, he spanned the space between them and pulled her and the baby into his embrace. Laying his cheek on the crown of her head, he choked down the grief that threatened to undo him. He was only distantly aware that

Sweetgrass, with Red Fox's wife Laughing Otter, and Spotted Pony's wife, Rain Woman, came to surround them.

After some moments, he cupped Blue Sky's chin in his hand and forced her to meet his gaze. "You know the British have a price on my head too. They almost captured White Eagle, and now they have Healer Woman. If they took the two of you, I'd—" He stopped, unable to continue.

Finally clearing his throat, he whispered, "For our son's sake, for my sake, dear wife, go to our people. Greet my father Grey Cloud and my mother Autumn Wind and tell them that I long to see them again. If they must take you farther west to keep you safe from the Long Knives, go with them without complaint. Though the miles may be long between us for now, never doubt my love. Never doubt that I will find you no matter where you go. Be content and trust Moneto to keep us safe until we can be together again."

"I must leave Little Running Heron, too, even though he is far away and will not know I am gone until he returns," Sweetgrass broke in, her round face creased with emotion. "I, too, must trust that he will come to me when Moneto wills. Until then, we will comfort one another," she added with a smile that reflected her kindly nature.

"See, Mary and her baby also go with us, and you will have them to comfort you as well, Blue Sky," Rain Woman urged as Carleton strode over to join them. "Together we will make the time pass quickly until Golden Elk and White Eagle and Healer Woman, too, are with us again."

"But He Leads the Way will forget his father," Blue Sky mourned, her voice muffled by sobs.

"A son does not forget his father," Laughing Otter scoffed. "Already he knows Golden Elk's scent and the sound of his voice, and you will see how he leaps for joy when his father comes home."

"I will send him to you as soon as he can be spared," Carleton put in. Taking the cradleboard from Blue Sky with a reassuring smile, he soothed the now whimpering child before looking up and saying firmly, "For now you must take your son where both of you will be safe. You do not want harm to come to him, do you?"

Blue Sky swallowed and shook her head. Andrews encircled her shoulders with his arm and led her to the horses, followed by the others. In bleak misery he wrapped her blanket coat more tightly around her.

"Always dress warmly in case you meet storms on the journey." His voice shook.

"We will care for her and the baby," Sweetgrass assured him to the assenting murmurs of the other women, "and there will be many Delaware and Mingo towns along the way to offer us shelter. Do not worry. They will be well."

Turning to Carleton, she said, "If Little Running Heron cannot come to me during the winter, I will return to him with the warriors in the spring. Tell my husband so."

Carleton put his hand on her shoulder. "I will send him to you with Golden Elk."

Mary drew her mount next to Blue Sky's and reached down to squeeze her hand, murmuring words of encouragement and comfort. Inconsolable, Blue Sky began to sob openly, head bowed. Red Fox, Spotted Pony, and the other warriors watched with open impatience, their faces dark at such display of emotion. But Blue Sky remained oblivious of their disapproval.

Taking the cradleboard from Carleton, Andrews kissed the top of his son's head and caressed his cheek, blinking back tears as he looked into the tiny, dusky face and the dark eyes that eagerly sought his own. At last he relinquished the cradleboard to the women, who quickly secured the straps around Blue Sky's shoulders and helped her to mount her pony.

The instant all the women were settled astride their mounts, Carleton raised his hand in farewell, and Red Fox signaled the company forward. Leaving the dawn behind them, they turned down the path into the shadowed woodland, Mary leading Blue Sky's horse, while she twisted in the saddle to reach back toward Andrews.

"Let us stay with you, Golden Elk! Please don't send us away—please, my husband! I shall be lonely!"

Blue Sky's cry echoed from the surrounding hills, and now the baby's loud wails joined hers. Andrews stood motionless, watching them disappear among the trees, heedless of the tears running down his face.

"She is strong. She will be comforted by our people." Carleton's words sounded forced, and uncertainty and sorrow edged his tone.

"And who will comfort me?" Andrews asked bleakly.

Carleton pulled him into a rough embrace. Shoulders heaving, Andrews stood with hands clenched and head bowed, straining to hear the last echoes of Blue Sky's heartbroken pleas, intermingled with his son's cries, until their voices faded out of hearing.

## Chapter Seven

*Sunday, 2 November*

Alarmed, Isaiah raised his hand to halt the six men who crowded on his heels. It was an hour before sunrise and deep shadows cloaked Montcoeur's back lawn.

"Soft, now," he commanded in an undertone as he motioned them back toward the line of trees that bordered the Hudson River's precipice. But too late.

"Well, come on!" called the brown, wren-like young woman who bustled toward them.

A bundle of what appeared to be bedding in her arms, she advanced from the rear of the elegant mansion Isaiah remembered well from the secret foray Carleton had led there the previous April. Where he had unexpectedly surprised Vander Groot in what appeared to be an intimate encounter with Elizabeth. And had taken him prisoner.

Isaiah exchanged glances with Captain Apollos Matheson, his second in command, whose coppery-brown complexion and the angles of his hawk-like visage reflected his mixed African and Cherokee blood. "You Mrs. Stebbins?" Isaiah asked politely.

"I am." She tilted her turbaned head and jutted her chin in the direction of the clapboard building at the rear of a much larger stone carriage house and stables of newer construction. "And I ain't scrubbed that ol' carriage house purty near all night to have you and your men shy off. Now get along."

Just then Vander Groot emerged from the black shadows of the building's open double doors, accompanied by a slender black man. He motioned to them.

"Thank God you're here!"

Relieved, Isaiah led his men across the lawn and inside the building. Mrs. Stebbins followed, closing the doors behind them before she hurried up a steep stairway to their left. In the gloom the men hastily saluted Vander Groot, then doffed their hats while he introduced Ben Stebbins and, when the woman returned downstairs, his wife, Sallie.

At closer range she justified Isaiah's initial impression: small and spritely as a little wren, but younger and prettier than he had first thought. She and her husband assured the men that they would do all they could to provide anything that might be needed, then took their leave.

"You're a welcome sight!" Vander Groot exclaimed when the couple had gone. "I've been imploring the Lord for your safety since I arrived last evening."

"We did our share o' prayin' too." Isaiah followed him around indistinct stacks of goods stored in the old building, then up the stairs, with his men pressing close behind.

They all hunched to avoid hitting their heads on the joists that defined a surprisingly spacious area under the building's gabled roof. The single window at each end had been heavily swathed, and a betty lamp flickered on a low table halfway down between pallets spread on the floor, each supplied with a pillow and a neatly folded blanket. A large, covered crock of water and a wooden box filled with food and utensils provided the room's only other furnishings.

When Isaiah asked whether the detail that had brought them across the river should stay to carry messengers back and forth, Vander Groot shook his head and told him to dismiss them. "Ben kept the *Implacable* seaworthy," he explained, referring to the small sailboat in which Isaiah's son, Pete, had transported Elizabeth on clandestine nightly forays while she and Tess lived at the estate. "He's able to sail her and will transport you and your men as needed."

He waited while Isaiah and his companions ranged themselves across the pallets. When they were settled, he asked Isaiah tentatively, "So . . . what was General Carleton's reaction when he learned I'd gone?"

Isaiah hesitated before saying carefully, "He afraid maybe you go to Howe to betray him. But when he read your letter, he be real sorry for doubtin' you. And now he worry about gettin' you out too."

Vander Groot studied him, certain he was not telling the full truth. Finally he said with a crooked smile, "That bad, eh?"

"He get over it." Isaiah shrugged. "He say to tell you he love you."

"It was worse than I feared, then," Vander Groot returned with a chuckle. He rubbed his eyes and stifled a yawn. "I didn't get much rest last night. I'm sure you didn't either, but we've no time to waste sleeping. You didn't run into any trouble crossing the river?"

"We come awful close to bein' cut off by a British schooner soon's we get halfway 'cross. Praise God they don't see us in the dark and our guides get us to shore quick." He gave Vander Groot a sharp glance. "You run into trouble at King's Bridge?"

Vander Groot massaged the taut muscles at the base of his neck and sat cross-legged beside Isaiah. "It didn't begin well, but Lord Howe's pass considerably improved the guards' attitude, and they sent me on my way."

Isaiah nodded. "Gen'l Carleton ordered me to send a report back soon's I find out what you learn and what you plannin'."

The doctor leaned forward tensely, glancing from Isaiah to his men. "Miss Howard is indeed here in the city. Ben and Sallie have connections with a multitude of black servants, some of whom work for British officers, which gives them access to a treasure trove of information. When I arrived last evening, they'd already learned of her arrest, though they haven't yet learned where she's held. But they appeared so genuinely distressed by the ill treatment she received that I confided our intentions, and they readily enlisted. Since then I've been trying to plot a strategy for getting to Miss Howard that has some hope of success.

"Ben's a blacksmith," he continued, "and he'll make grapnels and other equipment we'll need if she's held on one of the ships. He says many black sailors are also held aboard them, and in the worst conditions. In fact, he and several of his friends were trying to find a way to free them even before he learned of Miss Howard's plight. The trouble is they don't have the means—"

Isaiah grunted. "We supply that long as the gen'l ships get through. O' course . . . " he hesitated, then continued, "if she held somewhere else . . . "

Vander Groot made a dismissive gesture. "We'll deal with that if necessary. For the time being, we have to move ahead. What did you learn of the general's plans before you left him?"

After relating Carleton's plans and orders, Isaiah added, "Can Stebbins round us up some volunteers?"

"That's what he and Sallie plan to do." At Isaiah's broad grin, Vander Groot cautioned, "There's a great deal that must yet fall into place if this mission's to succeed."

Murmurs of agreement and eagerness to head into the city rose from the men gathered around them.

Vander Groot surveyed the worn but serviceable homespun they were clad in and nodded approval. "You'll easily pass as servants, which will allow you to move about the city without attracting undue notice."

He beckoned them to gather around and from his pocket pulled a rough map he had drawn of the city. Spreading it out on his knee, he noted where he wanted men posted at the docks and at Crown Point, directly across from Wallabout Bay, to take note of who came and went, where ships were anchored, and when any departed or arrived.

"We'll also need lookouts outside Clinton's headquarters, here. Glean as much information as you discreetly can from the conversations of those who go in and out and keep an eye on the general's movements. It's imperative that we find out exactly where Miss Howard and Captain Stern are held, whether a courier arrives from Howe and, if so, what orders he brings. That will determine our next steps."

For the next several minutes Vander Groot shared all he had gleaned from Ben and Sallie. In spite of General John Burgoyne's surrender of his entire force at Saratoga several weeks earlier; the city's isolation by land except for the main road to Philadelphia; and the swarms of privateers harassing British shipping, hampering the transport of supplies and reinforcements from England, the British still held a firm grip on the city. Its strong fortifications and the warships that crowded the harbor would make their mission hazardous in the extreme.

When he concluded, Isaiah said, "Atkin, nobody going to mark you, and you ride fast. Head back 'cross the river and make sure you report to the gen'l by nightfall tomorrow. Let him know everythin' we're plannin'."

"Yes, sir!" The slender youth scrambled to his feet, his face brightening.

Vander Groot regarded the corporal dubiously. Thin and short of stature, he appeared hardly old enough to qualify as a soldier. Yet there was a hardness in his gaze that indicated experience his age belied.

"We'll need you back here by Wednesday night with the general's orders, Atkin," Vander Groot said. "Can you do it?"

"I slept on horseback afore."

"Then godspeed."

After Isaiah returned upstairs from seeing the corporal off, Vander Groot told him, "Early tomorrow I intend to call on my associates at the hospital in my house," he told them. "And then I'm going to call on acquaintances still living here to determine whether any of them have heard rumors of my involvement with the army."

Isaiah rubbed his fingers along his jaw, his gaze growing sharp. "Maybe you stir somethin' up."

"I have to find out if I've been compromised before I attempt anything further. At any rate, there's no way to keep my presence in the city a secret—"

"You have to! If you forced to get out fast or be arrested, everythin' be lost!"

"That's not true. You'll simply have to carry on without me."

Isaiah slumped back against the wall. "And how we do that?"

"I'm not worried. You think on your feet. Besides, Ben and Sallie haven't heard anything about it or they'd have warned me. Once I confirm that I can safely go ahead, I'm going to make an appointment to meet with Clinton."

Isaiah straightened so abruptly that he struck the low angle of the ceiling. Rubbing the back of his head, he glared at Vander Groot.

"You want to hang?"

The other men joined in remonstrating with the doctor, but he remained unmovable. "If I can persuade Clinton of my loyalty and that I possess valuable intelligence concerning General Carleton, he might let fall some indication of where Miss Howard's held. I have to try, else we'll waste time attempting to locate her once the general's ships arrive, and an alarm will surely be raised. If that happens, there'll be little likelihood we'll succeed—or even make it out of the harbor."

# Chapter Eight

CARLETON RUBBED his burning eyes wearily. Deepening shadows lay long across the grass and pooled beneath the trees outside his chamber window, but he did not register the scene.

He had slept little more the previous night than during the two preceding it. His mind had stubbornly refused to quiet. The wrenching vision of Elizabeth in dire distress—or already dead—weighed on him until at last, compelled to rise, he had pulled on clothing and armed himself.

Flinging open his door, he had discovered his way blocked by four of Isaiah's largest, most muscular Rangers. They had remained impervious to his commands, and then to his rage.

Summoned from his adjacent room, Andrews stumbled into the passage, bleary-eyed, face etched with his own grief, to drag Carleton back inside by main force. "You saved my life, Jon," he had said, "and now I'm saving yours."

"I've no intention of surrendering myself to Howe," Carleton responded through gritted teeth.

Sweeping him with a glance that took in sabre and pistols, the colonel forcibly relieved him of his weapons and shoved him down hard onto the edge of the bed. "Even if you manage to get through his entire army and his personal guards and kill him, which is doubtful at best, you won't leave there alive."

"It matters not!"

"It does to me—and to Beth. If you die, who'll rescue her? Besides, if you should succeed in your goal, they'll execute her immediately."

At this Carleton had given way. Andrews sat with him until dawn, reasoning and praying with him until the cold clarity of sane judgment at length returned.

The shadow of those desperate hours had made it all but impossible for Carleton to attend to necessary duties during the day. He felt as though he had lost his way in a land totally foreign and bereft of any glimmer of a pathway home.

A knock on the door jarred him out of bitter introspection. He bade whoever was outside to enter, grateful for the interruption.

Andrews strode through the doorway, expression and movements under tight rein, as they had been since Blue Sky's departure. Hard on his heels came Carleton's agent, Louis Teissèdre, with McLeod following. Both men were rumpled and windblown as though from a hard, swift ride.

"As I said before, general," Teissèdre grumbled in French, without preamble, "you are an exceedingly hard man to find."

Carleton pushed out of his chair, reassurance flooding him at sight of his old friend. "Obviously not hard enough," he returned with a mirthless laugh. "At least not for Howe's minions—and you."

Teissèdre's stout form radiated energy from every pore. With a crumpled handkerchief he mopped beads of sweat from a bald pate that contrary to convention, Carleton knew, had never entertained a wig. He came to enfold Carleton in a hearty embrace, pounding him on the back.

"It'll all come right, my friend," he murmured in Carleton's ear. "We'll meet this challenge together, as we have before—more than once, as you'll recall."

It was impossible to hold onto despair in the face of such optimism, and Carleton managed a smile. "What would I do without you, Louis?"

Cocking his eyebrow, Teissèdre released him to indicate McLeod with a wave of his hand. "If I hadn't the fortune of calling upon General Washington just as the captain arrived, I'd have had no more idea as to where you were secreted than did your commandant. After James, here, treated us to a full report on the triumph at Saratoga, His Excellency made clear his orders were for you to return to him at the earliest instant. He's been wondering where you've been."

"We found the army on the march to White Marsh, where the General intends t' establish his headquarters," McLeod broke in. "I gave him your letter and explained the situation in full."

"He won't oppose us?"

McLeod directed a bland glance at Teissèdre. "He expressed deep concern for ye and Miss Howard and agreed to do all he can to help. He shared the latest developments in the Delaware campaign and promised to alert us to Howe's movements and anythin' else as may prove useful." The chaplain added dryly, "However, he did make mention that ye didna ask his permission before decidin' on this course."

Andrews snorted. "Sadly, we hadn't the time to write up a detailed report and send it on ahead, begging his approval."

Teissèdre's mouth quirked. "You may be interested to know that Washington confirmed his familiarity with the deplorable conditions your captives are subjected to. He's implored Howe to exchange them or at least allow his representatives to provide proper food, clothing, and medical care—all of which has fallen on deaf ears. Meanwhile, of course, Clinton fetes your General Lee as an honored guest and allows him to make free with the largess of the British treasury."

"No doubt either to tempt him back to the king's side or extract intelligence from him," Carleton returned sourly. "As far as I'm concerned, the British may continue to support Charles Lee and spare us the cost—not to mention his intrigues to supplant Washington as commander."

"I suspect Clinton will tire of him sooner or later and send him back to you."

"All the worse for us." With an effort Carleton shook off the fog that wrapped his brain. "I'm glad you've come, Louis. I'll depend greatly on your peculiar expertise when we sail into New York Harbor."

The Frenchman rubbed his hands together, glee and determination mingling on his features. "I admit I'm looking forward to our little charade. We enter the harbor under the British flag, yes?"

"We'll arouse fewer questions if we do." Carleton motioned them all to the table.

When they were seated, Teissèdre said, "Then, our pretext?"

"I'm thinking an urgent letter to Clinton from Lord Germain. We'll work out the details once we reach the rendezvous. Right now I just want to get there and see my ships on the horizon."

Teissèdre grinned. "If I know your Monsieur Stowe, they'll arrive without delay."

"If they're not becalmed, blown off course by a storm, or sunk by a British squadron," Carleton returned gloomily.

"Take courage, my friend!"

Apparently undaunted by the obstacles that lay before them, for the next hour Teissèdre regaled them with accounts of the successful attacks Carleton's privateers had undertaken against British shipping as well as actions involving the rudimentary Continental Navy. At some length he shared detailed intelligence on warships newly commissioned in England and others that were currently in port there. He went so far as to name their captains, their recent successes and failures, where they had come from, and where they were going. All information the British at New York did not yet have, he emphasized, which might prove useful when it came to devising assumed names for themselves and Carleton's ships as well as answering questions during encounters with naval personnel at New York.

"I tried to cover every eventuality," he concluded.

Clearly fascinated, Andrews burst out, "How in blazes do you know all this?"

Teissèdre leaned back in his chair, a cunning smile spreading over his face. "My dear colonel, my country has many highly placed . . . ah . . . friends . . . in England."

"Including at the very elbow of King George the Third," Carleton drawled. "And you have your fingers on the pulse of every one, no doubt."

Teissèdre gave an airy wave of his hand. "Britain has her own, shall we say, favorable contacts at the French court, as you know. Not to mention in your own Congress and military councils."

"We'll not mention that—nor that France does as well. In fact," Carleton added, regarding him with a sardonic smile, "I wouldn't be the least surprised if you weren't one of them. Considering the small sums I'm able to pay for your services, I don't flatter myself that I'm your only employer."

Smirking, Teissèdre threw him a sidelong glance. "Bah! I'm more than adequately compensated, general. But if your charge were true— and that's a point I don't concede—it would make me all the more useful to you, yes? For my part, I expect that you Americans have your own spies. Certainly in Britain and doubtless at the court of Louis the Sixteenth as well . . . the good Dr. Franklin being foremost among them."

"With the exception of Dr. Franklin, they're small fleas compared to the French and British spies. You're the true professionals."

Teissèdre conceded an expansive smile. "The trouble is that you Americans learn all too quickly. Such an enterprising people will ultimately invent methods to checkmate us."

Carleton's features hardened. "You may be right. For now, however, the only intelligence I care about is where Miss Howard is held. And how I can get to her with the utmost speed."

## Chapter Nine

*Monday, 3 November*

E ARLY THE NEXT MORNING, Vander Groot called at the mansion that had belonged to his elderly great aunt, Euphemia Van Cortland. It had passed to him on her death, and the previous winter, at Elizabeth's suggestion, the two of them had established a hospital there for the women and children of British soldiers, whose needs were sorely neglected by the army.

He was welcomed with surprise and pleasure by the doctors and nurses he had placed in charge after secretly deciding to join the Continental Army. His plan had been abruptly altered, however, when Carleton had unexpectedly slipped across the Hudson to Montcoeur and discovered him alone with Elizabeth. Instead of volunteering, the doctor had found himself a prisoner pressed into service with the Rangers. After a tense beginning, however, Carleton had won Vander Groot's genuine admiration and loyalty.

He spent much of the morning consulting on several critical cases. The manner of the doctors and nurses toward him provided ample assurance that none knew of his involvement with the rebels, and his confidence grew. After accompanying the senior physician on his rounds and offering recommendations, Vander Groot made his farewells shortly before noon and stepped into the large dining room at the front of the house to retrieve his coat and hat.

The tall windows were swathed in heavy draperies, and the room lay in semidarkness, the air cool and redolent of dust and little use. The long table with its chairs and the massive sideboard remained in their usual places as the space was now used only occasionally as a meeting room.

For several moments he stood motionless, pierced by an indefinable emotion. The familiar surroundings appeared unchanged from the last time he had entered there, shortly before going to meet Elizabeth on the fateful night that had changed his destiny forever. Looking about him, he felt a pang of loss and grief, sharper now for the contrast between the happy times that room had witnessed and the images of war he could not seem to banish from his thoughts.

For as long as he could remember, each week his Aunt Euphemia had held court at lively family gatherings in the expansive, ornately furnished room. Her absence from his life was a palpable one, especially as he had been prevented from being at her deathbed to bid her a last, loving farewell.

A host of cherished memories of the woman who since his childhood had been more confidante and mentor to him than merely relative flooded his mind. How he missed her and longed for her steady, wise counsel, her good humor and teasing, the laughter they had shared so often, the love she had offered unconditionally! Yet the sensation of her kindly spirit hovering protectively over him and the assurance that he would one day see her again warmed him.

His heart lifting, he caught up his greatcoat and pulled it on, settled his hat on his head, and, whistling softly, went out the door to call upon acquaintances who still remained in the city.

"I HOPE BY NOW YOU SEE the error of your ways in opposing your lawful king," the captain ground out, his fingers tightening around Elizabeth's frayed neckcloth until she fought to drag air into her lungs. He shook her roughly, the force of his grip lifting her until only her toes touched the deck. "Swear allegiance to the crown, wench, and you'll be shown mercy. Confess all you know of the rebel spies, and I'll personally see that you're released."

In spite of terror and pain, she was all too aware of the ragged men crouched around her, warded back only by the bayonets of a handful of sneering marines. "Never!" she croaked, breath rasping. "Even if I believed you, which I don't. Kill me if it pleases you. I'll tell you nothing."

He threw her back into the corner he had dragged her out of, giving a snort of derision when she banged her head against one of the hull's futtocks so hard that brilliant spots danced before her eyes. Josiah's arms were immediately around her, and Tom and Billy formed a protective barrier between them and the marines, faces contorted with equal fear and loathing. She could feel them trembling as much as she was.

"Had I known the full depths of evil you British have sunk to," she spat, her hand pressed to her aching head, "I'd have conspired against you even earlier than I did. I'd have done more and done it with a thousand times more passion! There's nothing you can ever do to me that will persuade me to harm those who oppose you or to give my allegiance to that tyrant who calls himself king. He is not my sovereign!"

The captain bent forward as though he meant take hold of her again.

"Leave 'er alone!" one prisoner cried.

"Shame to ye fer abusin' a girl, ye dirty coward!" another shouted over the chorus of angry murmurs that filled the hold. "Ye ain't got the guts to face real men!"

"Such as you?" the captain sneered. But he straightened as his uneasy men brandished their muskets threateningly.

The captain folded his arms, his dark gaze fixed on Elizabeth. "I swear you'll have cause to regret your stubbornness. And in the end you'll tells us everything we want to know anyway."

Turning abruptly on his heel, he motioned to his guard and led the way up the companionway. The torchlight diminished until the gun deck was once more plunged into grey gloom. Letting out a shaky breath, Elizabeth sagged against Josiah.

"Ye're all right?"

She looked up to meet his concerned gaze, and then Tom's and Billy's in turn before rubbing the knot at the back of her head ruefully. "It's nothing. I've suffered worse, though not nearly as much as you have."

Billy swore fiercely under his breath.

"The worst is there ain't nothin' any of us can do," Tom muttered, his tone bitter.

"Nor should you try," she returned with all the firmness she could muster. "You'll accomplish nothing but to bring reprisals down on your own heads and those of these men, and that won't help any of us."

Josiah released her and stared down at his clenched hands. Although he said nothing, she could feel his frustration at his helplessness.

She became aware that her skin prickled and shivered in disgust to feel the vermin crawling through the filth that crusted her body. Could she have been confined in this hellish pit for only a week? Josiah had told her so, but she had trouble believing it.

When she had first been dragged aboard the *Erebus,* more tomb than prison, she had determined to mark the passage of time if only to sustain some sense of connection with the outer world. But the scarcely perceptible passage of day to night and night to day, while autumn steadily declined toward the dark months of winter, combined with numbing boredom and physical discomfort to make keeping an accurate count all but impossible.

Never had she been subjected to such ill treatment. Day by day the weather was growing noticeably colder. Icy wind and water crept through the cracks in the ancient hull's rotted wood and crumbling caulking, and each morning the bilge had risen enough that sailors and the more able prisoners were pressed to manning the pumps.

Their ragged clothing was constantly damp and turned to ice when temperatures dropped below freezing. With no blankets to wrap their almost naked bodies, they huddled together in groups to keep as warm as they could. Most of the time the prisoners were not provided any charcoal with which to build a fire to cook, wash, or warm themselves. According to Josiah, if the previous winter was any indication, their situation would only grow more dire before warmer weather finally arrived.

From the talk of new prisoners, she had learned that they all passed through the *Frederick,* which functioned as both hospital and receiving ship, where their names were recorded before they were brought aboard *Erebus.* She, however, had been delivered directly there. Only those imprisoned with her, who had no hope of release, knew her name. And while other prisoners were at least allowed topside for short periods, a few at a time, to breathe fresh air and stretch cramped limbs, that privilege was denied her so that all she knew of life outside her grim confine was what Josiah and the others told her.

Clearly she had been made invisible, her captors determined not to hazard even the slightest possibility she might escape or to chance her identification by anyone who might be searching for her.

The knowledge Carleton must also be suffering caused her endless anguish. That he would likely alert her Aunt Tess, Elizabeth's fierce and loving ally in gathering intelligence, added to her burden. Once the news reached Roxbury, Elizabeth's parents and little sister, who by now must have returned home to Boston, would also know.

She was terrified not only that Carleton might deliver himself into Howe's hands, but also that the British commander would summon her parents and sister, and that they, not knowing the full extent of his treachery, would fall victim to his devious plot. At the very least, they would discover in the worst possible way the role she had played in the rebellion. She would not be there to defend her actions, and the thought of her father's devastation at learning how deeply she had been involved with the Sons of Liberty pierced her through.

Her capture had also done immeasurable damage to the glorious cause she fought for. Washington was now deprived of the critical intelligence only she had been able to supply with the depth of access she had to the highest levels of the British military.

The memory of the lies she had told and her brazenly seductive behavior toward so many of the British officers in order to elicit intelligence accused her as well. Could actions ordinarily counted unrighteous be justified in the service of a high cause? In a fallen world might it ever be right to violate certain of God's precepts in the effort to attain his will? Was it possible for human minds to comprehend the purposes of the great Being who created the universe and sustained it by his breath?

How she was humbled by the sickening realization that all along she had been played for a fool by General Howe and his mistress, Betsey Loring! Why else had they repeatedly sought her out, making her witness to scenes in which they revealed their malicious intentions toward Carleton?

Had not Carleton warned her? Had not her own intuition pricked her conscience? Yet, confident that her sex blinded her enemies to her covert role, she had once again pursued a willful course despite her vow to the Lord to follow his leading in all things instead of her own faulty understanding!

The bitter reflections that swarmed her mind would surely drive her mad. All she had clung to and deemed precious had been torn away as the result of her own foolish actions. And all the strength she had left was to cry out for the help for which it was abundantly clear she was unworthy.

## Chapter Ten

"I CONFESS I'M SURPRISED to see you," General Henry Clinton said, eyebrows rising as he took in Vander Groot's artfully disheveled appearance. "I assumed that after the great fire last fall, you and your family would remain in Philadelphia. As you can see, the city is a shadow of what it used to be."

Vander Groot took the chair indicated, forcing a smile to conceal his discomfort at the general's keen recollection. Indeed, now that he confronted Clinton in his own headquarters, Vander Groot's knees lacked their former steadiness and the scene he had so carefully rehearsed deserted him.

"You also lost everything, did you not?" Clinton prompted when he failed to answer.

"I . . . had particular reasons for returning," he began tentatively. *Lord, give me the right words—*

As none of Vander Groot's acquaintances remaining in the beleaguered city had known of or questioned his movements in his absence, he had wasted no time arranging a meeting with the general. Yet now it occurred to him that it was one thing to contemplate conning intelligence from the British commander, another altogether to carry it through.

A new appreciation for the roles Elizabeth and Carleton had played impressed itself on him. But with the thought of Elizabeth came a surge of love and fear for her—and renewed determination that he would not fail in his mission.

"Ah, your hospital, no doubt," Clinton was saying. "An admirable work. Knowing their women and children are well taken care of contributes enormously to my troops' steadiness." With a smirk he added, "The rebels will never gain control of *this* harbor as long as *I'm* in command."

Noting the general's emphasis, Vander Groot ventured, "I can't imagine those villainous patriots will hold the Delaware much longer against Lord and General Howe's assault."

Resuming his seat behind the writing table, Clinton snorted. "They're proving to be stubborn enough that General Howe's been forced to beg reinforcements. Just an hour ago I sent off as large a force as I could spare. My first responsibility, after all, is New York."

Vander Groot gave him a veiled look. So this was the reason for the sudden movement of troops out of the city, surreptitiously communicated by Isaiah as they passed each other down the street from Clinton's headquarters a short time earlier. Silently he prayed for guidance.

"Your family's well, I trust. Did they stay in Philadelphia or remove from the city for safety? We heard many loyalists fled before the battle."

"I've not been in . . . Philadelphia." Vander Groot put his hand to his head, feigning agitation.

Clinton's eyes narrowed. "I understood you intended to join your family there."

"I did, but . . . in fact, I didn't make it that far." He looked up. "I was taken prisoner by that villain General Carleton before I could leave."

The admission captured the general's full attention. Starting forward in his chair, Clinton stared at him, the color rising to his face.

"Perdition! You can't mean that he was here—in the city?"

Vander Groot's heart was pounding so heavily he had no need to pretend emotion. "Not precisely. You see . . . conceiving myself very much in love with Miss Elizabeth Howard, I called upon her at Montcoeur the night before I meant to leave for Philadelphia. While I was there, the general made a wholly unexpected appearance in company with several of his Rangers—"

"He was—he was on York Island then?" Clinton spluttered, his expression one of complete astonishment. "And he brought along a detail of his Rangers?"

Vander Groot nodded. "One can hardly credit it, but they managed to breach our lines undetected."

Clinton leaned back and regarded him as though thunderstruck. "And he captured you, you say? Where were you taken? How long were you held?"

"I was taken back across the Hudson to the Rangers' camp at Westfield, where I was forced to care for their sick and wounded. I made an attempt to escape as soon as I was able, but I was captured and beaten. Thereafter I was kept under such close watch that I'd no further chance of getting away. I finally determined to appear to join in their despicable cause in order to gain their trust, and in that I finally succeeded."

Clinton started out of his chair and took a turn around the room. "But surely your family marked your disappearance. As close as you've been to the Howes, I'd think they'd immediately have enlisted help to find and free you."

"Carleton forced me to write to them, claiming to have voluntarily joined the rebel army. They replied in complete dismay, as you may imagine, but my correspondence was so carefully monitored I wasn't able to alert them to my real situation. You can understand that they never mentioned my supposed change of allegiance to anyone for fear of repercussions if it became known that their son was a turncoat."

Clinton threw himself back into his chair. "But obviously you did get away."

Vander Groot took a deep breath. "Last Thursday night on the road back from Albany—his Rangers joined in the attack against General Burgoyne—Carleton was closeted with his officers on some matter or other. I took the opportunity to slip out of the camp and made my way here with as much care as possible to avoid attracting notice from any of the rebel militias."

Before Clinton could respond, he continued hastily, "I'm compelled to warn you that Miss Howard is a spy! You can't imagine how profoundly shocked I was that night when she openly admitted that she and Carleton are very much in love and that she's been working hand in glove with him to supply General Washington with intelligence. The worst is that she'd been using my family's relationship with the Howes for that very purpose.

"I don't know where she is now," he concluded, thickening his voice, "but I saw her with Carleton's Rangers at Bemis Heights in disguise as a man! You must believe me and find her, arrest her! Unfortunately I'm a physician, not a soldier, but such talents and abilities as I do have are at your service. I'd rejoice in nothing more than to see both of them hanged."

For a long moment Clinton fixed him in an assessing look that caused Vander Groot's chest to constrict. At last a smug smile spread across the general's face.

"My dear doctor," he purred, "I'm way ahead of you. General Howe had Miss Howard tracked after I became convinced that she must be that infamous spy Oriole who plagued us at Boston. You'll be relieved to know that I arrested her on her way back from Saratoga not a fortnight ago."

Vander Groot clasped his hands in pretended relief. "Thank God! You can't imagine the anxiety I've felt at thought of the harm her treachery has done our king and country! But you must exercise the greatest

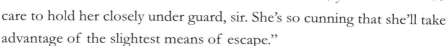

care to hold her closely under guard, sir. She's so cunning that she'll take advantage of the slightest means of escape."

Clinton's laugh was not pleasant. "I assure you, Dr. Vander Groot, Miss Howard has been secured where no means of escape exist. No one could ever get to her even if they learned exactly where she's held."

Vander Groot leaned forward. "Pardon me, but I'd not be so sure if I were you, general. If anyone could spring her loose, it's that devil Carleton. He's the most arrant and ingenious villain in existence. I'm convinced there isn't any place on earth he couldn't get to if he put his mind to it. And judging from his devotion to this woman, he'll move heaven and earth to find her."

Clinton leaned back in his chair, fingers steepled. "Aboard a prison ship in the middle of New York Harbor?"

Vander Groot arranged his features to reflect astonishment, then joined in the general's laughter with genuine delight. "In the very midst of the Royal Navy? Brilliant! I must concede to your genius. Not even Satan himself could get at her there." With satisfaction he saw that Clinton basked in his praise. "As much as she knows about the rebel army and their spies, she must have proven a veritable font of information," he added smoothly.

Clinton's preening faltered. "I'm afraid her treachery remains invulnerable, at least for now," he admitted with a scowl. "Let her but suffer a little while longer—and I assure you there's no place more guaranteed to break the resistance of even the most devout rebel than our prison ships—and she'll begin to see reason. In the meantime, Howe has threatened Carleton with her immediate execution if he doesn't give himself up. Either way, they're finished."

He rang a small bell on his desk, and in seconds a bewigged and liveried black servant appeared at the room's side door. At the general's order to bring tea, he disappeared as silently as he had come, returning moments later, bearing a well-laden tea tray.

At Clinton's invitation, Vander Groot joined him by the softly crackling fire. Seated opposite Clinton in a deep wing chair next to a small table, he accepted the steaming tea the servant poured. He stared into his cup, his stomach churning at the thought of Elizabeth's suffering while he and the general enjoyed the simple graces of warmth and food that she was denied.

When the man had gone, Clinton regarded him thoughtfully across the rim of his cup. "I greatly appreciate your offer of assistance, doctor. As a matter of fact, I believe your talents and abilities, as you put it, could prove invaluable to us." When Vander Groot eagerly assured him that he was most happy to oblige in any way, Clinton continued, "You've been with the Continental Army, with Carleton's Rangers specifically, and your recollections of what you've seen and heard while a prisoner may well be helpful in ending this unnecessary conflict."

Affecting a casual indifference, he continued deliberately, "Most particularly I'd like a detailed report of the action at Bemis Heights that led to General Burgoyne's surrender. We've gotten so many conflicting reports that it's impossible to sort it all out."

"It was an utter debacle." Vander Groot looked around as though to make sure they were alone, then added in a low voice, "I hate to say it, but our valiant men were ill used by General Burgoyne. If you ask me, sir, the responsibility for this shameful defeat lies in a want of the astute planning and strategy necessary for a wilderness campaign. If you'd been in command, I've no doubt the outcome would have been quite the opposite."

Equal glee at his rival's humiliation, dismay at the army's defeat, and gratification at the doctor's flattery waged war on Clinton's features. Vander Groot had much to do to keep from snickering.

"It occurs to me that there's another matter in which you might be of great use to us, doctor. Miss Howard has indeed proven quite resistant to divulging any information about General Carleton and the inner workings of the rebels' intelligence networks, information that would greatly benefit us. You had a very . . . ah . . . close relationship with her before you were taken prisoner, I understand."

Vander Groot drained his cup and set it back on the tray. "If you mean would it be possible for me to reestablish a relationship of trust that might yield fruit—"

"It did occur to me that if she believed you've gone over to the patriots she might let down her guard."

Vander Groot pretended to be taken aback. "She not only saw me being taken prisoner, but also knows my unalterable opposition to the rebels."

"It can't have been easy to persuade Carleton of your change of heart, but you managed it. Surely you can persuade that little chit too."

Again Vander Groot began to laugh, astonished that Clinton was making his task so easy. "She knew I had Lord Howe's pass to get back into the city, which will make my return unremarkable to her," he conceded. "And in her extremity she might well be highly vulnerable to the succor offered by an old friend."

A cunning smile spread over Clinton's face. "You can tell her that you're working with Carleton to rescue her. Did you know he's refitted a number of his merchantmen to serve as privateers and persuaded the rebel Congress to issue him letters of marque? The villain's already captured a number of East Indiamen fully loaded with goods worth a small fortune."

A chill settled in Vander Groot's breast at Clinton's open confirmation that British spies indeed operated in Congress. "The blackguard! I'd not believed even his villainy would extend so far."

"No matter. As soon as the rebels' Delaware defenses have been breached, Lord Howe plans to make it his express mission to either sink or take all that traitor's ships as prize, whether merchantmen or privateers. Of course, by then Carleton will have been hanged." He ground his teeth, eyes flashing. "Tell your Miss Howard that her lover plans to sail into this very harbor and pluck her out of our hands. She'll believe him capable of that."

It felt as though a vise squeezed the breath from Vander Groot's lungs. Fighting to keep the tremor from his voice, he said, "Even Carleton hasn't the temerity to try such a foolhardy scheme. But, yes, I believe I can convince Miss Howard of it."

He felt sick at heart. Whether Clinton truly believed Carleton would try to carry out such an attack, that the general had come up with the very strategy Carleton had decided upon, and thus might guard against it, increased the danger a thousandfold.

It would take two days for a messenger to reach Carleton with a warning, but until Atkin returned late in the day on the morrow they had no one to spare from keeping watch on Wallabout Bay and Clinton's headquarters. By then Carleton, knowing nothing of this new peril, might already have left Baptist Meeting House for the rendezvous.

Worse, it was already impossible to get a message to Boston in time to alert his ships. They would sail, unaware that the enemy might be on the prowl for them.

Andrews extended the letter he carried. "According to Sergeant Atwood, this is from Howe. His messenger is being held under close guard, though he protested mightily that he was ordered to deliver it in person."

Carleton snatched the paper from Andrews's hand. "Howe ought to know better than that. He'd do the same."

He directed an assessing glance toward the mounted patrol waiting for him in the windy twilight, concealed from the camp by a thick copse of trees behind the inn's stables. He could make out Teissèdre's rotund form as the Frenchman hoisted himself into the saddle.

Carleton snapped the letter's wax seal. Unfolding the page, he scanned it rapidly before handing it back to the colonel.

Andrews studied it, frowning. "It was sent from Philadelphia early this morning."

"You'll note that although he agrees to my terms, he states—rather carefully phrased—that it'll take several days for him to attend to the matter because he's tied up driving our little army out of our pathetic defensive line along the Delaware."

Andrews's mouth tightened. "The attitude certainly comes through, though he doesn't state it quite so baldly. I'd like to ask him why, if we're so contemptible, it's taking him so long to stamp us into the dust." He gave a grim chuckle and looked up. "At least he promises to send Caleb with a letter from Beth at the first instant. I care less for his gloating that it's a shame she's suffering while you drag your feet. What a gentleman."

"Curse his black heart," Carleton muttered, hardly able to speak.

Andrews snorted. "I'll add mine to yours. Obviously he wants you to think she's in Philadelphia, but I'll wager there's another messenger secretly riding hell bent for New York."

"Good of him to underestimate our powers of deduction."

"We'll take every advantage of it now that Isaiah and his men are safely in New York with Pieter, busily laying plans."

"Send McLeod to White Marsh at once to alert Washington to Howe's letter and our further plans and order him to meet me at the rendezvous with His Excellency's response." Carleton rubbed his throbbing brow. "Corporal Atkin was confident he'll be back in New York tomorrow."

Shivering in the cold wind, Andrews drew his cloak more tightly around his shoulders and took in the deepening shadows beneath the trees. "There's something about him that makes me believe he'll do it."

Carleton gave him a keen look. "No one in the brigade knows what we're about except those accompanying me?"

"I made certain of it. After you personally send Howe's messenger back to him, I'll spread the word through the brigade that you'll be cloistered in your chamber for a few days planning strategy."

Carleton glanced toward the western horizon, where the crimson sun was sinking into an incandescent cloud bank behind a thin line of leafless trees. "Our guides swear they'll get us to Squan Beach safely by Thursday dawn. We'll travel under cover of night and keep to back roads to avoid the notice of any loyalists along our route."

Andrews gave him a grave look. "Just stay on the alert."

"You know me well enough not to doubt that." Staring into the distance, Carleton added, "If I don't return, take the brigade to rejoin Washington's corps."

Andrews's jaw hardened and he saluted. "Yes, sir. And then I'll return to our people. There'll be nothing left for me here."

## Chapter Eleven

*Wednesday, 5 November*

"**H**AVE YE BROTHERS OR SISTERS?**"** Sensing that Josiah meant to distract her from the misery of their surroundings, Elizabeth forced a smile and looked up to meet his probing gaze. "One sister only. Abby's . . . twelve now."

Noting her hesitation, he guessed, "Ye been separated for a while?"

"She and my parents were returning this fall from an extended stay in London."

"Loyalists, then?"

"Papa was. But judging from his letters, his opinions have changed until they're quite the opposite of what they used to be."

She heard the captain's low chuckle. "From what I've heard o' London, I'd guess a stay there'd do that to a New Englander. But with Boston in our hands again, they'd have to secure passage from a port on the Continent, wouldn't they?"

She nodded. "Calais."

"Ye said Congress is tryin' to get the French on our side."

"They're already secretly providing us with supplies and munitions, while outwardly maintaining a pose of neutrality," she explained. "Our commissioners are trying to negotiate a formal alliance, and with General Burgoyne's defeat at Saratoga, success may finally be in sight."

"Hang it all, I wish I'd been there to see it!" he exclaimed, striking his knee. "That's the best news ye could o' brought us." He sobered. "But ye're sure the reports ye heard are true and not just rumors? The guards haven't so much as hinted at it."

She gave him a guarded look, thinking of the frightening days she had spent with the Rangers at Bemis Heights and the battle's final triumphant end at Saratoga, where the British had laid down their arms. "Oh, yes, quite certain. The British aren't exactly eager to talk of it, as you may imagine."

"Considerin' yer line o' work, ye ought to know," Josiah conceded, shifting awkwardly. "I didn't mean to question yer knowledge, Miss Beth. It's just that—"

"I understand. To learn the report was false would destroy the hope it's brought to all these men." She indicated their fellow prisoners. Heart contracting, for a moment she listened to the coughs, low groans, and mutters that filled the gun deck and drifted up from the ship's bowels. "The one who brought the report is trustworthy and was personally at the surrender."

A broad grin lit Josiah's face. "I know ye said Washington's corps lost Philadelphia, but as long as we've an army in the field, the redcoats still have to reckon with us."

"They do," she agreed, returning his smile.

He tilted his head. "It's clear from yer speech that ye're educated. I'm guessin' yer pa's a . . . lawyer or parson or some such."

"He's a physician, and a very good one. He taught me all he knows."

Again she glanced around at the dim forms of the men slumped across the crowded deck, then back at Josiah. He had developed a raspy cough. She had laid her head on his chest that morning to listen to his lungs and had felt a prickle of fear at the sound of congestion.

" 'T ain't nothin'," he had protested with a raw voice. "I coughed all last winter, and it didn't do me no harm."

Looking at his spare, wasted form now, however, she had a sinking feeling that if he did not get medical care, warmth, and nourishing food soon, the cough and sore throat would develop into pneumonia. Also worrisome, on waking that morning she had become aware of a faint flush of fever and aching joints.

What infection bred in her body? she wondered with a doctor's keenness. It could be anything from a simple cold to typhus or dysentery.

"If only I had my medical kit, I could do some good here."

At her sigh, he said quickly, "Ain't no good in pinin' for what can't be had. Best to just be thankful those ye love are where Howe can't get at 'em."

She could not speak for the lump in her throat, and after a long pause, Josiah teased, "I'll wager ye've a sweetheart too."

Tears flooded her eyes, and she nodded, mute.

Frowning, he bent to look into her face and drew in a sharp breath. "O' course. I'm a fool. He's in the army. And in danger."

"Yes," she whispered. "Howe wants him even more than me. I'm the general's weapon against him."

"Sure your sweetheart must be verra important if ol' Howe hisself is eager to catch him. What did he do to draw the gen'l's ire? Is he a spy like ye were?"

She cast a quick glance at Billy, on Josiah's far side with Tom beyond him. Both men had appeared to be dosing, but now sat up, considering her with increased interest.

As gently as possible, she said, "It's best for your own sake that we not talk of it. The less you know, the safer you'll be."

Tightlipped, Josiah admonished sternly, "She's right, Billy. Keep yer questions to yerself. 'T ain't none o' yer business."

Crestfallen, Billy looked down. After a strained moment, he murmured, "Fergive me, Miss Beth. Didn't mean no harm. It's just that time hangs heavy, and my mind gets to wanderin'."

"I understand. No offense taken."

Tom exchanged a glance with Billy. "Truth is, if we're honest, we all been prayin' for rescue. There's no way else out of here 'cept feet first, and if somebody important might be lookin' for ye . . . " He shrugged and let the words trail off.

"Now that's a downright fool idee," Josiah scoffed. "You think he'd sail right here into New York Harbor and take on the whole Royal Navy? Why, even if he had a squadron o' ships, they'd all get blown to pieces afore they made it through the Narrows."

Elizabeth's breath shortened. *Please don't let Jonathan try such a desperate course! Please, dear God, keep him safe!*

Yet if she were honest, the same desperate hope of rescue had taken residence in her heart.

The sudden thump of boots and flare of torchlight reached them from the companionway, and a detail of Hessian soldiers stamped down the stairs. "Elizabeth Howard," cried the sergeant in heavily accented English, "you come with us."

Dread clenched Elizabeth's chest. Before she could move, Josiah got to his feet, crouching to avoid the timbers overhead.

"What's she wanted for?"

As loud murmurs rose from the prisoners, the sergeant cursed furiously in German. "No matter! Get in way and it go worse for you."

Pushing Billy and Tom back with one arm, Elizabeth tugged hard on the tail of Josiah's ragged shirt with her other hand. "Don't risk your lives. There's nothing you can do."

Hastily she stood and gave them one last glance. "If I don't see you again . . . " The words choked in her throat. "I'll never forget you. Thank you for all you've done—"

The Hessian sergeant motioned impatiently. *"Heraus!"*

She stepped past Josiah, pretending not to notice the anxious look he gave her, while the painful throb of her heart blotted out all other sensations.

"EVIDENTLY OUR ACCOMMODATIONS haven't been to your former standards," Clinton sneered as he looked Elizabeth up and down, lip curling with distaste. "How far the lovely Miss Howard has fallen—or should I call you Oriole?"

Shivering, Elizabeth squinted at the general while holding one hand over her eyes to shade them. After a week's confinement in the *Erebus's* dank hold, the light reflecting from the harbor while she was being transported to the city and now streaming through the windows of the general's headquarters seemed exceedingly bright, even though the day was raw and cloudy.

She was all too aware of her fouled clothing, stained with all manner of filth; her tangled and matted hair; the dirt that soiled her face and hands. Moistening her cracked lips with her tongue, she glared at him, feigning the courage that threatened to fail her.

"I'm surprised you called me to this interview since I assured the captain you sent that I've nothing to tell you."

In spite of the inadequate fire and the room's chill, she felt overly warm. She wrapped her arms around her against the painful cramping of her stomach. *Dear Lord, don't let it be dysentery,* she pleaded silently.

She felt faint and lightheaded, terrified that Clinton would try to torture her into revealing information damaging to Carleton and to the rebel cause. In her weakened state she was fearful she would not be able to withstand such a trial. To her surprise, however, he merely smirked at her, then summoned a maid.

When a plump young woman in servant's dress appeared at the door, he waved a fastidious handkerchief in Elizabeth's direction before pressing it to his nose. "Take this . . . lady . . . to the kitchen and clean her up. Find her decent clothing. Nothing elaborate, mind you, but proper. Use your own, and I'll see the garments are replaced. Make sure she's clean and give her some food and wine. She looks about to expire, but keep a close eye on her. When she's presentable, bring her to me—and don't waste time about it."

He directed a coldly assessing look at Elizabeth. "This place is surrounded by guards, as I'm sure you noticed. You'll not escape, and if you're fool enough to try, I'll have you whipped."

Without answering, Elizabeth followed the maid out of the room and down a back stairway to the building's cellar, her legs trembling so much she had to cling to the railing to keep from falling. A bare passageway opened into an expansive kitchen lighted by windows high in the walls and a crackling fire on the huge hearth. The aromas of an elaborate meal's preparation brought the saliva into her mouth.

Wrinkling her nose in disgust, the maid motioned her to a stool in front of the fire. Elizabeth settled on it and bent over, clutching herself as another chill gripped her.

She was only vaguely aware that the portly cook at the table and her two female assistants regarded her with raised eyebrows. The maid made a hasty explanation to which the other women responded with clucking tongues and disdainful looks in Elizabeth's direction. They seemed to fade in and out of her vision.

When the maid held out a small glass of wine, Elizabeth started out of the stupor she had fallen into while gazing into the fire. The wine was near sour, but she swallowed it greedily to ease the rawness of her throat, grateful for the warmth that followed in the draught's wake.

Shortly, a large basin of steaming water appeared on the hearth in front of her. The plump young woman left the room and soon returned with lye soap, rough towels, and a small hand mirror and comb—like the fire, almost forgotten luxuries that Elizabeth took in with wonder.

She became aware that the maid had again disappeared. How long she had been gone, Elizabeth had no idea. Gathering courage, she lifted the mirror with a shaking hand and stared in dull dismay at her dirty, gaunt, hollow-eyed face.

" 'urry up now!" The maid commanded, suddenly at her elbow. "You heard wot the gen'l said. 'E wants you back w' no delay. 'Ere—gimme your clothes."

Elizabeth clutched her coat. "But it's all I have."

The woman grimaced as she placed an armful of clothing on a nearby chair. "They's dirty an' crawlin' w' vermin. Besides, they's men's gear. I brung you a clean gown like the gen'l ordered."

"You'll give these back to me, won't you?"

Without answering, the woman began to unceremoniously drag off Elizabeth's clothing using only the tips of her fingers. Too weak and ill to offer resistance, Elizabeth allowed herself to be stripped. A hot flood of humiliation rose to her face at being exposed before these strangers.

"Please, not my boots!" she pleaded when the maid piled the footwear on top of the discarded clothing.

The woman's only answer was to impatiently order to her to wash and again bustle off, clearly eager to be rid of her unwelcome charge.

Keeping anxious watch for any men entering or passing by the door, Elizabeth loosely wrapped a large towel around her and hastily washed away as much of the filth that crusted her body as she could. The cook and her assistants continued to hurry to and fro, apparently indifferent, only occasionally casting her a scornful look.

The exertion exhausted her, but when the maid returned, Elizabeth pointed to the muddy water in the basin and meekly asked for clean water to wash her hair. Although the young woman carried the basin away grumbling, she soon returned with fresh water.

It was necessary for Elizabeth to soak her hair and comb it out several times to remove most of the tangles, dirt, and lice, while the disgruntled servant repeatedly urged her to make greater haste. All the while she wondered why Clinton wanted her clean and in feminine dress. Fearful questions teemed her mind as to what she might be forced to endure now.

Feeling so weak she feared she would fall off the stool, she managed to draw on shift and stockings and step into shoes a size too large. With the maid's help to stand, lace the stays, and don a plain blue petticoat and bodice that hung on her despite being tightened as much as possible, she was at last clad with reasonable propriety. She sank back onto the stool so spent she feared she would lose consciousness.

The maid bustled around the kitchen and at length delivered a bowl of soup and a crust of bread. Elizabeth received the meager meal with gratitude and savored each mouthful. Although apparently leftovers from the midday meal as the soup had gone cold and the bread dry, the food tasted more delicious than her favorite dishes ever had.

She stopped mid bite when the maid gathered up the discarded clothing. "Please keep them for me until I find out what the general intends. If he sends me back—"

"These things is only fit for the fire—and I'll have to bathe afterwards." Nose wrinkled, the maid swept out the door.

Elizabeth's heart sank even farther as she stared down at her attire, unable to still her shivering. Finding it strange to be clad in gown and stays after wearing men's garb for so long, she felt unaccountably exposed.

The gown's fabric was thin, threadbare in places, as was the shift. Along with the worn stockings and shoes, they would afford little warmth aboard the *Erebus*.

The angry voices of the two assistant cooks behind her brought her warily around. The older of the two berated the younger for not carrying out trash she had been ordered to remove the previous day. Elizabeth followed her angry gesture toward the overflowing wooden box in front of the hearth within arm's length of her feet, unnoticed earlier.

Clearly resentful, the younger woman complained about always being assigned the most menial tasks, to which the cook interjected that as the younger she was obligated to follow her superior's orders. She softened the blow by telling her young assistant to first fetch parsnips and cabbage from the pantry and ordered the older woman to bring rosemary and thyme from the kitchen garden for the evening's roast.

With a triumphant glance toward her tormentor, the younger woman flounced through the pantry door. Equally disgruntled, the older assistant headed out the kitchen's main door, while the cook returned to kneading a lump of dough, her back to Elizabeth.

Careful not to tip the soup bowl on her lap, Elizabeth leaned over the box to peer at the contents, wondering whether she might find something that would be useful to her or her friends aboard the *Erebus*. A small, ornate, lacquered box partially covered by the welter of objects inside immediately captured her attention, and her heart began to race.

She was sure it was the one she had seen in Clinton's office on the day Howe had interrogated her and revealed his malicious plan. Then it had held the silver Indian jewelry Carleton had sent her from Ticonderoga. And the miniature portrait of him as a youth that Andrews had brought to her from Carleton's Virginia estate after he had disappeared into Ohio Territory.

All stolen from the baggage she had shipped home to Boston before she left Philadelphia to join Carleton with the Northern Army at Bemis Heights. Evidence of their treasonous relationship.

Heart pounding, breath choked, she glanced quickly around. She could hear the younger assistant shifting something heavy in the pantry, and the cook was still occupied with the dough.

Snatching the box, Elizabeth flipped it open. The Indian jewelry was still inside with the miniature on top. Hungrily she gazed down at Carleton's face, anguish stabbing through her.

Footfalls approached the pantry door. In breathless haste, she grabbed the miniature, closed the box, and set it back in its place, in the same movement thrusting the miniature down the neck of her bodice and into her stays with her other hand.

When the young assistant walked into the kitchen carrying a basket filled with vegetables, Elizabeth was swallowing her last bite of soup, the spoon poised in her hand. She looked up, fearfully seeking evidence of suspicion in the young woman's features. To her relief she found only annoyance there.

VANDER GROOT STEPPED UP into his carriage and settled on the seat. Glancing toward Isaiah, who lounged nearby with Matheson, he gave a jerk of his head.

Isaiah shuffled to his side, shoulders hunched. "Ye've work for me, sir?" he asked plaintively, speaking loudly enough to be heard by the detail of soldiers marching briskly by.

"I might, boy," Vander Groot responded with equal volume, "depending on your experience . . . " He let the words trail off as the soldiers passed out of earshot.

Isaiah leaned into the carriage while keeping the detail in the corner of his eye until they moved out of sight. "They bring Miz Howard in a carriage round back o' the mansion. Me an' Atkin follow, and he tell me they take her off the *Erebus.*"

He nodded toward the corporal. Hands in pockets, Atkin shifted idly from one foot to the other as he lingered on the edge of a group of roughly garbed laborers across the street in front of the mansion that served as British headquarters.

*"Erebus?"* Vander Groot exclaimed. "A foul name for a foul vessel! She's the worst of the prison ships. I got aboard her last spring, and the prisoners are held in shocking conditions—though I suppose that's true of the rest as well. Did you get close enough for a good look at her?"

Isaiah's face set in tight lines. "Close enough to tell it be her, though she be in men's dress. She look sick, and one o' the guards have to support her."

Before Vander Groot could respond, another detail of soldiers escorting a shackled prisoner approached the cluster of laborers and turned onto the walkway that led to the mansion's front door.

"Captain Stern," he said under his breath. "Looks like he can hardly walk."

When Isaiah turned, Matheson met his gaze and without a word sauntered across the street to join Atkin and his companions. He reached them just as Sergeant Prince drifted into the group from the direction the detail had come.

His mouth set in a hard line, Isaiah asked, "You still meetin' with Clinton today?"

Vander Groot shook his head. "I tried to persuade the aide of the urgency of our meeting and to allow me to wait until the general's free, but according to him, Clinton's cancelled all appointments and is closeted in his office. He refused to say why, though I believe we can guess."

"Then what 'bout that pass for you to get aboard the ship?"

Thoughtfully Vander Groot studied the solders swarming in and out of the British headquarters. "I'm to come round in the morning. Clinton's aide assured me that he'll provide the passes I requested for my 'hospital assistants'. I told the general that as long as I'm making the pretense of visiting all three prison ships to treat those with infectious diseases, I may as well inoculate any who need it against the pox. That'll give us the perfect pretext to board the *Erebus* anytime we want without arousing suspicion."

"Atkin say Gen'l Carleton plan to bring his ships in Saturday night so long as they get to the rendezvous in time," Isaiah reminded him.

"That gives us little more than three days to prepare." Vander Groot chewed his lower lip. "Any delay in our getting the passes or in the ships' arrival at the rendezvous may well compromise our mission or, at worst, make it impossible for us to proceed."

"We got to find a way no matter what happen!" Isaiah snapped. Noticeably containing his agitation, he continued, "According to Atkin, the gen'l concerned about bad weather keepin' his ships at Boston or drivin' 'em off course. Or them bein' intercepted by the enemy on the way to the rendezvous."

"From what Clinton told me, he's wise to be concerned about the latter, but all we can do is pray." Gazing through the leafless treetops, Vander Groot assessed the thin plumes of clouds high in the pale azure sky. "I can't vouch for Boston or the Jersey shore, but as far as the weather's concerned, there's been no sign of any storms here since I arrived although it's been cold. We only need things to remain quiet for the next few days."

Vander Groot glanced across the street to where Sergeant Prince loitered with the other two Rangers. "You're sending Prince to intercept Caleb after Clinton sends him off?" When Isaiah nodded, he said, "Fill him in on every detail of what I told you and have him make a full report to General Carleton. We've no way to warn *Destiny's* captain, but if they can reach Squan Beach, it's imperative they exercise the greatest caution from there back to New York."

He gathered the reins in his hand. "If I stay any longer, I'll attract notice. I'm heading back to Montcoeur to check on Ben and Sallie's progress in recruiting more men."

"Tell 'em I want to meet with their recruits tonight."

Vander Groot nodded. "Report to me as soon as Caleb's sent off and Prince after him, but first make sure Miss Howard is returned to the *Erebus.*"

With a wary glance at the soldiers gathering on the steps of Clinton's headquarters, he pulled on the reins and turned the carriage back the way he had come.

## Chapter Twelve

NOT LOOKING UP from his correspondence, Clinton motioned Elizabeth impatiently to a chair placed at the end of the table nearest him. He continued to write while she huddled there for some minutes, shrinking from him as she fought painful cramps. And tears.

While imprisoned, she had wanted nothing so much as to be removed from the ship's terrible confines. Now she longed desperately to return there. As appalling as conditions aboard the rotting hulk were, they were familiar and safe compared to the unknown horrors she imagined the general must have in store. And her friends were there. To be separated from them, not knowing whether she would return, had been truly wrenching, and she had been hard pressed to not weep when the guards led her away.

She jumped when a knock sounded at the door. At Clinton's command, it was thrust open. A guard entered, arrayed in brilliant regimental dress with powdered hair and musket in hand. He was followed by another who jerked Caleb inside, his hands and feet shackled.

Catching her breath, she started to her feet, hand pressed to the throbbing pulse at her throat. Her thirty-year-old cousin, a captain in the Continental Army, had ostensibly served as butler to her and her Aunt Tess. In reality his true assignment had been to assist Elizabeth in planning and carrying out her clandestine activities. Taciturn, level-headed, and daring, he had proven himself invaluable in that role.

Now he appeared as dirty and ragged as she had been. In the fortnight since their arrest, the flesh had noticeably wasted from his sturdy frame. An unkempt beard covered his jaw; his dark hair was clotted with sweat, blood, and dirt; and the purpled bruises and crusting scrapes of a beating marred his face and arms.

Clinton wiped the nib of his pen on a cloth and looked up, scowling. "Put him there." He indicated a chair at the end of the table opposite Elizabeth, then barked at her, "Sit!"

She sank back into her chair as the guard shoved Caleb into his. Each of them regarded the other hungrily.

Her heart ached at the evidence of his suffering. Because of her.

"Don't talk!" Clinton snapped before either could speak.

After dismissing the guards, he deliberately pushed a fresh sheet of paper in front of Elizabeth, along with the pen and ink bottle. Sitting back in his chair, he steepled his fingers and regarded her with what she could only interpret as malicious satisfaction.

He gestured at the objects in front of her. "Write what I say." When she hesitated, glancing apprehensively at Caleb, Clinton barked, "I don't have all day!"

Mouth dry, she grasped the pen and dipped it in the ink.

"I am in good health and am being treated well."

Hunched over the paper, she wrote, her hand shaking so much she had trouble making the words legible.

"General Howe has given me his sworn word, on his honor as a gentleman, that he will release me as soon as the stated terms are met."

She felt the blood drain out of her face, and her eyes flew to Clinton's. Mute, she shook her head.

Half-rising, he leaned toward her, hand raised. She whimpered and shrank away from his blow, heard the scrape of Caleb's chair as he levered himself to his feet.

"Leave her be, you coward!" he rasped.

Clinton rounded on the captain. "Shut up or I'll have you given a hundred lashes," he hissed, livid. "I doubt you'll survive that."

"Don't!" Elizabeth cried when Caleb flushed and opened his mouth to respond.

With every evidence of reluctance, Caleb resumed his seat. Shaking, he crossed his arms on the table and lowered his head onto them as though he had not the strength to hold it erect.

Clinton turned back to her. "Write what I say if you want him to live: I have General Howe's sworn pledge, on his honor as a gentleman, that he will release me as soon as the stated terms are met," he repeated slowly, each word enunciated with precision.

*Oh, Jonathan, no!* Gone entirely numb, Elizabeth wrote blindly.

"I have every confidence that General Howe will keep his word," Clinton concluded, and when she had finished, added, "Now sign it."

For a long moment she stared at the words scrawled unevenly across the page in an uncertain hand. *He'll know it's all a lie, that I've been forced to write this, that I'm not well. But will that keep him from surrendering to Howe?*

Slowly she inscribed at the bottom: Elizabeth Anne Howard.

She slid the page toward Clinton. While the general scanned it, Caleb straightened and glanced at her. She met his tortured gaze and surreptitiously jutted her chin toward the window, directing a meaningful look toward the ships visible in the bay. He followed her glance with a veiled one, then his mouth tightened and he gave an almost imperceptible nod.

"Good enough. Guard!" When the guards reappeared, Clinton sealed the letter with wax, imprinted it with his signet, and handed it to the higher ranking of the two men. Indicating Caleb, he said, "You've my orders. Take him away."

"MATHESON AND ME OVERHEAR the guards talking when they bring Captain Stern out," Isaiah told Vander Groot after hurrying back to Montcoeur. "He look awful weak, and they say they got to feed him afore they take him 'cross to Staten Island or he may not make it. Orders are to take him to Amboy, supply a horse, and send him on to Gen'l Carleton at Baptist Meeting House. I doubt he be on the road afore sundown." Hands unconsciously clenching, he watched Vander Groot pace the length of the mansion's rear parlor.

"Did you see a letter? He has to bring a letter from Miss Howard in her own hand."

"When Prince and me pass by, I see one guard hand the other a folded paper that have a seal, but we don't dare linger any longer."

"You sent Prince off, then?"

Isaiah stretched and rubbed the back of his neck. "Ben takin' him 'cross the river right now. He ought to get to 'Lizabethtown afore sundown, and from there he ride fast to Brunswick Road to intercept Captain Stern. As bad as he look, it goin' to take him a while to get far, so I doubt there be any chance Prince'll miss him."

"If the ride to Squan Beach is too much for him, the ships may get there before they do."

"I tell Prince to get him there by nightfall tomorrow if he have to carry Capt'n Stern on his back," Isaiah growled.

Vander Groot responded with a short laugh, then sobered. "You impressed on him the extreme urgency of staying on the lookout for British patrols, I trust. The closer he gets to Brunswick, the more likely he'll run into trouble."

"The British don't stray far out o' their camps, and nobody pay attention to a black slave ridin' on a errand for his master nohow."

Despite the years since his escape from bondage as a youth, the words *slave* and *master* brought back the searing humiliation of the auction block and all that had followed and struck Isaiah like a punch in the gut. To his relief, Vander Groot showed no sign that he noticed.

The doctor pulled out his handkerchief and wiped his brow. "I hope you're right," he said with a grimace. "Atkin verified that they took Miss Howard back to *Erebus?*"

Isaiah answered in the affirmative. "They put women's clothes on her, and the stuff look thin. It be bad enough afore, but she gonna freeze in this weather with no more coverin' 'n that."

Dropping into a chair, Vander Groot muttered, "How much longer can she hold on?"

"I tell Prince wait till the gen'l's ships arrive, then get back here as fast as his horse can travel. No use us tryin' to board the *Erebus* if the ships don't make it to Squan Beach."

"Clinton should have our passes ready first thing in the morning. He's eager for me to begin interrogating Miss Howard, but first he wants to question me in detail about my 'enforced' sojourn among the Rangers. I'm hoping he won't keep me overlong. We need to get aboard *Erebus* as soon as possible."

Isaiah eyed him dubiously. "You tell him everythin'?"

Vander Groot returned a cold smile. "My plan is to provide information that'll thoroughly unnerve him—and hopefully fix his attention elsewhere long enough for us to rob him of his prize."

" 'Tis a shame they took yer warm clothing. Had I a coat, I'd lend it to ye gladly."

Elizabeth gave Josiah's ragged shirt, worn breeches, and bare legs and feet a meaningful glance and forced a smile. "You need a coat more than I do. And shoes."

"We're sure glad they brought ye back," Billy put in fervently.

"Not that we want ye to suffer any longer in this pit. We was afraid they'd abuse ye, and that we'd never know what happened to ye."

"I'm relieved they brought me back too, Tom," Elizabeth admitted. "Strangely enough I feel safer here. I'd have missed you if I'd never seen you again." She included them all in a warm glance.

"What did Clinton want?" Josiah pressed. "He didn't mistreat you none?"

Before she could answer, a paroxysm of coughing wracked the captain's gaunt frame, echoed by many others all across the hold. Billy and Tom bent over Josiah helplessly, their expressions anxious.

Billy's nose was streaming, and time and again Tom was forced to drag his weakened frame to the overflowing necessary tubs. Dread settled over Elizabeth. If only she had some of her herbs and tinctures with which to treat their illnesses! But as Josiah always pointed out, there was no use wishing for what was beyond possibility.

Finally Josiah's coughing eased. He cleared his throat and wiped his dripping nose on the crusted remnant of his shirtsleeve.

Haltingly she described her interview with the British commander. When she finished, Josiah silently mulled over her account.

"Ye think the letter is meant for yer friend, then?" he said at last.

"Howe told me he'd summon Jonathan—" She broke off and pressed her hand hard to the small lump the secreted miniature made beneath her stays. It was the first time she had spoken Carleton's name, but after a brief hesitation, she went on, "He said he'd threaten him with my execution if he didn't surrender himself. But, of course, Howe means to execute us both as soon as he has Jonathan."

The glance the three men exchanged held a rising hope, and Billy spoke for them all. "Leastwise yer cousin's free now. That's good in itself, but if he figgers out where they're holdin' ye, then maybe he can do somethin'—"

"What?" she demanded angrily, trembling with another chill. "Urge Jonathan to take on the entire British navy?"

Eyes closed, Josiah slumped back against the hull. "All hopin' fer rescue'll get us is distractin' us from doin' what's needful to get through this day. An' the next. An' the next."

Billy looked down disconsolately and muttered, "I just keep thinkin' o' my Mam an' Pap."

Looking from one discouraged face to the next, Elizabeth could tell that each thought of his family. She had learned from their conversation that Billy, a sailor who had been captured from a Continental schooner sunk by the British, was also from Boston, where his parents and two older sisters tended a small tavern in the North End, while a younger brother served with the Massachusetts militia. Tom, a veteran with the Delaware Continentals, had lost two brothers in battle, and his widowed mother, sister, and two youngest brothers struggled for survival managing a small farm outside Wilmington.

While serving with a Connecticut regiment, Josiah had been wounded and taken prisoner at White Plains after Washington's army was driven out of New York the previous fall. Both parents were dead, and although he spoke little of his concern, he could not entirely conceal his constant worry about three younger sisters of whom he had heard nothing since his capture.

Her heart ached. Their stories were reflected in those of all the men aboard the *Erebus* and the other prison ships anchored in Wallabout Bay—men whose plight she had known nothing of until the previous spring when a young woman had called upon her and Vander Groot, desperately seeking aid for her imprisoned brother.

Most likely few of the prisoners' families knew what had happened to their missing loved ones. Even those who did were allowed to visit them only rarely and had no power to ease their suffering.

Was there anyone else who knew? Were any efforts being made to save them? Or had they been entirely forgotten, abandoned to this hellish existence . . . and to inevitable death?

For three years she had done and endured what few women were capable of. Never before had she lost all hope. But now, in a mere fortnight, she realized with despair, none remained.

She had not expected to be broken so quickly and so completely.

## Chapter Thirteen

*Thursday, 6 November*

CARLETON'S PARTY REACHED the designated rendezvous on the New Jersey coast at dawn on the second day. They had followed the road from Princeton through Monmouth, then southeast, riding by night at all possible speed and lying in concealment by daylight.

For the past hour they had been bedeviled by gusts of sleet slanting out of the north. All were saddle sore and bleary eyed, their buckskins slicked with rain and stiff with cold. Inured to fatigue and discomfort by too many sleepless nights, however, Carleton was conscious only of the goal that brought them there.

As arranged, the guide who had gone in advance met them at Manasquan River bringing the assurance that the patriot leaders in the area had warned local residents to stay well away from the bay and take no heed of unfamiliar ships. Nevertheless, Carleton insisted on scouting the area carefully, until, satisfied that the area's scattered villages and saw and grist mills lay at a safe distance, he called a halt.

They made a secluded camp within a dense thicket of wind-gnarled cedars at the head of Barnegat Bay and hobbled the horses in a nearby clearing. The site lay on the western bank of a creek that divided the mainland from the narrow length of the wind-raked, sandy barrier known as Squan Beach.

By now the sleet had blown away to the south. At Carleton's command, the weary troops gratefully substituted dry clothing from their packs, hung their wet buckskins over the interlaced branches overhead to freeze dry in the east wind, and rolled up in buffalo robes or bearskins beneath the cedars' shelter.

Paying no attention to Teissèdre, who trailed him, Carleton crossed the shallow creek and stopped where the trees gave way to an expansive view of beach and ocean. Before him the restless sea reflected the leaden clouds that streamed across the brightening sky.

He trained his spyglass on the horizon, feeling his agent's sympathetic gaze on his back. The Jersey coast was beset by treacherous rip tides and crosscurrents, but Teissèdre had insisted that *Destiny's* new captain, William Eaden, was well familiar with the region and would keep the ships out of danger.

It was impossible for Stowe and Briggs to have reached Boston earlier than the previous day, Carleton reminded himself. If his ships had been in port and sailed immediately, they would not reach the rendezvous until after sunset the next day—and later if they encountered storms at sea. Or the enemy. Still, disappointment cut through him as he scanned the empty expanse of heaving, wintry ocean, its seething waves shimmering back the intermittent rays of the rising sun.

At length he returned to the camp with the Frenchman padding silently along behind him. Their companions all lay motionless as though they had fallen asleep the moment they lay down. Reluctantly Carleton wrapped his bearskin around him and made a bed on the sandy ground a short distance from Teissèdre, turning his back to discourage any attempt at conversation.

It was his last sensation. For the first time since receiving news of Elizabeth's capture, he fell at once deeply asleep, lulled by the crash of the waves, exhaustion overwhelming even the urgency to get to her.

✳ ✳ ✳

IT WAS PAST ELEVEN by the time Vander Groot, Isaiah, Matheson, and Atkin, settled into the cutter that would take them to the *Erebus*. While the sailors manned the sweeps, Vander Groot seethed silently at the time wasted by the long interrogation he had been subjected to. At the same time, he was confident that the information he provided Clinton would cause him much concern, while revealing nothing ultimately harmful to Carleton or the patriot cause.

When the general had been finally satisfied, to Vander Groot's surprise he confided what had occurred the previous day. "Deuced fool nonsense to negotiate with a traitor," Clinton had ranted. "But would Howe listen to me? Of course not—no matter that I'm the only one in command who has any sense at all!"

"I told you Carleton's a very devil," Vander Groot responded, ignoring the general's self-serving remark. "But considering how slippery he is, what choice does General Howe have if he means to get his hands on him?"

Hands on hips, the general had embodied the image of disgruntlement. "Can you imagine the arrogance of the man? The life of the woman he claims to love weighs in the balance, but he insists on setting terms."

"I can't say but I'd do the same," Vander Groot admitted with a shrug.

The general had given him a sidelong glance, an ironic smile twisting his mouth. "The villain clearly trusts us as much as we trust him. Had we not secured Miss Howard where even he can't get at her, I'd worry that complying with his demands will only give him the advantage in whatever game he's playing."

Vander Groot's laugh had been genuine and quickly stifled. "By his own account General Carleton trusts no one—including himself. But I can testify that he does indeed love Miss Howard. He'd never jeopardize her release, and he'd freely give his life to save hers."

*And she'd do the same for him,* he thought now, staring across the water to the rapidly nearing dismasted bulk of the old frigate. His heart contracted painfully. *I can't let that happen to either of them.*

When the boat bumped up against *Erebus's* darkly weathered hull, he drew in a steadying breath, met Isaiah's narrowed gaze, and gave him a firm nod.

BY SLOW DEGREES Elizabeth returned to consciousness. Even before she unwillingly forced open her eyes, she ached to return to the stupor that had enveloped her.

Her head throbbed and chills succeeded waves of fever. Her throat's rawness made it difficult to swallow, and a foul-tasting crust coated her tongue.

*Typhus,* she thought in dull resignation.

To add to every other discomfort, her time of the month had come. Mercifully there was little flow. With abstract indifference, she calculated that meager, rotten food; foul water; exposure to cold and vermin; and lack of fresh air and sunshine had sapped her strength to the point that her body could no longer fight off infection and was losing the ability to maintain its normal functions.

Would Carleton notice her attempt to warn him? she wondered. Knowing that Clinton would read the missive she was forced to write, she had risked much in hazarding even that one subtle signal. Thankfully, he had noted nothing amiss . . . but then neither might Carleton.

Seeking comfort, she pressed her hand to the slight bulge the miniature made under her stays, as she had often since returning to the *Erebus.* The maid had laced the garment tightly to keep it in place on Elizabeth's shrunken figure, and she longed to remove or at least loosen it so she could breathe more freely. But she was afraid the tiny portrait would slip out, that she might lose it or someone might notice and ask questions, perhaps take it from her. As long as it was there, pressed tightly against her breast, she felt closer to Carleton and that the bond between them could not be broken by time or distance or even death.

Unable to force down more than a mouthful of the water Billy offered, she sank back against the greasy deck, haunted by the memory of Carleton's vow: *I'll never let anything hurt you, Beth. I swear it. No matter what happens, no matter where you are, you've only to send for me and I'll come at once. Never doubt that. Never.*

*If he keeps his promise,* her muddled mind protested dully, *he'll only fall into Howe's toils. And then he'll die too. Perhaps he already has . . .*

For an indeterminate period she lay insensible. At last she roused at the sound of a voice above her, one it seemed she had known a lifetime ago.

She forced her eyes open. She had to squint against bright torchlight and, trembling, she pressed her hand to her aching head.

"Pieter," she whispered in wonder when her eyes met the clear blue ones that regarded her with unmistakable love and anguish.

Surely she dreamed. She was certain of it when her blurred gaze shifted to the black face that hovered above Vander Groot's shoulder.

"Isaiah? But . . . you can't be here . . . "

Vander Groot knelt beside Elizabeth, barely able to contain the fury that seared through him. Isaiah's massive hand, squeezing his shoulder with painful force, made it clear that the same emotion possessed him.

"Beth, hush," Vander Groot soothed, keeping his voice low so no one else could hear. "We're not ghosts. We're really here, and everything's going to be all right."

She struggled to lift her hand and touch his face. Joy leaped into her eyes, succeeded at once by horror.

"Oh no! They've captured you too—"

He touched his finger to her lips. "We're not prisoners. We've come for you."

She stared at him as though his words made no sense. Then disbelief gave way to stunned comprehension, and she began to weep.

He gathered her in his arms, burying his fingers in her tangled hair and pressing her head to his shoulder. Too weak to hold her body erect, she clung to him as to a lifeline, only pulling back once to look into his eyes, before again stifling her sobs against his neck. It was all he could do to keep from breaking down as well, while Isaiah knelt beside them, his strong arms encircling them both.

*Jon, where are you? How much longer . . . ?*

Swift calculation reminded Vander Groot that Carleton's ships could not possibly reach the rendezvous earlier than the next evening. That is, if Stowe and Briggs had gotten through. And if every detail of their plan worked perfectly . . .

His stomach lurched. "Don't be afraid, my love," he whispered against Elizabeth's cheek, fighting down doubts and fears, his throat so tight he could hardly speak. "You're safe now. You're going to be safe—and all these men—I swear it." He prayed fervently that his promise would not prove hollow.

His assurances caused her to weep the harder. He cradled her, his heart overflowing with love and gratitude and supplication.

"But how?" she managed to ask between sobs. "If Clinton learns you're here—"

Again he touched her lips, and forcing a smile, brought his mouth to her ear. "Shhh. He sent us. I persuaded him I'd charm intelligence out of you."

He became aware that the murmur of voices had grown louder. Glancing around, he noted gratefully that Josiah, Billy, and Tom formed a barrier around him and Isaiah, with Matheson and Atkin stationed behind them to block the view of the weak, wasted men who crowded the hold. The two soldiers firmly warded back several prisoners who had crawled forward, staring in amazement, weakly trying to press into the circle and determine who the strangers were.

Vander Groot covered Elizabeth's fevered brow with his hand, then gently laid her back against the deck, dismayed to see that her gaze drifted away to fix vacantly on the shadows. He directed an anxious glance at Josiah, wondering how far he could trust the man.

As soon as they had descended the companionway, the rebel captain intercepted them and, on learning that Vander Groot was a doctor and that he sought Elizabeth, had immediately led them to her. From his manner, Vander Groot gained the impression that the gaunt officer held authority over the prisoners and that he had made himself Elizabeth's protector. Yet the doctor remained wary of confiding his mission to any of the captives.

In spite of Vander Groot's attendance on the hulk's hard-drinking commander during an illness the previous spring, and regardless of the orders Clinton had sent along, Captain Villers had clearly been suspicious of the doctor's presence. That Vander Groot brought along three black "assistants" and intended to treat not only sick sailors, but also prisoners, had not helped. Villers had spouted language that caused Vander Groot to cast an apologetic glance toward Isaiah and his men, but their expressions had remained blandly unreadable as though such abuse was not unfamiliar to them.

It had taken considerable persistence on the doctor's part to persuade the blustering captain to allow them access to the decks where the prisoners were held. Convincing him that a guard was unnecessary had required every ounce of Vander Groot's patience, inventiveness, and, finally, outright bullying.

If any of the prisoners caught wind of what they were really about, Vander Groot feared, it would not take long for their guards to sniff it out. And then the news would reach Villers in a flash, and their carefully laid plans would unravel.

His first concern for Elizabeth, Vander Groot took her pulse and bent to listen to her heart, then gently coaxed her mouth open and checked her tongue. She made no resistance to his ministrations. Indeed, except for a low moan, she seemed unaware of them.

Overcome by dread, he opened his medical kit, explaining to the gathered men that she had typhus, that he would administer cinchona bark to relieve her fever along with laudanum for pain. It required considerable effort for Elizabeth to swallow, however, and much of the draughts, mixed with fresh water from the canteen he had brought, dribbled down her jaw.

When Isaiah asked anxiously whether he would bleed her, Vander Groot shook his head. "The infection's too far advanced, and she's too weak to bear it." With a quick glance around, he added in an undertone, "And this isn't an environment in which I'd do such a procedure anyway even if I felt it would do her good—which I don't. Normally I'd prescribe a cool bath and emetics followed by a low diet. But that's impossible here."

Noting that Elizabeth had slipped into unconsciousness, he removed his coat and wrapped it around her, making her as comfortable as possible. Through another fit of coughing, Josiah thanked him fervently and repeatedly, with Billy and Tom joining in.

Conscious of how much time had passed, Vander Groot directed Isaiah and his men to quickly check the condition of the rest of the prisoners, starting with Josiah and his assistants, then moving to the berth deck and hold. Astounded at how many prisoners were packed onto the ship, Vander Groot dispensed the drugs he had brought to the sickest, while taking mental count of those who were strong enough to endure transfer to Carleton's ships when they arrived. Isaiah estimated that more than two hundred men suffered in the makeshift prison.

Josiah's cough worried him the most. From the sound of the captain's chest, Vander Groot suspected pneumonia, practically a death sentence in his weakened condition. Yet they would need Josiah's help in accomplishing a rescue. Clearly that would have to happen with as little delay as possible, for every day brought the deaths of more men. If they did not receive proper treatment soon, both Elizabeth and Josiah might well be among the victims.

Vander Groot finally decided against sharing any hint of his true mission until it became absolutely necessary. While he calculated the odds they faced, the tramp of footfalls down the companionway announced the arrival of a Hessian detail. They delivered Captain Villers' message that the doctor and his assistants were taking too long and that the detail was to escort them off the ship directly.

Vander Groot bent over Elizabeth one last time to listen to her chest, his heart constricting when she made no response to his tender farewell. He kissed her brow, then lightly brushed her lips with his. At last he pushed to his feet, fighting to mask his emotions, and motioned for Isaiah and his men to follow.

WAN GHOSTS PRESSED CLOSE about him: gaunt, ragged men who reached out to him as though in supplication. Carleton could not see their faces nor hear their voices, but he knew with certainty that they appealed to him for succor, deliverance, justice.

The whisper unheard for months took gradual form in his mind: *". . . bring out the prisoners from the prison, and them that sit in darkness out of the prison house . . . "*

Abruptly awake, he wrenched upright, shoved aside his bearskin, and looked about him, dazed. From the angle of the light filtering through the canopy of the low trees, he judged it to be past midday. He had slept for hours.

A preternatural hush lay over the clearing. Around him, still wrapped in their robes, his companions lay motionless. No breath of wind creaked through the branches overhead to disturb the stillness. Although the beach lay no more than five rods distant, he could not hear the boom of surf that had lulled him so quickly to sleep.

Despite the day's damp chill, he felt a strange sensation of warmth, a deep consciousness as piercing as the vision given him the night he had ridden behind Washington on the way to Trenton: a presence profound and holy that caused his skin to prickle and the hair to rise on the back of his neck.

"Beth . . . " he whispered, realizing with sudden foreboding that she had been absent from his dream.

Immediately a harsh wind rattled the treetops and raised a fine veil of dust from the sandy soil. At his back the breakers roared against the shore, shattering the disquieting thrall that had briefly held nature suspended.

As he turned toward the sound, beside him Teissèdre rolled over, yawned and stretched, and then sat up to eye him speculatively before looking around the camp with wry expectancy. "What, no food prepared, and not even a fire for cooking?" he grumbled in French, raking his fingers through his sparse hair and setting it on end.

"No fire," Carleton returned gruffly in the same language, sitting up. "The smoke may attract attention."

Teissèdre sighed. "I suppose cold viands are better than none. We do plan to break our fast before the day is out, I trust."

Carleton allowed a faint smile. "You French. Always concerned with food—and women."

With a shrug, Teissèdre spread his hands. "When a man cannot have the one, then at least he can take comfort in the other."

Jaw clenched, Carleton stared at the breaking surf visible between the gnarled tree trunks. *What comfort can there possibly be in food when the one you love is lost?*

The rest of the party had begun to awaken, and Teissèdre glanced toward them, then back to Carleton, his gaze sharpening. "Don't despair, my friend," he said gently, reaching to clamp his thick hand over Carleton's knee. "Never fear. Your ships will be here on the morrow, and then we'll go reclaim your lady."

## Chapter Fourteen

*Friday, 7 November*

"TWO RIDERS APPROACHING, SIR."

Looking up from the kettle bubbling over the small fire he had finally allowed due to the piercing cold, Carleton returned the picket's salute. He could hear muffled hoof beats approaching at a trot, just audible above the rattle of the wind through the tangle of cedars and underbrush and the tide's restless seethe against the shore at his back.

Standing, he pulled his bearskin around his shoulders and squinted through the pale sunlight toward the sound. In moments two riders emerged into the clearing, preceded by another of the pickets.

In the lead Carleton recognized Sergeant Prince. He led a horse whose gaunt rider slumped in the saddle as though he remained astride only by dogged determination.

When Prince dismounted, the man lifted his head to gaze at Carleton and his companions in dull amazement. The sergeant moved to catch him before he fell from the saddle, and Carleton ran to his side. Teissèdre followed on his heels, along with McLeod, who had ridden in an hour earlier.

Clutching Caleb in his arms, Carleton strained the younger man to his breast, emotion rendering him speechless. At last he stepped back to take him in, while support the captain at arm's length.

Caleb met his anxious gaze with a weary one, then, stroking his bearded jaw in dazed wonder, turned his attention to the tidy, compact camp. "Blessed be the good Lord!" he croaked. "When Sergeant Prince . . . waylaid me on the road north . . . out of Amboy . . . he said you planned our rescue. I could hardly credit it, but . . . here you are! Unless you're spirits—"

"I assure you, captain," Teissèdre broke in kindly, "we're flesh and blood."

"Ghosts or men . . . you're a most welcome sight." His voice choking, Caleb added, "I'd given up all hope. I thought for sure Beth and I were lost."

It was all Carleton could do to motion McLeod to bring water. The chaplain quickly fetched a bucket and dipper.

"We'd o' been here sooner, sir," Prince apologized, turning to Carleton and hastily saluting, "but the capt'n be in bad state when I find him. We ride most o' last night, but I's afraid he'd not make it if we press too hard."

Carleton returned his salute. "You did very well in getting him to us safely."

Caleb emptied the dipper twice, then cleared his throat. "I doubt I'd have had strength to ride half this far if Sergeant Prince hadn't nursed me along like a helpless babe."

Prince scratched the back of his head and gave a rueful chuckle. Sobering, he turned to Carleton.

"We learn where Miss Howard be held. Major Vander Groot guess right 'bout them prison ships. She aboard one called *Erebus*."

Stiffening, Carleton exclaimed, "*Erebus?*"

"It appears our plan may yet have good hope o' success," McLeod exulted. "But we'll nae count our chickens afore they're hatched, eh?"

"Then let's get to hatching," Carleton responded, his voice hardening. "If her name's any indication, the sooner we get Miss Howard off that cursed hulk, the better."

He dismissed the two guards, fighting to hold his emotions under tight rein. "Once you're warmed and refreshed, I'll hear your report, Captain Stern. We were just ready to eat, and doubtless both of you are ravenous."

"Starved—literally," Caleb conceded with a short laugh. "Sergeant Prince kindly insisted I eat every bite of his provisions on the way, but I could've swallowed twice as much and not noticed." He pulled a letter out of his coat pocket and held it out to Carleton. "You'll want this right away, I reckon."

Carleton took it, mouth dry, and frowned down at the wax seal. Satisfied that the stamp was Clinton's, he said with an effort, "You saw her write this?"

Caleb nodded, the muscles tightening in his jaw.

Although he wanted nothing more than to read the missive, Carleton tucked it into the pouch that hung from the woven sash girdling his waist. He waved his companions to the fire. After McLeod blessed the food, all were quickly seated and helping themselves to cups of strong black coffee and bowls of stewed beans and parched corn, supplemented by the fish the Frenchman had caught in a nearby stream, spitted on sticks, and set to roast over the hot coals. Teissèdre immediately occupied himself in preparing the rest of his catch for roasting.

"Ye need to take it slow," McLeod cautioned as he ladled a small helping of beans and corn into a bowl and offered it to Caleb. "As little nourishment as ye've had, eatin' too much at once may sicken ye."

Caleb swallowed a bite of fish, then took the bowl in hands that trembled. "I'd forgotten food could taste this good. Clinton's commissary doesn't believe in feeding prisoners overmuch. There were at least a hundred of us squeezed into a space that'd cramp half that number. We counted ourselves blessed when we got a mouthful of salt pork and a moldy biscuit, with half a cup of dirty water to wash it down."

After swallowing a spoonful of the stew, he added, "They gave me what they called a meal before releasing me. It was little better than what

I'd gotten in prison, and I might as well have thrown a drop of water down a dry well."

"Doubtless Clinton doesn't want us to gain the mistaken impression that the British treat their prisoners with any less than a mother's tender care," Teissèdre returned with a smirk.

Carleton listened to their banter absently, his emotions in turmoil. Unable to force down even a mouthful of food, he pulled the letter from his pocket. For some moments he could only stare at it, unable to breathe.

It was from her hand. Perhaps the last communication he would ever receive from her.

A sickening urgency overcame him. He snapped the wax seal and unfolded the page to hungrily scan the lines that wavered across it. The shakiness of the hand that had formed the words deeply grieved him.

With his finger he traced her name: Elizabeth Anne Howard. He drew in a slow breath and let it out, but his racing pulse refused to ease.

When he looked up, he caught Caleb watching him. Although the stocky captain was cleaner and more respectably clad than Carleton would have expected—doubtless at Clinton's duplicitous behest—his hollow cheeks and dull eyes, along with yellowing bruises and scrapes only beginning to scab over evidenced the abuse and deprivation to which he had been subjected.

Gratitude for Caleb's release and the success of their plan so far was tempered by the same agonizing questions that had tormented Carleton since the hour he had learned of Elizabeth's capture: *What must Beth be suffering even now? Will we reach her too late—or at all?*

He turned his gaze to Prince. "Your report."

The sergeant complied, relating all that had occurred from the time he and his companions had joined Vander Groot in New York until the arrival of Howe's messenger and the prisoners' summons to the British headquarters. Tersely he warned Carleton that the British were well aware that Carleton had received letters of marque from Congress, and of Lord Howe's intention to either destroy or take all Carleton's ships as prize, both privateers and merchantmen.

*"Mon Dieu!"* exclaimed Teissèdre, turning abruptly to Carleton. "Your merchantmen too! We must—"

Carleton cut him off, not shifting his gaze from Prince. "We must rescue Miss Howard. When she's safe in my arms I'll think about my ships. Until then, God and their captains will have to care for them."

"Accordin' to the major," Prince broke in, "Clinton make a joke o' you attemptin' to invade New York Harbor."

"He was serious?" Teissèdre asked sharply.

The sergeant shrugged. "Major Vander Groot don't think so, though he advise you take account o' it. Clinton tell him no enemy can get into the harbor."

Carleton exchanged a hard glance with Teissèdre, who threw back his head, eyes glittering. "Bah! It's nothing to counter this flea Clinton. Have no worries. I'll take care of it."

Thoroughly familiar with Teissèdre's talents, Carleton dismissed the matter from his mind and leaned tensely forward, his gaze fixed on the sergeant. "You saw her with your own eyes."

"They bring her 'round back o' Clinton's headquarters in a carriage, sir, and I catch a glimpse when they take her inside. She be filthy, still in men's dress, and one o' the guards support her to keep her from fallin'." Puzzlement creased Prince's brow. "When they bring her back out it look like she washed, and she wear somethin' like a servin' girl's gown."

"No doubt to make it appear to Captain Stern that she's being treated like a queen." Sarcasm edged Teissèdre's tone. "You verified that she was returned to the *Erebus?*"

"And a worse wreck I never seen," Prince affirmed. "She anchored on the outer side o' Wallabout Bay, some apart from the rest, which goin' to make it easier for us." He took a stick and scratched a rough chart in the dirt in front of his feet, showing the positions of each of the ships in the small bay. "You smell the stink of them boats all the way from the East River docks. Not just waste, gen'l. Dead bodies. Buzzards hover thick o'er the bay."

*If she dies before I reach her, they'll cast her body into the water with all the others. And I'll not even be able to bury her.*

Carleton stared down at his clenched hands, a dull roaring in his ears blotting out the fire's muted crackle and the surf's seethe. In that moment rage and hatred rose in him so powerfully that he could taste blood.

At the cross Jesus had asked the Father to forgive those who crucified Him, he reminded himself. The Savior had commanded his disciples to forgive if they wished to be forgiven. To do so was not an option.

Carleton admired that kind of forbearance. He acknowledged that someday he should be that strong.

But not now.

Today, now, this moment, every nerve ached for retribution. He wanted to get to Elizabeth's tormentors by any means possible, to capture and humiliate them as they had done to her and to all the soldiers who suffered with her, then to kill each one by slow degrees with the exquisite torture at which his warriors were so expert. He longed to look into their eyes and exult in their agony and terror as hell engulfed their souls.

He became aware that he was shaking. Drawing a searing breath, he swallowed the acid taste of bile. When he turned to Caleb, he feared even that slight movement might cause him to shatter.

"How long . . . were you with her?"

Almost he could not speak. His voice sounded brittle in his ears.

Caleb dropped his gaze. "Only long enough for Clinton to dictate the letter. He wouldn't allow us to get close and ordered that we keep silent and not talk to each other. We only exchanged a couple quick glances across the table. After she wrote what he told her to, he called the guard to take me away. That was the last I saw her."

Hands clenched, Carleton forced himself to ask the question whose answer he most feared. "How was she? The truth."

Still Caleb avoided Carleton's piercing gaze. "Looked like she'd been allowed to wash and she had on a clean gown, like Prince said. But her eyes were over-bright and she was flushed, feverish-like. That worried me considerable."

Carleton indicated the letter. "Clinton dictated this."

Caleb looked up, his eyes haunted. "She didn't want to write it, gen'l. She shook her head when he said the part about her being released once the terms were met. But he threatened to strike her, and when I tried to stop him, he said he'd have me given a hundred lashes. Then she gave over and wrote it."

Sick with rage and agony, Carleton thrust the letter at Teissèdre. He and McLeod bent their heads together to scrutinize the writing.

After a moment, Teissèdre glanced up and asked, "This is how she writes her name, yes?"

Carleton rubbed his brow in an effort to ease the throbbing ache centered there. "I don't know. Because of the danger of interception, her messages were always either verbal or in code."

Caleb frowned. "Clinton just said to sign it."

"See there," McLeod said softly to Teissèdre, "at the end o' her middle name, Anne. The line breaks between the two n's, and the e looks to me more like an o."

"Her hand shook while she wrote," Teissèdre suggested.

"But she doesna break a word at any other place," McLeod pointed out. "Not in the whole o' the letter."

Carleton held out his hand, and Teissèdre surrendered the paper to him. McLeod, Caleb, and Prince crowded around to look over his shoulders. "It's hardly noticeable, but you're right. One could read those two letters as the word *no*."

They all exchanged sober glances. "The question is whether she wrote it that way intentionally," said Teissèdre.

McLeod resumed his seat, his expression thoughtful. "If she did, what exactly did she mean by it?"

"Don't come?" Caleb guessed. "Don't try to rescue her? Better than anyone, she knows the risks—and that you'll try it, sir."

"Don't turn yourself in t' Howe," Prince suggested.

Eyes narrowed, Teissèdre stroked his long nose. "That surely. Possibly all of it."

Carleton folded the letter with careful deliberation and tucked it back into his pouch. "She knows I'll come. I swore I'd never forsake her, and that's a promise I mean to keep. But after this business is finished and she's safe, I'll make it my personal mission to attack and sink every one of the warships Lord Howe commands."

He stared, unseeing, into the fire, feeling as though above him swung the razor-keen blade of the sword of Damocles, suspended by a single hair. Fear and resolution welled up in equal measure.

He became aware that his companions had resumed their seats, and that each one studied him with concern. With great effort he summoned strength to shake off his stormy thoughts and mask the emotions he knew must show on his face.

With a calmness entirely foreign to what he felt, he explained to Caleb and Prince that McLeod had arrived that morning with a message from Washington detailing the disposition of Admiral Howe's fleet in the Delaware and British progress in driving the American force out of their river defenses blocking access to Philadelphia. "General Howe was seen observing the action, which means one less concern for us. With the army pinning him down there and Clinton convinced that no one can get to the prison ships, the chance for our success is greater. If my ships arrive yet tonight, we'll sail tomorrow afternoon. That will put us in New York Harbor by nightfall as planned. Pray that Captain Eaden gets them here."

He rose and strode across the beach to the edge of the water, trailed by the others. The surf washed over his boots, and the keen wind cut through his buckskins, stinging his face and hands. Taking his spyglass from his pouch, he extended it and for long moments studied the horizon.

"No sign of a sail?" Teissèdre asked, squinting at the distant edge of the heaving water.

"Not yet," Carleton answered. "But the wind's steady out of the north. If all's gone well, they'll be running before it and making good speed. By God's grace they'll be here by nightfall."

"CAN YE DO NO MORE FOR HER?"

Vander Groot looked up to meet the captain's tortured gaze. "Considering the circumstances, I'm doing all I can, Josiah. She's unable to swallow any food, and certainly what you're given here would do her more harm than good."

He returned his gaze to Elizabeth's flushed face. In her delirium she had not recognized him and remained insensible to Josiah and the others as well. Moaning, she rolled her head restlessly from side to side, eyes closed.

He dampened his handkerchief with clear water from his canteen and wiped away the moisture that beaded her brow. "Just breathing this foul air does her harm. But all we can do is to continue the cinchona and laudanum and wait for the infection to run its course."

Billy and Tom pressed close. "She'll . . . not die?" Billy faltered.

The young Irishman's expression reflected Vander Groot's fear, and desperation squeezed his chest. "There's no way to tell yet, Billy. But she's dangerously weak . . . " He bit his lip and let the words trail off.

Just before noon he had met with Clinton to assure him that Elizabeth was far too ill to respond to any probes for intelligence. He had delicately brought up the possibility of moving her to the nearby *Frederick,* where conditions were marginally better, but Clinton's vehement objection immediately quelled the possibility of protest.

Howe had directed that she be removed from the *Erebus* only at his express order, Clinton emphasized, and he completely concurred. Howe had ordered her to be brought to Clinton's headquarters under heavy guard only long enough to meet with Captain Stern and write the letter Carleton demanded. She was then to be returned to the *Erebus* with utmost speed. No further exceptions would be granted.

Concerned that to press the issue would only compromise his already tenuous position, Vander Groot had pretended complete agreement with the general's outburst. He promised to do all he could to obtain intelligence from her quickly in case she died, and the subject was dropped.

From Clinton's headquarters Vander Groot had gone immediately to the *Erebus,* this time leaving Isaiah and his men behind in hope of gaining greater cooperation from the hulk's captain. He had found Villers in his cabin, deep in his cups. When the man hardly responded to Vander Groot's insistence on examining Elizabeth, the doctor abruptly left, only to be accosted by a couple of Hessian soldiers, and then one of the marine guards on his way to the hatch leading below. Vander Groot told each of them in plain fury that he followed orders issued by General Clinton and, if they had any opposition to it, to take their concerns to the general. Then he strode by them with a stare that dared them to block his way.

Now he tenderly cupped Elizabeth's sunken cheek in his hand, wincing to feel the fire that raged in her. Becoming aware that Josiah watched him intently, Vander Groot glanced up to meet the captain's assessing gaze. And understanding.

"Ye love her," Josiah said softly. "Yet I know the man she loves is named Jonathan." When Vander Groot compressed his lips, the captain continued, " 'Tis impossible for ye to get aboard this ship 'thout Clinton's allowin' it, yet I've no confidence he's suddenly developed a conscience where we're concerned. Who be ye really, doctor? And what be ye doin' here?"

Gently Vander Groot settled Elizabeth back against the deck and covered her loosely with the blanket he had smuggled aboard in his medical pouch. Turning to the captain, he looked from him to his mates and back again.

"You're right, and I'm going to need all the help you can give me. But you must guarantee that not another soul aboard this ship will hear the faintest whisper of what I'm about—nor anyone connected to the British in any way. Only the four of us. Can I trust you?"

CARLETON STOOD MOTIONLESS, braced against the steady wind, his spyglass trained to the northeastern horizon. Around him shadows slanted long across the sand and pooled beneath the tossing limbs of the trees. At the far edge of the ocean, the sky held the dusky pink and blue tints of twilight.

"Ships?"

"One, hull up on the horizon. She's crowding sail."

Teissèdre clapped him on the shoulder. "Did I not tell you they'd come yet today, my friend?"

"As I said, there's only the one, and she's nowhere near enough to identify yet. She could be British for all I can tell."

"Bah! Ye of little faith!"

Lowering the spyglass, Carleton glanced at his agent. "I admit there are times when I'm sorely lacking in that department. This is one of them."

Teissèdre fixed him in a piercing look. "I suspect you're not lacking in faith so much as that you fear to be disappointed in God should you trust. Is it not man who has disappointed you? But God is not a man."

"He is not," Carleton agreed, "but his ways are inscrutable, at least to me." He turned his back and again raised his spyglass. He tensed and after a long moment said, "There's a second. The first, I think . . . " He hesitated, then muttered, "Yes. Three gun decks."

*"Destiny!"* Teissèdre exulted. "What of the other?"

"Her hull's just come above the horizon, a little distance back from the first." Moving the spyglass slightly, he drew in his breath. "There's a third set of sails behind her, almost blocked from view. They're on a heading in this direction, but slightly south. Toward the inlet, I'll wager."

"How many gun decks?"

"Two for the second," Carleton responded after a long pause. "I can't make out enough of the third to tell."

"Shall I have the men light the fire?" Teissèdre thrust his chin toward the dry branches and underbrush piled high a short distance down the beach.

"Wait. If they're not mine, we don't want to attract their attention."

Teissèdre made no response, and for some moments Carleton drank in the sight of the three vessels skimming across the ocean's swells and troughs as they ran before the wind. Tall racks of snowy sails were full spread, and they cast high plumes of white spray from their bows. He watched for other sails to appear, but except for these three, the horizon remained reassuringly empty.

"They're flying the French flag."

Teissèdre eagerly held out his hand and, when Carleton surrendered the spyglass, trained it on the ships. "The first I know to be *Destiny* from her new colors. You'd not recognize her, of course, since she was refitted this summer. The other two are 74s, thus *Liberty* and *Invictus.*"

Carleton again scrutinized the rapidly closing ships through the spyglass, his heart lifting when the awaited signal winked from a shaded lantern at the bow of the largest. *"Destiny's* signaling. Have the men light the fire at once."

The older man hurried off, and within minutes a bonfire pushed back the gathering darkness. Keeping watch from the edge of the trees with the rest of his party while the three ships corrected their course to sail directly toward the beach, Carleton fought back stinging tears.

*Thank you. And forgive me. Despite my lack of faith, You've not forsaken us.*

Leaving the others, he returned quickly to the camp and roused Prince, who had settled down to a deep sleep soon after they had finished their meal. He carefully outlined his orders to Vander Groot, then directed the sergeant to take a fresh horse and ride at all speed back to New York.

"Take especial care to avoid any British patrols," he emphasized, "but it's urgent you reach the city before nightfall tomorrow. Your detail must be in control of the *Erebus* when my ships enter the bay. We'll have no time to waste if we're to get all the prisoners off."

Prince assured him that he would not stop until he delivered Carleton's orders. Grabbing his pack, he disappeared into the night, headed toward the clearing where the horses grazed.

Carleton returned to the beach. Within half an hour, the three privateers, darkly shadowed by encroaching nightfall, began to lower sails and slowed, one of the 74-gun ships in advance of the others. A voice singing out the depths reached the watchers on the shore, while the ships edged as close as they dared. At last they hove to and cast out anchors, *Liberty* and *Invictus* taking up posts on opposite ends of *Destiny*.

Carleton took in the fine, raked lines of his ships, feeling breathless. It was the first time he had seen any of them since his maternal uncle, the French admiral le comte de Caledonne, had overseen the refitting of a portion of Carleton's merchant fleet into privateers. Indeed, he had not seen any of his ships since his life had undergone a drastic change three years earlier.

*Destiny,* with her figurehead of an ethereal water sprite holding a globe as she emerged from a wave, especially evoked a turmoil of emotions. He and Andrews had sailed to Virginia aboard her in the fall of 1774. Then, the joy he should have felt at his homecoming after ten years in England had been obscured by a deep fog of grief at the sudden, unexpected death of his paternal uncle and adoptive father, Sir Harrison Carleton. Learning that Sir Harry had died at the hands of British soldiers as the result of false charges of smuggling, Carleton had vowed undying enmity to king and ministry and secretly resumed the command in the Virginia militia he had neglected to resign when joining the British 17th Light Dragoons. He had subsequently allowed himself to be persuaded by Patrick Henry and George Washington to use his position as a British officer to gather intelligence for the Sons of Liberty while stationed in Boston.

Discovered and arrested, he would have been hanged for treason had not Elizabeth, in her guise as the nefarious rebel spy and courier Oriole, plucked him out of British hands with an audacity that enraged generals Gage, Howe, Clinton, and Burgoyne. General Washington had immediately sent Carleton to negotiate the native tribes' support for the American rebels—an assignment that had led to his capture and enslavement by the Seneca, his rescue and adoption by the Shawnee, and his rise to become the tribe's war chief in the bitter fight against encroaching white settlers. It had been Elizabeth again, along with Andrews, who had found him after more than a year and brought him back.

*From the pot into the flames.* Carleton let out a sigh. *It seems I'm incapable of staying out of trouble. And now Beth's life is in danger because of me.*

His reverie was broken when *Destiny* lowered her cutter. Swiftly the small boat danced across the waves and drew up near the shore. The officers aboard waded through the surf and were instantly swarmed by the waiting party. Carleton followed more slowly and returned the salute of the officer in charge, introduced to him as First Lieutenant John Stanisbury. After ordering, the rest of his party to stay on alert for any intruders, he and Teissèdre boarded the cutter to cross to the great warship riding at anchor a safe distnce off the sandy beach.

## Chapter Fifteen

T HE IRONY OF BEING CEREMONIOUSLY piped aboard his own ship by the bosun's whistle while clad in the plain linen hunting shirt and weathered buckskins of a frontiersman was not lost on Carleton. Stepping through *Destiny's* entry port into the ship's waist, he threw a wry glance at Teissèdre and received a grimace and shrug in response.

Carleton's gaze swept the seamen and officers who crowded the broad forecastle, quarterdeck, and poop deck and spilled into the ship's waist. They stood at rigid attention in precisely ordered ranks—nearly 1,000 in all. Since being converted from merchantmen, his privateers' crews had been bolstered dramatically, and the multiplied ranks were an impressive sight in short blue jackets and blue-and-white striped slops.

As on all his ships, *Destiny's* crew included large numbers of French, Dutch, Spanish, and African, as well as American, seamen. Many had been freed from forced impressment on British vessels and had eagerly joined their liberators to wreak vengeance on their former oppressors. Also among them were young boys who served as powder monkeys and carried out other light duties; older youths and young men holding midshipmen's rank; and a number of the seamen's women, who filled the roles of nurse, laundress, and the children's teachers and caretakers.

He noted with approval that Stowe, Briggs, and the detail that had accompanied them to Boston waited at the near end of the first line. Pete Moghrab stood farther down the line among the midshipmen, looking resolutely straight ahead. Here and there, however, some of the crew took Carleton's measure with sidelong glances. Considering his rough garb, he could not blame them.

While the red-clad marines presented arms, he allowed his gaze to stray upward along the shrouds and the length of the masts all the way to the tops that swayed against the night-shrouded heavens. From her newly coppered bottom, gleaming dark blue oak hull, and polished oak decks trimmed in ivory and crimson, to the tops of her three towering masts decked with snowy sails, now furled on the yardarms, and networks of taut rigging, she was even more breathtakingly beautiful after refitting than he remembered her to have been as a merchantman. Flanking her fore and aft, the two 74s, *Liberty* and *Invictus,* were accoutered identically, although on a smaller scale, giving the same striking impression of grace and power.

He became aware that several officers advanced toward him, none of whom he recognized. The man leading the party he assumed to be William Eaden, *Destiny's* new captain. Carleton was instantly impressed by his confident manner and the sense that his abilities justified it. His companions were undoubtedly the captains and first lieutenants of the two 74s, brought over in the ships' longboats for this meeting while Carleton and Teissèdre crossed in the cutter.

Coming to a halt, Eaden touched his fingers to the forepoint of his cocked hat. "We're honored to have you aboard, General Carleton." When Carleton returned his salute, Eaden bowed to Teissèdre. "Monsieur Teissèdre. It's good to see you again."

After a brief exchange of pleasantries, Eaden introduced *Liberty's* captain, Philippe Souvage, and First Lieutenant Mathieu Blanchard; then Captain Fernando Rodrigo and First Lieutenant Alfredo Ballesteros of *Invictus.* Wasting no further time on ceremony, Eaden dismissed the crew either to their duties on the dogwatch or to a delayed dinner, then invited Carleton and Teissèdre to join him and the other officers on a tour of the ship.

Full night had by now fallen, and for the next hour they traversed the vessel by lantern light, while the seamen stood watch, took their turn at mess, or busied themselves mending clothing, rigging, or sails. The usual custom of singing and dancing on deck during peaceful evenings was neglected that night—not only due to their employer being aboard, Carleton guessed, but also because the gravity of their mission had been made clear. The face of every crewman he encountered was soberly, but resolutely, set.

Eaden led the party to inspect the dispositions of the hundred guns on the upper, main, and lower gun decks, the tidy berths and officers' cabins, the neatly stowed supplies, and fully stocked magazine. While at Boston, the captain explained, he had cleared *Destiny* of everything not strictly necessary for their mission and had brought her to full fighting trim.

It quickly became clear that Eaden ran a tightly disciplined ship. In fact, Carleton would have expected no more from a British or French ship of the line arrayed for battle.

Judging by the speed at which *Destiny* must have traveled to reach the rendezvous in time, Eaden either exercised draconian measures to control his crew, had gained their unqualified allegiance by his fairness and justice, or was a miracle worker. That the men they passed nodded to their captain with both respect and liking and extended to Carleton the same easy, but grave, deference spoke well of the way Eaden exercised authority. Of course, Carleton reflected wryly, the rich prize money the crew had shared in over the past few months certainly would not have dampened morale.

As he moved about the ship, he recognized suddenly, with unexpected pleasure, that without being conscious of it he had instinctively adjusted his stride to the once-familiar movements of a ship at sea. A flood of both happy and painful memories of summers spent aboard his uncle's flagship as an adolescent washed over him. He had taken to sailing with such enthusiasm and native talent that Caledonne had urged him to enter the French *gardes de la marine* as a cadet on Caledonne's sponsorship and on graduation to sail under him, making a career in the French navy.

It was a plan Sir Harry peremptorily vetoed the instant he heard of it. Although Carleton had not learned the truth until years later, Sir Harry had decided to send him off to Harvard in hopes of separating him from his maternal uncle. Sharp words passed between Sir Harry and Caledonne as a result, creating a long-standing rift between them so bitter that Carleton had been torn between these two men he deeply loved and respected, feeling that to please the one was inevitably to displease the other.

Carleton himself had at last indirectly settled the dispute without realizing it. Over those years the lure of the wilderness had begun to draw him ever more powerfully to the native peoples. He kept the extent of his forays into Shawnee territory from Sir Harry as much as possible, finding in the sachem Black Hawk, who years later adopted Carleton into the Kispokotha sept, the uncumbered acceptance and affection he longed for.

By the time he was eighteen, his course had been irrevocably set away from the sea—and, as well, from Sir Harry's cherished intention for his adopted son to take over control of his merchant fleet—and to the wilderness.

The sea had never entirely relinquished its hold on him, however. Thirteen years earlier, before leaving on that fateful crossing to England to the death bed of his natural father, Lord Oliver Carleton, he had persuaded Sir Harry to build *Destiny* according to a design he had devised with Caledonne's secret guidance. And as Carleton had predicted, she had brought in enormous profits for Sir Harry's import business during the years of Carleton's absence in England.

Large for a merchantman and built in the most advanced French style, *Destiny* was gracefully raked, while having a broader bottom than did British ships. The design resulted in greater speed, maneuverability, and stability than the largest ships of other nations, which wallowed like sows in heavy seas. It also provided greater cargo capacity and allowed her to carry a formidable complement of guns and marines for protection against pirates. It had thus been a simple matter for Caledonne to have her refitted as a privateer, along with other vessels in Carleton's fleet also built to French design.

For all the good the effort would do, Carleton thought, a sick feeling churning his stomach. For now the British knew, much earlier than he had hoped, of his involvement in American attacks on their shipping. And not only was Lord Howe determined to wreak all hell on Carleton from that quarter, but now Clinton had casually made a mocking reference to the exact plan Carleton had put in motion to rescue Elizabeth.

He would have despaired of both their lives were he not so confident of Teissèdre's covert craft. Yet come what may, no choice was left him but to play the game through to its end.

THE TOUR OF THE SHIP ended in the expansive wardroom, where the rest of *Destiny's* officers joined them, including the surgeon, slender, dark-haired, dark-eyed Dr. Jean Lemaire. After Eaden led them in a prayer, they took their seats at table. Eaden waved his hand at the heavily loaded platters of food his steward and assistants hurried to set before them, while the space filled with rich aromas that would have made Carleton's mouth water but for the turmoil that twisted his stomach.

"Caledonne saw us supplied not only with generous stores of food, but also with excellent cooks. When we're not otherwise engaged, we dine like kings."

"That would be my uncle," Carleton acknowledged, forcing a smile. "I've fond memories of his penchant for fine cuisine."

Eaden cast a frowning glance across the groaning board. "I'd have puddings and custards to offer you too if we hadn't offloaded our goats at Boston when your orders arrived. I deemed it prudent to minimize our distractions. The chickens and pigs went by the by as well, so unfortunately this is the last of our poultry. It'll be salt pork, beans, and biscuit until we can resupply."

"Exactly what I'd have counseled, Mister Eaden," Carleton approved. "As I'm sure you know, we'll need the ships as light as possible to cross the Bar into the harbor. And if we don't accomplish our purpose tomorrow night, there'll be no need to resupply." His gaze briefly turned to Lemaire. "We've experienced surgeons aboard *Liberty* and *Invictus* as well, I take it."

"The best available, along with a full complement of surgeon's mates. Again, Caledonne saw to our every need." Eaden fixed him in a keen look and lifted his wineglass. "To your health, general."

"And to yours."

They all emptied their goblets. Carleton set his beside his plate and transferred his gaze from one face to another around the table, feeling of a sudden that if he was to have any hope of succeeding in his goal, these men were the ones he wanted with him. The discipline, resolve, and professionalism each conveyed by his manner impressed him—though also being well familiar with his uncle's astuteness in choosing officers for his own ships, Carleton had expected no less. And judging by the shrewd glance Teissèdre returned, he shared Carleton's assessment.

*As usual, You've gone before,* Carleton thought, humbled once more.

The fear for Elizabeth that constantly nagged at the back of his mind soon returned in force, however. As the others attacked the food with gusto, while conversing about inconsequential matters, he silently choked down what he could of the succulent roast chicken and vegetables, knowing that he needed strength for the task that lay ahead of him. But it all might as well have been dust.

At length Carleton turned to Eaden and said gruffly, "I've neglected to thank you for coming so quickly."

Eaden grinned. "We're at your beck and call, sir."

"A squadron of British frigates off Nantucket Shoals wished ardently to make our acquaintance, which did much to speed us on our way as well," Souvage explained, giving a short laugh that was echoed heartily by the others.

"Doubtless they took our trade for what it is, but *el dios bueno* gave us swifter wings than theirs and let us fly away."

With a nod at Rodrigo, Carleton echoed softly, "*El dios bueno,* indeed."

Eaden sat back in his chair, his hand covering his smile as he stroked his chin. "God and Caledonne, to be sure." He sobered. "I'm sorry for the circumstances that necessitated this mission, but be assured that we'll do all in our power to rescue your lady and all those with her."

Carleton conceded a curt nod. "Your crews understand the extreme danger we're sailing into and the odds against our success?"

Eaden's clear blue eyes brightened in his deeply tanned face. "They do. And there's not a man who isn't eager to invade the lion's den and rob him of his prey."

He spoke with a relish that brought to Carleton's mind the circumstances that had caused one of the Royal Navy's most brilliant captains to leave his country's service in order to take command of an American merchant vessel. With a promising career stunted for some years due to naval politics, Eaden had grown disillusioned enough to seek new opportunities, a vulnerability Sir Harry had cannily exploited to lure the captain into his employ as captain of his second-rated ship, *Black Swan.*

Since then, Eaden had developed deep sympathies with the plight of the American colonists and, from what Teissèdre had told Carleton, was more than eager to apply his talents to visiting retribution on his former countrymen. His abilities had earned him command of *Destiny* late the previous summer when her former captain died in an accident, and Eaden had already more than justified the confidence placed in him.

"The situation's become more complicated since I summoned you," Carleton told Eaden. After warning the officers of Howe's threat to all of his ships and Clinton's reference to their attacking New York Harbor, he continued grimly, "The task we've before us is not only to enter the bay and rescue the prisoners, difficult as that is, but we may also be sailing into a trap. Should we succeed in our goal, in order to get away we'll then have to sail all the way back through the harbor since it's impossible for ships of this size to make it through Hell Gate, especially on an inrushing tide. If we're discovered, we'll be forced to fight, with the odds very much against us."

Over the next hour, while they finished the meal and the dishes were cleared away, Carleton directed the officers in planning the coming action. Beginning at first light, the carpenters would repaint the ships to make them appear as newly minted British warships, while ballast was redistributed to ensure the greatest stability and speed. They would sail in early afternoon, flying the British ensign, so they would reach Sandy Hook around nightfall.

Caledonne had supplied Carleton's ships with detailed charts of all major ports, and both Eaden and *Destiny's* master, a stocky, middle-aged New York Dutchman named Ezekiel Kuthoopen, were well acquainted with New York Harbor. Finding their way to Wallabout Bay without escort would be an easy matter.

They spent some time discussing the transfer of prisoners. Sergeant Prince had supplied an estimate of how many were held aboard *Erebus,* and it was decided that the sickest would be taken aboard *Invictus,* while those able to walk under their own power would board *Liberty.*

"The women aboard each of our ships are well experienced in nursing the sick and wounded," Eaden assured Carleton.

"I'll interview them on the morrow when I inspect *Liberty* and *Invictus,*" Carleton responded. "The captive I seek, Miss Howard—" He broke off, the words sticking in his throat.

"We received a report today that she's fallen gravely ill," Teissèdre put in, his hand closing over Carleton's arm. "As you can imagine, it's of immense import that we reach her without delay."

Carleton downed the remaining wine in his goblet, its fiery trail through his veins steadying him. "I want her brought aboard *Destiny.* And I want the woman with the most experience in nursing to attend her."

"That would be Marie Glasière," Eaden said. 'She's here, and we'll speak with her tonight."

Realizing that he had kept everyone later than he intended, Carleton pushed stiffly out of his chair. All around the table, the officers got to their feet.

"Gentlemen, we'll finalize details in the morning. After I inspect *Liberty* and *Invictus,* we'll meet back here."

As Teissèdre and the officers filed out, Pete slipped inside the wardroom and gave a brisk salute. "General Carleton, forgive my interruption," he said breathlessly, casting an apologetic glance at Eaden. "I'd like to speak with you at your convenience if I may."

Before Eaden could object, Carleton laid his hand on the youth's shoulder. "If it's news of your father you're wanting, Pete, he's with Major Vander Groot at New York, along with a number of his troops." Briefly he outlined their mission. "They'll join us here aboard *Destiny* when all the prisoners have been taken off *Erebus.*"

Concern etched Pete's face, but he forced a smile. "Yes, sir. Thank you, sir."

Thoughtfully Carleton watched the youth stride out of the wardroom, then turned to Eaden. "He saw his brother killed in battle at Long Island."

Eaden's expression cleared. "Ah, that explains it. Well, then . . . "

"I want him with the detail boarding *Erebus.*"

"He's earned the assignment." Eaden gave Carleton a keen look "You're not planning to accompany them, I hope. You're far too valuable a target, and if anything were to go wrong—"

"I'll be with them," Carleton cut him off abruptly. Swinging on his heel, he made for the companionway.

Carleton bade McLeod farewell and turned to Caleb as the chaplain mounted. "I'm not giving you a choice, captain."

"But sir, I'm fully capable of—"

"You'd only slow us down. The ride back to Baptist Meeting House will be ordeal enough after all you've endured. You'll be ready for action again soon enough, and besides, you can be of greater service to Colonel Stern right now," he added, referring to Elizabeth's uncle, Colonel Joshua Stern, with the Massachusetts brigade. "Report to him when you return to the corps. Tell him I'll speak to him directly if we've further need of you."

Caleb's face fell. "Yes, sir." Reluctantly he mounted and took his place in the line of troopers.

"I'll take good care o' im, gen'l," Briggs assured Carleton as he pulled his mount up behind Caleb's.

"Thank you, Briggs." He included McLeod in his glance. "Be sure to give Colonel Andrews a full report."

"That I will, sir," McLeod answered.

Carleton strode to the head of the line where Captain Farris waited. "Tell Colonel Andrews to take the brigade immediately to White Marsh to join General Washington's corps. I'll send Isaiah back to him as soon as possible with a report on our mission."

Captain Farris saluted. "I'll tell him, sir, and God grant you good success. I'll personally see to Devil," he added, referring to Carleton's tall, black-stockinged bay stallion, on a lead behind him.

Carleton thanked him, and the lean, buckskin-garbed officer mounted. He glanced back down the ranks of the waiting Rangers before returning his concerned gaze to Carleton.

"Godspeed, general." He waved the guard forward, and they spurred off through the trees, quickly vanishing from sight into the restless night.

Private James Stowe came to Carleton's side. Middle-aged, his thinning brown hair threaded with grey, the servant gave the impression of a bulldog, with a stout body, thick neck, brawny arms, and bandy legs. The livid, puckered scar that ran from his left eye to his jaw lent him the appearance of an unsavory character, though his eyes and crooked smile conveyed amiability. Long Carleton's servant, the previous year Stowe had become his adoptive Shawnee brother as well, receiving the name Little Running Heron for his slight stature and hunched back.

"What do you think of Eaden?" Carleton asked.

Stowe had doused the small campfire of the now abandoned camp. In the starlight that dimly illumined the clearing, Carleton could see his grin, which puckered his livid scar even more.

" 'e's a good man, sir. Never saw nobody move so fast—'ceptin' fer ye, o' course."

"It appears he made all the decision I'd have," Carleton allowed. For some moments he remained silent, then said with an effort, "Dr. and Mrs. Howard had returned to Boston?"

"Yes, sir."

"You told them everything?"

"As much as we 'ad time to," Stowe answered gruffly. "The elder Miz 'Oward promised as how she'd fill 'em in on the whole lot."

When he did not elaborate, Carleton asked, "How did they take it?" Dreading Stowe's answer, he was yet anxious to know the truth.

In the darkness he made out the flash of Stowe's eyes and the tensing of his features. "They was . . . in some distress, o' course, sir. Like ye'd expect. Took some talkin' t' persuade Dr. Howard t' sit tight for the time bein'. 'E 'ad . . . 'ard things to say."

Carleton stared through the trees bordering the beach to where the cutter's crew waited to convey them back to *Destiny*. Mentally he braced himself for the reception that would likely greet him at Boston.

If he could get to Elizabeth. If he could get her off that cursed ship alive.

Should she die in the attempt, he thought bleakly, her parents could say and do what they would. It would not matter. Nothing would matter ever again.

And his own death would be a mercy.

## Chapter Sixteen

"CALEDONNE WAS RIGHT. You'd have made a fine naval officer. At least you have the look of one."

Carleton met Teissèdre's amused gaze with a grimace and flicked the sleeve of the gold-trimmed dark blue uniform coat in which he was clad. "First I'd need a uniform that fits—and not a British one."

It had been the Frenchman's suggestion that, due to the risk of Eaden's being recognized by former colleagues in the Royal Navy, Carleton stand in as *Destiny's* captain in any encounters with the British. When Carleton readily agreed, Eaden had lent him the British captain's uniform he kept on hand for such contingencies. The coat's sleeves barely reached to Carleton's wrists, however, and strained at his broad shoulders, as did the shirt, which, along with the white waistcoat, hung loose at his waist. To add to his discomfort, with every movement, the matching breeches uncomfortably constricted his thighs.

"As *le capitaine* said, any irregularities will be hidden by the darkness, *mon general.*"

Carleton glanced at the dark-eyed young woman who stood on his left, wrapped in a heavy cloak, her softly curling black hair bared to the elements. He had been taken aback at his first meeting with Marie Glasière, who had turned out to be a slip of a girl of about nineteen, small and delicately beautiful. Despite his initial hesitation, after speaking with her privately he had been won over not only by Lemaire's recommendation, but also by her unexpectedly modest, unassuming manner and the steely core he sensed in her that would keep her steady if it came to battle.

"I hope you're right." He forced a smile and returned to his moody contemplation of the indistinct New Jersey shoreline gliding slowly past off *Destiny's* larboard bow.

As though reading his thoughts, Marie said quietly, "I have great admiration for the calmness and fortitude you display in such a time of distress."

He met her sympathetic gaze with a masked one. He had never felt less calm, less sure of his course and the outcome of it, and in spite of her carefully chosen words he had the uncomfortable feeling that she read his inward turmoil.

During the interminable hours since departing Squan Beach, while time hung suspended on the wintry sea, he had been overcome by the piercing realization that it was wholly beyond his power to save Elizabeth or any of the others aboard the hell-bound ship that was their goal. Even if by a miracle they made it into Sandy Hook Bay and past the batteries at the Narrows without arousing suspicion, that they could navigate undetected all the way around Long Island to Wallabout Bay past long ranks of Royal Navy warships was highly doubtful.

Should they accomplish that improbable feat, taking Elizabeth and her fellow prisoners off the *Erebus* would be a Herculean task. Yet once begun, they could leave no one behind even if it came to a fight. They would then have to sail a second time through the harbor's full length, avoiding dangerous shallows and threading constricted roadbeds where they might be waylaid a dozen times over before they could escape into the open sea.

It was a daunting mission for a full naval squadron. The odds against three privateers succeeding in such an endeavor were unimaginably high.

The Savior alone could accomplish a rescue so manifestly impossible. For there to be any hope of success, Carleton had to rely utterly upon the Almighty to guide and care for each of them at every step along the way.

While he watched the seemingly endless ocean rush by, conviction had held him in its unyielding grip: If he refused to obey the Lord's clear command to forgive as he had been forgiven, how could he plead for his Master's help? The only course possible was to relinquish all thought of vengeance, trusting that as well to the Father, and focus on the needs of each moment as they arose. Yet how could he foreswear retribution when rage at the monstrous violation Elizabeth suffered so consumed him?

In the end, that she was so dear to him, that his Savior was yet more dear had finally led to an agonizing surrender. He had felt then—would feel so until he held Elizabeth safe in his arms—as though he had taken a hard blow to the heart.

Four and a half hours after they sailed, Eaden had made good on his promise that they would reach the harbor at nightfall, nor had any enemy ship appeared on the horizon to challenge them. It was not by chance, Carleton felt certain.

*Vengeance is yours alone, Lord,* he repeated now, throat aching painfully. *If you but save her, I swear by your Name that for all the days left me I'll never seek vengeance against any man who's had a hand in this.*

Off to their left the sun's rapidly fading rays cast in sharp silhouette the long curving spit of Sandy Hook, framed by desolate marshland along its coast and night-black cedar forest farther inland. Closer at hand bobbed the shadowy buoy that marked the shallows of Middle Ground, a broad, treacherous, sandy expanse that lurked beneath the sea's surface at the mouth of Sandy Hook Bay. The buoy's twin to starboard warned ships away from the East Bank's extensive areas of still-submerged mud flats, which slipped smoothly past on their right.

With *Liberty* and *Invictus* following at a safe distance, *Destiny's* master expertly guided the close-hauled vessel through the roadbed's constricted channel into the vast Hudson River estuary, tacking against the ebb tide and a freshening wind that portended a coming storm. The bosun broke the stillness as he called out the depths, his voice underlaid by the muted boom of wind in taut rigging and sails, the creak of deck and mast and yards, the sibilant hiss of the ship's prow cutting through the water, the brisk movement of seamen at their duties. Beneath these familiar sounds Carleton could hear the occasional faint screech of gull or shore bird bound for its nightly roost.

Teissèdre leaned on the weather rail at his right. "A storm's brewing."

"You expected smooth sailing?" Carleton responded caustically.

His mouth tightening, he glanced toward the threatening bank of inky clouds rising in the west-southwest, steadily blotting out the last of the sun's failing rays. *Why is it the heavens always seem intent on making a challenging mission even more so?*

As if in answer to his doubts, the image of the wild nor'easter that had battered the army on the march to Trenton rose immediately to his mind. The reminder that the Lord of storms had used the elements' furies to grant them a signal victory stirred a thread of hope and relieved his tension.

He lifted his face to the wind. It had turned perceptibly warmer, he noted. *Thank God for small favors,* he thought with black humor. *If we're to be drenched, at least we'll not be entirely frozen.*

Turning, he directed an assessing glance the length of the deck. While still at sea, the three ships had cleared for action as much as possible without arousing suspicion: sails trimmed for a fight and upper decks stripped, wetted, and sanded; loose objects secured on the lower decks; the surgeon's station prepared; and powder, shot, and tackle distributed to the guns. Their crews casually loitered around them, and to either hand Carleton could make out faint coils of smoke twining into the air from the slow matches in their tubs of wet sand, shoved out of sight against the hammock netting that lined the bulwarks, along with ammunition, sponges, rammers, and other tackle for loading. He was relieved to see that at a short distance the drifting smoke dissolved into the gathering darkness.

Beyond the ship's bow the expanse of Sandy Hook Bay opened before them just as the fiery light at the western horizon extinguished, obscured behind the cloudbank swiftly overtaking the sky. Staring into the harbor's indistinct expanse, he had the momentary impression that they sailed into the impenetrable darkness of a valley cleft through deeply shrouded uplands where dangers crouched, as yet unseen.

*Yea, though I walk through the valley of the shadow of death, I will fear no evil: for Thou art with me; Thy rod and Thy staff, they comfort me. . . .* The scripture floated into his mind, and inexplicable warmth possessed his chest, dispelling the unsettling impression.

They entered the harbor boldly, bow and poop lanterns flaring to guide their way. Off their larboard bow the bright beam from the Hook's lighthouse also suddenly winked into the gathering night above a black mass of low scrub cedars.

"Seventy-four dead ahead."

Pete's hushed call reached him from the maintop seconds before the light sent a gleam across the black bulk of the British 74 that crept from the shadows beyond the lighthouse a quarter mile in front of them to block the roadbed into the bay.

"Lower sails," he heard Eaden command from behind him. "Bring her about and heave to."

His orders were repeated across the deck to the pipe of the bosun's whistle. The midshipmen sprang with their crews up the ratlines to the yards, with Stowe and Briggs surging past amid of a clutch of sailors racing to their stations.

All three ships slowed. *Destiny* came about until she lay abreast of the 74, a ship's length between them, and dropped anchor.

"Please go below, Mademoiselle Glasière. Stay there until I bring Miss Howard aboard."

He watched the young woman's graceful retreat until she disappeared into the hatch's gloom. Straightening, he readjusted his cocked hat and cast a sidelong glance at Teissèdre.

The Frenchman responded with a wolfish smile. "Remember: Answer no question that remains unasked." He stepped back, his form melting into the shade of the foremast rigging.

Across the water a slight figure at the 74's quarterdeck weather rail lifted a lantern. "Who goes there?"

"Captain Edwin Shaw of His Majesty's ship *Albion* out of Portsmouth, escorted by *Whippet* and *Northumbria,*" Carleton said crisply. "Who are *you,* sir?"

"First Lieutenant Alfred Canning of the *Invincible,*" the voice responded in a saucy tone. "What's your business entering the harbor at nightfall?"

"We carry an urgent message for General Clinton, Mister Canning. I request immediate passage."

There was a hesitation, then, "You fly the Union Jack, but your ships have the lines of Frenchmen."

"So they are. Taken prize and rebaptized for more honorable service."

"Sweet," Canning said, admiration replacing suspicion. "I'm sure they sail like swans."

"They do indeed. But you'll pardon me if I've no time for pleasantries. Afford us passage at once."

There was a short interval marked by the movement of men along the 74's deck before a taller form replaced that of the lieutenant.

"Captain Merritt here. The tide's ebbing and it's already full dark, Mister Shaw," he said with asperity. "Even without a storm coming on, you'd run into trouble making it through the Narrows into the upper bay with a ship of that burthen, and there's no pilot available to guide you this time of night. I'm afraid you'll have to wait out the night here and enter on the morrow."

"The ebb's hardly beyond the midpoint, Mister Merritt. My master knows this harbor well and assures me he'll bring us safely through before the storm hits."

"I suspect I may know these waters better than your master. Whatever business you have can wait for the morning, urgent or not."

The wind suddenly picked up, forcing Carleton to hold onto his hat. A spattering of rain sprinkled his shoulders and briefly drummed across the deck.

He directed an assessing glance at Eaden, who eased closer to him. "It'll take too long for my ships to make it all the way to York Island on the morrow," Carleton returned, his voice steely. "General Clinton will be considerably less than pleased at the delay when he receives Lord Germain's communication, as will Germain when he learns of it. Our orders are to deliver the message directly into the general's hands at the earliest possible instant and upon receiving his response immediately to sail to the Delaware to deliver Germain's orders to General Howe."

"Germain?" It was clear that Merritt was nonplussed, as Carleton meant him to be. "Is Howe being summoned back to England? It's no secret there's no love lost between him and the secretary."

"I didn't make that my business, sir. It's a matter between the general and Lord Germain." Carleton's stiff tone implied that it was not Merritt's business either.

"I'll have to see your credentials before I clear you to enter the harbor," Merritt huffed. "We've been warned that American privateers may be planning to breach our defenses in the next few days."

"American privateers?" Carleton drawled, his stomach clenching. "Surely you jest."

"I'd have thought the same, but Clinton appears to be taking the threat seriously. Those are my orders, Mister Shaw."

Carleton motioned to Eaden. With a satisfied smile, the captain pulled a packet of papers from his pocket and ordered that one of the longboats be lowered. What felt like an interminable period wasted away until Stanisbury, rowed across by a small crew, sprang up the 74's ladder to present the papers to her captain with a bow.

More moments dragged by in a tense silence that plucked at Carleton's already taut nerves. Merritt first appeared to study the packet's wax seal, evidently impressed by the official insignia of Prime Minister North's Cabinet, which Teissèdre had come into possession of by some clandestine means. Finally Carleton saw him snap the wax and open the packet.

To his satisfaction, Merritt stiffened while scanning the papers' contents. Knowing Teissèdre's work had, as usual, been impeccable and that the signature on the documents purporting to be Lord Germain's was virtually indistinguishable from that of the British Secretary of State for America, Carleton surmised that Merritt assessed the consequences of denying them passage over the secretary's express orders, while weighing the possibility that they were, in fact, privateers.

Carleton wrestled the impulse to command that *Destiny's* guns be run out on all three decks to speed the captain's decision. Before he could give in to temptation, Merritt returned the packet to Stanisbury and dismissed him.

"Well, then, if the matter's so urgent, be on your way." the captain called across the water haughtily while the lieutenant descended the ladder to the boat. "You'll present these to the harbormaster, of course. You know where to find him?"

Carleton bit his lip to quell an openly insolent response. "Certainly. He and my master are old friends."

"If you run aground, don't expect any aid until daybreak," Merritt returned. "I can't warrant anyone'll be available to help you before then."

"Thank you, Mister Merritt." For good measure, Carleton threw in: "And there'll be no need to hail us on our way out. We'll be in a rush."

"No doubt," Merritt growled. "A good night to you, Mister Shaw."

❋ ❋ ❋

THE TIGHTLY PACKED BOAT ground against *Erebus's* hull, rising and falling with the steepening swells that raced, wind-driven, across Wallabout Bay. Only with difficulty did the oarsmen manage to keep their light craft from either being borne away from the larger hulk's side or crushed against it.

Vander Groot clasped Prince's arm. In spite of eyes bleary and heavy-lidded from lack of sleep and the punishing ride from Squan Beach, the sergeant returned the doctor's look with a reassuring grin.

"Don't worry none 'bout me, major. I's rarin' to go. Ain't nobody leavin' me behind on this mission."

"We're going to need all the strength you've left, sergeant," Vander Groot assured him dryly.

When they left the docks, he had noted that with the storm's approach, the British men of war usually posted in the East River had removed to deeper waters at the mouth of the Hudson and now lay out of sight of the prison ships. A welcome miracle he reflected uneasily, considering that it was by now almost an hour past the time Carleton's message had set for them to take control of *Erebus*.

Of the twenty recruits Stebbins had promised, only seventeen had appeared, though all bore knives or clubs as ordered. Prince's late arrival had raised Vander Groot's concern further. Shepherding men and tackle stealthily through the town to the deserted shipyards across from Wallabout Bay had slowed them even more. None of which boded well for the night's endeavor.

Most unsettling of all, Carleton's ships, which Vander Groot had expected to find already in the bay by the time they got there, were still nowhere in sight. And now the threatening storm complicated everything.

He muttered a fervent prayer that it would not break upon them until all the prisoners had been transferred to the ships—but first, that the ships would get through the length of the bay to them. And most of all that Elizabeth's condition had not worsened since yesterday, and that he could quickly get her off the hulk to safety.

He forced the anxious thoughts to the back of his mind. "The men are fully briefed on the ship's layout and know their stations," he said to Prince, fighting to keep his balance against the boat's tossing. "When we board, Captain Hutchinson and his men are going to force their way on deck. Some will create a diversion, while others help Major Moghrab's party over the larboard side.

"You'll lead the second squad, sergeant." He turned to Matheson. "And you'll command the first. Once we get aboard, give the enemy no time to react. It's imperative we catch the *Erebus's* crew by complete surprise and take over the ship without any guns being fired to attract attention."

Both men answered with sober nods and gathered their men around them in the heaving vessel. Vander Groot hailed the *Erebus,* raising his voice over the wind.

"Who's there?" the first lieutenant called from above after several moments.

"Dr. Vander Groot here, with my assistants. General Clinton ordered me to inoculate the new prisoners for the pox so this epidemic won't spread to the sailors and the guard details."

The lieutenant leaned over the railing beside the waist entry port, dimly outlined by the hulk's wavering lantern light. "You can't seriously mean to board this late with a storm blowing in, doctor. We've had no incidents of pox aboard *Erebus* so far, thank God."

"If we don't inoculate the new arrivals, we can't guarantee that'll continue," Vander Groot shouted back. "The infection's already gained a foothold on shore, and someone's bound to carry it here."

"How do you expect to inoculate men in these rough seas?" the lieutenant scoffed. "Come back tomorrow."

Vander Groot waved his hand toward the west, where distant flashes of light sporadically lit up the horizon. "We'll manage it, lieutenant. The storm won't reach us for another hour at least, and I've brought a number of assistants, so it won't take long. We just left the *Frederick,* and as long as we're this close I want to finish before heading back to shore."

He heard a muttered oath from above. "Very well, then. If you're mad enough to be out on the water in dirty weather, you might as well come—though I advise against lingering if you mean to make it back to shore tonight."

*We're not leaving until our ride out of here arrives. And if Jon's ships don't make it through . . .*

As though in echo of Vander Groot's thoughts, Prince asked hoarsely. "The gen'l's ships ought to've been here by now. What'll we do if they don't get through?"

In the faint flicker of lightning, Vander Groot took in the dark forms of the men hunched all around him. Most of the volunteers attached to his party were hardly more than boys, the rest no older than their early twenties. Every face was glazed with anxiety at the daunting prospect of attacking a British ship, even such a sorry hulk as this one. The doctor's churning gut and shortened breath testified to his own fears.

The image of the even greater suffering the choppy waves must be causing Elizabeth and her fellow prisoners hardened his resolution. He included all the boat's occupants in a fierce glance as the ship's ladder descended, rocked violently by the turbulence of wind and waves.

"They may have run into some trouble. I don't doubt that they'll get through, but if worse should come to worst, we'll spirit as many prisoners away as possible if we have to row through Hell Gate and all the way across the Sound to Connecticut to get them to safety."

He strained to grab hold of the ladder and in a low voice commanded, "Courage and speed!"

✺   ✺   ✺

STANDING SHOULDER TO SHOULDER, Isaiah and Atkin maintained a perilous balance against the boat's pitch and yaw, planting their hands against *Erebus's* hull to keep the small vessel from slamming against it. "Don't make no sound," Isaiah ordered in a low growl.

"How you expect to take over a British warship with no more'n the likes o' us, major?" demanded a burly volunteer poised on the thwart behind them.

Isaiah swung his head around to glare at the complainer. "This ain't no warship. It be a hulk. Don't even have masts. Got a skeleton crew, and lucky for us that Hessian grenadier guard rotate off yesterday. We only got to take down a few light infantry and a handful o' sailors. If all us together can't do that, we be worthless."

"You all getting' paid good for this job," Atkin reminded the men. "Ain't got nothin' to complain 'bout."

"You never say what we be paid," one of the younger men pointed out testily.

"What do it matter when you ain't got money comin' in nohow?" Atkin threw back.

"Won't matter if we all die," grumbled a third.

"Keep this boat 'longside now!" As the men wielded their oars to stave off another collision with the larger vessel, Isaiah added, "How 'bout ten dollar and a land grant at the end o' the war?"

Another of the men chuckled uneasily. "Sound like we be joinin' the army."

Isaiah and Atkin exchanged glances. "You ain't joinin' no army," Atkin assured him.

"Naw, they joinin' the Rangers," Isaiah muttered under his breath to Atkin's muffled laugh. "And by the time I get through with 'em, they be good ones."

"Hey, how we gonna get them prisoners away?" the third man broke in. "These little boats ain't big 'nuff to take 'em all off."

"Where you 'spect to take 'em anyways, major?" demanded the burly one. "And what 'bout us? The British sure be all riled up when they find out what we done."

"We got ships comin' with room 'nuff for them and us too." In the faint lightning that briefly flickered across the bay and shore, Isaiah read astonishment and disbelief on the upturned faces of the recruits.

"You better pray they get here," Atkin said under his breath before grabbing his oar and returning to his seat. "We be in a world o' trouble if they don't show up."

"No way a Continental ship goin' t' make it into this harbor through the whole dang British Navy," the burly recruit objected.

"Ain't gonna be no Continental ship," Isaiah returned. "An' this ain't the whole British Navy."

The scoffing men abruptly silenced. All of them felt more than saw a huge form loom over them, blacker than the seething night. The boat bobbed violently on the ship's wake as a massive volume of water displaced all around them with its passage.

A deafening crack of lightning close at hand illumined the night, shivering air and water and causing Isaiah to start powerfully. He gained a fleeting impression of a great warship's gracefully curved hull, the British jack snapping in the wind, and three long gun decks stretching the length of her sides below soaring masts that towered high into the stormy sky.

The flash of light immediately extinguished, but as his eyes again became accustomed to the dark, he made out two smaller, but still enormous, ships following close behind the first. They broke from her course to come swiftly around, close on either side of the *Erebus,* while the larger vessel hove to off the hulk's larboard bow at a safe distance to prevent the gale from driving her afoul of the other ships.

*Sweet Jesus, let 'em be the gen'l's ships and not British!* Isaiah breathed fervently.

"We been discovered!" one of the men exclaimed, panic lacing his voice. "They gonna blow us to kingdom come!"

Isaiah caught the measured blinking of a shaded lantern at the largest warship's bow, and exultation rose in his breast. "Those ain't no British ships!" he told the men as a furious clamor broke out on *Erebus's* opposite side. "Time's wastin'! Let's move!"

He grasped the coiled rope at his feet and swung it high. The grapnel at its end spiraled upward to fall over the hulk's weather rail, indistinct in the gloom.

A muffled thunk and the scrape of iron biting into wood summoned a number of dark forms to the entry port above them. Just then a brilliant webwork of lightning sizzled overhead, revealing the jubilant black faces that peered down, interspersed by the haggard, bearded visages of prisoners. Grasping hands hauled on Isaiah's rope and those immediately thrown up by his companions.

In moments the boat's occupants had abandoned the small craft and flooded onto the hulk's deck. Wasting no time, they raced to join the furious struggle Vander Groot's detail was waging to wrest control of the vessel from her crew and guards.

*Chapter Seventeen*

A BLINDING FLASH SPLIT THE DARKNESS that cloaked them, illuminatiing the entire harbor and revealing everything. Praying that no enemy had taken note, Carleton was the first to reach the entry port at the ship's waist, with Teissèdre close behind, while the cutter was being lowered from its tethers along the vessel's larboard side.

Euphoria had filled him at their success in gaining entry to the harbor in spite of the warning Clinton had put out. It was quickly succeeded by frustration. By the time they cautiously worked their way between the batteries at the Narrows against the out-flowing tide and passed into the upper bay, the heavy layer of clouds rising from west-southwest had entirely obscured the sky. The wind had stiffened, and with only a jib and partially reefed foresail and spanker hoisted, the ships slowed even more.

Considerable time had been consumed in navigating through the upper bay, taking care to steer well clear of the faint pinpricks of lantern light that marked the long rows of warships riding at anchor along the Staten Island, Long Island, and Jersey shores. When his privateers at length wore into the East River and, shortly thereafter, hove to by *Erebus* at the outer edge of Wallabout Bay, Carleton again anxiously consulted his pocket watch, relieved to see that only a quarter of an hour remained until the tide's turning.

Eaden materialized at his side. "Since the marines from *Liberty* and *Invictus* will board, I'm only sending a small crew across on the cutter."

"Our marines would only overcrowd *Erebus's* deck," Carleton agreed. "If we're discovered, we'll need them here."

He had discarded the troublesome cocked hat and replaced the constricting British uniform with buckskins, covered by one of the generously cut oilskins Eaden had supplied him and Teissèdre. The loose skins offered not only warmth and protection from rain and sea spray, but also greater ease of movement, for which Carleton was most grateful. Impatiently he waited for the bosun to drop the ladder, nerves stretched taut as a bowstring.

It was well past the time he had set for Vander Groot and Isaiah to begin the assault on the *Erebus,* but he could make out no unusual movement on the hulk's deck. Every possibility that might cause their mission to go awry crowded his mind. For the first time in memory, the high tension that preceded violent action, causing his heartbeat to slow and breathing to steady, had the opposite effect now.

"Where are they?" he growled. "They should have control of *Erebus* by now. If Prince didn't make it back in time, or they were overcome—" He broke off as another flash of lightning lit up the bay, followed closely by a boom of thunder that shivered the air and jarred through the planking under his feet.

Jutting his chin toward the hulk, Teissèdre said, "Look—they're boarding!"

Long yards away, illumined by brief flashes of lightning and the bobbing pinpricks of lanterns, dark figures poured over the hulk's near side. Instantly Carleton moved toward the brink of the entry port, only to have Eaden catch him by the arm and pull him out of the way of the men who crowded together, waiting their turn to descend to the cutter.

"No, general. You're of too great value to risk losing you—"

Teeth gritted, Carleton jerked out of the captain's grip. "Get out of my way."

Teissèdre stepped between them. "Listen to reason, Jonathan. If by some accident you're lost, our mission will be inalterably compromised."

"I'm going to get Miss Howard."

He stepped again toward the port, but as Briggs disappeared over the side, Stowe took Carleton by both arms and maneuvered him back. "Ye'll only be in the way, gen'l," he soothed, nodding toward the *Erebus,* from which sounds of a fierce altercation now rose. "The majors'll 'ave things in 'and shortly. We'll bring Miss 'Oward to ye straight away. Rest easy now."

"I've no intention of waiting on the sidelines—" Carleton began, voice rising.

Pete appeared at his elbow. "Pa'll get her off safely. Let us take care of it, sir. You're needed here."

They were over the side, while Teissèdre's arm lay firmly around Carleton's shoulders and Eaden stood in the entry port, blocking his way. As the captain shouted for the cutter to cast off, Carleton tore free and shoved Eaden to one side.

Against the black sea Carleton made out the pale, square patch of the vessel's sail bobbing across the heaving water toward *Erebus.* He swung around, cursing furiously.

"Securing Miss Howard is the easiest part of our task, Jonathan," Teissèdre said forcefully. "If she's to be gotten out of this harbor, we need you here to direct the action as difficulties arise. Were you to fall, your lady's sure to be lost, and everyone else as well."

Carleton sucked in a deep breath, fighting to contain rage and terror. He bit his lip hard and glanced toward *Erebus* as a brilliant strike over the distant city silhouetted sky, bay, and surrounding shore in a flat blue light.

*Liberty* and *Invictus* already lay lashed to the hulk on each side by grapnels and ropes. Their marines poured onto *Erebus's* deck, where the majors' squads had pushed the hulk's crew and guards to her bow. Planks were swiftly being laid between the three vessels' entry ports for prisoners to be carried across to the privateers, while on the water below, *Destiny's* cutter veered toward the hulk's stern and vanished from sight around *Liberty's* bow.

All three men started powerfully as a musket report reverberated across the water. Close upon it echoed a deafening peal of thunder.

In the blackness that followed, Carleton glanced around toward the scattered ships that lay between them and the Long Island shore. He caught the flare of a lantern a second before a torrent of rain descended to obscure it.

THE SUDDEN SHARP REPORT of gunfire from somewhere above wrenched Elizabeth from feverish dreams of battle, borne on what sounded like the rolling mutter of cannon fire. The confused noise of pounding feet, shouted curses, and blows reverberated through the planks overhead. Her heartbeat, already racing, increased in tempo.

She raised unsteadily on one elbow, her limbs stiff with cold, her other hand pressed to her throbbing head. The ship heaved in short, choppy movements different from its usual free pitch and yaw, giving the impression that it was somehow tethered.

Nauseated, she squinted at the blurred flashes that glanced intermittently down the companionway. They flared suddenly into swinging shafts of lantern light, revealing a large body of marines who hastened down the stairs on gusts of wind and rain. As they called unintelligible orders to the rousing prisoners, she pulled back into the shadows, whimpering.

In seconds mingled questions, cries, and pleas filled the hold, and the invaders began roughly to lift and carry the prisoners up the stairs. Elizabeth tried to cry out for them to leave the men alone, but terror choked her raw throat.

Two men descended the steps behind the marines and began to push through their rapidly moving ranks, one holding up a torch as though looking for someone. "Gently now! Gently!" the taller urged each one, his voice vaguely familiar. "Make sure all the sick, are removed, Josiah. I want this deck cleared within the quarter hour and none left behind except the dead."

"Miss Howard's worse—delirious," Josiah's gruff voice answered. "Didn't want to move her afore ye got here."

Confusion tangled Elizabeth's thoughts. "Josiah?" she whispered, her voice a hoarse croak. "What's happening?"

"I'll bring her." The man began to move in her direction. "Get these men and yourselves onto the ships as quickly as possible. We've not a moment to spare. That gunshot may attract attention."

Vander Groot shook off the rain that streamed from hat and coat, while Stowe held the guttering torch aloft. Kneeling beside Elizabeth, the doctor noted unhappily that her eyes were unnaturally bright, her face deeply rosy with fever.

"Pieter?" She moistened her cracked lips, confusion dulling her gaze. "What are you doing here? Did they capture you too?" Clutching his coat, she began to sob convulsively.

His heart sank and tears blurred his own eyes. "Beth, we've captured the ship as I told you we would. See, here's Stowe. We've come to take you home."

"Easy, Miss," Stowe murmured, bending to awkwardly pat her shoulder. "We'll 'ave ye out o' here right quick."

Recognition flickered in her eyes but as quickly extinguished. She shook her head and weakly reached out to the prisoners who were being led away.

"I'll not leave them. They're all I've left."

"Shhh. Don't worry, dearest. They're all being taken off—Josiah, Tom, Billy too. We're freeing the entire ship and taking you back to Boston. You'll be with your parents soon, and Abby."

"I spoke to 'em and yer aunt a few days ago," Stowe broke in. "They're more'n anxious t' have ye 'ome wi' 'em."

When Vander Groot gathered her in his arms, wrapped in her dirty blanket, and pushed to his feet, she cried out and fought against his hold. "Who are you? What you doing? I'll tell Clinton and Howe nothing! Let go of me—"

"I'm taking you to Jon," Vander Groot assured her, heart breaking.

She stared at him as though he were a stranger. "Jonathan? But . . ." Her voice dropped and despair etched her face. "Howe hanged him. He's dead."

"Nay, Miss, the gen'l's alive an' waitin' fer ye aboard *Destiny*."

"He brought his ships to free you."

"I've lost him," she mourned, her eyes growing vacant. "Save my friends, please. They've suffered so. But there's nothing left for me."

Vander Groot laid his cheek against the clotted hair at the crown of her fevered head, ignoring Stowe's keen gaze. "You're safe now. Both of you."

The tension left Elizabeth's body, and her eyes drifted shut as though agitation had worn her out. Seeing that she had sunk into unconsciousness, Vander Groot bent to tenderly brush his lips across hers.

"I love you so, Beth," he whispered. "I'll love you always. Your happiness is my greatest joy."

"I DON'T SEE WHAT CHOICE we have now but to take her aboard *Invictus*," Vander Groot shouted above the storm's din. He braced against the beat of rain and wind that swept the streaming deck in waves. "With the ships blocking both entry ports, we'll have the devil of a time lowering her into the cutter."

"Bind 'em and confine 'em below in the wardroom!" Isaiah shouted hoarsely to the passing marines, who urged the remainder of *Erebus's* crew and guards along at gunpoint.

A short distance away the hulk's captain lay where one of the marines had felled him as he charged, waving a pistol. The last of the prisoners were being carried or led through the entry ports onto the two 74s, a treacherous task as the ships tossed in wind and surging waves, alternately grinding together and bucking apart to the length of the tethering ropes' give.

Isaiah steadied the doctor with one arm and bent over Elizabeth. Seeing she was insensible, he met Vander Groot's gaze with a worried one.

Gusts of freezing rain sluiced off both men's hats and shoulders and drenched Elizabeth through the thin blanket. "We can't keep her out in this storm!" Vander Groot shouted over the gale. "Sick as she is, she'll die of exposure if we don't get her into shelter quickly."

Pete intercepted them. "Sir, the sickest prisoners are aboard *Invictus,* and she's preparing to cast off now. The last of those who can walk are being taken onto *Liberty.* I've ordered all our men aboard as well. She'll cast off as soon as everyone's secured."

"I think ye be right, major," Isaiah agreed. "It be too dangerous to try gettin' her down to the cutter in this weather even from the entry ports."

While he was still speaking, *Invictus* slipped free of the hulk. Vander Groot cursed and swung toward *Liberty.*

"I'm going to take her aboard now!" he called as he hurried toward the remaining ship. "We can transfer her to *Destiny* once we're well away. The general's going to be beside himself, but I won't risk losing her."

"Ship off the starboard bow!"

At Stowe's shout they all swung around in alarm. To their right a frigate materialized through the rain, advancing cautiously toward *Invictus,* her flaring bow lanterns lighting the British Union that fluttered from her jackstaff.

EADEN WAS THE FIRST TO SEE the signal flags that snapped upward along the lines secured to *Liberty's* mizzen mast. He leaned on the weather rail, squinting to make them out by the repeated bolts of lightning that illumined the night, then turned sharply to Carleton and Teissèdre.

"Enemy off *Erebus* to starboard."

All three men turned their attention to the shadowy spars just visible against the darkness on the hulk's far side.

Teissèdre's mouth hardened to a thin line. "It appears we're going to have a fight after all."

"I'd hoped the thunder covered that gunshot. What's taking them so long to bring Miss Howard away?"

Teissèdre grasped Carleton's arm. "*Invictus* has hoisted sails and cast off." He nodded toward the ship now moving into position to oppose the advancing enemy.

"All hands to their stations!" Eaden commanded briskly. "Clear for action and run out the guns."

Seamen and marines raced across the deck and up the ratlines all around them, while the crews serviced their guns with furious speed. Below his feet Carleton could feel the multiple vibrations of *Destiny's* gunport covers snapping open.

Cursing his enforced inaction, he watched helplessly while *Liberty* cut off from the hulk's larboard side. Commands rang across her deck and gunports sprang open as her courses unfurled to capture the wind.

He could scarce breathe, could not tear himself from the railing while the two warships glided through the water in a deadly, synchronized dance. Gathering speed swiftly, *Liberty* moved to sweep around *Erebus's* bow, exposing the cutter bobbing on her wake below, and the small cluster of men who huddled on the hulk's quarterdeck above.

And, cradled in the arms of the figure he identified as Vander Groot, a limp, motionless bundle.

# Chapter Eighteen

"NO—WAIT!" Vander Groot cried. He stared in dismay after the departing *Liberty*, then swung around to see *Invictus* cutting across the smaller, 50- gun frigate's bow as she brought her guns to bear.

"Avast! Identify yourselves and your business here!"

Multiple shafts of lightning sizzled across the sky, drowning the angry shout from the frigate in a deafening roll of thunder that caused everyone aboard *Erebus* to crouch involuntarily. *Invictus* answered close on, the roar of her broadside swallowed by the heavens as she raked the frigate from bow to stern. Fiery balls plowed lengthwise through the enemy's hull, while chain and grapeshot ripped through her rigging, sheets, and yards; splintered her foremast; and exploded wreckage across her upper deck.

Furious, incredulous shouts and screams rose from the frigate, immediately carried away by the howling wind. Within seconds her remaining bow guns responded in sporadic rhythm.

"Dear God, no! The sickest prisoners are aboard her!" Vander Groot groaned. To his relief, the shots did no damage to *Invictus* that he could make out beyond shredding a couple of sails and tearing through some rigging.

"She be firin' too high," Stowe growled.

*Liberty* had rounded the hulk and now came broadside to the frigate. Before the doctor could draw breath, she unleashed a flaming barrage full into the enemy's hull and across her deck. The frigate's mainmast swayed, cracked, then collapsed off her larboard side, crushing a length of bulwark and bearing it away.

Instantly the vessel listed heavily. In the flickering lightning Vander Groot could make out crumpled bodies all across her ravaged deck, while her surviving crew scrambled franticly to get clear of the tangle of fallen rigging, spars, and sails.

The clash of thunder and cannon startled Elizabeth awake, gasping. Soaked hair plastered to her cheeks, she clutched Vander Groot convulsively as repeated tongues of fire rained from the heavens, echoed by the deluge's tattoo and thunderclaps that jolted the deck beneath Vander Groot's feet like hammer blows. He sheltered her against his chest, trying to comfort her while glancing anxiously toward Stowe.

The older man hung over the bulwark, shouting orders laced with extravagant invective to the cutter's crew below. Straightening, he grabbed Briggs by the arm and motioned him toward the entry port.

Briggs raced to it, sliding across the slippery deck. He managed to maintain his balance and disappeared over the side just as the frigate's bow guns loosed dying shots. They screamed across *Invictus's* deck and tore away a section of the mizzenmast's rigging and sails before plowing full into *Erebus's* bow. All of them ducked as knife-sharp splinters of wood erupted into the air.

"Let's go!" Isaiah shouted over the reverberation of *Liberty's* second broadside.

He shepherded the small party to the hulk's entry port in urgent haste, everyone blinded by horizontal sheets of rain. He and Pete steadied Vander Groot on each side to keep him and his burden from tumbling onto the rain-slicked planks, while Elizabeth huddled against the doctor, her arms around his neck, her face pressed to his shoulder.

When they reached the entry port they met Briggs scrambling up from below, dragging an unwieldy bundle after him. By a miracle he avoided being cast into the sea by the wildly flailing ladder. Stowe and

Pete wrenched him over the top, and he collapsed across the planks, looking half drowned, breath coming in loud rasps.

Stowe knelt, knife in hand, to slit the bundle open. "Cutter's spare sail," he explained at a shout above the storm's din. He threw open the square of canvas and slit a large strip from it. " 'Ere, wrap 'er in this!"

As Vander Groot gently unclasped Elizabeth's arms from his neck, she cried out, distraught. Isaiah took her and quickly laid her onto the strip of canvas.

While the others knelt around her in an effort to provide a shield against the storm's onslaught, Stowe expertly swathed her in the heavy cloth, fashioned a flap to cover her head, and secured the length of sail around her by long strips cut from the remainder, leaving her arms and legs free.

"How are we going to lower her to the cutter?"

Vander Groot's companions exchanged glances, each face reflecting the same helplessness. Stowe alone appeared unperplexed.

"Cargo net," he snapped, waving Briggs and Pete toward the windlass used to haul supplies on board. "Ye should find the tackle stowed inside that 'atch by the winch. Move!"

The two men were forced to crawl across to the winch against the raging gale and the deck's violent pitch. Vander Groot threw an anxious glance to starboard. In the flare of lightning he could make out *Invictus's* sailors swarming across her deck and up the ratlines to make hasty repairs while *Liberty* lay protectively by.

Beyond them he saw no mast or sail to mark the location where the enemy frigate had been.

"Ship to starboard!" A midshipman's voice reached them from the foretop.

For the past half hour, Carleton had watched in an agony of fear and frustration as the assault on *Erebus,* followed by the battle with the frigate, unfolded long yards distant while he stood idle, able neither to reach Elizabeth nor join the fight. Now he swung round, breath constricted, to stare into the darkness off *Destiny's* right side.

Teissèdre and Eaden raced to join him from opposite ends of the ship. A tense interval passed before the unsteady light of a bow lantern emerged from curtains of rain and fog, inching toward them as the enemy ship gradually began to assume solid shape.

A sudden, brilliant flash of lightning revealed her fully, and Carleton's heart dropped even further. Substantially larger than the frigate, though smaller than *Destiny,* she appeared to be a second-rate ship of the line and, he estimated with a quick glance along the three gun decks that furnished her hull, carried ninety guns.

"I'll signal *Liberty* and *Invictus*—" Eaden began.

"Ahoy the ship," called a commanding voice. "What's afoot here?"

"Hold!" Carleton cautioned Eaden in an undertone. Certain the warship's appearance was more evidence of Clinton's measures to secure the harbor against a rescue attempt, he shouted, "The prisoners aboard *Erebus* attacked their guards. They've been put down, and we've set everything's back to rights."

"Any help needed?"

A glance toward the *Erebus* revealed by flickering lightning something like a bundle of cargo being lowered over her side to the cutter, while several figures cautiously descended the ship's ladder. It appeared that the middle figure held tight to the cargo net with one hand to keep it from swinging wildly with the hulk's tossing, and with a closer look Carleton made out another figure who rode in the net, holding in his arms the bundle that could only be Elizabeth.

"Don't trouble yourselves," Carleton responded, maintaining a confident tone even though he felt entirely breathless. "Everything's back in order. We're preparing to return to our berth in the river before this infernal storm grounds us on the lee shore."

"I could swear I heard cannon fire." Suspicion tinged the officer's tone. "Identify yourself."

"Captain Shaw of *Albion*." With a glance at his companions, Carleton gave a hoarse laugh. "The thunder's certainly loud enough to give the impression of battle. I was beginning to think so myself." A loud clap punctuated his words as though in affirmation.

The warship drifted nearer. "I've never heard of you or your ship. What's that cutter doing over there?"

"Bringing my crew back." Carleton directed a fearful glance at the small vessel, which had at last cast off from the hulk with everyone aboard.

"We're wasting time! Give me the order to fire!" Eaden pled under his breath.

"I say, why've you run out your guns if it was only an attempt at escape? What are you about? Surely you didn't mean to fire on an unarmed hulk."

The warship had ceased her forward motion. Wallowing in the bay's choppy waters while fighting a wind that had turned fluky and the tug of the incoming tide, she began to revolve sluggishly, coming oblique to *Destiny*.

"She's riding so low," Carleton muttered, "that she won't be able to make use of the guns on her main deck."

"We can bring all three of our decks to bear. Let us fire the instant she comes all the way about!" Eaden importuned.

Still yards off *Destiny's* larboard bow the cutter, impossibly small, achingly vulnerable, rocked dangerously on the stormy sea, cresting the incoming waves as she beat toward them. Carleton stared at the fragile craft, fingers clenched over the railing, heart pounding wildly, soul screaming, *Lord God, hold them back!*

For an instant of disbelief, it seemed to him the cutter hung suspended atop a wave, then slanted sideways as the turbulent waves sucked her back toward *Erebus*.

From the warship rang the command, "Answer, you scoundrel, or by God I'll give the order to fire!"

Carleton turned back as lightning illuminated sailors swarming around the lighter guns on the enemy warship's upper deck. To his relief, the ports of the main gun deck below remained closed on the ship's heaviest cannon.

"Fire!" he groaned.

Eaden ran off, shouting the command, and a broadside from all three of *Destiny's* gun decks followed within seconds. Carleton staggered as the ship gave a powerful lurch, saved himself from falling by clenching both hands over the railing. Blinding, choking billows of gunsmoke enveloped him, pierced almost instantly by the roar of their opponent's fire and a flaming hail of shot that arced through the space between the two vessels.

Instinctively he crouched against the bulwark, hands over his ears to muffle the fierce drumming of cannonballs against *Destiny's* hull, the shouts of sailors, the crack and splinter of wood on every side. The acrid stench of gunpowder burned his throat and lungs with every jagged breath.

The ship righted and settled with gratifying rapidity. He straightened cautiously, squinting through the battle smoke already shredding in the shrieking wind.

It was immediately evident that except for minor damage to her upper deck, a number of riddled sails, and patches of rigging torn away, *Destiny* remained relatively unscathed. Her thick, seasoned, oaken double hull, hard as iron, had repelled most of the enemy's solid shot, with only a few cracked planks visible from where he hung anxiously over the rail.

The scene opposite stood in stark contrast. *Destiny* had wreaked staggering carnage across their opponent's upper deck with chain shot and canister and in several places had blown gaping holes in her hull at the waterline with solid ball. Agonized screams and furious profanities reached Carleton, along with the frantic order to reload and prepare to fire—a task that would be greatly complicated by the wreckage *Destiny* had inflicted, but would surely be completed with all possible speed.

This time, the enemy's main deck gunports flung wide in spite of the surging waves that threatened to spill inside. An alarmed glance at *Erebus* revealed the masts and sails of *Liberty* and *Invictus* sweeping around opposite ends of the hulk, bringing into reality Carleton's worst imaginings.

He sought the cutter in desperation, dread clenching his chest. The small vessel was nowhere in sight. Noting that Teissèdre crouched at the larboard waist entry, Carleton raced to him and saw that he had cast out the ladder and that the cutter bobbed far below.

"Hasten! There's no time to waste!" the Frenchman urged her crew.

Briggs sprang to the ladder and scurried upward, Pete crowding his heels. Isaiah followed closely with Elizabeth bound to his muscular back by broad strips of canvas, Stowe right behind them. On the cutter's heaving deck, Vander Groot and a couple of the crew hung onto the ladder's end to steady it against the shifting wind, while watching the climbers in breathless suspense.

Together Carleton and Teissèdre jerked Briggs, then Pete over the top. As they sprawled onto the deck, Carleton immediately turned to look down.

Isaiah labored to climb the last yards, sweat and rain sluicing down his furrowed face, Elizabeth's arms clutched around his neck as she gazed up at Carleton, confusion and fear in her eyes.

"Jonathan?" The word came out in a hoarse, disbelieving whisper. "You . . . you're alive!"

Knifing wind and rain had shocked her to full consciousness from what had seemed like a dream. Her heart leaped, and when his gaze met hers, tears overflowed. She reached out to him, fearful that he was but a fever-borne image, that she had again fallen into delusion.

"I'm here, dearest one!" he cried from high above her, his voice shaking. "Hold fast! A moment more and you'll be safe!"

*Jonathan! Oh dear God . . . dear God . . .*

She clutched Isaiah with the last of her waning strength, her gaze fastened on Carleton's face, feeling that he drew her upward by his love. Waves of joy and gratitude flooded over her, blotting out even the cruel lash of the storm.

Eaden rushed to Carleton's side. "They're preparing to fire again!"

*"Do—not—fire!"* Carleton shouted at him. He tore off his gloves and leaned as far over the side as he dared, Briggs and Pete hanging onto him from behind, and reached for Elizabeth.

"Take my hand, dear heart!"

She reached for him across Isaiah's bulging shoulder. Their rain-slicked fingers grazed.

Carleton sucked in his breath as Isaiah's hand slipped from the ladder. Straining every muscle, the major regained purchase.

Carleton was distantly aware of the furious activity that engulfed the ship all around him, of Eaden and the other officers barking orders, of crewmen scurrying to ready guns, strain at ropes, or scramble into the tops. He knew only that Isaiah fought another foothold higher, that Elizabeth twisted to look back down at the cutter, that far below Vander Groot still clung to the end of the ladder, staring up at them, a pale shadow partially obscured by the sweep of the rain.

"Go on, Beth! Hurry!" Vander Groot called. "Jon, get her!"

Carleton threw an agonized glance toward *Liberty* and *Invictus,* who now angled toward the enemy warship, felt Eaden grasp his shoulder in a painful grip.

"We can't delay any longer!"

"Pieter, come!" Elizabeth cried, reaching out to Vander Groot.

"I'm right behind you—haste!" The doctor's shouted reply reached them only faintly, whipped away by the storm's assault.

"Beth, take my hand!"

She wrenched around to look up at Carleton, then to his relief clawed for him. This time their fingers met and he clasped her small hand in his.

"We have to fire, sir! Now!" Eaden's tone was frantic.

"A moment more!" One hand clutching Elizabeth's, his other grasping Isaiah's arm below the shoulder to steady him, with Teissèdre hauling on the major's other arm, Carleton fought the ship's pitch and yaw to draw Isaiah and his burden the last impossible distance upward.

Through the savage wind that boomed through the rigging, flailing them with pouring rain, stinging sleet, and gusts of hail, he felt more than heard the rolling, echoing thunder of the British warship's broadside. Beneath him a deep, grinding tremor shook *Destiny*. The others crouched over him as shrieking noise and debris enveloped them all.

Rending blows splintered the deck's oaken planks to Carleton's left and right, stinging his back with razor-sharp fragments through the heavy oilskin, while blazing arcs overtopped them. Fiery shot blew out the port lanterns and ripped away rigging and yards before casting up spouting fountains just beyond the violently rocking cutter.

"Pieter!" he shouted as Vander Groot was thrown to the cutter's deck.

At the same instant, Isaiah lost his foothold. He slid backward, desperately clutching the ropes, face contorted in pain as the rough cords tore his palms, while the ladder bucked and swayed and banged against the hull, then away from it. Clinging to his back, Elizabeth screamed in terror as she swung out into space, very nearly wrenched from Carleton's grasp, the strips of canvas that bound her to Isaiah coming loose with the writhing of their bodies. Carleton bit his lip so hard he tasted blood, fought to block out the bolt of fiery pain searing from his fingers to his shoulder and keep his grip on her hand, on Isaiah's arm.

" 'old on! I got 'er!" Stowe shouted reassurance from below them as *Destiny* steadied in the bay's swells.

"*Liberty* and *Invictus* are closing to rake the enemy," Eaden shouted in Carleton's ear. "She's seen them and is preparing to fire!"

The crash of the privateers' almost simultaneous broadsides and the answering report that followed a fraction of a second later from the enemy drowned out Carleton's bitter profanities. With the ships so closely clustered, the wave of sound was a physical force rolling across the waves to envelop them. Again wreckage flung through the air like bludgeons and knives.

Eaden swung around and shouted the command to fire. Below Carleton, Isaiah had no sooner dragged Elizabeth under his arm to shelter her against the coming carnage than Armageddon unleashed.

The night was filled with a horror of destruction as *Destiny's* second broadside answered the warship's third. Solid shot screamed outward from both vessels on gouts of flame and clouds of gunsmoke, the thunderous shocks that followed causing the privateer to buck and plunge.

Gasping, Carleton instinctively pressed his eyes shut and cringed away from the red-hot ball that exploded into the gun to his right, blasting the crew and their shattered cannon with its splintered wooden truck through the bulwark to plummet at full force into the cutter directly below. Deadly missiles of wood and iron flung outward and upward, whirling to every side. His arm gone entirely numb, teeth clenched until his jaw ached, he somehow kept hold of Isaiah and Elizabeth, who twisted around.

"Beth, don't look down!"

*"Pieter!"*

Her anguished scream tore the breath out of Carleton.

Bleeding face contorted, Isaiah wrenched Elizabeth upward, with Stowe shouldering them hard from below. With his last strength, ignoring the tearing pain of arm and shoulder, Carleton hauled her higher until she clasped the jagged bulwark weakly with her free hand. She also bled from cheek and hand and arm, and he struggled to gather her in through the entry port, to keep her from turning to look back.

"No, Jonathan, no! Don't leave him!" she sobbed. "Please—please!"

An incandescent zigzag of lightning illuminated the night, closely followed by a jarring peal of thunder that shook the ship. "Pull!" Pete shouted. "Now!"

It felt as though time unwound with furious speed, at the same time stood still. As Pete and Briggs dragged him back from the entry port by main force, Carleton blocked out consciousness of the gun crews to each side who wielded sponges and rammers like madmen and applied the glimmering ends of slow matches to touchholes. With a final heave, ears ringing from the ships' simultaneous broadsides, back hunched against the mangled rigging, blocks, yards, and sails that showered over and around him, Carleton wrenched Isaiah and Elizabeth through the entry port, Stowe scrambling after them, all tangled together as they spilled across the deck.

"Thank you, God, thank you!" Carleton whispered, his throat raw.

Distantly he heard Eaden exulting, "Well done, men! We've hulled the enemy. She's settling."

With Teissèdre madly wrenching away debris, Stowe drew his knife and quickly slit the heavy sailcloth strips that bound Elizabeth to Isaiah. Carleton laid her, all but senseless, onto the lurching deck, while Pete and his father clutched each other, both gulping in harsh breaths.

Carleton made sure Elizabeth was breathing before levering upright to lean with the others over what remained of the splintered bulwark. Stabbing shafts of lightning revealed the cutter wallowing clumsily in the turbulent waves below, broken in two at the center. In the water on either side where the impact had thrown them, her crew fought to stay afloat amid the limp bodies of the gun crew that bobbed face down.

In the vessel's shattered bow, appearing dazed, Vander Groot struggled vainly to drag himself free of the fallen mast that pinned him to the ruptured deck. Carleton went cold through to see what appeared to be a dark stain advancing across the doctor's shirt with each painful movement.

"I have her, Pieter! She's safe!"

As the wreckage of the small boat settled rapidly deeper into the boiling water, Vander Groot's failing gaze met Carleton's. His lips moved as though he answered, but no sound reached Carleton. Then the doctor's eyes became fixed.

While Carleton watched, feeling as though the heart had been torn out of him, the remains of the cutter lurched violently on the foaming maelstrom. With shocking suddenness it disappeared from his sight, swallowed whole by the churning tide.

# Chapter Nineteen

HOW HE HAD COME TO HIS CABIN he had no recollection. All he knew was that he held her safe in his arms—though not truly safe, not yet. And that both of them had suffered a great wound.

Dr. Lemaire and Marie helped him lower Elizabeth gently onto a sheet spread across the deck's planks, where a basin of water and toweling lay by. Kneeling at her side, Carleton took her in hungrily in the wavering bars of muted light cast by a single lantern swinging from a beam overhead with the ship's movements.

He had steeled himself against this moment, but his worst imagining could not have prepared him to see up close, beneath the filth that smeared her, the emaciation of her body, her sunken cheeks and eyes, the deep flush of fever that suffused her face. A groan wrenched from him, and he cursed to heaven the wretches who had done this to her.

Slipping his arm under Elizabeth's shoulders, Lemaire carefully raised her, while Marie coaxed her to drink from the cup she offered. Elizabeth swallowed convulsively, the fluid dribbling from the corners of her mouth. When they laid her back, Carleton wiped the moisture away with his fingertips and bent to brush his lips across her cracked ones.

Weakly she lifted her hand to touch his cheek, tears trickling down her dirt-smudged cheeks. "You're bleeding."

"It's nothing."

"Dearest . . . how I prayed you'd not come . . . not into such danger . . . " She could hardly mouth the words.

"How could I abandon you, dear heart?" He enclosed her hands in his, fighting back his own tears. Thinking not of how she had stood between him and death when he had been grievously wounded on the road back from Concord, nor of the day she had, at great peril, boldly rescued him from hanging as a traitor, but of all the days that had followed, he whispered, "You saved my life."

"I love you so." For a moment her eyes grew vacant, then again fixed on him, pain darkened. "We've . . . lost Pieter?"

He nodded, overcome, and drew her into his arms, rocking her against his breast, his tears mingling with hers. "If I'd lost you too . . . "

"Come now, Jonathan. These good people must care for your lady. She'll be well as long as we get out of this harbor."

Feeling Teissèdre's hand on his back, he looked up into the Frenchman's kindly face and nodded, unable to speak. The sounds of shouted commands and multiplied footfalls pounding back and forth across the decks on every side, the drumming of rain and beat of wind, the jarring thunder and the ship's sharp rocking impressed themselves on his consciousness.

It was the hardest thing he had ever done to relinquish Elizabeth into Marie's hands. Had her tender solicitation not been so evident that Elizabeth's fears, and his, were calmed, it would have been impossible to let go of her.

Banished from his cabin to allow Marie to strip and bathe Elizabeth, Carleton sprang up the companionway with the Frenchman crowding on his heels, while Lemaire hurried off to his surgery, where the surgeon's mates and women were already at work. On the upper deck, seamen carrying the wounded below pushed by, while others swarmed the decks and masts of all three ships to shouted commands, rushing to hack away wreckage with axes and heave debris overboard, splice shredded rigging, and make other critical repairs.

Carleton wove through the crush to Eaden's side, where the last of the cutter's crew were being hauled on board, while their mates huddled nearby beneath blankets in the driving rain. Carleton was numbly grateful that all of them had been saved. At the same time sorrow filled him at thought of the lost gun crew and other casualties surely suffered.

The one loss most vivid was also the most crushing, save if, in the end, Elizabeth did not survive. It was all he could do not to give way to rage and grief. Forcibly he suppressed the images that seared his mind, knowing that to give them purchase would drive him to the vengeance he had forsworn.

Only one emotion could possess him now: to get his ships out of this enemy harbor and to the open sea no matter what was required to accomplish it.

Eaden turned from the entry port as the last man came aboard. "General, I apologize for going against your orders—"

"You did what was necessary," Carleton said gruffly, knowing there had been no alternative, that he would have done the same under the circumstances. "Never apologize for that."

"We'll make it back out to sea, come what may," Eaden assured him with a keen look. "We've both faced stiffer challenges, I'll wager."

Carleton inclined his head, nerves steadying, emotions gone cold and hard. "If anyone gets in our way, blast them to Hades."

A broad grin spread across Eaden's face, and he said with relish, "It'll be my pleasure, sir."

ANXIETY WOULD NOT ALLOW Carleton to stay apart from Elizabeth for long. As soon as he was assured that repairs were underway, he left Eaden's side to hurry back to his cabin. Below deck, the concentrated reek of gunpowder assaulted his senses. In his cabin these mingled with the bitter odors of cinchona and laudanum and the spirits used for cleansing.

He found Marie bending over Elizabeth, sponging her face and arms with a wet cloth. She had been bathed and clothed in a clean shift, and now lay insensible in the hammock bed, which was securely tethered to prevent its swinging wildly with the ship's movements.

He was shocked to see that her hair had been cut, leaving only a short cap of dark ringlets. There was no question of its having to be done because of her fever and the vermin that had beset her. But for her to be so shorn pained him almost as much as the visible ravages to her slight body.

"How does she?" he asked gruffly.

Marie wrung out the cloth in a basin. Turning her grave gaze on him, she said softly, "We will hope for the best, *mon general.*"

Coming around the bed, she took his hand and pressed into it a small porcelain oval framed in gold filigree. "I found this concealed in her stays and thought perhaps you might want to keep it for her."

Carleton stared down at the almost forgotten miniature portrait Sir Harry had commissioned for Carleton's twentieth birthday. The reminder of the hope and innocence of his younger self stunned him, as did the evidence that it had come into Elizabeth's possession and that she had managed to keep it with her in a time of gravest danger.

*Charles,* he thought, gratitude welling up. *He was at Thornlea before they found me with my people. He must have brought it to her, knowing what it would mean.*

"I'll return it to her when she wakes," he said, his voice ragged. "Call me at once if her condition changes."

DESTINY IN THE LEAD, the privateers crept out of Wallabout Bay, lights quenched, each nursing multiple wounds.

With the immediate danger overcome, Carleton had chafed mightily as time dragged out until the ships could sail. By the time he had left Elizabeth, the force of the gale had begun perceptibly to diminish. In the pouring rain he accompanied Eaden and his officers in the longboat to assess the damage to *Destiny's* hull.

Reassured that she could quickly be made seaworthy, they had boarded *Liberty* and *Invictus* to determine how repairs were progressing and the number of casualties suffered. Their situation had been serious enough, but thankfully not fatal.

Three-quarters of an hour later, *Destiny's* mangled bowsprit was finally repaired and the bobstays replaced, her splintered figurehead strapped down, new foremast shrouds set, and maintop platform reinforced. A replacement for *Invictus's* shattered foretopmast had been swayed onto the cap and secured. On all three ships, torn rigging had been spliced, new yards and sails substituted where needed, damaged masts braced, and all shot holes below the waterline plugged.

Much yet remained to be done. The danger of further discovery, however, allowed no more time to linger. As they slipped down the East River, crews manned the pumps on *Invictus,* which had suffered the greatest destruction, and on all three ships the carpenters and their mates continued to work feverishly to complete other critical repairs.

The privateers passed unnoticed into the Hudson's channel and cleared Governor's Island, tacking against the wind and the estuary's rapidly inflowing current. The wind was growing colder, steadying in the western quarter, where the declining half moon cast occasional spars of silver light through breaks in the clouds. By degrees the weather moderated to squalls of rain laced with stinging sleet, while lightning and thunder rumbled eastward toward the Atlantic, leaving the vast harbor swathed in relative darkness and quiet.

As they slipped cautiously past Oyster Bay back down toward the Narrows, an urgent voice from the maintop suddenly broke the stillness. "Enemy frigate off *Liberty's* larboard stern!"

Heart pounding, Carleton followed Eaden at a run up the companionway onto the poop deck. Carleton jerked out his spyglass and quickly found the shadowy bulk of a frigate bearing toward them from the direction of the Hudson River docks, ghostly in the moonlight that glimmered through the scudding clouds.

The frigate closed rapidly, and her challenge reached them, wind driven. Eaden's response was to call out orders that within seconds also echoed across the two 74s' decks. In concert, on all three ships, topsails bellied out above courses, jibs, and spankers. Through the planks beneath his feet, Carleton felt *Destiny* leap forward like a living thing, the hissing rush along her hull increasing in tempo and volume as she sliced through the water.

The strengthening wind bore the privateers in a phalanx down the constricted passage toward the Narrows that lay yet four miles ahead, the trailing 74s shifting to *Destiny's* port and starboard. Briefly losing ground, the frigate hoisted topgallants and cut the gap. Her warning shot fell short of *Liberty,* but Carleton noted that the warships anchored along the shore to both sides came immediately alive.

Eaden's grim gaze met his. "We can't risk another battle, or the whole fleet'll be on us like a swarm of hornets. We have to make a run for it. I just hope *Invictus's* foretopmast holds."

Carleton directed a speculative glance at the 74. "Looks steady so far. We'll pray it remains so. Take *Destiny* as fast as she'll go."

In moments full racks of canvas blossomed high above to the topgallant yards, stark against the seething black clouds as the wind thrummed through taut rigging. Her escorts instantly followed suit.

Carleton clenched his hands over the taffrail, pulse thrilling to the powerful draw of the sails and the great ship's dramatic increase in speed. *Come,* he thought, fierce anticipation burning through every nerve. In that moment he cared nothing for the carnage required to gain the open sea, only that they reached it still alive and afloat whatever the cost to his ships and to the enemy.

They were flying recklessly fast for the darkness and the roadbed's narrow channel, but Kuthoopen's hand remained steady on the wheel. Beside Carleton, Eaden leaned far back against the bulwark, his gaze fixed on the tops, while the great ship cut a straight white wake through the water with the 74s following hard.

With the Narrows looming a mile ahead, Carleton said coldly, "While we're at it, reduce those batteries to rubble," and was answered by the glitter of the captain's eyes and his thin-lipped smile.

The privateers wore leeward well ahead of the frigate, tracing the bulge of the Long Island shore. In single file they swept into the Narrows, broadsides erupting to pound its defending batteries and the line of warships riding at anchor. The sight of their crews scrambling for cover by the flash of gunfire gave Carleton intense satisfaction. But his spyglass revealed that now three sets of sails shadowed the frigate.

The privateers wore south southeast, cut a tight curve back to the southwest, then south, quartering before the wind as they passed between the East and West mud banks. At last they gained Sandy Hook Bay, steadily spreading the distance between them and their pursuers.

AFTER ANOTHER BRIEF VISIT to his cabin to assure himself that Elizabeth's condition remained stable, Carleton returned to the upper deck. He found Eaden and Teissèdre standing together on the forecastle and immediately saw what held their attention. From the far side of Sandy Hook's curving black expanse, two enemy 74s loomed into their path to block their way to the Bar and, beyond it, to the sea.

Eaden's narrowed gaze told Carleton that he intended the maneuver that also leaped to Carleton's mind, and he nodded fierce assent. In short order, signal flags fluttered from the mizzen mast, and *Destiny's* escorts again spread out to port and starboard.

The gunners aboard the British warships were servicing the bow guns in furious haste when *Destiny* raced between them at breathtakingly close quarters, with *Liberty* and *Invictus* keeping exact pace along the two warships' outer sides. Their guns echoed the deafening roar of *Destiny's* double broadside.

Before their opponents could get off their shots, mortal carnage enveloped their decks. Exultant, Carleton saw through the shifting gunsmoke that most of the enemy's guns had been blasted apart and both ships had been hulled below the waterline by multiple shots. With the sea pouring into their shattered holds and their decks tangled in fallen spars and rigging, they swung helplessly on the surging flood tide, while seamen leaped into the water or struggled to lower the few longboats that had escaped destruction. By the time the privateers fully cleared the wreckage, the two enemy 74s were rapidly settling.

Along with Eaden and Teissèdre, Carleton hurried back to the poop deck and watched in an agony of suspense, while the pursuing vessels swept within gunshot. His spyglass now revealed yet two more warships navigating between the mud banks a distance behind them. *Liberty* and *Invictus* lagged to the rear, their stern chasers resuming a heavy fire, while the enemy responded with their bow guns.

At that moment, with startling suddenness, *Invictus's* foremast cap splintered under the press of sail, causing her hastily replaced foretopmast to collapse. The falling spar dragged crosstrees, foretopgallant yard, sail, shrouds, and rigging with it, breaking the foretop. The tangle crashed into the sails below, sending two seamen plummeting into the bay. Eaden and Teissèdre loosed simultaneous oaths as the foremast swayed, causing the ship to falter and begin to fall back.

Through his spyglass, breath choked, Carleton watched men crawling precariously up the foremast's sagging ratlines in a desperate effort to bring down the wreckage and the remaining sails before they caused the weakened mast to fall. At the same time the frigate closed like a spaniel on a scent, coming around *Liberty's* stern to rake her, while the British 74s behind her spread out to intercept *Invictus* and *Destiny*. Farther back, the trailing warships cleared the mud banks and swept into the bay. ·

Carleton slammed his fist on the taffrail, cursing at the agonizing thought of Elizabeth helpless below in his cabin and the sick prisoners aboard *Invictus.* "We can't allow *Invictus* to be taken—or sunk," he growled to Eaden, avoiding the Frenchman's sickened gaze.

"You and Miss Howard cannot be captured!" Teissèdre protested vehemently. "It is impossible!"

Carleton gritted his teeth. "Slow and let her come around us."

Eaden paled, and Teissèdre threw up his hands.

They descended to the quarterdeck together. Eaden's reluctant commands sent seamen springing up the ratlines to back the sails, while the young powder monkeys dragged ammunition to the cannon and the gun crews prepared to fire with demonic speed. Receding behind them, the deep-throated roar of *Liberty's* guns reverberated through the night as, surrounded, she warded off three attackers with a ferocious response.

A desperate glance toward the bow told Carleton that they were within a pistol shot of the narrow channel over the Bar. Even with sails backed to slow them, the wind drove the privateers forward against the force of the flood tide. But the enemy's canvas, full spread, drove them faster, and they closed in a rush.

After what must surely have been an eternity *Invictus* crawled past. *Destiny* gained the Bar so close on her stern that Carleton feared a collision. The black waters of the Atlantic were opening out in front of them, their closest pursuer's bow guns waging a thundering duel with *Destiny's* stern chasers, when from the foremast top Pete screamed, *"Four ships dead ahead!"*

His warning was punctuated by a fiery shot that raised a tall plume of water less than a yard off *Destiny's* stern. Carleton drew in a sharp breath, calculating that the next barrage would smash through the stern gallery into Eaden's quarters. Behind which lay Carleton's cabin.

He instinctively shifted his stance as *Destiny* heeled to starboard. Following the channel's curve, she gained an achingly slim advantage over her pursuers.

In blind terror, he ran down the steps and pushed his way through the moving tide of seamen in the waist to reach the forecastle. The indistinct but unmistakable black forms of four large ships materialized out of the night, still out of range of their bow guns, but sweeping toward them with breathtaking speed.

*Invictus* slipped clear of the channel, yawing wide in the attempt to maneuver out of *Destiny's* way, while turning her side to the oncoming enemy in what was surely a fatal maneuver for the crippled ship. The British 74s closed on *Destiny* like a swarm of hornets as she swept through into open water, Eaden screaming orders to the gun crews over the din of cannon running out on all three decks.

Dismay washed over Carleton, succeeded by despair. "Lord, have you brought us this far only to abandon us now?" he groaned.

The prayer had hardly left his lips, when Stowe's voice rang from the top of the mainmast: "*Black Swan* and three others with 'er!"

The breath went out of Carleton. As Eaden and Teissèdre raced up onto the forecastle to his side, he focused his spyglass on the approaching ships, then began to laugh exultantly, his companions joining in with equal glee as they pounded one another on the back.

"Hold your fire!" Eaden shouted to the gun crews.

"Stowe!" Carleton called, swiping the rain from his eyes as he looked up to the maintop. "Why do I suspect you're responsible?"

He could hear the smile in Stowe's voice when he answered. "Thought as 'ow we might come in need o' reinforcements, so I left a message fer any o' yer ships as made port t' follow hard after."

Gathered with the others at the bulwark, Carleton watched ninety-gun *Black Swan* bear into the channel to interpose her finely raked form between *Destiny* and the closing enemy. Sweeping past her on the rising tide, two more of his 74s, accompanied by a 50-gun frigate, raced toward *Liberty*, which had beaten back her attackers by main force, only to be beset by two more, just now coming into position to join the fray.

The shock of multiple broadsides split the night. Faced by *Black Swan's* firepower, the enemy ships dropped back and began to form a battle line, a maneuver that allowed *Liberty* to disengage from the action.

She made her way over the Bar, too scarred by the encounter to continue the fight.

Shepherding *Invictus* between them, the privateers surged ahead with as much speed as they could safely muster. Within moments the only evidence of the battle raging behind them was the rapidly diminishing, repeated pulse and faint, reflected flash of gunfire.

Undetected, they vanished into the night-shrouded, misty reaches of the sea.

ELIZABETH HAD BEEN AWARE of someone ministering to her, of gentle hands bathing her, then of sobbing inconsolably as they cut away her matted hair and being tenderly comforted. To be clean and dry and warm, mercifully rid of the tormenting vermin, wrapped in soft linens that cushioned her aching body, and laid upon a rocking hammock bed was incomprehensible luxury.

She was forced to swallow a bitter draught, then later, warm, salty broth. Both hurt her throat, but soon eased its rawness. For an indeterminate time she drifted in hazy dreams.

"It was too much of a strain in her weakened condition." A man's voice, the physician, speaking in French, penetrated the fog that enveloped her. "The rescue has done as much harm as imprisonment in those deplorable conditions."

"Ah, but he couldn't have left her, never to know her fate," murmured a low, feminine voice.

The beautiful young woman who had handled her so gently, Elizabeth thought. Marie. Or was she dreaming?

She felt a cold, wet cloth blotting her fevered brow and cheeks. "Her fever continues to rise, Jean. I fear for her."

Every joint and muscle felt raw and burned with the slightest movement, with every breath. Excruciating pain stabbed Elizabeth's abdomen and pounded in her skull. Nauseated, she writhed and began to retch.

The doctor lifted her head and shoulders and gently wiped away the foul fluid that dribbled from her mouth.

"We'll do all we can, but I can't guarantee she'll live." His voice held genuine concern.

"At least he can be with her if . . . " Marie let the words trail off.

*Am I so ill then,* Elizabeth wondered dully.

She could feel the fire kindling steadily higher in her body, doubtless ignited from its embers by the icy wind-driven rain that had soaked her. Yet worse was the great weight of anguish that pressed upon her heart until she feared it would crush her.

She heard the doctor reply but could not comprehend what he said. Mercifully, cool, damp cloths again soothed her scalding flesh, briefly holding the conflagration at bay.

From time to time the deafening din of cannon fire reached her as though from far away, along with a flurry of footfalls across the deck and shouts and screams. Then Marie held her steady in the rocking bed against the ship's violent pitch until consciousness faded once more.

She roused from welcome insensibility to find a loving presence hovering over her, one she sensed had been there often. She felt his light kiss upon her brow, her lips.

Warm, strong hands whose touch she could never forget enclosed hers. How she longed to cling to them! But her fingers refused to respond to the prompting of her will.

Was he indeed a corporeal being—or merely a spirit returned from the dead to comfort her in her delirium? She was terrified the latter might be true, pleaded that if it were so, she might go where he was.

Yet time and again his dear voice, choked with inexpressible emotion, murmured endearments of such sweetness that they called her back again from the dangerous, fevered tide drawing her ever farther toward a dark and distant shore.

## Chapter Twenty

*Sunday, 9 November*

Andrews stared hard at Spotted Pony. "What's gone wrong?" he demanded hoarsely in Shawnee. "Blue Sky—"

"She and your son are well, Golden Elk," Spotted Pony assured him hastily. "Blue Sky appears often sad, but she now says she is eager to be among our people again. The women also stay close and help to care for He Leads the Way."

Andrews let out his breath, almost laughing as relief battled a new anxiety that Blue Sky would become too reconciled to his absence.

As though reading his thoughts, Spotted Pony said with a broad smile, "She also speaks with longing of the day when her husband will come home to her."

Curbing his emotions, Andrews turned his attention to Spotted Pony's companions. He nodded to the two Delaware scouts, who had joined those accompanying Red Fox's party on its way west. The other four, strangers to him, were Shawnee, judging by their dress and manner.

"If nothing's the matter, why did Red Fox send you back?" he asked, eyes narrowed.

When the warrior's visage hardened, Andrews's gut clenched again. Spotted Pony hesitated and directed a questioning glance toward the troops who passed around them on every side, hurrying through the orderly maze of tents sprawled across the field behind the inn. The biting northeast wind and leaden skies portended a downpour, and the men were busily engaged in transferring equipment and supplies into wagons beneath canvas covers.

"You break camp?"

By now several of the warriors who had remained behind with the brigade had drifted over, and Andrews said in a guarded tone, "White Eagle ordered me to take the brigade to Washington's camp at White Marsh. We move out at daybreak tomorrow."

Spotted Pony's eyebrows rose. He began to speak, then with a sidelong glance toward the men pressing close around them, quickly introduced his four Shawnee companions, all members of the tribe's Chillicothe sept.

An indefinable sense of dread settled into Andrews's chest as Spotted Pony continued, "We met these men on the far side of the Susquehanna at the door to Delaware lands. They were sent by Black Fish to tell us that he and a large party of his warriors have carried out raids in Kain-tuck-ee . . . using weapons supplied by the British."

When Andrews stiffened, Spotted Pony hurried on. "Black Fish's intention was to wipe away all the forts and towns of the Long Knives in our sacred hunting grounds. They succeeded in driving many back over the mountains and carried a large number of scalps to Chillicothe."

The expressions of the Chillicothe Shawnee confirmed his words. Andrews stifled a groan.

With barely suppressed intensity, Spotted Pony continued, "Cornstalk would not join with him because of the treaty he signed with the white chief Dunmore, who prevailed against us three years ago. Although Black Fish's warriors fought valiantly, without Cornstalk's help he was unable to take the two strongest Long Knife forts."

"There are great warriors among these Long Knives," Roaring Waters, the leader of the Chillicothe Shawnee admitted grudgingly. "They did not seem to sleep, and their bullets killed many of our men from hundreds of paces away, one of Black Fish's sons among them. Our clan grieves and cries for vengeance."

"Why have we heard nothing of this?" Andrews demanded.

Spotted Pony shrugged. "No one knew where we were so that Black Fish might send us word. And after his attacks against their settlements, it was too dangerous for messengers to search for us in Long Knife territory. Roaring Waters and the others talked with some of our Delaware brothers after the victory over Burgoyne and were on their way to find us when our party met them."

"Whatever possessed Black Fish to do the bidding of the British? They only use us to distract the Long Knives from fighting against their king, and we are the ones who will suffer for it!" Looking from one to another, Andrews growled, "Have the Long Knives yet come against our towns since these attacks?"

The warriors exchanged uneasy glances. "No, Golden Elk, but surely after our great victories they will not dare to cross the *Pelewathiipi* again and murder our people," Roaring Waters burst out.

"Either you have not heard White Eagle's counsel or your ears have been shut tight against it! If not this winter, then when *Shkipiye kwiitha,* the Sap Moon, returns and the winds begin to warm, the Long Knives will come across the mountains and rivers like starving wolves." Andrews glared at Roaring Waters. "Where are Black Fish and his warriors now?"

"They returned to Chillicothe to hunt so their families will have food for the winter," the warrior returned sullenly.

"Red Fox and the rest of our warriors are eager to reach Chillicothe in order to learn all that happened and what Black Fish plans." The fierce light in Spotted Pony's eyes reflected his own eagerness.

By heroic effort Andrews restrained the impulse to curse. "Thinking to protect my wife and son, I've instead sent them into even greater danger! Red Fox is taking them—along with your wife and children, Spotted Pony, and all the others—straight to the very place the Long Knives are most likely to strike!"

"Only a small party will turn aside to Chillicothe with my brother," Spotted Pony explained. "The rest will ride ahead to Grey Cloud's Town. As soon as I return, I'll urge Grey Cloud to take the women and children to the upper *Miyamithiipi* where they will be safe."

"Will our people find any place safe from the Long Knives?"

Sinking Ground, one of the two Delaware warriors, exclaimed, "We must tell White Eagle at once what has happened, Golden Elk! These men say Black Fish wishes for both of you to come to Chillicothe before the winter snows set in and counsel with him."

"How can White Eagle go to Chillicothe now?" Andrews snapped. "The British offer much gold for him, as Black Fish well knows—and yet he allies with them!"

Horror reflected in the warriors' eyes. "Neither Black Fish nor any of our people would sell White Eagle to the British," Roaring Waters protested.

"Would they not? Some have already tried—or have you forgotten?" Andrews exchanged a heated glance with Spotted Pony, then conceded bitterly, "But it matters not. White Eagle is not here."

"Aieee!" exclaimed Brown Bear, one of the Rangers' Shawnee scouts who had gathered around the newcomers. "I knew he was not keeping to his room all these days to set down words on paper for Washington when we are so close to his camp." His eyes narrowed. "Has he gone to join him?"

Andrews blew out a breath. "He has not. I do not know where he is . . . nor even whether he still lives."

Sharply indrawn breaths met his words. From their expressions, Spotted Pony's lack of surprise was not lost on the rest of the warriors.

He indicated the bustling camp with a wave of his hand. "But you say he commanded you to go to Washington's camp."

"Captain McLeod arrived with Captain Stern a couple of hours ago, bringing his orders. They left him Friday night after his ships arrived at the rendezvous. That much of our plan, at least, succeeded. White Eagle meant to sail for New York Harbor yesterday afternoon. Beyond that, I know nothing more."

Bewildered, the rest of the warriors insisted on an explanation. Andrews gave a terse account of Elizabeth's capture by the British and Carleton's efforts to rescue her.

Roaring Waters threw up his hands in an angry gesture. "If the British fathers have done such a shameful thing to Healer Woman in order to capture White Eagle, how can we ally with them any more than with the Long Knives?"

"Tell that to Black Fish," Andrews responded caustically.

"It is as White Eagle has said," Spotted Pony broke in. "We must join with our brothers and uncles to walk in our own path. None of the white faces will ever be our friends when it is so greatly to their advantage to be our enemies."

## Chapter Twenty-One

*Monday, 10 November*

Squinting against the pale noon-day sunlight, Carleton turned from the middle-aged man who blocked his way like a bantam cock and cast a grim glance back down the length of Long Wharf to where *Destiny,* along with *Liberty* and *Invictus,* was docked. *Black Swan,* the sleek 74s *Hornet* and *Eagle,* and the 50-gun *Columbia* lay at anchor beyond them in the bay.

They had made Boston Harbor an hour earlier. Mindful of the meeting with Elizabeth's parents that must soon follow, he had taken care to replace his ragged hunting shirt and worn buckskins with full uniform, for whatever advantage appearance might give him in the difficult encounter that lay ahead.

By the time he disembarked with Elizabeth swaddled against the biting wind and cradled in his arms, the wounded seamen and freed prisoners were being taken off *Destiny* and her escorts for transport to a nearby warehouse, where Stowe had arranged for a hospital to be set up. That concern, at least, had been taken care of.

Stifling a sigh, Carleton met Dr. Samuel Howard's hostile gaze.

"You've done quite enough harm, sir," the doctor said, his voice trembling. "Now give me my daughter and begone."

Carleton carefully shifted Elizabeth's blanket-swathed form more securely against his chest, his jaw hardening. A confrontation was the last thing he needed after the acute torture of the past day and a half, fearing at every moment to lose her—and his ships and crews as well.

Fighting the stiff northeast wind that succeeded the storm, the small convoy had been forced to slow even further to allow their crews to make what repairs they could at sea. As soon as they had been well away, *Black Swan* and her escorts broke off from the battle and with their greater speed eluded the enemy, cloaked by a renewed deluge. An hour before dawn they had intercepted the crippled ships off Cape Cod and formed a protective wall around them.

Although they struck British colors and hoisted the French flag, Carleton and his captains were intensely conscious of the danger that Clinton might send pursuers after them *en masse* or that a roving British squadron might happen upon them by accident. In that case, the damage to the privateers would be a dead giveaway and a renewed engagement inevitable and disastrous.

With his mind befogged by concern for Elizabeth, Carleton had repeatedly been drawn away to make critical decisions. Prime among them had been that he would not abandon *Invictus,* which had suffered the most grievous destruction during the race back through the harbor, made worse by the existing damage from the battle at Wallabout Bay. Although the other ships could divide *Invictus's* crew between them, attempting to transfer the sickest of their passengers on the stormy sea would take the better part of a day, were it even possible in their fragile state. Thus with crews ceaselessly manning the pumps, the battered 74 had limped into Boston Harbor guarded by her escorts, half a day later than Carleton had hoped.

"We're wasting time," he said now, tight-lipped. "We need to get Beth into shelter at once."

When Elizabeth's father moved to wrest her from Carleton's arms, he stepped out of the older man's grasp.

Startling, she roused and clutched the facing of Carleton's uniform coat. "Jonathan! Don't leave me—"

At the panic in her voice, he bent his head over hers. Even through her heavy wrappings he could feel the heat of the fever that ravaged her.

"Never, dear heart," he soothed. "I'm here. I swear I won't let you go." A bout of coughing wracked her, and he gathered her more tightly in his arms.

Quietly Lemaire said to Mrs. Anne Howard, "We've had no success in relieving her fever, madame. This wind can only do her more harm."

"Please, madame, monsieur," Marie echoed, "let us get her inside."

Carleton directed a glance of desperate appeal at Anne. To his relief, her delicately modeled features softened and she straightened, dabbing away tears.

"Samuel, put your anger aside for our daughter's sake. We can't keep her out in this cold."

As though he did not hear their pleas, the doctor raked his fingers through his curly black hair, searching Elizabeth's shadowed face hungrily before looking up to meet Carleton's smoldering glance. "Are you such a monster, sir, as to deny a father his sick child? You're to blame for this—"

"You've no need to remind me of it. I know it very well. My concern is for her alone."

"Samuel, this does no good! If not for General Carleton, our girl would still languish aboard that foul ship."

"Were it not for him, she'd not have been there!"

"Tess said herself she was the one who persuaded Elizabeth to become a spy," Anne pleaded.

"He's responsible for her continuing until Howe captured her." Visibly shaking, Dr. Howard turned back to Carleton. "Give her to her mother and me and leave us in peace so we can try to undo the damage you've caused. You, sir, are not welcome in our home!"

Elizabeth stirred. "Papa . . . "

He stepped forward to bend over her. "My dear girl—"

"My fault . . . don't . . . please don't . . . send him away . . . " Again her head drooped against Carleton's breast, and she let out a sigh, her eyes drifting shut as though she had not strength to hold them open.

"I won't allow it, Samuel, no more than I'd allow anyone to send you away were I ill," Anne said firmly, placing her hand on Carleton's arm and drawing him toward the chariot that waited nearby. "He'll be the best medicine for her, as you always are for me."

Angrily Dr. Howard brushed away the tears that trickled down his cheeks. His mouth clamped in a thin line, he turned on his heel and led the way.

They detoured around wheelbarrows, carriages, hogsheads, piled boxes of goods, and wagons bearing the rescued men, pushing through the throng that continued to swell as news of the ships' mission and their human cargo spread through the town. Although forced to move with great care for fear of jostling Elizabeth, Carleton was gratified to see that Boston's citizens showed every sign of welcome for men they clearly considered heroes and vied with one another to render assistance.

Dr. Howard held open the chariot's door, and Carleton climbed inside, settling Elizabeth across his lap. Marie took the seat beside him, and Elizabeth's parents arranged themselves opposite, with Lemaire pressing in next to Dr. Howard.

As though only now becoming aware of the two strangers, Dr. Howard included them in a haughty stare. "We've not been introduced. Who are you?"

"I am Dr. Jean Lemaire, and this is Mademoiselle Marie Glasière, who serves as my nurse. We've had the privilege of caring for your daughter these past two days."

"Dr. Lemaire is *Destiny's* surgeon," Carleton explained gruffly, "and a distinguished graduate of the Naval Medical School at Rochefort. Were it not for the care he and Mademoiselle Glasière provided, I fear Beth would have . . . " He stopped, unable to speak the word.

Dr. Howard's demeanor perceptibly softened as he studied Lemaire. "I'm very grateful, sir. And to you as well," he added, nodding to Marie.

Anne leaned forward to run her fingers through the short, dark-auburn curls that were all that remained of Elizabeth's long tresses, her expression reflecting tenderness and fear. "Jonathan, I'm afraid we have to take her to Tess's home in Roxbury. The repairs to Stony Hill haven't been completed, and we've been staying there since our return from London."

When Elizabeth moaned, Dr. Howard reached to capture her hand and clung to it, rubbing it between his own. "We've got to bring this fever down."

As the chariot jolted and swayed, Carleton glanced out the small window beside him. They had turned from State Street onto Cornhill and now threaded their way through even heavier traffic at the intersection with School Street, which after a short distance angled into Beacon. This street ran between the expansive, grassy Common and Beacon Hill.

"What about your town house?" he suggested quickly. "It's close by."

Chewing her lip, Anne lifted her worried gaze from her daughter's face to Carleton. "Unfortunately it was let to new tenants last month."

To keep his fearful thoughts at bay while the the others talked in hushed tones, Carleton forced his attention to the town's narrow, winding lanes and alleys. Shaded by the overhanging second stories of the red brick buildings that crowded to the edge of the cobblestones, the warren of streets always reminded him of the ancient towns of England and the Continent. The cacophony raised by passers-by, the rattle of wagons and clop of hoofs, and the scrape and thump of wheels bumping over the cobbles filled the chariot.

More than two years earlier, he and Andrews had been billeted in the Howards' town house at the far end of Beacon Street, while Carleton served as an aide to British commander General Thomas Gage. And, unknown to anyone except the rebel leader Joseph Warren, Carleton had also acted as the spy Patriot, sent by General Washington to assist Massachusetts' beleaguered Sons of Liberty.

Shortly after arriving in Boston, on the night of April 18, 1775, Carleton had been assigned to accompany a British detachment to Concord to ferret out and destroy the rebels' secret stores of ammunition. On their way the column had passed through Lexington and, in spite of Carleton's efforts to avert disaster, had touched off a firestorm on its Green, a conflagration on which the soldiers had thrown fuel at Concord Bridge.

Consequently the British column had been hounded on the road back to Boston by a swarm of militia that rapidly increased in numbers as the day progressed. At Menotomy, in a moment of blackest irony, Carleton had taken a bullet in the chest from one of the militia soldiers he had come to serve.

The memory of that night when Elizabeth, along with Andrews and their servants, had brought him from the hospital set up for the wounded to the town house along this same street flooded back with vivid intensity: the agony searing through him like a burning poker with every jolt of the carriage; the wretched dizziness and nausea from loss of blood; the unwilling acknowledgement through a haze of pain that in spite of his strongest defenses Elizabeth already owned his heart.

He had come perilously close to death then. But she had persuaded her father not to give up on him, and together they had nursed him back to health.

At least, he told himself, he had brought her back to her parents so they would be with her if the worst happened.

His mind shrank from the thought. He was alive because of her. He could not, would not give her up.

The rest of the drive through Boston's narrow, crooked lanes passed in a blur. The two doctors conferred over Elizabeth's care, heads bent together. Each time she moaned or coughed, Anne or Marie anxiously caressed her brow or hand or tucked her wrappings more closely around her.

Little of it registered. With Elizabeth cradled protectively against his breast, he drank in the delicate lines of her sweet face as he had at every unoccupied moment since he'd first gathered her safe in his arms. Despite her hollow cheeks and the flush of fever, she was yet incomparably lovely to his sight, and so would she always be.

Not caring what the others might think, he bent to kiss her brow. When she stirred and cried out, such pain seized his heart that he could not breathe.

To his intense relief, the carriage finally rattled through the city gates and past the abandoned British fortifications, then ascended narrow, sandy Boston Neck connecting the peninsula to the mainland. The mud flats of the Back Bay crowded close on their right, while the broad harbor opened out to their left, with Dorchester Heights looming ahead.

In a sheltered hollow below the small village of Roxbury, he caught a glimpse of the Howards' home, Stony Hill. The structure was newly rebuilt after being badly damaged in a cannon barrage during the siege of Boston, and then burned to the ground by the British.

There, following Easter services on the day after their first meeting, he and Elizabeth had raced their horses. And in a blow to his pride that now made him smile, she had bested him.

Along the road through Roxbury they passed rebel fortifications thrown up during the siege and fallen into disrepair in the year and a half since the British were driven out of Boston. It seemed an eternity until they turned onto the carriageway leading to the home of Elizabeth's aunt, Tess Howard, on the near bank of Stony Creek opposite old Pierpoint Mill's weathered structure.

The sight of the mansion brought more painful memories crowding thick and fast. Elizabeth had brought him here after plucking him boldly from a British gaol and spiriting him out of Boston less than an hour before he was to be hanged for treason. And later, heart breaking, he had watched from the mansion's tall cupola, with its expansive view of Boston and the surrounding mainland, while Elizabeth and Tess returned to peril in Boston to continue spying on the British—at Washington's behest and over Carleton's adamant opposition. Shortly thereafter, against every instinct, he had obeyed his commander's orders to travel far to the west among the Indian tribes to negotiate their neutrality or support in the war against Britain.

All that had flowed from each decision he and Elizabeth had made, each step they had taken, both good and ill, now pierced him through. He searched her face, hardly able to tell whether she breathed, and at last tears spilled.

"If you leave me, dearest, how can I go on?"

He hardly realized he had whispered the words or that Anne and Marie enfolded them both in their arms, while Lemaire regarded him with sympathy and Dr. Howard sat with arms crossed, stubbornly glaring at him through the moisture that glimmered in his eyes. Carleton did not look up until the carriage jerked to a halt with a jingle of bridles and stamp of hooves, and the door was flung open.

He waited for the others to climb out, then followed blindly, taking pains not to jostle the dear burden he carried. He was immediately engulfed in Tess's arms, with slight, twelve-year-old, blonde-haired Abby pressing against him, crying out tearfully, "Beth—oh Beth!"

Elizabeth let out a shuddering breath, but did not rouse. Her face lined with anguish, Tess turned to Anne.

"As soon as we got your message that the ships arrived, I sent for Joshua. I thought it best for him and Jane to come right away."

Anne stepped into the older woman's arms. "Thank you. Surely it was God's doing that he was granted a furlough to come home just now."

Feeling numb, Carleton swung toward the house. Tess led the way inside, with Abby pressing close at Carleton's side, her small hand clasped over his arm. Sarah and Jemma Moghrab, Isaiah's wife and seventeen-year-old daughter, who served as the Howards' housekeeper and Elizabeth's maid respectively, met them at the door.

Isaiah and Pete were well and would come as soon as their duties allowed, Carleton assured them distractedly. "Had it not been for Isaiah and Pete's help, we'd have lost her," he said, his voice breaking.

Sarah gave him a grateful look. She briefly bent her turbaned head over Elizabeth, her coffee-colored face creased with worry, then hurried to usher them upstairs, where a crackling fire took the chill from a spacious chamber at the head of the stairs. The heavy draperies of the four-poster bed were drawn open, the linens turned back. Gently Carleton laid Elizabeth on the mattress, soothing her when she cried out.

Dr. Howard abruptly pushed his way between them. Carleton began to protest, but Marie insistently guided him to a deep wing chair near the window. He suffered her to expertly divest him of gloves, cloak, and helmet, all his attention fixed on Elizabeth.

"No more cover than this," Lemaire cautioned when Jemma and Abby tucked the sheet around her. "She must be bathed regularly with cool water. We must bring her fever down quickly or I fear it'll not go well with her."

Abby's face crumpled. She bent over Elizabeth, clinging wordlessly to her older sister with tears coursing down her cheeks until her mother gently drew her back.

For several minutes the two doctors consulted in hushed tones. Then Sarah was sent off to prepare a tea of yarrow, black elder, and peppermint, while Jemma took Abby with her to fetch towels and a bucket of cold water.

While Lemaire sorted through the vials in his case, Dr. Howard pulled Carleton aside. "I'll talk to you now, sir." He directed a quick glance at the bed, where Elizabeth lay unresponsive. "Downstairs if you please."

Anne hurried to her husband's side. "Samuel—"

"Please call me if her condition changes," Carleton cut her off, with difficulty controlling the tremor of his voice.

She nodded, distress darkening her eyes. He followed the doctor from the room to the spacious downstairs parlor, where, sparing no time on niceties, Dr. Howard demanded of him explanations and answers.

Pacing the length of the room, head bowed, Carleton gave an abbreviated but unsparing account of why he had agreed to spy for the rebels, how he had discovered Elizabeth's ties to the Sons of Liberty too late, and how she had rescued him from hanging; and that because of him she had been drawn ever deeper into the maze of subterfuge and lies that had ended in her capture.

"Last spring, after returning from the Shawnee, I pleaded with her not to continue, but she felt strongly that this was her calling. Indeed, she was very good at it, and she saved many lives because of her bravery. I thought it right then to respect her decision to continue in the course she felt God would have her to follow."

He added a terse description of the assault upon New York Harbor that had resulted in many casualties—and, worst of all, Vander Groot's death. He offered no excuse or justification for his failure to protect Elizabeth from the consequences of the perilous role she had played.

"I should have done more to persuade her to stop," he concluded painfully. "Beth's not to blame in any of this. She acted always out of unwavering allegiance to the cause of liberty."

Dr. Howard heard him out without interruption. A tense silence ensued, and at last Carleton said in a choked voice, "I don't deserve it, sir, but I ask your forgiveness for all I did that went wrong."

The doctor made no answer. He stared at Carleton for several moments, his expression unreadable. Then he turned on his heel and walked out the door.

Limbs leadened by emotional and physical exhaustion, Carleton sat at Elizabeth's bedside, his despairing gaze fixed on her face. Her breathing was shallow and labored, and she rolled her head restlessly from side to side, her flushed face glossed with moisture.

Several times during that interminable afternoon, he had waited outside the door, while Sarah and Jemma bathed Elizabeth with cool water, supervised by her mother and Marie and attended by a tearful Abby. Each time he returned as soon as they finished their ministrations. He spoke to no one, grateful that Dr. Howard made no move to bar him from the chamber, although he refused to relinquish his post on the opposite side of the bed.

Carleton was vaguely aware that Isaiah and Pete had arrived at mid afternoon; that Stowe had come, bringing Carleton's packs and weapons; that Lemaire had borrowed a horse to ride into Boston to an apothecary for a tincture he thought might break Elizabeth's fever and meant to briefly check on the care of the injured seamen and freed prisoners while there. The welfare of the hospitalized men and concern for repairs to his ships hovered at the periphery of Carleton's fearful thoughts and prayers, distant but nagging.

According to Stowe's report, the damage to *Black Swan* and her escorts was minimal, and they would quickly return to sea. Repairs and repainting *Liberty* to her original colors would take little more than a week, then she, too, would sail.

The destruction done to *Destiny* and *Invictus,* however, required that they be careened for repair. Then after they were again launched, they had yet to be painted, rigged, and supplied. The process would take six weeks or more.

Carleton had sent Stowe back with orders for *Hornet, Eagle,* and *Columbia* to sail for Charleston, South Carolina, as soon as possible to avoid the worsening weather and to intercept his merchantmen returning along the southern sea roads. The privateers were to divide the merchantmen between them, taking them in convoy on their regular routes for protection against Admiral Howe's threatened attacks.

Refusing to intrude on Elizabeth's family during her illness, Teissèdre had insisted on staying in town to supervise the work at the shipyard until *Black Swan* and *Liberty* were seaworthy. His intention was to return to France aboard *Black Swan,* with *Liberty* as escort.

Carleton had bidden him a reluctant farewell before leaving *Destiny* with Elizabeth to find her parents unexpectedly waiting at the wharf. Stowe had alerted them to the approximate date Carleton meant to attempt Elizabeth's rescue, and they had lodged near the docks the previous night anxiously awaiting his ships' arrival—or news that the attempt had failed and Elizabeth had been lost.

The sudden opening and shutting of the front door below, followed by the commotion of voices, roused Carleton from his anxious thoughts. Anne hurried from the room, and within moments rapid footfalls pounded up the steps.

Carleton started to his feet as Tess, pale and grim-faced, ushered Colonel Joshua Stern and his wife, Jane, into the chamber, with Anne following. Abby ran to embrace her uncle and aunt, while Dr. Howard came around the end of the bed and reached to grasp his brother-in-law's extended hand.

Plump, motherly Jane Stern hurried to the bed, arm in arm with Anne. For a brief moment Stern turned on Carleton a piercing gaze in which he read anger.

Weeks had passed since the last time they met, then in much happier circumstances. Today the portly colonel's square, normally genial face reflected his surname, and his unruly mop of iron-grey hair stood on end, whether from the wind or because he had pulled at it as was his habit when seized by emotion.

He returned his attention to Dr. Howard. "How is she? Any improvement?"

Able to bear no more, Carleton bolted into the passage outside. A hand caught his arm from behind.

"Jon—"

He jerked away from Tess's hold and descended the stairs, bypassing the dining room for the chilly, shadowed morning room at the mansion's rear. Halting at the bank of windows at the room's far side, he stared through the panes, oppressed by black desperation.

Beneath scudding grey clouds, dusk wrapped the bleak, frost-blighted gardens. The massive, ancient barn beyond it that sagged at the edge of the bluff blocked the expansive vista of Boston peninsula spreading out below, yet he had no need to see it. Unbidden, the vivid image of the bay with its verdant islands and the hilly, wooded mainland that surrounded it, cleft by rivers and steams and dotted with tidy villages and farms filled his mind.

The town had served as home for him from time to time in the years before he had gone to England. Indeed it had been one of his favorite places. Now he felt an alien here, unwelcome and unwanted.

He had at his disposal every means to flee to the farthest reaches of the earth. He would have done so had it not meant abandoning Elizabeth. The anguish of never knowing whether she lived was all that stayed him.

Outside the door he heard Tess speak to a servant. Footfalls pattered away down the passage. After a moment someone entered quietly—Tess, he assumed.

He did not turn, did not move. For some moments all remained silent, then a chair softly scraped across the floor close behind him, and he heard the rustle of her gown as she sat.

To his gratitude, another interval passed unbroken. Throat painfully tight, he had no idea what to say or how to answer the questions she would undoubtedly ask.

At length someone entered, and soft footfalls moved around the room. He heard the clink of dishes on the table, and after a moment candlelight flared. Soon a fire on the small hearth joined in dispelling the shadows to the room's corners and warming the space. Finally the intruder withdrew, and he heard the sibilance of liquid being poured into a cup.

"Sit with me, Jon," Tess said kindly. "Have some coffee while it's hot."

He took a shaky breath and let it out. He could not stand there forever, he reasoned, and at last he turned, wishing for nothing more than that she would go away. She met his despairing gaze with one of kind appeal and beckoned him to the chair next to her. When he slumped into it, she set a delicate china cup of steaming coffee before him.

For a long moment he stared at the dark fluid, finally took the cup between trembling hands and gulped down a mouthful, welcoming the scalding trail it left.

"Stop berating yourself. It isn't your fault."

"Samuel thinks so. And the others. I see it in their eyes. And I feel it in my heart."

"Beth made her own decisions. They all know that, including Samuel, regardless of what he said to you earlier. They've no reason to blame you. You rescued her, after all."

"I should have dissuaded her from continuing."

Tess harrumphed. "I know my niece better than that. You couldn't have dissuaded her from what she felt compelled to do. And you respected her enough to allow her to make her own decisions." Tess took a sip from her cup and set it down. "You aren't at fault. If anyone is, it's me. And Joshua too. We drew her into the work with Dr. Warren long before you arrived in Boston. We encouraged her to continue with you and Washington." Her voice broke. "She was simply too good at what she did for us to do without her."

He waved her words away with a painful gesture. "It's because of me—because of our love—that Howe had her captured. She was his only sure weapon against me. I taunted him, and he'll never forget that. I made him want me badly enough that he'd do such a monstrous thing to a woman."

Tess leaned forward and laid her hand on his arm. "Jon, you couldn't help whom you'd love or that she'd love you in return. And we all do things we later dearly regret, whether rightly or wrongly. Your taunting

Howe in a moment of passion doesn't justify his and Clinton's acting beyond all reason."

Sitting back, she sighed and turned to the darkened window. "Oft times our emotions convict us of guilt that isn't ours," she said as though to herself. "I long blamed myself needlessly for Daniel's death . . . "

He studied her, wondering who Daniel was. When she returned her gaze to him, her features softened.

"No matter what happens, don't despair. You're not to blame for their actions. You did what no one else could possibly have done to save her. And you succeeded. She's alive, and with God's mercy, she'll be well again because of you."

For some moments he said nothing, his vision blurred. "Thank you," he whispered then. "You've no idea how much your friendship means to me."

Behind them the door creaked softly open, and Stern stepped into the room. When Carleton pushed back his chair and began to rise, Stern motioned him to remain seated and came to take Carleton's hand between his, tears welling into his eyes.

"Thank you for rescuing my niece. We owe you a debt we can never repay."

Shaken, Carleton gripped the older man's hand. "How does she? Has she awakened?"

Stern glanced at Tess and shook his head. "Samuel said he gave her a decoction that might break her fever, but he fears a crisis is near. You'd better go to her. The sound of your voice may keep her . . . " He choked, letting the words trail off.

Chest clenching, Carleton sprang to his feet and crossed to the door, with Tess and Stern following. In the entry they met Lemaire coming in.

The doctor gave Carleton a sharp look. "She's worse?"

Carleton nodded, mute. He took the stairs, two at a time, the others pressing close behind. In the upper passage, he pushed past Sarah and

Jemma, then came to an abrupt halt on the threshold of the candlelit chamber.

Across from him, Anne and Jane stood at the near side of the bed in each other's arms, heads bent together, while Abby lay with her head on Elizabeth's pillow, sobbing. Dr. Howard sat motionless in a chair drawn close to the far side of the bed, his head buried in his hands.

Uncovered, clad only in a thin shift, Elizabeth lay motionless. Beneath her sunken eyes, the skin appeared darkly bruised, and the fever flush that had suffused her face had given way to a deathly pallor.

## Chapter Twenty-two

A NDREWS'S RAMROD-STRAIGHT STANCE wilted under the force of his commander's glare. "Your Excellency, there simply wasn't time for General Carleton to send word begging your advice or approval. General Howe commanded him to appear at his headquarters within two days or he'd execute—"

"I understand, but that is not the point." Forty-five-year-old, auburn-haired General George Washington's piercing blue-grey eyes narrowed, and he emphasized each clipped word. "I do not appreciate one of my generals embarking on such drastic action against the enemy without the courtesy of consulting with me. Especially when it involves sailing blithely into New York Harbor to assault the British Navy with— what? *Three ships?*"

Andrews's gut clenched. The General's immense physical energy seemed to overflow the small chamber. Andrews felt distinctly like a hapless sparrow skewered in an eagle's talons.

He swallowed, wishing mightily that Washington's aide had at least given him time to change out of sodden, muddy buckskins into a uniform before dragging him to the General's headquarters. " I assure you the decision was not made blithely, Your Excellency. Forgive me, but I was under the impression—I mean, sir—Captain McLeod and Monsieur Teissèdre assured General Carleton that—"

Washington drew himself to his full six-foot-three height, his voice as icy as the gust of wind that rattled the bare trees outside. "You expect me to criticize a general officer in front of one of his subordinates? And particularly before his French agent—whom I highly suspect of being a spy for the court of Louis the Sixteenth—all while Congress's commissioners are in Paris, engaged in negotiations to conclude a treaty with his government?"

Andrews briefly pressed his eyes shut. "Of course not. My apologies, Your Excellency."

*A dressing down. Lovely. The perfect finish to a perfect day.*

The chill draft that pervaded the shadowy parlor, enlivened only by the faint glow of the seething embers on the hearth and the single guttering candle on the writing table, caused Andrews to shiver involuntarily. With the conviction that he took his rank, not to mention his life, in his hands, he drew a breath and plunged ahead.

"I believe you'd agree that Miss Howard's efforts have been of considerable value to our cause, and that you're aware of General Carleton's deep attachment to her. Were Mrs. Washington caught in such danger, would you not move heaven and earth to secure her from harm?"

The General stiffened, high color suffusing his cheeks. "I do not need you to remind me of my responsibilities to my wife." In spite of his severe tone, Andrews sensed a softening in his demeanor, and he quickly conceded, "I do not deny that Miss Howard has been of great service, nor that efforts ought to be made to rescue her. My greater concern is that . . . " He cleared his throat and turned partially away so that Andrews could not read his expression. "I fear that not only will she be lost, but with her an excellent officer and a good friend."

"I also stand to lose them," Andrews reminded him, his voice tight. "But what other choice was there for Jon to make?"

His deliberate use of Carleton's first name had the effect he hoped. Washington turned back and fixed Andrews in a look that could not entirely conceal sympathy.

"General Carleton included a report when he ordered you here?"

Nodding, Andrews briefly recounted Caleb's release, the arrival of Carleton's ships, and the plans that had been laid, concluding, "Major Moghrab confirmed that Miss Howard was held aboard a prison ship called *Erebus.*"

Washington's eyebrows rose. *"Erebus!"*

"Aptly named, no doubt." Wearily Andrews scrubbed his hand over his face. "He and Major Vander Groot were gathering volunteers and planned to have control of the ship by the time General Carleton's privateers arrived. If they made it through. More than that, I don't know."

Andrews jerked his rain-stiffened buffalo hide around his shoulders. "You could at least have given me time to change into dry clothing, Laurens. If I'm to walk into an ambush, I'd appreciate doing so in uniform."

Pausing in the doorway of the narrow dining room, Washington's affable twenty-two-year-old aide craned his neck into the passage to throw a wary glance up the stairway, where Washington had disappeared moments earlier. Reassured, he advanced into the room, grinning.

"A tad testy this evening, is he?" Laurens' low voice brimmed with mirth.

"Frankly, *testy* isn't the word that sprang to my mind."

"You were lucky. It's one of his better days." Tall, thirty-two-year-old Tench Tilghman's mouth appeared suspiciously puckered.

"I can't say I've had the best day myself," Andrews growled, hoping to steer the conversation into safer waters. "I meant to arrive by mid afternoon, but the Delaware was running high because of the rains. Getting our wagons, cattle, and pack horses across the ford turned into an ordeal. Two of our wagons overturned and their contents were swept away. Consequently, we were fair frostbitten by the time we got to that godforsaken hill where we're expected to make camp—in the dark."

Laurens's grin reappeared. "Ah, so that explains why your brigade didn't seem to be overflowing with joy when I tracked you down. But where's General Carleton? He hasn't gotten himself into trouble again?" he added with unmistakable glee, ignoring the annoyed frown Tilghman cast him.

Pretending not to hear, Andrews jammed his slouch hat onto his head and turned to Spotted Pony. Wrapped in his buffalo robe, the warrior stood just inside the door as stiffly erect as a carved statue, arms folded. He met Andrews's gaze with an impassive one.

"Doesn't your scout speak any English?" Laurens tried, tone and look innocent as a dove. "He refused to say a word while you engaged in your pleasant visit with His Excellency."

Andrews managed to squelch a guffaw. *And I'll wager you made every effort to loosen his tongue.*

Tilghman gave an impatient sigh. "Give it up, John." He strode around the table to Andrews's side. "I apologize for this young pup. He's been thoroughly spoilt by—at his young age—being privileged to be in the middle of everything that goes on around here and in Congress as well, since his father's serving as president. The General's kept mum about why your Captain McLeod popped in last week with a Frenchman in tow, and it's driving John mad."

"I say, Tench, you're being mighty unfair. It's our business to make ourselves useful by helping the General in any way we can, which means we need to know what's going on. You have to admit that I hold everything I hear very close."

"That's your one saving grace," Tilghman conceded with a superior tone, jabbing his finger at the younger man.

Ignoring him, Laurens narrowed his eyes. "Carleton isn't somehow involved in the negotiations for a treaty with the French, is he? He did call on Congress during the summer, and it's common knowledge he has high-level ties in France."

Andrews winced. *Obviously there's a great deal more about Jon that's common knowledge than I'd supposed.*

"That's an understatement, considering that his uncle is le comte de Caledonne. It doesn't get any higher than that except for a direct line to Louis the Sixteenth. In fact, Caledonne appears to *be* a direct line to the king."

"I'm afraid you're considerably overstating General Carleton's connections, Tilghman," Andrews objected as he pulled on his gloves.

Laurens regarded him with a wry expression, then shrugged in defeat. "Sorry to press you on the matter. I suppose you aren't authorized to divulge details any more than we are."

It was Andrews's turn to snicker. "I assure you it isn't personal. I've been in the same position myself on occasion, which makes your discomfiture all the more entertaining."

Laurens's grin reappeared, and he abruptly changed the subject. "I hope the accommodations I found for you and your officers are suitable. The house is even more cramped than this one, but unfortunately there aren't any other unoccupied farmhouses in the vicinity. You will want to stay on your toes. In spite of their protestations, I'm fairly certain the owners are rabid loyalists."

Andrews grimaced. Laurens's unexpected kindness had made it impossible for him to turn the favor down even though he preferred to make use of Carleton's marquee and share his troops' misery as long as they were forced to live in tents.

"I suspect they'll be more loyal to Spanish doubloons, but I'll post a strong guard about the place just the same."

"It must be nice not to be dependent on Congress's largesse," Tilghman put in sourly. "Of course, what little Continental scrip they're willing to part with from time to time isn't worth a fig. And on top of it, the British keep flooding the market with counterfeit bills to further undermine confidence in our currency."

"They've taken to counterfeiting?" Andrews burst out, incredulous.

Tilghman's mouth quirked. "All in the service of our supposed sovereign."

"The area's awash in everything the army needs," Laurens grumbled. "However, our wealthy Pennsylvania friends—the Quakers prime among them—are too busy selling their goods for British coin to spare us any. Profit's their king."

"Every day our patrols capture both men and women smuggling their wares into Philadelphia. And without a doubt, intelligence too."

"What exemplary patriots!"

Tilghman raked his fingers through his hair and puffed out a breath. "You know Congress hasn't the authority to levy taxes, Andrews. And they baulk at confiscating goods even from Tories."

"The politicians consider it political suicide. The result is that the army goes naked and starves."

Tilghman frowned at Laurens. "As His Excellency continually points out, the surest way to lose the support of our fellow citizens is to treat them as the British do. And how, pray tell, would you enforce the collection of federal taxes from the states when they already refuse to turn over any monies in spite of Congress's continual nagging and pleading?"

Laurens waved his words away with an airy gesture of his hand. "Since their vaunted militias are so eager to rush to our aid and spill their blood in defense of their country, the army isn't needed at all. And naturally true Whigs happily pay their tithe to maintain the war out of pure, unspotted virtue. No self interest for them."

"An ideal that's been amply proven a delusion—especially in regard to the Pennsylvania militia—though our New England representatives seem oblivious to reality."

Andrews looked from one to the other, unable to suppress a chuckle. "That bad?"

"That's not the half," Laurens grumbled. "Congress continues to stall action on the General's recommendations for improvements we desperately need to the commissary and quartermaster departments, with the consequence that the army's numbers continue to decline through starvation, illness, and desertion. In other words, nothing has changed from the beginning."

Tilghman directed a cautious glance toward the stairway before speaking. "It's even worse than that. It appears there's a cabal building to unseat His Excellency and replace him with the mighty victor of Saratoga. No doubt you can guess who's behind it."

Andrews stiffened. "If truth be told, that victory belongs to General Arnold far more than to Granny Gates. Had it been up to the latter, we'd still be crouched behind our defenses on Bemis Heights, waiting for Burgoyne to make a move—even though he'd far outrun his supply lines and both food and ammunition were scarce in his camp."

"Ah, but you see, if you'd simply waited, Burgoyne's men would've starved by now," Laurens crowed, "giving us a bloodless triumph."

Andrews snorted. "They'd have escaped back to Canada to fight another day, and Gates would have been deprived of the victor's laurels. I'm not a fan of Arnold's, but he did our country a great service, for which he was rewarded by being shunted aside in the most despicable manner possible. He's an active officer who holds the entire loyalty of his men, and the Army will rue the day he was so unjustly treated."

As HE CLOSED THE DOOR of the house behind them, Andrews gave Spotted Pony a wry look. "I was surprised to hear you don't speak a word of English. My impression was that you'd become rather fluent in the tongue, but evidently I was mistaken."

His visage hard, Spotted Pony returned, "I do not speak to Long Knives without a weapon in my hand."

Andrews cast him a meaningful glance, then strode to where his servant, Briggs, waited holding the reins of their mounts. The three men mounted and spurred their horses to a trot, Briggs lagging behind. For some minutes they rode down the shadowy, winding road toward the wind-swept field where they had left the brigade pitching camp.

"I'm glad you and Sinking Ground stayed behind when the others left," Andrews said at length. "When do you mean to go?"

"When Roaring Waters and the others brought Black Fish's message, Red Fox and I agreed I would stay until we learn of White Eagle's fate."

"It may be long before word reaches us. Even if White Eagle succeeds, I know he'll delay his return, especially if it is not well with Healer Woman. I'll not send Black Fish's message to him while he's away. We must tell him face to face. By then it may be *Washilatha kiishthwa,* the Eccentric Moon."

Spotted Pony dismissed Andrews's words with a wave of his hand. "It's unlikely the British will seek out our people before the spring, *Melo'kami.* There is yet time for White Eagle to counsel with Black Fish before they appear—and before the Long Knives come seeking revenge."

"I know you thirst to drive the *Shemanese* out of our lands, Spotted Pony, even as Black Fish and his warriors do. But White Eagle is right. Another war with the Long Knives will be disastrous for us, especially for our elders and women and little ones." Andrews continued with fierce emotion, "If we could keep them safe, I'd be the first to set my foot upon the war path. But now Blue Sky and my son are also in the line of fire, and I'm not there to protect them."

The warrior stared down the moonlit road, his jaw hardening. "If we do nothing, the Long Knives will wrest from us everything worth living for—our land, our homes, our families, our freedom. Then what will our lives be worth, Golden Elk? Is it not better to die as warriors than to live like dogs?"

# Chapter Twenty-three

*Tuesday, 11 November*

SHE STILL BREATHED.

His entire world hung on the labored, almost imperceptible rise and fall of her bosom. Head bowed, he cradled her slack hand between his own and pressed it to his lips as he had a hundred times.

Mercifully, her fever had been broken by the decoction of boneset Dr. Howard had administered shortly before Carleton left the room. Although she did not rouse or respond to his touch, her skin remained cool, and in that he took courage. And redoubled his prayers.

At length he lifted his eyes from her still face to glance fearfully toward the eastern windows. The tentative, pearly light of dawn had just begun to dispel the sky's inky hues and faintly brighten the shadowed chamber.

Across from him, Dr. Howard sat slumped in a chair, eyes closed, surrendered to exhaustion. Lemaire stood with Marie in front of the highboy behind him, his hand on her shoulder as they quietly conferred with Jemma. Abby lay asleep, curled up on a cot pushed against the bed beside Carleton, while Tess, Anne, and the Sterns had retreated to garner what sleep they could until the others gave out.

Carleton released Elizabeth's hand to rub his burning eyes, then massaged the tension from his neck. Days of intense action with little or no sleep or food, succeeded by the wrenching strain of hours spent in agony at her bedside, had left him so lightheaded he feared he could not remain conscious much longer. His hands shook, his head pounded, and nausea roiled his stomach. Coherent thought and speech seemed impossible to form. Yet he feared leaving her for even a moment.

The harsh intake of her breath, followed by a slow, muted sigh as she let it softly out, brought him upright, bending over her, feeling as though the floor had given way beneath him. For a terrifying, suspended moment, she neither breathed nor moved.

He had given up all hope when she suddenly drew in a shuddering breath and turned her head on the pillow, her eyelids fluttering.

"Beth," he managed in a hoarse whisper, clutching her hand as though it were a lifeline. "Dear heart, I'm here."

Both doctors were immediately at the bed, bending anxiously over her, with the women crowding close behind them.

"Daughter," Dr. Howard pleaded. "My girl, can you hear me?"

Elizabeth's breaths shortened, and Carleton noted with a surge of relief that the slightest tinge of color came into her ashen cheeks. With an effort she forced her eyes open, struggling to focus on their faces as she turned a bewildered look from one to the other.

At Carleton's knee, Abby thrust aside her covers and scrambled onto her knees. Rubbing her eyes and pushing her disheveled hair out of her face, she leaned onto the bed.

"You're awake!" She threw her arms around her sister and buried her face against Elizabeth's shoulder.

Tears slanted down Elizabeth's cheeks. "Abby . . . sweet sister . . . "

Gently Carleton brushed away her tears. When Elizabeth struggled to clear her throat, Abby sprang from the cot and took the glass of water from the small table at the head of the bed. Smiling down at her, Carleton slipped his arm around Elizabeth's shoulders and carefully raised her while Abby held the glass to her lips.

She drank, then mouthed, "Thank you."

He settled her back against the pillow, and Abby and Marie tucked the covers around her.

"How do you feel?" Dr. Howard asked anxiously.

Lemaire felt her brow, then took her hand. "The fever has not returned. Does anything hurt you, mademoiselle?"

A smile touched her lips, and she turned her head slightly from side to side. "No . . . only weary . . ." Her eyelids drooped.

Carleton bent to touch his lips to her brow. "Rest now. You're safe— and your friends from *Erebus* too." Her gaze fixed on his face, and when he saw sadness come into her eyes, he whispered, "Don't grieve, dear one. He's in God's hands now."

Gulping back a sob, she nodded. "Caleb?"

"Safe and well. I sent him back to his regiment."

Marie wrung out a cloth in the basin of water on the dresser and came to blot her face as gently as though she handled an infant. "You've only to think about getting well now."

Opposite them, Lemaire clasped Dr. Howard's shoulder. "*C'est un miracle*, Samuel! I must have some of the herb you gave her. What do you call it—boneset?"

Dr. Howard dashed the tears from his eyes. "The Indians use it for all manner of ailments, including severe fevers. I purchased a supply before we sailed to London and found it very helpful for several of my patients there. Yesterday, after you left, I remembered I still had a small quantity on hand. Thank God I did!"

Jemma had slipped quietly away and now ushered Tess, Anne, the Sterns, and Sarah inside. Carleton moved back while they gathered around the bed, and for some moments soft exclamations of relief, joyful thankfulness, and praise to God filled the chamber. By one accord, they bowed their heads while first Dr. Howard, and then Stern offered up prayers of gratitude and petitions that Elizabeth would soon be restored to full health.

When all had echoed the amen, Marie sent Sarah to bring a cup of a nourishing broth she had prepared earlier at Lemaire's direction.

For Carleton, words had ceased to make any sense. The floor swayed beneath him, and he was forced to take hold of the bed's headboard to hold himself upright.

Anne and Marie appeared at his side and he heard Sarah say, "I readied the chamber 'cross the passage. I go call Stowe," before bustling out the door.

He shook his head and bent to capture Elizabeth's hand. "I won't leave her—"

"It'll do her no good if you fall ill," Anne answered firmly. "We'll simply have two to care for instead of one."

"Jonathan . . . please rest," Elizabeth whispered. "You look . . . so terribly . . . worn."

"Indeed, general, you must take care of yourself, for her sake as well as for your own," Marie's gentle voice echoed. "You can do nothing more here for now. I promise we will take good care of her, and you will only be a few feet away. Sleep, and we shall call you if you're wanted."

"They be right, sir," Stowe said, appearing suddenly at his elbow. The older man's arm was around Carleton, insistently urging him toward the door. "I'll stay by to wake ye if need be."

Elizabeth gazed up at him, concern etching her features as she silently formed the words *I love you.*

Too exhausted to protest more, Carleton kissed her hand, then released it and allowed Stowe to lead him, blindly, from the chamber. Dr. Howard had gone out just ahead of them, and they met him in the passage at the head of the stairs.

"I'll leave as soon as Beth's better," Carleton offered hoarsely. "I fear if I go now while she's still so weak, it'll cause her too much distress."

Dr. Howard's stern look softened. "Regardless of the differences between us, sir, I wish you to stay as long as you're able. I may be a stubborn man, but I'm not heartless. You saved our daughter's life, and her mother and I are greatly in your debt. Beth's given her heart to you, and it's clear you love her," he added gruffly, moisture brightening his eyes. "What kind of father would I be if I'd rob her of that?"

Carleton pressed his hand to his aching head. "Thank you."

Giving the doctor an abrupt nod, Stowe led Carleton into the chamber opposite Elizabeth's, where a fire leaped on the hearth. Outside, the sun had risen, and the glow that outlined the drawn curtains at the windows was so bright it hurt Carleton's eyes.

Stowe pushed him into a chair and wasted no time prying off his boots and stripping off his clothing. After pulling back the covers of the high, tester bed, he returned to help Carleton to his feet.

"Stowe . . . I . . . " The words hovered at the edge of consciousness, impossible to summon to his tongue.

The servant patted his arm. "There be plenty o' time to talk later, gen'l."

Supported on his arm, Carleton made it to the bed and sprawled across it. The moment his head touched the pillow, he was aware of nothing more, not even of Stowe drawing the blankets over him.

CONSCIOUSNESS FILTERED BACK in fragments. This time opening her eyes did not require the effort it had earlier. Despite the fitful dreams that tormented her while she slept, Elizabeth remembered immediately where she was and that Carleton was there, and her family.

She drew in a shaky breath and focused on her father's face hovering over her, lined with deep furrows of weariness and worry. "Papa," she whispered.

Smiling, he laid his hand on her brow, then against her cheek. "Good. The fever's not returned, and there's a bit of color in your cheeks."

"Jonathan?"

"He's asleep. Hasn't moved since he lay down, according to Stowe. Lemaire and Marie have gone down to the hospital in Boston, and now that you're on the mend, they'll only return if needed. The others decided to get what rest they could while you were sleeping."

He pulled out his pocket watch and glanced at it. "It's just past three. I'll have cook heat up more broth for you. Proper nourishment is the best antidote to infection, my girl." He kissed her brow and straightened her covers before leaving the room.

She took in her surroundings with a sense of wonder. All was, as usual, neat and pleasingly arrayed. The mattress, linens, and blankets felt heavenly soft after having slept so long on hard planks without any cover except for her tattered clothing. Before she had fallen asleep again, she had been bathed, her shift replaced with a clean one. As if by a miracle, no comfort had been neglected.

She stretched tentatively, grateful that although her joints and muscles still ached, the agony of movement that had plagued her had eased. *Dear Father, thank you. Paradise could not be sweeter.*

Her father strode in the door. "Jemma will be right up. This evening I think we'll see if your stomach can hold down broth with a bit of bread soaked in it. And in the morning, perhaps a bite of coddled egg and toast."

"That sounds wonderful."

"It's a good sign you're hungry. Lemaire insists it's best for you to sit up as much as possible and for the chamber to be thoroughly aired each day." He helped her to sit up and propped pillows behind her, his arm encircling her shoulders to hold her steady until dizziness eased. "I must admit he's taught me a few things. And I flatter myself that I've returned the favor."

"You must share everything you've learned with me."

Smiling, he pushed his fingers through his curly hair. "When you're well again. You gave us an anxious time, you know."

A lump formed in Elizabeth's throat. The grey strands that had streaked his temples before he had gone to England now threaded through the rest of his black hair, and the fine lines at the corners of his eyes had deepened.

"I'm sorry, Papa. Truly."

Jemma entered quietly, bringing a cup of steaming broth that made Elizabeth's mouth water. When she set the tray on the table beside the bed, Elizabeth reached to draw her into her arms and kiss her, and for a moment they clung to each other.

"We were so worried about you, Miss Elizabeth," her dark, finely featured countenance creased. "I'm glad you're better."

"You're a good part of the reason. Thank you for your care." Elizabeth released her. "Your father and Pete . . . are they here? I want to thank them for all they did."

"They're gone back into Boston but plan to come again tomorrow afternoon." Jemma tilted her turbaned head toward Dr. Howard. "They're anxious to see her, too, once she's strong enough, sir."

"Tomorrow should be fine, Jemma. She's making good progress."

The maid nodded, smiling. She helped Elizabeth to drink the broth and when she had finished bore the tray away, closing the door quietly behind her.

Again Elizabeth scanned the chamber, her gaze finally resting on her father's face. "I've never felt so . . . safe . . . and loved." Overcome by sudden emotion, she burst into tears, covering her face with her hands. "Please forgive me. I never meant to hurt you and Mama so."

He gathered her into his embrace. "I cannot find it in my heart to condemn you, dear Daughter. Yes, your mother and I were appalled to learn of the risks you took, but Tess explained your reasons for your course—and Jon's too. And he related more to me yesterday as well. I confess, at first it was hard for us to swallow, and I'm afraid I was overly harsh with him. But my opinions about the rebellion have changed over these past two years. And now, seeing to what lengths the British will go to force us into subjection to a monarch unworthy of allegiance, I have to say that I've come to agree with you."

He settled her back against the pillows and resumed his seat in the chair pulled close to the bedside. With a rueful chuckle, he added, "It's strange that it took going back to England after all these years for me to realize that I'm an American—and glad of it!"

"Oh, Papa! I'm glad too."

Pulling out a handkerchief, he gently wiped away her tears, while regarding her with loving concern. "I wish mightily that you'd been more careful, Beth. But I can't fault your determination to serve the great cause of our nation's liberty or the skill with which you did so. Indeed, Jon told me your actions saved many lives, and I can't help being proud of you."

When she again began to weep, he took her hand. "What troubles you?"

"It was horrible," she managed through sobs. "You can't imagine the conditions our imprisoned men endure. Why would God allow anyone to suffer so? And Pieter—oh, Pieter!"

"Tess told us what he did. An admirable man. I wish I'd had the chance to meet him."

"He was like a brother to me. He reminded me so of you, Papa. You'd have loved him like a son. Why did he have to die? Why am I spared? The cost is too high!"

He let out a sigh. "Life has taught me that it's impossible for man to understand the ways of the Almighty. Not that he intends evil for us or that evil is in some way good—it isn't—but I'm learning that he'll use it in our lives to accomplish his own inscrutable purposes if we but trust him."

He reached to the bedside table, where his old, well-worn Bible lay. Leafing through its pages, he said, "You remember how, many years after Joseph's brothers sold him into slavery in Egypt, he rose to become second only to Pharaoh?"

She nodded, puzzled.

"This is what he said to his brothers when they stood before him, fearing that he would bring just retribution upon them for their cruel mistreatment of him: 'Ye meant evil against me; but God meant it unto good, to bring to pass, as it is this day, to save much people alive.' "

He looked up. "I'll admit I was very angry when I first learned about your and Jon's . . . involvements. And I accused Jon of evil. But after hearing him out, I realized that his faults are no greater than mine. My refusal to listen to you made it impossible for you to be honest with your mother and me." His face contorted and he fixed her in an anguished look. "If only I'd heard you out, opened my mind and heart to yours, mine might have been changed. Instead my harsh attitude forced you to keep secrets. And this is the result."

"How I hoped and prayed that someday I could confide in you! I should have done so anyway, Papa. I know in your heart—"

He shook his head regretfully. "My heart was exceedingly hardened against the patriots, daughter, and if you had, who knows what I might have done in passion. In truth I had suspicions, but you played your part so well that I discounted them."

He patted her hand. "Despite our faults, the one who knows each heart is merciful. Perhaps, in this case too, it was God's purpose to turn what others meant for evil unto good so that he might save all these men alive. And you, dear Daughter. He used both Jon and Pieter to accomplish his purpose, and how can we question his will?

"But here," he interjected quickly, "all this talk has worn you out."

Unable any longer to fight the weariness that overwhelmed her, she smiled up at him as he helped her to lie down again. "I'm glad we talked, Papa." She squeezed his hand. "You're a great comfort to me."

She sank again into healing slumber, hearing him whisper, "I love you, my girl. Rest now. I'll be here when you wake."

❋  ❋  ❋

"WHAT TIME IS IT, STOWE?" Still groggy after soaking in a hot bath, Carleton took in the peaceful, orderly chamber, noting that no light showed around the edges of the draperies that swathed the windows against drafts.

"Nigh eight o' the evening, sir. Been asleep the 'ole day, and I'd say the rest did ye some good."

The abrupt cessation of the strain Carleton had been under for so long was disorienting. Had the past two weeks been a dream? he wondered. Or was he dreaming now?

He pushed back his damp hair and hastily stepped into drawers, then his uniform breeches before bending so Stowe could pull a shirt over his head. "You've seen Miss Howard? She's doing well?"

"Dr. 'oward said she woke a while back and took more broth. She's sleepin' now." Stowe cocked his eye while Carleton carelessly buttoned his shirt and shoved the tail into his breeches. "She'll be right as rain soon. Just give 'er time—'ere, sir." He tidied the shirt's drape, helped Carleton into his waistcoat, and buttoned it for him.

"Rest and nourishment is the best medicine," Carleton agreed, relieved.

The servant motioned Carleton to sit, then brushed his hair and tied it neatly at the nape of his neck with a black ribbon. Retrieving Carleton's uniform jacket, he assessed it with a frown.

"I cleaned and pressed yer uniform as best I could, but both breeches an' jacket are near threadbare, and new linens are wanted too. This last campaign put considerable wear on yer clothin'."

"I'll stop at the tailor's tomorrow, then." With a lazy smile Carleton rose and turned so Stowe could slip the uniform jacket over his arms.

Stowe clucked his tongue as he settled the jacket across Carleton's shoulders. "And yer buckskins, sir! They be so disreputable they ought t' be chucked."

"No worry on that score, Stowe. Laughing Otter, Rain Women and the other women were particularly industrious while we were at Bemis Heights." Carleton moved to the mirror to assess his appearance. "I'm well supplied, not only with hunting shirts, leggings, and moccasins for the winter—all properly fringed, beaded, and quilled—but also with a rather impressive match coat. They helped equip Charles, too, since Blue Sky had the baby to care for. But keep these for the ride back to camp. I'm rather fond of them. They've just gotten perfectly worn in."

"I know wot ye mean. Sweetgrass made sure as 'ow I'll look a right smart Shawnee." Stowe's grin faded.

Carleton gave him a keen look in the mirror, while he tied his stock. "I'm sorry you weren't there when she left with Red Fox's party. She said to tell you that if you don't come to her during the winter, she'll return with the warriors come spring. I promised Charles I'd try to send him to Grey Cloud's town this winter, and if it's possible, you'll go along."

Stowe's face brightened. " 'ow long do ye plan to stay 'ere?"

"That may depend on how long Dr. Howard is willing to put up with me."

It suddenly struck Carleton that Dr. Howard's hostility was no longer due to his spying for the patriots while serving as aide-de-camp to British General Thomas Gage, and then defecting to the Continental Army. Some months earlier Elizabeth had confided that her father's letters from London made it clear his opinions had changed drastically on that score as well as on the merits of the rebellion.

The cause of the current tension between them could only result from Carleton's part in leading raids against the white settlements as a war chief of the Shawnee—a minor detail that, along with her own involvements, Elizabeth had promised to reveal in person on her return to Boston in hope of allaying her parents' concerns before Carleton joined them. Her capture had made that impossible; however, according to Stowe, when he delivered the news of Elizabeth's capture, Tess had promised to disclose everything Elizabeth had meant to.

What had most likely been a hurried account at such a time must have caused quite a shock, nor could Carleton blame the Howards for their reaction. He would have to tread cautiously if he were to regain their good will—if that was even possible, he reflected glumly.

Stowe buttoned Carleton's jacket and stood back to study him. "Ye look well enough, but ye can't wear uniform all the time, gen'l. Ye'll need ordinary dress too, particularly as 'ow ye'll have a British target on yer back after this last little escapade. There's doubtless some as is still loyal to the crown 'ere, and ye've no need to draw their attention any more than's unavoidable."

Carleton dismissed his troubling thoughts with an airy wave of his hand. "I'll order a full complement then. In the latest style." More soberly he added, "By the way, Stowe, thank you for your foresight in arranging for the hospital, not to mention everything else you've done. As usual, I'm greatly in your debt. We'd never have succeeded without your efforts."

"Ah, ain't no 'count, sir. Nothin' more'n my duty."

"But you always go beyond mere duty. You think of every detail." Carleton stretched, a smile tugging at his mouth. "I knew there was a reason why I adopted you as my elder brother. Are you finally going to allow me to promote you to sergeant?"

Stowe stepped back, his expression reflecting alarm. "Oh, no, sir! All that responsibility at my age, sir?" He shook his head vigorously to emphasize the point. "I'm not up t' the task—no way."

"No man, regardless of rank, could possibly handle any more responsibilities than I've already laden you with," Carleton scoffed. "Besides, you more than deserve an upgrade in pay. You've never failed to carry out every task I assigned, and very well too. I'd be helpless as a babe without you."

Stowe raised his hands and continued to back away. "Ye take good care o' me, and like I told ye many a time, I'll stick w' ye as long as I got breath. Don't need no promotion t' ensure that."

Carleton folded his arms, regarding him fondly. "Corporal, at least."

"No, no. I'm well content with where I am. Nobody pays no attention to a mere private." He grinned, the scar that marred his cheek puckering further to make him look even more villainous.

Carleton threw up his hands in mock frustration. "By now I ought to know better than to argue with you, Stowe. You're even more stubborn than I am."

THE DOOR TO ELIZABETH'S CHAMBER stood ajar, and Carleton eased it open to find Sarah coming toward him carrying a dinner tray. Anne and Abby occupied chairs drawn up to the bedside, where Elizabeth sat propped against pillows and swathed in the thick bed rug, wan and hollow cheeked. A smile curved her lips as their eyes met.

Abby turned and saw him in the doorway. She ran to clutch him around the waist.

"Thank you for bringing Beth home . . . Jonathan."

At her hesitation in speaking his name, he smiled down at her, then bent to enfold her in his arms.

"Abby," Anne reproved gently, "it's General Carleton, please."

He cupped Abby's face in his hand. "Let her call me by my given name. It pleases me."

Anne dimpled, clearly pleased as well. "Very well, then."

Abby threw her arms around his neck and kissed his cheek. "You're my brother now."

"I'm honored. I've always wanted a sister, and there couldn't be a better one than you."

He returned her kiss. Releasing her, he strode to the bedside. Not caring that the others watched, smiling, before looking discreetly away, he bent to lightly touch his lips to Elizabeth's.

"It's so good to see you sitting up," he murmured. "I love you with all my heart."

Weakly she trailed her fingers feather soft across his cheek. "You look more rested, but there's still a shadow in your face. I fear you suffered too much for me."

"I'd gladly suffer anything, dear heart. To see you smile means more to me than all the treasure in all the world."

He slipped the miniature from his pocket, pressed it into her hand, and closed her fingers around it. "Marie found this when we brought you aboard *Destiny*. I thought I'd better keep it until you were safe at home."

She opened her hand and gasped. "Oh, how I feared it lost! Thank you, dearest. It was all I had of you for so long, and it helped me to feel you near. I'd not give it up, ever."

"I'm glad you had it."

Sarah had waited patiently while they talked. Now she said, "Gen'l, I'll bring you up a tray. Looks like you in need o' some nourishment."

He straightened, grinning. "Thank you, Sarah. It suddenly occurs to me that I'm ravenous as a wolf."

Anne raised her eyebrows, mouth quirked. Chuckling, Sarah reached for Abby's hand.

"Miss Abby, you better come with me and leave the grown-ups to talk."

Abby's brow creased. "Mama, please—"

Anne gave her a reproachful look. "You heard Sarah. I expect you to obey."

"But I'm twelve now, and—"

"Your father like to share supper with you, Miss Abby, since he been so preoccupied with Miss 'Lisabeth for days now. He be missin' your times together."

"It is getting late, Abby," Elizabeth broke in gently. "Go to Papa, and I'll see you in the morning. I love you."

After kissing her, Abby reluctantly followed Sarah to the door. When she glanced imploringly back at him, Carleton winked. She put her hand to her mouth to stifle a giggle and hurried after Sarah.

"Joshua and his wife have gone?"

Anne motioned him to take the seat the child had vacated. "They have, but he plans to stop by the end of the week when he leaves for White Marsh. He's recruited a company of men to fill vacancies in his regiment and is eager to muster them in as quickly as possible since a number of his regiment's enlistments expire at the end of the year."

"A continuing problem." Carleton settled into the chair. "During the winter there are always more desertions. Men become war weary or disillusioned or anxious for their families. Or they simply cease to care. It's hard to carry on a war without a trained and disciplined force."

"I suppose . . . you'll have to return to your brigade soon too." Elizabeth met his gaze, then quickly looked down and concentrated on rolling the edge of the bed rug between her fingers.

"How long do you plan to stay?" Anne prodded.

"Charles is more than capable of commanding the Rangers in my absence. I thought perhaps . . . I might stay through Christmas as long as that's agreeable to everyone."

Elizabeth clasped her hands. "Oh, Jonathan, do, please! We've had so little time together. It's all right, isn't it, Mama? I know Aunt Tess won't object."

"Of course, dear. Jonathan, stay as long as you can. You'll always be welcome here—you know that."

"If Dr. Howard's not opposed—"

"He won't be," Anne returned with a serene look. "Just a little while ago, he spoke to me quite approvingly of your devotion to Elizabeth. Samuel can be prickly at times, I admit, but he truly is a very good man at heart."

"He is, Mama! We had a long talk earlier, and he was such a comfort to me." She gave Carleton a warm smile.

He let out his breath slowly, exulting at the evidence that the Lord was working to soften her parents' hearts toward him. Concerned that they would never accept him, he had hesitated to broach the subject of his staying, but now he was glad the opportunity had arisen. Tess had always been kindness itself to him, and clearly he had won Anne and Abby over as well. That left Dr. Howard.

Taking to heart the doctor's assurance that he would not rob Elizabeth of Carleton's love, he reflected that perhaps God meant to knit them into a family after all. In that case, he would exercise patience. He would curb his tongue and avoid sensitive issues, while at the same time being prepared to address objections forthrightly, but tactfully, if asked.

In a burst of exuberance, he turned a glance on Elizabeth that brought a blush to her cheeks and mischief to her eyes. He grinned in return, resolved to resort to the weapon that had never failed of success when he availed himself of it.

He would charm her father into submission.

## Chapter Twenty-four

D UMBFOUNDED, Andrews clenched his teeth to keep his jaw from dropping. Taking a tighter grip on his mount's reins, he blurted out, "An attack, you say—on New York Harbor?"

Washington had appeared unexpectedly, riding alone, moments after Andrews arrived at the camp from his headquarters with the sun's red edge barely above the horizon. He had immediately drawn Andrews apart to a cluster of gnarled pines at the camp's perimeter where they could talk without being overheard.

The General pulled his tall bay partially around and for a long moment seemed to assess the orderly sea of tents that washed across the barren hill. The smoke of campfires curled peacefully upward in the still morning air, and a disciplined tide of troops moved along the pathways. Details rode out to picket and forage duty, while others lined up to drill to the shouts of sergeants, dug fortifications, cared for horses, or hustled about the brigade's other common daily routines.

After a moment he transferred a speculative gaze back to Andrews. "Perhaps you are aware that Major Clark has sent a number of spies into Philadelphia." When Andrews nodded warily, Washington continued, "One of them gained access to the house on Market Street that Howe occupies with his mistress."

Andrews narrowed his eyes. "A servant would have the greatest freedom of movement."

Washington conceded a noncommittal shrug. "As you can imagine, talk is loose in what one would conceive to be a secure environment. Early this morning I learned that an express arrived from New York yesterday bearing a report from Clinton that put Howe's staff in quite a clamor. Our contact managed to get a look at it. Clinton claims that a squadron of at least half a dozen privateers gained entry to the harbor during a storm Saturday night. The ships flew the British flag and carried an urgent message with Lord Germain's signature that appeared so authentic they were immediately passed through."

"Saturday night?" Andrews exclaimed. "Then he's done it! But . . . half a dozen ships? The last report I received from General Carleton stated that the three ships he expected reached the rendezvous. He mentioned no others."

A smile tugged at the corners of Washington's mouth. "Perhaps more came in . . . or perhaps the British cannot count."

Andrews gave a short laugh. "They're not likely to admit there were only three, Your Excellency. But what of the outcome?"

"The attack appears to have been a brilliant success. According to Clinton, this force took possession of one of the prison ships and carried off every prisoner aboard . . . including Howe's most particular object."

"Miss Howard!"

Washington allowed another faint smile. "He claimed the Navy discovered the privateers and attacked them, but they put up a fierce resistance. Apparently in the process of fighting their way out of the harbor, they reduced the batteries at the Narrows; however, Clinton maintained that the ships suffered severe damage and a couple were sunk."

Crestfallen, Andrews managed, "He's undoubtedly overstating the case, but if even one was sunk, they lost many men. And we've no way of knowing who survived. Or died."

Washington's mouth hardened. "Clinton may be in error on that score too, or he may have indulged in wishful thinking. I fear we will remain in suspense until we receive a true report from General Carleton."

Andrews looked away, feeling sick. *Of course, if one never arrives . . .*

"The report also stated that the rest of the privateers escaped when another large squadron joined them beyond the Bar. The pursuing ships also suffered damage in the battle, nor were they supplied for a major naval engagement. And with the storm they were forced to turn back."

"Nothing but excuses." Andrews scowled. "I hope Clinton's trying to conceal the fact that Jon sent a large number of them to the bottom of the bay."

Washington gave him a keen look. "Interestingly enough, my contact says that Clinton's missive heaped blame on Howe for the debacle—the consequences of dealing with the devil, as he phrased it. As to be expected, the talk at Howe's headquarters was all about Clinton's incompetence in maintaining security."

"Regardless of the result, creating dissention within enemy ranks is a worthy accomplishment in itself." Andrews gave a caustic laugh. "Neither Clinton nor Howe is likely to take responsibility for such a spectacular defeat—by privateers, no less."

Washington's lips pursed. "Despite my concerns, General Carleton has apparently done our cause a great service, for which he deserves the highest commendation. That one of our generals breached New York Harbor and brought away a large number our prisoners is an enormous coup, but hold this information close until we have confirmation of exactly what happened. In the meantime, we will pray that he and Miss Howard made it through safely, and that his ships did not suffer extraordinary damage."

A troop approaching up the muddy road drew Andrews's attention. The horsemen turned into the camp and halted, while their leader looked around as though searching for someone. After a moment he spied the two of them and, motioning for his troop to wait, he spurred his mount forward to join them. His face ruddy from the early morning chill, handsome, twenty-three-year-old Major Benjamin Tallmadge of Colonel Elisha Sheldon's Second Dragoons pulled his mount to a halt and gave a brisk salute.

"Good morning, Your Excellency." He nodded to Andrews. "You're still riding out with us, colonel?"

Andrews directed a questioning glance at their commander, who waved them off. "That's all I have at the moment, Colonel Andrews. Since your brigade will bolster Colonel Sheldon's in picket duty along Philadelphia's perimeter, I think it good for you to accompany Major Tallmadge for the day to get an idea of what we're up against."

Andrews saluted. "Yes, sir. Thank you, sir."

After Washington had ridden off, Andrews motioned Tallmadge to follow and led the way to where Captain Farris had drawn up his mounted troop. With Tallmadge's detachment joining them, they turned their mounts onto the main road to Philadelphia.

They had not ridden far when Andrews felt the younger officer's sidelong gaze. "His Excellency seemed in fine fettle this morning. I presume it's something to do with General Carleton—"

"Don't start, Tallmadge," Andrews cut him off. "I've already gone a round in the ring with Laurens and Tilghman, and I can't tell you any more than I could tell them."

The major's eyebrows rose. "Now I am intrigued. It must be a highly sensitive matter if neither of them know about it."

"You wouldn't believe the half of it."

Tallmadge laughed good humoredly as he studied the road ahead of them. "Well, you're not going to believe what we encounter either. Nine major roads and uncounted byroads ring Philadelphia, and we're charged with guarding all of them with only the help of Major Henry Lee's troops and General Armstrong's Pennsylvania militia. Needless to say, we're delighted to have your brigade join us."

"We're more than happy to oblige."

Tallmadge grinned. 'Then you're in for a treat. Every day I discover new occasions for amusement or outrage, leavened by a hearty dose of cynicism, at the debased state of human nature."

"Laurens and Tilghman alerted me to the fanatical patriotism of the locals," Andrews replied with a smirk, very much liking Tallmadge's cheerful attitude and obvious competence. "I have a feeling it's going to be an interesting, if not thoroughly amusing, day."

"I guarantee you won't be bored," Tallmadge answered, returning a smug grin, "and it isn't just the locals. Be sure to stay on the lookout for Howe's light horse units. They appear to resent our roaming the area and getting in the way of their movements, and we do everything in our power to justify their objections."

"I believe I'm going to enjoy this assignment, Tallmadge," Andrews said with a laugh. "Lead on."

## Chapter Twenty-five

M OODILY CARLETON STUDIED the clouded morning through the library window, drapes half-drawn against drafts from the gusty winds that occasionally shook the house. With a sigh, he returned his gaze to the letter he held, his last communication from Vander Groot, written at Baptist Meeting House just before the doctor slipped secretly away to New York. Reading it again, Carleton was struck by what he had not recognized then: his friend's firm determination to rescue Elizabeth even at the sacrifice of his life.

At length he handed the sheet across the writing table to Stowe. "Ask Colonel Andrews to take this to the Vander Groots when he calls on them at Lancaster. I hate to give it up as it's all I've left of him. But it details Pieter's reasons for doing what he did, and his family deserves to have it. Perhaps it'll soothe their grief in some measure."

"The news'll be right hard for 'em t' bear."

"It will. I'll call to offer my condolences in person after I return to camp. It's the least I can do."

Stowe took the letter, grim faced, and tucked it into his saddle bag. Next to him, Isaiah shifted his stance.

"Jemma write you that copy?"

"She did, Isaiah. Thank you for the suggestion; she has a very fine hand. I know Miss Howard will cherish it."

Carleton took a thick packet of papers from the table and handed it to Isaiah. "These are the reports for Colonel Andrews and General Washington detailing the attack and my plans to stay here for a few weeks."

Rising, he came around the table and gave Stowe a pouch filled with coins. "This should be enough to provision the brigade with food and forage until I come. I've ordered Andrews to have our clothier requisition new uniforms, weapons, and other necessaries from my Baltimore warehouse. There'll be no need for you to ride all the way back here, by the way. The ladies are making sure I'm well taken care of, and you'll be of more use to Colonel Andrews until I come."

He turned back to Isaiah. "I'm sorry to send you off again when you've had so little time with your family."

"I don't expect to stay home safe and warm while the rest o' the brigade be on duty, sir. Pete'll stay till *Destiny's* ready to sail. That comfort his ma."

"How are your new recruits shaping up?"

The major smiled broadly. "Capt'n Matheson got 'em well in hand. They beginnin' to get the idea."

"Brilliant of you to enlist them. We couldn't have gotten control of the ship and taken the prisoners off so quickly without the strong force you and Pieter assembled, and it's a double benefit to end up with replacements for some of the troops we've lost over the past few months. I commend you. I only wish Pieter were here to share in it."

Gruffly Isaiah said, "We make a good team."

"Ye goin' down to the warehouse today?" Stowe broke in.

"After I stop by the hospital and the shipyard. I'm quite pleased to hear that business is back to normal in spite of the office being shut down so long during the blockade and siege."

"*Faire Winds* just brung in a new shipment yeste'day, and the place was 'oppin'," Stowe noted with satisfaction. "I give the manager a full list o' yer needs, and 'e promised t' 'ave everthin' ready for ye. Talked to the tailor too, and ye've but t' let 'im measure ye and 'ave the cloth sent over."

"You'll have me presentable with a minimum of effort on my part, as usual, Stowe," Carleton said with a chuckle.

He saw the men off as the clock struck eight, then hurried upstairs to see whether Elizabeth had awakened.

AS ALWAYS AT FIRST SIGHT of Carleton, Elizabeth's heart leaped when he strode into the chamber, his movements panther lithe. She drank in his tall, lean form, struck again a subtle force in him that effortlessly commanded his surroundings. As though drawn by it as well, her mother, sister, and aunt immediately turned welcoming smiles on him.

Sitting propped up on pillows in a dressing gown, with a bed tray across her lap, Elizabeth eagerly reached out to him. When his deep blue-grey eyes met hers, the emotion in them sent a thrill through her veins. He paused long enough to give the others a graceful bow before crossing to the bedside to take her hands in his.

Elizabeth's mother set her sewing aside and rose from her chair. "Good morning, Jonathan. You look much rested. You had a good sleep, I trust."

"Like the dead," he drawled, releasing Elizabeth and smiling down at Abby, who had popped up from her chair to take his hand.

Tess gave him a reproachful look. "We missed you at breakfast."

"You've had nothing to eat?" Elizabeth chided. "You must be starving."

"I couldn't delay any longer sending Stowe and Isaiah off with my report to Charles and General Washington. They've a long journey ahead of them."

"I'm so glad I was able to thank them in person for all they did before they had to leave."

"I'll have Sarah bring up a tray," Anne broke in, taking the bed tray.

She motioned to Tess and Abby to accompany her. The three disappeared into the passage, the older women hiding sly smiles and ignoring Abby's protests as they shepherded her from the room.

Elizabeth reveled in Carleton's laugh, and his kiss. When he straightened, he glanced after the women.

"It's becoming a habit for everyone to scamper off the moment I appear. I'm beginning to think I've lost their favor."

She gave him a knowing look. "I suspect the real reason is that they think we'd rather be alone."

"They might just be right." Sobering, he took one of the vacated chairs and gave her a keen look. "You look stronger today."

"I'm feeling much better," she said brightly. "I had a coddled egg a little while ago, along with a bite of toast and a swallow of tea."

"You've been so strong all the time I've known you that it hurts terribly to see you confined to bed."

"I'll be well again—very soon. I promise."

"Your father warned me that it'll take months for you to fully regain your health, and that in the meantime you must take extra care to avoid infection. I love your independent spirit, Beth, but until you're fully well, please promise you'll follow his instructions exactly. For my sake, if nothing else. I can't bear your being so ill and fearing every moment I'll lose you."

His voice shook, and she stared down at her clasped hands. "Then you can imagine my panic at the thought that you might surrender to Howe."

"There was no danger of that," he said gruffly. "Please, Beth. Swear to me you'll do everything your father advises."

She returned her gaze to his and smiled deeply into his eyes. "I will, dearest. I've no intention of becoming an invalid. There's more yet to be done and our whole lives ahead of us. I want more than anything for us to meet the future together without any restraint."

Seeing a shadow fall over his face, she rushed on, "Papa told me that Aunt Tess disclosed everything we've done, including our reasons. He confessed that at first he and Mama were deeply distressed and that he spoke quite harshly to you. He was sorry for it and assured me that his opinions have undergone a great change, that he and Mama are reconciled to the course we've chosen—though it worries them, of course."

He let out his breath and sat back in the chair. "You told me they'd understand. Truly, I didn't believe they ever would."

"Knowing Papa as I do, I can only believe that God smoothed our way." She gave a merry laugh. "His heart can be as willful as mine—I am my father's daughter after all—but I'm confident that he'll come to love you as much as I do."

"I hope so with all my heart."

She patted the covers beside her. He came to sit on the edge of the bed and drew her into his arms.

She caught the spark of mischief in his eyes and stiffened, too late. Before she could pull away, he snatched off the demure cap that covered her short curls. She clutched for it, but holding it out of her reach, he tossed it across the bed, laughing.

She pressed her hands to her hair. "Oh, Jonathan, don't! I look horrible with my hair all cut off."

"My love, I'd find you alluring even were you bald," he teased, tugging at a wayward curl. "But having it cropped makes you look so infinitely sweet that I can hardly keep my hands off you. Did I not love its glory so, I'd insist you always keep it cut. Once other women saw how dear you look with those ringlets clustered about your face, I swear they'd all insist on having their hair shorn."

She pushed him away, pretending annoyance. "Must you always be such a scoundrel?"

He sobered and gave her a languid, brooding look that caused her heart to pound and brought heat into her face. "I'm afraid it's ingrained in my nature, *enfant*. Did I not tell you the night of General Gage's ball that a mere child like you oughtn't to be left alone with me."

He was not teasing now, and that first endearment, which once had annoyed her beyond measure, now left her without defense. He drew her hands away from her hair and, bending over her, buried his fingers in the glossy tresses.

She trembled at the feel of the hard, corded muscles beneath his uniform coat. When she turned her face up to his, he caught his breath and lowered his mouth to hers. As their lips touched, she felt as though a bolt of lightning surged between them. Lightheaded, she slid her arms around his neck and drew him down beside her, trembling to feel his passion rise swiftly to match hers, all caution abandoned.

He trailed kisses across her cheekbones, to the base of her ear and down her throat to its hollow, every feather-light touch robbing her of breath. By degrees, his arms tightened, one hand following the curve of her back to her waist, each kiss more sensual and intense than the previous one. She gasped and arched against him, shuddering.

Abruptly he pulled away, appearing as shaken as she was. She sagged back against the pillows.

"Jonathan—"

He stood abruptly, putting space between them, and resumed his seat on the chair. For some moments he remained silent, fixing her in a haunted gaze.

"I don't want to hold back any more than you do," he said at last, "but you're too weak for this, Beth. If we go farther, it'll do you harm— in more ways than one."

She looked down, blinking back tears of frustration, unable to deny his words. All the strength had left her, and she trembled in every limb.

He took her hand between his and held it tightly. "We'll always be one in spirit and mind, heart of my heart. God grant that we may soon be so in body as well."

She drew him insistently back to her. "May it be so! And for now . . . only one more kiss."

Relenting, he yielded. But as footfalls ascended the stairway, he again drew quickly back. Seconds later Jemma entered, bearing a covered tray from which wafted rich, mouth-watering aromas.

He pulled the small side table in front of his chair for Jemma to set the tray on, his expression supremely innocent. When she removed the cover, he took in the plate brimming with poached eggs nestled next to a thick slice of perfectly browned ham and a generous portion of buttered brown bread; the bowl of creamy porridge and small pitcher of milk; and the cup of steaming, black coffee.

"As my friend Teissèdre is wont to say, when one cannot have love, food must suffice," he observed with a lofty wave of his hand.

Elizabeth managed, with considerable difficulty, to strangle her laughter, while Jemma slanted a prim glance in Carleton's direction, a blush rising to her dusky cheeks. Promising to return in a little while to fetch the tray, the maid retreated from the chamber.

"You *are* a scoundrel!" Elizabeth accused, giving in to mirth.

He grinned and concentrated on devouring his breakfast. Between mouthfuls he answered Elizabeth's eager questions about Andrews and Blue Sky, explaining why Andrews had sent her back to Grey Cloud's Town with Red Fox and Spotted Pony's party.

"Oh, poor Charles and Blue Sky! I understand all too well what they're suffering so far apart, not knowing what their future may hold or even whether they'll ever see each other again."

He set down knife and fork his expression grave. "Your capture impressed on me that Washington foresaw things we couldn't at the time. If we were married and had a child . . . " He broke off and shook his head.

"There's still your—our people's council," she amended hastily. "Will they grant us permission to wed even when the war is over?"

Clearly he noted the slip, though he made no reproach. "Red Fox is confident they will in time."

She forced a smile. "Well, until then we'll take all the joy we can in the time we have together. Now tell me of your meeting with Isaiah and Stowe."

He gave a brief account of his conversation with the two men, adding that he planned to go into Boston for the day.

"When you stop by the hospital, please find out how Josiah, Tom, and Billy are doing," she pleaded. "Tell them when they're better they must come to see me."

He readily agreed, then returned to his seat on the edge of the bed and drew a folded paper from the pocket of his uniform coat. "This is a copy of the last letter Pieter sent me. I knew you'd want to have it, but I'm concerned about giving it to you while you're still so weak. If it's too upsetting, I'll keep it until you're stronger."

She reached out. "Please. I want to read it now."

He surrendered the page. Her sight blurred as she read.

*Jon,*

*By now Isaiah will have told you why I've gone. Both of us know that without someone inside the city who can move openly and freely, finding Beth—much less rescuing her and the prisoners with her—will be difficult if not impossible. I'm the only one with any hope of accomplishing it, and I'm resolved on this course whatever the cost. Please believe that you couldn't have changed my mind and that if I fail in the attempt, I'm the one at fault, not you.*

*God go with you both! You have all my love, as does Beth. He's given you to each other, and I rejoice in being of some use in restoring her to your arms.*

*If we never see one another again in this world, I trust we'll meet in a better one someday. Take courage and act boldly, and may our Lord bless you always.*

*With every regard, I am your most devoted friend,*
*Pieter*

Tears overflowed. "He knew," she whispered. "And yet he went."

" 'Greater love hath no man than this,' " Carleton quoted, his voice muffled.

He took the letter from her and laid it on the bedside table, then gathered her into his embrace. For some moments they clung to each other, unable to speak.

At length Elizabeth brushed away her tears and touched his cheek, letting her fingers trail along the line of his jaw. "You've long doubted God, yet your faith seems stronger now."

"You and Pieter have done much to restore it."

On the staircase landing, the case clock struck the first quarter after nine. He took her hand and pressed her palm to his lips, then reluctantly released her and rose.

"I've much business to be about, and you're already wearying. You need rest."

She pressed her hand to her bosom. "Oh, I forgot! There's something I meant to give you this morning."

"What is it?"

"You'll have to wait now until this evening to find out," she teased. "The sooner you take care of your business, the sooner you'll return."

"Then I'll hurry back," he promised, smiling, and with a final kiss took his leave.

CARLETON SPENT MORE than two hours at the makeshift hospital along the wharves, accompanying Lemaire on his rounds. The large space was clean and orderly, and doctors and nurses recruited from Carleton's ships and from the town moved between the cots, the latter under Marie's close supervision.

Many of the freed prisoners appeared dangerously ill. Lemaire informed Carleton that several more, for whom little could be done, had died, in addition to those who had not lived through the battle. The

264 ❋ J. M. Hochstetler

survivors were clean, however, their rags replaced with warm, serviceable clothing through Carleton's provision and generous donations by the town's citizens.

Carleton made a point of speaking to as many of the men as possible, both former prisoners and his seamen. From the former he received almost worshipful gratitude, which he invariably turned aside with firm courtesy. Thank God alone, he told each one.

In the surgery set up at the building's rear, they found Elizabeth's father preparing to amputate the infected arm of one of *Invictus's* seamen wounded in the battle. They stopped to confer for some moments, and Dr. Howard's calm, forthright manner set Carleton at ease. Pleased, he concluded that Elizabeth was right and that he and her father would surely regain the warm friendship they had enjoyed before the Howards moved to London.

He asked Lemaire whether letters were being sent to the men's families as he had directed, to which the doctor responded in the affirmative. Although the number of patients made it a daunting task, those who could write to their relatives had been given paper and pen to do so. The nurses were recording the others' information as quickly as they could and had begun to send out notifications.

At last Lemaire conducted him to the beds of Captain Josiah Hutchinson, Ensign Tom Spencer, and Seaman Billy Finnegan, whose mother and sisters clustered anxiously around his cot. Like their fellows, the three men were hollow-eyed, so gaunt their bones stood out beneath their skin. But each already showed enough improvement that Billy's mother hoped within a fortnight to take him home to their North End inn, where she and his sisters could manage his care. Carleton was quickly impressed by the intelligence and spirit of Elizabeth's guardians and thanked them earnestly for all they had done for her and for joining in the takeover of the *Erebus*.

Hunched on the edge of his cot, Josiah spoke for all of them when he said, "It's ye we have to thank, gen'l. Why, ye risked everythin' by invading the very nest o' the enemy in order to bring us out. How could we do any less? As for Beth—Miss Howard—why, she wahr like a sister or a sweetheart to us. There wahrn't a one aboard that hulk that would-n't ha' given our lives for her."

"Beth feels the same way toward you." Carleton included Billy and Tom in his glance. "She told me of your kindness and that she'd not have survived had it not been for your care and protection. I can't tell you how deeply grateful I am."

"How is she, sir?" Billy blurted. "Dr. Lemaire told us she's doin' a mite better, but she were real sick, and we been worryin' 'bout 'er ever since we were took aboard yer ship."

"She's out of danger, Billy, but I'm afraid she has a long recovery ahead of her."

"Might it be possible for the three o' us to call on her soon's she's well enough for visitors, sir?" Tom asked. "That is, if she'd like to see us, and it's not too great an imposition."

"She wants very much to see you and asked about you just this morning. But first she must get stronger, and all of you must be well enough to bear the ride to Roxbury in the cold."

"O' course, sir," the men echoed, beaming. "Just give us the word when the time's right."

"We'd given ourselves up for lost, gen'l," Josiah broke in. "When your ships showed up—well, it wahr a miracle straight and simple." He indicated their surroundings with a wave of his hand. "This place's like heaven itself compared to where we wahr held. We're all prayin' that none ever has to endure such misery again in all the world."

"I'll gladly join you in that prayer," Carleton returned. "And may God grant it in his mercy."

CARLETON LEFT THE HOSPITAL to find Eaden and Rodrigo waiting for him, along with their first lieutenants. Riding in the chariot Tess had lent him, they headed north toward Thornton's shipyard, stopping along the way for a congenial lunch at the Salutation tavern. An hour later they traveled the short distance to the shipyard where *Destiny* and *Invictus* lay on their sides, rigging and masts removed, with workers crawling over their exposed hulls at work on repairs. Satisfied at the progress being made, Carleton took leave of his companions and headed back to his warehouse just off Long Wharf.

It was a blustery overcast day with the cold wind gusting out of the northwest. As the chariot turned south past the North Battery onto Ship Street, sunbeams slanted through the threatening clouds, bringing the four-mile compass of the expansive harbor into vivid focus.

Where Ship curved into Fish Street, he ordered the driver to a halt in front of Paul Revere's silver shop and left the chariot to walk a short distance out onto Hancock's Wharf. He took in a deep breath of the air, heavily tinged with the odors of smoke and salt water and tar; canvas and hempen rigging; decaying wood, seaweed, and fish. A welter of memories assailed him.

More than a dozen islands studded the bay. Standing a league distant, Castle Island was crowned by the charred remains of Fort William, whose formidable compliment of cannon had guarded the port's only roadstead for ships of burthen until the British destroyed it with a flaming barrage when they abandoned the town.

Boston, with its narrow, crooked streets; quaint, crowded buildings; and tall church steeples occupied an arrow-shaped, hill-studded peninsula that jutted into the bay. High bluffs encircled the harbor all along the mainland's expansive curve, from Dorchester Heights to the south, to Charlestown peninsula and Noddle's Island close off the North End, to Hog Island and a narrow strip of mainland to the northeast that gave way to the ocean at the harbor's broad entrance.

Most of the town's inhabitants had returned since the end of the siege. Carleton noted with satisfaction that the destruction the British had inflicted during their occupation was steadily being repaired.

Seamen, businessmen, and shoppers swarmed along the waterfront with apparent good cheer, while ships lined up at the wharves to disgorge their wares.

In spite of the worn fabric of his uniform, evident close up, his tall figure and the flowing crest of his helmet drew many glances and the arch looks and smiles of passing women as he returned to the chariot. The equipage followed the peninsula's gradual eastward curve to Dock Square; past Fanueil Hall, the scene of many inflammatory rebel meetings leading up to that disastrous confrontation on Lexington Green; and finally to Long Wharf.

Over the door of a large warehouse that stretched along the south side of the dock, fronting on Kilby Street and directly across from the Bunch of Grapes tavern, swung a modest sign in the form of a globe with a ship emblazoned across it and the inscription Carleton Imports. Closed when the British shut the harbor down in 1774, following the destruction of a shipload of tea, it had reopened in late 1776, some months after Washington had taken command of the rebel force besieging the town and had driven the British out.

The sun hung low over the southwestern hills by the time he emerged. Although he was all but certain the new manager Teissèdre had installed was a player in the Frenchman's intrigues, Carleton was greatly heartened by the man's competence and the volume of business the office handled after being so long shuttered.

Two more of his merchantmen had arrived earlier in the day with holds full of goods from the Orient. From their cargo he had chosen bolts of cloth to be sent to his tailor and a number more to be delivered to Roxbury.

He stopped by the tailor shop on Court Street to order new clothing and the men's furnishings shop next door for shoes, boots, and other necessaries. At a gunshop he found a finely crafted, German-made Pennsylvania long rifle with a matched set of rifled pistols, and from one of the numerous bookstores around the corner on Cornhill, he purchased a Bible to replace the one he had given Red Fox. At last, with dusk falling, he climbed into the chariot and eagerly directed the driver back to Roxbury.

# Chapter Twenty-six

"OH, JONATHAN!" Elizabeth gasped, gathering the generous length of luxurious, shrimp-colored silk brocade into her arms. "I've never seen anything so exquisite!"

Curled up warmly bundled on a deep wing chair next to the drawing room fire, she fingered one of the scattered clusters of embroidered flowers that interspersed the creamy stripes running the fabric's length. When she looked up, the emotion she read in Carleton's eyes brought a blush to her cheeks.

"I couldn't resist. It had to be yours."

Anne and Tess, seated on the nearby sofa with Abby, Sarah, and Jemma kneeling on the floor in front of them, exclaimed in wonder as they sorted through the bolts of rich fabrics, silk fly fringe, French and Italian lace, buttons, and other trims that had been delivered to the mansion shortly before Carleton returned from town.

"Sir, we simply can't accept such generous gifts," Dr. Howard remonstrated, though Elizabeth noted a reluctance in his voice and the pleasure he could not quite conceal.

"Papa, how can we refuse Jonathan's kindness?" Elizabeth pleaded.

"I'd be quite pleased if you'd indulge me."

"But the cost—"

"—is not great, truly." Carleton left his post beside Elizabeth's chair to join her father, who stood behind Sarah, surveying the treasures spilled across the floor. "My agents get very good prices on the goods they purchase. These just arrived in shipments from Canton and Nantes. When I saw them, I thought of all of you immediately and had to have them."

Elizabeth laid the cloth across her lap. "But your own wardrobe is . . ."

Carleton laughed. "Deplorable? I know. Stowe minced no words in ordering me to amend my slovenly ways. Be assured that I've ordered new linens, suits, uniforms, even boots and shoes, and every possible accoutrement for myself. In short, I shall soon be a veritable paragon of fashion, I promise."

"No doubt you'll burst upon our quaint local society like a regular macaroni," Elizabeth teased. "I shall be reduced to beating off my rivals with my parasol."

Turning a significant look on her that deepened her blush, he murmured, "My love, you have no rivals."

"Samuel, this moss-green wool is perfect for a new suit for you—which you're much in need of for the winter!" Anne rose to drape a length of fabric over her husband's shoulder. "It'll be so fashionable, and warm too."

"Oh, and look at this!" Tess held up a length of striped silk. "It'll make an elegant waistcoat, don't you think?"

"Exactly my reasoning." Carleton bent to hand Abby a length of heavyweight sky-blue silk interwoven with gold metallic thread that shimmered in a delicate floral pattern. "I thought you might like this."

She clutched it, looking up at him in delight. "Oh, thank you! It's just what I wanted, but I thought surely it couldn't be for me."

"The color's perfect for you."

"You'll look like a princess, Abby!" Elizabeth exclaimed.

Indicating a shot silk taffeta brocade striped in colors of blue, cream, and maroon and thickly sprinkled with off-white asters that made Elizabeth sigh, Carleton said, "Perhaps this for you, Anne."

"I confess I had the very same idea," Anne conceded with a dimpled smile.

"And if you like the faille, Tess—"

Sarah appropriated the royal blue fabric, hand-painted with flowers and ornate scrollwork. "Couldn't be better with your coloring, Miz Howard, and I got the perfect pattern in mind."

Tess stroked the supple length. "I haven't had anything so fine since I left England, and that's been a long time. Thank you, Jon. It's lovely."

She seemed preoccupied, Elizabeth thought, studying her. Since Carleton's arrival, her aunt had hardly spoken and avoided his gaze.

Before Elizabeth could question her, however, Jemma asked shyly, "What of these?" as she turned over bolts of soft ruby and indigo wool.

"I wondered if you and your mother might make good use of them."

Jemma gathered the bolts possessively to her breast, and both women beamed at Carleton. "Thank you, gen'l," Sarah said. "You be too kind."

"Papa, don't you dare forbid us to accept these! You'll have a mutiny on your hands if you do," Elizabeth warned with mock ferocity.

Samuel threw up his hands, unable to suppress a smile. "It appears I'm overruled. Well, I know better than to oppose the ladies."

"I'd be quite disappointed if you refused to accept these small tokens as a measure of my gratitude for your kind hospitality—not to mention your work at the hospital, Samuel. The welfare of my crews and the men we freed is quite dear to my heart, and I very much appreciate your efforts in their care."

Mollified, Dr. Howard waved his words away. "Not necessary. Not at all. But . . . thank you, Jon."

He was enthusiastically echoed by the women. Delighted by the warmth of her father's tone, Elizabeth reluctantly surrendered the shrimp-colored silk to Sarah, who, with Jemma, had begun to gather up the cloth and trims.

"I send for the seamstress first thing in the mornin'," Sarah told her. "She need to take new measurements for you."

"Let me have this, Sarah. I'll cut and sew Dr. Howard's suit myself." Elizabeth's mother relieved the housekeeper of the green wool, and the women retreated up the stairs in the direction of the sewing room.

"And now, my girl, it's past time for you to be abed. I'm afraid my doubts about bringing you down so soon were warranted. I don't like those dark circles under your eyes."

"No, Papa, I'm fine, truly. Please let me stay and have dinner with everyone."

"It's an hour yet until dinner," Dr. Howard reminded her sternly. "You've been up for more than two hours already, and I don't want you to suffer a setback."

Carleton stroked her cheek with the back of his hand. "Your father's right. You're worn out. It's been hardly more than a day since your fever broke."

Elizabeth surrendered with a sigh, but insisted that she was strong enough to walk without assistance. When she rose with Carleton's help, however, dizziness overcame her, and she would have fallen had he not supported her. Giving her a reproachful look, he swept her up into his arms and carried her upstairs.

"No more protests, dear heart," Carleton commanded. "Jemma's bringing up a tray, and I'll sit with you while you eat. Then you must go to sleep."

"I am tired," Elizabeth admitted. She settled back against the pillows and gave him a knowing look. "I have to say you're exceedingly clever in managing Papa."

Carleton conceded a chuckle. "Now, it wasn't entirely subterfuge meant to draw attention from my giving you such a personal gift. I'm blessed to have the means to give nice things to the people who mean a great deal to me, and I take delight in doing so."

"I know you do." She pursed her lips. "And, of course, you knew it was the surest way to accomplish your goal."

He folded his arms, regarding her with smug satisfaction. "It worked, didn't it?"

Elizabeth could not suppress a smile. "Your charm is quite irresistible when you mean it to be. Why, Abby's entirely smitten with you."

He chuckled. "I'm smitten with her too—though even more so with her sister. She's going to be as beautiful as your mother when she grows up, and as sweet tempered."

"Don't you ever dare say that one day she'll make someone a fine wife!"

He gave her a languid look. "The thought hadn't crossed my mind."

She drew away from him with a flounce. "That's what all men say. As if the only thing a woman is capable of is marrying advantageously."

He drew her back into his arms, laughing down at her. "Someday you'll make me a very fine wife, though I'm well aware that there's much more that you can do. And as a Shawnee wife, you'll certainly have all the independence you could ever want."

"And I mean to make full use of it too," she answered saucily.

No longer able to resist, he bent to silence her with a kiss, and her passionate response drove every other thought from his mind. At length he reluctantly pulled back, the sight of her rosy cheeks and heaving bosom leaving him dizzy with desire. It required considerable effort for him to regain control of his emotions.

"You know how to please me too," she murmured, touching his lips with the tips of her fingers.

He captured her hand. "My dearest wish is to spend all my life pleasing you."

He released her quickly when Jemma entered, carrying a bed tray laden with a small teapot and cup, a bowl of hot chicken broth, and a wedge of toasted brown bread. When Elizabeth had eaten, she motioned to Jemma to wait before removing the tray.

"I told you I have a surprise for you," she said to Carleton.

"You need rest now," he objected, frowning. "Whatever it is, it can wait until morning."

"I've waited too long already. Jemma, will you bring it, please?"

Carleton glanced after the maid as she hurried to the large armoire across the chamber, then turned back to Elizabeth, eyebrow raised. "You're quite mysterious."

"Close your eyes," she admonished. "And don't you dare peek."

Amused, Carleton complied, leaning back in the chair, eyes firmly closed. He heard Jemma return to the bed, then quietly withdraw from the chamber.

"You can open your eyes now."

He did so—and stared at the object Elizabeth held out to him, stunned. "My violin!" he exclaimed, taking the case eagerly. "You've kept it all this time. I assumed it had been lost."

"I'd never turn loose of it except to give it back to you. During those dark days after your disappearance, when I most feared what your fate had been, this was my only comfort. I used to hold it to my breast like a babe. It bears your touch and your spirit, and from time to time I drew the bow across the strings, certain that it would cease to play if you were not still alive."

His throat too tight for speech, he laid the case on the bed and opened it to reveal the gleaming instrument inside, still disbelieving. Drawing it out, he caressed the mellow wood.

"When I was a child, Sir Harry gave me a small violin just my size and taught me to play," he explained. "I was very young and, I confess, more than a little rebellious at the beginning, but he made a wonderful game of our lessons. Playing our violins together taught me to love him even more, to own him as my own dear father, and to feel I could do nothing wrong in his eyes."

"How you must miss him!"

"I do, very much." He looked up, sadness giving way to happy memories. "For my tenth birthday, he took me along to Italy on a business trip. He bought this for me in Rome, and when we returned home, he engaged an excellent teacher for me. Striving for mastery of the violin became one of the greatest pleasures of my life."

He stood, tucked the violin under his chin, and took up the bow. As he pulled it across the strings, he marveled that although the instrument needed tuning, the purity of its clear tones remained unchanged from the last time he had played it.

"I wanted to return it to you earlier, but I'd left it here for fear it would suffer damage from cold and damp while we traveled or that it might be lost or stolen," she explained. "So I decided to say nothing until I could give it back to you."

"Thank you, dearest, for keeping it safe! All the years I was in England, believing the lies my elder half-brother told me, there were times when this was my one true companion and solace, the only thing I could trust. It's more precious to me than I can say."

"I've longed so dearly to hear you play it again."

He grimaced. "It remains to be seen whether I can still play tolerably. I'm woefully out of practice, and you might be less than thrilled."

He applied resin to the bow and drew it across the strings, wincing as he adjusted the tuning. After several false starts, he succeeded in playing through the scales without hitting too many sour notes. Pacing back and forth across the chamber, he played them again several times, more slowly, adjusting his fingering and the movement of the bow, until he was pleased at his improvement.

"See, you're doing better already," she said approvingly.

"I suspect everyone will be a great deal happier if I practice where no one can hear."

She laughed. "I asked Mama and Papa, and they suggested the library. They're delighted at the prospect of having someone to play for us in the evenings. Papa loves to sing, and he has a fine voice."

"Then I'll bend every effort to improving my abilities."

"Do you remember the first time I heard you play, that night at Gage's ball before the march to Concord? I was certain it was a trick meant to lure me into dancing with you."

"It was the only thing I could think of that might tempt you into my arms," he admitted with a laugh.

"And I was so cruel to you. Surely you know it was because I was already falling in love with you. I didn't want to—or so I kept telling myself. You were a British officer, after all, and I was terrified you'd discover my involvement with the patriots."

He returned the violin to its case. Sitting on the bed beside her, he took her in his arms. "I was already head over heels when we collided that afternoon and I held you in my arms for the first time. Looking down into your sweet face, I knew at once you were the one. But you were a loyal Tory, and I kept telling myself I could never have you."

"If only we'd trusted the Lord enough to open our hearts to one another then, we'd have spared ourselves so much pain."

He tipped up her face to his, murmuring, "But God had his way after all."

"That he did."

She melted into his arms, and again he forgot all else.

*Chapter Twenty-seven*

*Tuesday, 18 November*

ANDREWS DIRECTED a sidelong glance at Isaiah and Stowe, who waited motionless beside him in front of Washington's writing table. They stared straight ahead, their expressions blank, and Andrews suspected that both men shared his emotions. Carleton's triumph over the British felt bittersweet, for exultation mingled with grief over Vander Groot's death.

While the General finished reading the report they had delivered, Andrews noted with sympathy that his brow was furrowed with lines of strain and weariness. The previous Saturday a brutal British bombardment had finally driven the tenacious American defenders out of Fort Mifflin on the Delaware. For months the fortress had anchored the Continental Army's defenses below Philadelphia, preventing the Royal Navy from clearing the river channel of obstructions laid by the American force. With its destruction, Admiral Howe would be able to freely supply the city—and his brother's troops—by sea.

Washington suddenly looked up, a fierce smile lighting his eyes. "This is most welcome news coming on the heels of Fort Mifflin's fall. Very well done, gentlemen."

Isaiah glanced cautiously at Andrews, and at his nod, said, "Thank you, Your Excellency."

"What of Miss Howard? Her health was improving when you left?"

"It was, sir," Stowe acknowledged. " 'er fever broke the day afore, but looked as 'ow she still had a long ways to go."

"We will trust that the Almighty will quickly restore her to health." Rising, Washington came around the table. "The death of Major Vander Groot is especially regrettable, considering that his efforts were invaluable in carrying out this mission. Losses are inevitable in such actions, but I know this is a great one to the brigade, as to his family. You will call upon his parents personally, Colonel Andrews?"

"I plan to go to Lancaster tomorrow to offer General Carleton's condolences and my own." Dread filled Andrews at the prospect.

"Please add mine as well."

After he dismissed Isaiah and Stowe, Washington's visage relaxed into a rare smile. "General Carleton has struck a great blow for our cause, and I will make certain this news is widely spread. There is no need for you to keep this matter silent any longer, Colonel Andrews. I will send a copy of the report to Congress immediately, and I am sure they will make the best use of it, as I urge you to. With Congress having sent the Articles of Confederation to the states early this week," he added, eyes narrowing, "it may be that this victory, added to that at Saratoga, will encourage the legislatures to make no delay in ratifying them."

"I'll sow the news to the wind," Andrews promised, smiling.

"General Carleton intends to stay at Boston to oversee repairs to his ships."

Andrews cited the damage to *Invictus* and *Destiny* and Carleton's concern for the injured sailors and the sick among the freed prisoners, in addition to Elizabeth's fragile health. "His report to me indicated that he'll likely be needed at Boston through Christmas," he concluded cautiously.

As he had feared, this news did not please Washington. He conceded grudgingly, however, that as long as there was no indication that the

British planned a concerted effort to break out of the city, Carleton could be spared a while longer.

"My source at General Howe's headquarters reports that the reward for General Carleton—whether dead or alive—has been doubled."

Andrews's chest tightened. "Not unexpected, sir."

"I plan to send an express courier to General Carleton later this week detailing the situation here, and I will add a warning, though I am sure he is well aware of the dangers. I assume you wish to write to General Carleton and perhaps Miss Howard as well, and if so, give any letters to Laurens as soon as you return from Lancaster. He will include them with mine."

"I'll do so, Your Excellency. Thank you." Certain Washington meant to read his correspondence before releasing it, Andrews kept his expression neutral.

"As far as Miss Howard is concerned . . . " Washington paused before continuing, "well, we can only hope that the British command will consider her inaccessible now."

Andrews read the same skepticism in his commander's gaze that he felt. "She wasn't the one who so publicly tweaked their noses." he responded hopefully.

"I believe this was more than a tweak to the nose."

Andrews gave a short laugh. "The troops we captured during skirmishes with Howe's light horse were already aware of General Carleton's attack. Rumors also reached a number of the local loyalists intercepted on our patrols. None of those we interrogated had anything kind to say about the folly of Clinton and the brothers Howe."

"Then it is already affecting our enemy's morale," Washington returned with satisfaction. "I am confident it will have a more salutary effect on the corps and our friends."

To Andrews's surprise, he continued, "Colonel, you've impressed me with your abilities and dedication in commanding the brigade in General Carleton's absence. The discipline, order, and morale of your troops are an example to the army as a whole. And your efforts in patrolling your sector have shut down significant traffic in and out of Philadelphia."

Andrews's mouth dropped open, but he quickly clamped it shut. "Thank you, Your Excellency."

Another faint smile softened the weary lines of Washington's face. "Now, both of us have work to do. Good day, Colonel Andrews. Please send Mr. Laurens in on your way out."

Andrews choked back a laugh. He saluted and went out. In the passage he found Laurens leaning against the wall next to the door, his aspect forlorn.

"I can't bear this suspense much longer, Andrews," he complained. 'If someone doesn't tell me what's going on soon—"

Grinning, Andrews cut him off, jerking his head toward the room he just had vacated. "I think you're about to find out. He wants you."

He headed outside, chuckling as behind him Laurens threw open the parlor door and said brightly, "How can I be of assistance, sir?"

TRUE TO WASHINGTON'S WORD, bolstered by Andrews's efforts, news of Carleton's audacious raid on New York Harbor raced through the corps. It caused a sensation that soon had the entire camp in a tumult.

Within an hour officers and enlisted men alike from the other brigades besieged the Rangers' headquarters, gleefully demanding firsthand accounts of the action from Isaiah, Stowe, Andrews, and anyone else they could corner. For their part, the warriors strode proudly through the camp, pointing out to any who would listen that it was their war chief White Eagle who had accomplished this triumph.

Wednesday morning, knowing the meeting with the Vander Groots could not be delayed, Andrews left for Lancaster, escorted by his guard. He took Isaiah and Stowe with him in the hope that their account of the major's vital role in the attack would offer some comfort to the bereaved family. McLeod also accompanied them for the solace he might be able to offer.

Slowed by a drizzle that turned the roads to mud, they arrived on the afternoon of the second day and were quickly directed to the estate of Martin Lamb, the fiancé of Vander Groot's sister. The interview that followed was even more wrenching than Andrews had feared.

Angry, outraged, and overcome by grief at the unexpected news, the elder Vander Groots bitterly questioned the reasons for their son's involvement in a perilous mission made necessary by the roles Carleton and Elizabeth had voluntarily chosen as spies. Vander Groot's effects and final letter only caused greater pain. McLeod's gentle ministration soothed their distress to some degree, and their younger son, Christiaan and his sister, Isobel, along with her fiancé, strove to comfort them as best they could from the depths of their own grief. But all their efforts had little effect on the rawness of Mr. and Mrs. Vander Groot's emotions.

All Andrews and his companions could do was to offer words of condolence that sounded hollow. To the family's demand to speak directly to Carleton and Elizabeth, Andrews answered that Carleton would call upon them upon his return from Boston, but that Elizabeth was far too ill to travel for the foreseeable future.

Although he understood the Vander Groots' anguish and could not blame them for their anger, the encounter hung over Andrews like a heavy weight and affected his companions in equal measure. It was late by the time they left Lamb's estate, and with the rain increasing to a downpour, they found lodgings in Lancaster, speaking little of the matter or any other that night.

The detachment had just set out the following morning under clearing skies, when they were abruptly halted by a sudden severe shaking of the earth that caused the horses to neigh and fight the reins, ears laid back and eyes rolling wildly. It took all their efforts to keep the animals under control, but at last the earth settled and their mounts quieted. Exchanging alarmed looks and with nerves on edge, they rode on.

They reached the Rangers' camp shortly before noon on Saturday to find Colonel Tilghman impatiently pacing up and down in front of Andrews's headquarters. Taking one look at the aide's face, Andrews said grimly, "What now?"

Tilghman shook his head. "The General will explain."

After dismissing the rest of his party, Andrews accompanied Tilghman to Washington's headquarters, wondering bleakly what new disaster had befallen. The news could hardly have been worse.

"I'm beginning to believe that earthquake this morning was a portent of renewed disasters," Washington told him, appearing more shaken than Andrews had ever seen his commander. "Yesterday the British burned Hazelwood's navy in the Delaware. Then just a little while ago I learned that Howe has set a number of mansions in Germantown to the torch as retaliation for all the skirmishes he's had with our cavalry."

Cutting off Andrews' exclamation of angry disgust, he continued heavily, "But that's not the worst. This arrived from Governor Henry last evening." He extended a letter from Virginia governor Patrick Henry. "Cornstalk was murdered at Fort Randolph a fortnight ago."

Stunned, Andrews took the letter and sank into a chair. He scanned the closely written pages, fighting to make sense of the words, while refusing to accept their meaning.

Cornstalk, the great Shawnee sachem and warrior had gone to Fort Randolph to warn its commander that he could no longer control his people's war faction. Along with large numbers from many other tribes, Shawnee warriors were flocking to ally with the British. Attacks led by Black Fish on the American settlements along the Ohio that summer were only the first wave of what he feared was to come.

The fort's commander, Captain Arbuckle, had immediately taken Cornstalk hostage, along with Red Hawk, another notable Shawnee sachem, and a warrior named Petalla, knowing that the Shawnee sachem was held in such high regard by all the tribes that they would stay their attacks as long as he was held in custody. And when Cornstalk's son Ellinipisco came to visit him, Arbuckle detained him as well. Yet Cornstalk willingly cooperated with his captors, hoping to hold back the rising tide of war.

Then disaster intervened. Soldiers from the garrison brought into the fort the body of one of their number killed and scalped by Indians. In blind rage they broke into the blockhouse where Cornstalk and his companions were held and, although they offered no resistance, brutally executed the unarmed men with a volley of bullets.

" 'Vile assassins,' Governor Henry calls them," Andrews said, bitterness lacing his tone. "An apt description, considering that Cornstalk and his companions were held prisoner in the fort at the time the soldier was murdered. But doubtless they think that four innocent red men is not too high a price for one white man."

Washington stalked around the room, radiating suppressed fury. "Governor Henry promises that he will investigate the incident fully and bring the murderers to justice."

Andrews gave a contemptuous laugh. "You think any of their fellows will testify against them? Nothing will be done."

"I fear you're right," Washington conceded, his face darkening. "Without testimony against them, Governor Henry's hands are tied. The truth, however, is that much of the responsibility for Cornstalk's death must be laid at the feet of Black Fish. The soldiers were doubtless on edge because of his recent attacks on the border settlements. Governor Henry is concerned enough that he delegated a man named George Rogers Clark to raise a regiment of militia to put down these attacks."

"Well, that justifies the murders then," Andrews retorted with scathing sarcasm. "No matter that Cornstalk used his influence to oppose this very thing because of his treaty with Lord Dunmore. Had the settlers respected the treaty as much as he did and kept out of Indian lands, Black Fish would have had no reason to ally with our enemies."

Washington stared out the window, rubbing his brow. "Be that as it may, all hope of securing Shawnee neutrality may well be entirely lost now. In one fell swoop, these miscreants wiped away the advantage they held, and who knows what retribution the tribes will exact for it."

He rounded on Andrews. "I am sending a courier off to Boston as soon as possible with orders for General Carleton to return immediately." Abruptly he added, "I will also notify him that Congress approved my recommendation for his promotion to major general and yours to brigadier."

*How thoughful of you to cast us a bone to distract us from this outrage.*

Andrews bit his tongue to suppress the caustic reply. He gave his superior a look that Washington countered with an icy one.

"In the meantime, I do not wish General Carleton to learn of Cornstalk's death until I can discuss it with him face to face. You are to tell no one of this. Do I make myself clear?"

"I won't conceal this from my warriors," Andrews snapped, stiffening. "For one thing, they'd never trust me again. And to be quite frank, I'm not capable of covering up an injustice of this magnitude."

"Sir, you have my orders. Take care, for you tread very close to insubordination."

"If you insist on my silence, you place me in an impossible position. There is an authority greater than yours, Your Excellency. And that I obey."

Washington regarded him, tightlipped. "I need not remind you of the destruction another Indian war will cause. If you have any concern for your wife and child—"

Livid, Andrews rasped, "Don't reproach me with that! There's nothing more dear to me than they are. There's not a second when their safety is not on my mind."

Sick at heart, he locked his gaze with Washington's hard stare. Although terror for Blue Sky and their son overwhelmed him, he knew absolutely that on this point he could not yield.

At length Washington gave an impatient shrug and said sharply, "Very well. In this one instance, then, I give you leave. But you must swear to me on your honor that you will not speak of this matter to the rest of your brigade nor communicate it to General Carleton until I meet with him. And if you do not keep control of your warriors, I assure you, sir, there will be grave consequences for you personally."

Andrews hesitated, furious, yet feeling he had nowhere to turn. Finally he conceded a curt nod.

"I'll do as much as I can, but I'll not answer for my warriors' reaction. Every one of them may well desert us at once, and how am I to stop them? Indeed, I wouldn't blame them. And I'll not hold them hostage even had I the power to do so."

Washington flinched, clearly stung by the jab. "That's enough, sir," he reproved, his visage hard as adamant. "I expect you to bend every effort to persuade them to stay at least until General Carleton returns."

"That may not be possible. This will come as a hard blow—not only to our warriors, but also to General Carleton. He admires and loves Cornstalk deeply, and I fear—" Andrews stopped abruptly, shaking his head.

"That is why I wish to talk to him first," Washington said, his harsh tone softening. "He holds a unique position of influence with the Shawnee and may be our only hope of avoiding a war that will be ruinous to everyone concerned. Indeed, I would not have him act rashly for his own sake, and perhaps I may be able to prevent that."

EVERY WARRIOR WHO HAD REMAINED with the brigade crowded into the cramped parlor of Andrews's headquarters. The air was charged with grief, fury, and cries for vengeance. Andrews directed an alarmed glance at Spotted Pony, who met it with one of such dark savagery that his breath constricted.

"Before the sun rose high in the sky yesterday, did not the earth itself cry out because of the murder of Cornstalk and Ellinipisco?" demanded Brown Bear, shaking his fist in emphasis.

"We Delaware are as insulted by these Long Knives' evil deeds as you, our brothers!" Sinking Ground cried, striking his breast with his fist.

"Do any of us believe these *motchitteheckie* will ever punish the murderers?" another warrior shouted. "They are *wannine!*"

Andrews raised his hands to still their cries. "Governor Henry is as outraged as we are, and he promised to investigate the matter—"

A tumult of angry protests immediately cut him off. "He swore to send this man Clark against us to destroy our villages and kill our women and children," Brown Bear said fiercely.

"There will be no justice from the Long Knives," Striking Snake, one of the Mingo warriors growled.

"All of us must return at once to our people." Spotted Pony's voice shook with emotion as he continued, "We Shawnee will counsel with Black Fish and Blue Jacket. You, brothers, must consult your councils and decide what course your people will follow."

Andrews rounded on his friend. "Will you also turn your back on White Eagle—and on Cornstalk? Did not both of them counsel us against war with the Long Knives?"

"White Eagle is not here," Brown Bear pointed out, "and Cornstalk has gone to the wigewas of Moneto. We must make our own way now."

Andrews stared at him in disbelief. "Then the Long Knives will surely overcome us. It is only in our unity that we have any hope of prevailing."

He looked from one warrior to the next. The tears of grief that glistened in many of the men's eyes caused his throat to tighten.

"Washington is sending for White Eagle to come at once. He will surely return early in *Washilatha kiishthwa,* the Eccentric Moon. My brothers, let us wait until we can counsel with him. He will help us to determine the most prudent course."

Brown Bear raised his tomahawk and shook it over his head. "The most prudent course is war!"

Andrews glanced at Spotted Pony. As their eyes met, to Andrews's relief, the warrior's stance relaxed. Spotted Pony lowered his chin in a grudging nod, then lifted his hand to cut off the shouts of agreement that answered Brown Bear's outcry.

"No, my brothers, Golden Elk speaks wisely. This is indeed the way of ruin as we have all seen many times. Let us wait until White Eagle returns. The winter snows and the hunger time are almost upon us, and our people must eat and secure their lodges against the cold if they are to endure until the sun strengthens again. Neither we nor the Long Knives can take up the tomahawk before *Pooshkwiitha,* the Half Moon. If we are to have any hope of prevailing over the Long Knives, we must counsel together to plan a wise course, and then make preparation to follow it."

It was dusk before the warriors finally calmed enough to pledge that they would stay until White Eagle's return. When he was alone, Andrews slumped into a chair, his head in his hands.

For some moments he mused on his promotion to brigadier. There had been a time when that would have meant everything to him. But now . . .

That he felt a deep allegiance and responsibility to the Rangers was without question. In spite of their very real differences, he also respected and admired Washington greatly, as well as Patrick Henry and other patriot leaders he had come to know. He believed with all his heart in the fight for freedom they had undertaken.

There was the rub.

The truth was that by his marriage, and especially in the birth of his son, he was now as inextricably bound to the Shawnee as was Carleton. He could not imagine taking his wife and son away from them—from their heritage—to live among the Whites. Indeed he rejected the possibility.

When he was with them, he not only spoke the Shawnee tongue, but had begun to think in it as well, reasoned increasingly as they did. He answered to the name of Golden Elk with as little thought as he did to his English name. And now his conscience accused him of betraying his new kindred by yielding to Washington's demand that he persuade them to stay with the corps and be tamely resigned to the murder of their great leader.

Were the native peoples not as justified in seeking to protect their homes and families—and their freedom? he quesstioned. Was it not rank hypocrisy for the Whites to deny them this, while claiming to fight for the glorious cause of liberty?

He sat up and raked his fingers through his hair, releasing a sigh of frustration. Some months earlier he had sworn that when this war ended he would return with Blue Sky to their people and not walk among the Long Knives again. Yet then he had sensed only dimly what that decision meant. Now he felt it viscerally, not just with his head, but in his heart and in the depths of his soul. And he despaired of continuing to walk a course between the Shawnee and his white life when daily it became harder to justify and maintain.

Concern and love for Blue Sky and He Leads the Way consumed him, and with an intensity he had never known, he longed to go to them, to guard their safety and fight for their freedom. He would gladly give his life if need be. Day by day the loneliness that oppressed him in their absence grew less tolerable until he felt his deepest being cut in twain as if by a sabre's strike.

Would Carleton heed Washington's summons to leave Elizabeth and return to the corps right away, when he had no knowledge of the reason? At the earliest, even if he left immediately on receiving the message, a fortnight would pass before he reached them. And then how would he react to the news of Black Fish's war and the deaths of Cornstalk and his companions?

Andrews got up and moved restlessly around the darkening room, feeling foreboding shadows gather around him. Like the others, he had no choice but to bide his time for now. But as he brooded over the days to come, the certainty overwhelmed him that the war Black Fish had begun and the murder of Cornstalk and his companions that followed could only give birth to monstrous and bloody offspring.

# Chapter Twenty-eight

*Thursday, 27 November*

"Josiah!" Elizabeth laid aside the book she had been reading while curled up in the wing chair in front of the fire. Pushing aside the blanket, she sat up, hastily straightening her cherry-colored caraco and striped, quilted petticoat, and eagerly reached out to the lean soldier who hesitated on the drawing room's threshold.

"Tom—Billy!" she exclaimed when they stepped into the room behind Josiah. "Oh, how well you all look!"

Edging farther into the room, the three men bowed, to all appearances intimidated by their surroundings. When Elizabeth beckoned them, they cast apologetic glances in the direction of the other women, then hurried to her side to take her hands.

Anne, Tess, and Abby immediately put down their sewing and came to join them, while Sarah and Jemma pulled chairs close to Elizabeth's before quietly withdrawing. When Elizabeth had introduced everyone and they were all seated, Abby squeezed next to her on the chair and shyly nestled her head against Elizabeth's shoulder as she drew her into her embrace.

"Aw, you put me in mind o' my littlest sister, Miss Abby," Josiah ventured, drawing the young girl's blushing smile. "She's right about your age and 'most as purty."

"They've found your sisters?"

He beamed at Elizabeth. "Thanks to Gen'l Carleton. They're livin' with a distant cousin, and they're all right and doin' just fine. They been told I'm comin' home."

"General Carleton promised to bring you out today," Tess broke in, her glance warm. "I'm glad you've come. We're truly honored to have you with us."

"We can't thank you enough for caring for Elizabeth despite your own suffering," Anne added. "She told us of your kindness and protection."

"Ma'am, it wahrn't more'n any man'd do, and we counted it a privilege," Josiah protested, directing a grateful glance at Elizabeth. "Miss Beth is a right angel. She took care o' the sick and encouraged those as was losin' hope until she got too sick herself to do more. It's us as wahr blessed by havin' her with us."

Billy and Tom fervently echoed his sentiments, bringing a blush into Elizabeth's cheeks. Earnestly she studied the men she had until now seen only briefly by torchlight and by flashes of lightning during the rescue. At first sight of their clean-shaven visages, she had almost not recognized them. Josiah's craggy features had filled out pleasingly, as had those of his companions, and he breathed easily again, with only an occasional cough. She was surprised to see that his hair gleamed a rich mahogany and that his eyes were a warm hazel.

Tom she found to be quietly handsome, a couple of inches shorter than Josiah, with sandy hair and mild blue eyes. And Billy sported freckles and green eyes in addition to hair the color of polished copper.

"Papa and Dr. Lemaire are taking very good care of you it appears."

The men did not spare any praise for their doctors and nurses, but especially for Carleton. The hospital was to be shut down at the end of the month, Josiah reported, with those who were well enough being transported to their homes. The few in need of continuing care would be transferred to a private home Carleton had bought to convert into a hospital for ill and injured sailors.

The women exchanged glances. "He never said a word about this," Anne exclaimed, directing a smile at Elizabeth. "But we're coming to expect such reticence from the general about his good works."

The men murmured agreement. Then Billy proudly announced that he had been home with his family for more than a week and that he had signed up to serve on *Invictus* when she and *Destiny* sailed. Tom added that he was leaving for his Delaware farm the following day along with several others headed that direction, and Josiah explained that he would join his sisters in Connecticut as soon as he was released from the hospital. Both had enlisted with the Rangers. Josiah was to report in early March if he was well enough, while Tom had been given leave to report for duty after planting the spring crops for his widowed mother.

Elizabeth looked up as Carleton stepped into the room and for a moment lost her breath. He wore an immaculately tailored suit of fine blue-grey silk that perfectly matched his eyes and intensified the color of his sun-streaked hair. An elegant cream-colored embroidered waist-coat contrasted with the deeper color of coat and breeches, while snowy linen and hose and silver-buckled shoes of fine leather completed his attire. Although he entered quietly as though loath to draw attention, the others immediately turned to him, each face reflecting pleasure and welcome.

"There you are," Elizabeth murmured. Releasing Abby, she reached out to him.

He came to kiss her hand, the light in his eyes causing her heart to leap. At the same time he covertly tugged one of Abby's curls with his free hand. She squirmed and playfully batted his hand away with giggling protests.

"I was wondering where you'd gotten to," Elizabeth murmured.

"I didn't want to intrude while you visited with your friends."

"Dearest, you never intrude."

Sarah appeared in the doorway. "Miz Tess, tea been laid in the dining room. Dr. Howard just ride in from Stony Hill."

Tess rose, the others following her lead. "Please do join us for tea," she said to Josiah, Tom, and Billy. "We'd be greatly honored if you'd visit with us for a while."

When they hesitated, Carleton added his insistence that they stay, noting that the chariot waited to take them back to Boston whenever they were ready. Eagerly the men adjourned with them to the library, where tea had been laid. There followed a happy hour of fellowship and an array of food and drink that the former prisoners clearly found gratifying.

At length Elizabeth ushered her friends to the door and bade them a reluctant farewell, embracing each with tears and whispered thanks and blessings and hopes that they would meet again before long. Carleton escorted them outside to the chariot and saw them off, then returned inside to gather her into his arms and dry her tears. Arm in arm, they joined the others in the drawing room, where Dr. Howard was in the midst of detailing progress on rebuilding the mansion at Stony Hill.

"I'm afraid it's going to be well into spring before our home is habitable," he concluded, directing an apologetic glance at Anne. "I've stormed and blustered, but the workmen haven't even begun to plaster the walls, and now it's unlikely it can be done until the weather warms again. The stables are only half built, the foundations of the barn and other outbuildings haven't been laid, and as to wallpaper, paint, and furnishings for the house . . . " He blew out a breath in frustration. "I've had what's been delivered so far—and that's little enough—held at the warehouse. It appears you won't be relieved of us anytime soon, Tess."

"Have you heard me complaining, Samuel?" Tess demanded, pretending to be indignant. "I'm perfectly delighted to have all of you stay through the winter . . . though once summer arrives, I can't promise this old woman won't evict you in order to return to her solitary ways."

Elizabeth laughed with the others, knowing her aunt's sociable nature.

"Old woman indeed," Carleton chided. "I've never known anyone younger in spirit than you, Tess."

Elizabeth felt a twinge of discomfort that, although Tess chuckled and returned a humorous retort, she again appeared to deliberately avoid meeting Carleton's gaze.

*I must talk to her and find out what's wrong,* she decided. The thought was quickly forgotten, however, when Dr. Howard eagerly suggested that Carleton play for them that evening.

ELIZABETH'S PRESENCE ALONE could soothe the restlessness that plagued him the way playing the violin did, Carleton reflected as he dressed for dinner, assisted by Dr. Howard's servant. Visits to the hospital to monitor the care of the patients and the efforts to contact relatives and arrange for the recovering men's return home consumed every weekday morning. The rest of the waning daylight hours he divided between his warehouse offices and the shipyard, often not returning to Roxbury until past sundown.

He chafed at spending so much time away from Elizabeth now, when his return to the Rangers and the concerns of war loomed over him with increasing urgency. In addition, a nagging foreboding about the state of affairs along the western frontier left him on edge.

He had received no word from the Shawnee since the beginning the summer campaign, when Red Fox and Spotted Pony had returned from Grey Cloud, bringing more warriors with them. They had reported that, in spite of the efforts of Cornstalk, the Shawnee's principal sachem, to maintain their people's neutrality, an increasing number of warriors were allying with the British to war against the Long Knives.

With his Rangers constantly on the move in rapidly developing skirmishes and shifting battles, he had received no further news. Instinct warned him, however, that, as he had feared, during the year of his absence the relentless raids he had waged against white settlers intruding on Shawnee lands had spun into a destructive cycle of retribution on both sides that might at any time explode into a widening and ever more bloody war.

Or already had done so.

To keep at bay a frustrating sense of powerlessness to avert this disaster, Carleton devoted every spare hour to regaining his former skill on the violin. His greatest pleasure became the intimate evenings after dinner when Elizabeth's family relaxed together in the drawing room, the women with warm dressing gowns wrapped over their night dresses, he and Dr. Howard wearing casual banyans over shirt, waistcoat, and breeches. After playing several songs, he accompanied them as they sang, led by Dr. Howard's strong, fine baritone. Along with the work at the hospital, this had led to a genuine, and encouraging, friendship between Carleton and Elizabeth's father.

Elizabeth, Carleton had been especially delighted to learn, had been quite accomplished on the pianoforte when she was younger. "I've always thought it a shame that by the time she was seventeen she'd lost confidence in her ability and ceased to play, regardless of her mother's and my encouragement to continue," Dr. Howard had told him, with a gently reproachful look in Elizabeth's direction.

She had bitten her lip and looked away, and nothing more was said of the matter. Although Carleton hesitated to broach the subject with her for fear of bringing back unhappy memories, he could not help wondering whether the cause was not the malicious verbal abuse to which her former fiancé, David Hutchins, had secretly subjected her until her father discovered and put an end to it. And whether this painful experience had pushed her into the reckless acts of daring that had made her infamous among the British.

Another concern that had lately begun to nag at him was that lately Tess exhibited a strange reticence that stood in puzzling contrast to the friendship and encouragement she had at first extended. Although her manner was invariably kind when he sought her out, it was becoming increasingly evident that she deliberately avoided him. The only reason he could think of was that he had outstayed his welcome.

The prospect of leaving Elizabeth before circumstances required it, in addition to the unavoidable responsibilities that occupied his days, kept him from speaking frankly—and privately—with Tess, however. And as he went downstairs to join the others for dinner, he again pushed the matter out of his thoughts.

Later, as they gathered around the fire in the drawing room, he decided to play a tune that had first come to him during the darkest period of his captivity among the Seneca. He had worked out the composition in his mind over the intervening months, and in the fortnight since Elizabeth returned his violin, he had practiced assiduously, taking care to do so when no one would hear so that he might surprise them.

ELIZABETH LAY CURLED UP in the chair, eyes closed, with Abby cuddled in her arms. Against the backdrop of the shadowed room, illuminated by muted fire- and candlelight that wavered in the drafts from the gusty wind buffeting the house, the haunting strains of the violin held her in thrall.

The melody Carleton played awakened in her the sigh of wind and rain through forest treetops. Then, over several measures, the music subtly transformed into a lilting Scottish jig before softening to evoke misty highland and moor. The sibilance of ocean waves and a distant melody of sea chanties succeeded, melting into flute-like tones that evoked endless woodlands and native peoples. At last the song faded into a deep, mournful, receding drone that left her throat painfully tight and breath constricted.

"Oh, Jonathan," she breathed, "you've taken me far away. Your playing is better for me than any medicine."

"How exquisite!" Anne murmured. "I didn't realize you compose in addition to playing so exceedingly well."

"It quite touches the heart," Dr. Howard agreed gruffly. "Very well done, Jon."

Carleton gave a half bow, his expression unreadable. "The tune's been in my mind since I was with the Seneca. I didn't have a violin then, of course, so I memorized what I heard in my head. I wasn't certain how it would turn out when actually played."

When Abby ran to him, his stiffness eased. "I could see pictures in my mind while you were playing," she told him.

He brushed the curls from her face, smiling down at her. "I hoped you would."

Elizabeth sat up to study him intently. "It reflects all the different worlds you've known, doesn't it—Scotland, the sea, the Shawnee?"

His glance told her she had touched a deep chord in his heart, but he turned away before she could read more.

"Indeed it does seem to cover all the parts of your life, Jon." Although Tess's tone was warm, she kept her gaze on the embroidery she had taken back up again.

Dr. Howard left his chair to add a log to the seething embers on the hearth. "Thank God you were able to get away from the Indians and come back where you belong." He straightened and stretched to ease his back, hands braced at his waist.

"Tess told us that Charles married an Indian woman and that they have a baby."

"You'd love Blue Sky, Mama! She's very dear to me. The two of them are exceptionally well suited and so strongly attached to each other that it's a joy to see. Perhaps Aunt Tess told you that I helped to deliver their son,"

Elizabeth threw an apprehensive glance at her aunt. When Tess kept her head bent, apparently concentrating on her embroidery, Elizabeth concluded with forced cheerfulness, "They named him He Leads the

Way because on the night of his birth he reached for a moonbeam. He's the most splendid child."

"I'm very glad they're happy. I've heard of others who've married Indian women, of course, but as for me, I simply don't understand why one would want to marry into a culture so at odds with their own, especially one that's warred against them."

"Now, Samuel, there are good Indians too," Anne remonstrated.

Carleton started to speak, but when his gaze met Elizabeth's, his mouth tightened and he held his silence. Dr. Howard turned back to him.

"From what Tess told us, we gathered your time among the Indians wasn't a happy period of your life, to say the least."

Carleton's brow furrowed, and Elizabeth bit her lip. She was relieved when he said simply, "My experience among the Seneca was certainly the most painful of any I've endured. But then, I can't imagine that anyone enjoys being held a slave."

"I can hardly think of the horrors you must have suffered," her mother exclaimed.

Dr. Howard made a dismissive gesture. "All I can say is, you're well out of all that, Jon. Undoubtedly the less said about it, the better."

The guarded look Carleton directed at her father increased Elizabeth's discomfort. Hoping to distract them from a discussion that threatened to delve into matters better left unsaid, she impulsively blurted out the first thing that came into her mind.

"You told me once you'd love to take me to Scotland. Do think that once the war is over and all is settled and at peace again, it'll be possible for you to return? I know it still has a claim on your heart."

She saw at once that she had only made things worse.

"I always assumed I'd go back some day," he answered after an uncomfortable pause, not meeting her gaze. "I'd particularly like to visit Stoughton Hall again and see if my memories are accurate. I was only three years old when I was . . . taken away. Of course, it belongs to my half-brother Edward now." He stopped, then added softly, "But since I'm a traitor in the eyes of the British, I'm afraid my bridges are burned forever."

Was this true of her too? she wondered. Certainly she could never return to the clandestine role she had undertaken for the patriots. And after sharing the horrific suffering of the prisoners aboard the *Erebus,* she could not help wondering whether it would ever be possible for her reclaim the innocent courage and idealism with which she had entered on that perilous path.

Exhaustion claimed her suddenly, and she sagged back into the chair, too weary to think any more of the matter.

She started when Sarah and Jemma rushed into the room, followed by Tess's maid, Mariah. "Come outside quick!" Sarah ordered, her expression registering alarm. "There's strange lights flickering in the sky—I never seen the like!"

Amid the flurry of gathering coats and cloaks to rush outside, Elizabeth struggled to her feet, limbs impossibly heavy. "Only for a moment, Jon," she heard her father say behind her. "I don't want her in the cold air too long."

"I completely agree," Carleton answered. He was beside her then, ignoring her half-hearted protests as he wrapped her in a thick cloak and tucked the hood around her head.

"But I'm fine," she said when he gathered her up in his arms. "You needn't carry me."

He brushed a kiss across her cheek and murmured in her ear, "You're hardly able to hold up your head, dear heart. You ought to have been abed two hours ago." He strode outside after the others. "I'm sure it's the aurora, and I don't want you to miss it. But then I'm going to carry you directly upstairs."

She yawned and nestled against his chest, reveling sleepily in the feel of his strong arms around her, keeping her warm against the icy wind that buffeted the night, clear and cold as crystal. When they joined the rest of the servants at the center of the yard, she looked up past his shoulder and gasped, her breath pluming in the air.

Across the star-studded indigo bowl of the heavens infinitely high above, brilliant curtains and streamers of red, yellow, blue, and green fluttered and twisted, advanced and receded in silent, ghostly dance. All around her the others exclaimed in amazement, fear, and delight.

"Oh, how lovely!" For several minutes she watched, entranced, finally asked, "What causes these strange lights?"

"No one knows for certain," he answered. "Some people think it's a portent of evil things to come."

For several minutes longer she watched in wonder as glorious folds of color continued to arc and swell in ceaselessly changing vistas across the night sky. "Such beauty couldn't portend evil," she ventured, her voice muffled against his coat. "I think they must be the curtains of heaven. Do you suppose God is favoring us with a glimpse into his realm?"

He bent his head to smile down at her. "I'd like to think so. But now it's time for you to go to bed. And may heaven's curtains wrap you in sweet dreams tonight, dearest of my heart."

# Chapter Twenty-nine

*Friday, 28 November*

"W HAT DO YOU MEAN you didn't tell them? Mama and Papa obviously know about Jonathan being Shawnee." Elizabeth regarded her aunt with alarm, the color draining from her face.

"They don't know that he's a famous—or infamous, if you will— war chief."

Elizabeth's mouth dropped open. "Papa said you told them everything!"

Motioning her to lower her voice, Tess waited until Jemma's footfalls completely faded down the stairway and quiet reigned downstairs before crossing the chamber to softly close the door. Then she hurried to take a chair at the window beside Elizabeth.

"Naturally he'd have thought so, but how could I tell them the rest?" Tess hissed in an undertone. "They'd just arrived the day before Stowe and Briggs delivered Jon's letter telling us of your capture—"

"Exactly what did you tell them?"

"All I felt I could, including that Jon was adopted by the Shawnee. I didn't know how to fully convey what that meant, and it didn't seem to register with either of them. Seneca, Shawnee—" She waved her hand dismissively. "It was all too confusing. You said you'd explain things in a way they might accept, but you understand Jon's thinking much better than I do. And you were there with the Shawnee—"

"Did you tell them I accompanied Charles to find him?"

Tess let out a sigh and stared down at her hands. "I couldn't. They'd have been horrified, and I was afraid I'd only make a hash of it in the attempt. Naturally they wondered why you weren't here, so I told them I'd come ahead because of the problems with construction on Stony Hill, and that you'd stayed behind to close up the house in Philadelphia—as you did, more or less."

"Then you said nothing about my being with Jonathan at Bemis Heights last month?"

Tess rubbed her brow. "Not until later. After we learned of your capture, I had no choice. At first I only said that you'd been temporarily forced to stay in the city because of the British occupation, but that you were safe and would come as soon as you could get a pass to leave. Which was at least partially true. That much alone caused them considerable distress. Of course they knew of your sympathy with the patriots, and Samuel already suspected you of some direct involvement."

"Mama more than suspected, but she was careful not to ask questions. I don't think she wanted to know the full truth." Elizabeth sprang to her feet and began to pace the room.

"She has her own loyalties," Tess observed, eyes narrowed. "But as for the rest, I thought it better for you tell them what you felt appropriate."

"Appropriate! I hoped we were at last done with secrets and lies, but it appears not. What did Jonathan say in his letter?"

"It was written in invisible ink. Stowe showed us how to hold it over a candle flame to read it. That raised eyebrows to be sure. Jon wrote only that Howe had captured you and Caleb as spies. He pleaded with us not to comply with any demands Howe might make and not to leave the area under any circumstances until we received further word from him."

"Thank God he thought of that! I worried constantly."

Tess gave Elizabeth a sympathetic look. "He asked for our prayers, of course, which we continually lifted up from that moment on. At that point I had no choice but to confess the extent of your involvements as a spy and that you were with Jon at Saratoga when Burgoyne surrendered."

Elizabeth groaned and buried her face in her hands. "I can't imagine their reaction."

"I won't repeat what was said in the heat of the moment. And then Stowe told us that Howe demanded Jon's surrender, promising that he'd release you at once if he complied."

"They understood that Howe would never have released me, that he'd simply have executed both of us if Jonathan gave himself up?"

"Stowe made that point very strongly—bless him—so that none of us could doubt it. When he told us Jon intended to sail into New York Harbor and rescue you and the prisoners with you, we were all in despair. It was unimaginable that such a mad plan could possibly succeed. So you see why I hesitated to confide that the man you love and plan to marry is the war chief White Eagle who carried out raids against the settlers moving into Ohio Territory. I simply couldn't find the words."

Returning to the window, Elizabeth pushed back the heavy draperies to look bleakly out at the brightening morning. "Yes—yes, I understand. Papa would have been beside himself."

"My brother can be quite choleric when roused," Tess agreed wryly. "Your mother won't be at ease with this either. They've simply set the matter aside because Jon managed to carry through his plan and brought you safely home—which in their eyes covers a multitude of sins on both your parts. And now they've been completely captured by the force of his charm."

Elizabeth cast her a rueful glance. "He's nigh impossible to resist when he makes up his mind to win you over."

"We've all felt the effect of that," Tess conceded with a chuckle. "At any rate, I've been praying that their good will remains strong enough to also cover his actions as a war chief when they learn of it. But after last night, I realized I'd better warn you as soon as possible."

Feeling lightheaded, Elizabeth returned to her seat. Tess placed her hand over hers, and she became aware that she was shaking.

"If I'd confided in you as soon as you began to get better, perhaps we could have found some way to tell them that they could accept. Now, after weeks have passed, I'm afraid they'll feel as though they've been lied to."

"Which they have been!" Elizabeth let her shoulders slump. "It's my fault, really. I should have understood how difficult this would be for you and made certain that they'd been told everything. I admit there were a few times when I wondered, but it's been such joy to have Mama and Papa and Abby home again and Jonathan with us and everything in such harmony after all the animosity Papa felt toward him." Pressing her hand to her head, she said, "I've been stretched on this rack for so long, and I simply wanted to believe that at last there's peace between those I love the most."

"I'll not share the blame with you," Tess objected. "You've been quite ill, and you're yet a long way from recovering completely."

"This is why you've been avoiding Jonathan."

"I can't tell you what a state of panic I've been in that he'll either suspect I'm keeping something from him or unwittingly let fall some unguarded word about . . . about the rest to your parents."

Hope rose in Elizabeth's breast. "Perhaps they do know! Papa said that he and Jonathan talked right after we arrived, and he told Papa more of what happened."

The two women stared at each other, considering this possibility. Then Tess shook her head.

"If he had, we'd all have heard the explosion."

The absurdity of their situation struck Elizabeth suddenly, and she doubled over, fighting to suppress a gale of laughter, while Tess also gave way to mirth. At length Tess cleared her throat and dabbed the tears from her eyes.

"There are times when you have to laugh to keep from weeping."

Elizabeth sobered. "Well, so far Jonathan's not broached the subject with me, even privately, and there's no reason for him to mention it to them. I've never seen him so happy and at ease as he's been these past weeks. He's grown quite close to Mama and Papa, and Abby adores him. It's not natural to him to speak freely about things so close to his heart, as you saw last night. From what was said, he's likely concluded that they do know the whole story but, as you said, have simply set the matter aside. I can't imagine he'll willingly challenge them on it if only for my sake."

"But the truth will out sooner or later, and the longer until it does, the greater the shock will be. We simply can't keep such an enormous secret forever! I constantly feel as though I'm walking on eggshells. And if we don't tell them soon, the truth is bound to come out at the worst possible time in the worst possible way."

"Where's Papa?"

"He's calling on that new patient in Brooklyne, and afterward he meant to stop at Stony Hill again. He probably won't be back until this afternoon. When I came upstairs, your mama was in the drawing room sewing, while Abby finished the sketch she started yesterday."

Elizabeth rose and went quietly to crack open the door. She could hear the faint murmur of her mother's and sister's voices from the back of the house. Softly closing the door, she returned and sank back into her chair.

"Has Jonathan already gone into Boston?"

Tess nodded. "He had to be at the shipyard early. He'd have come up, but you were still asleep. He didn't want to wake you so he asked me to give you his apologies."

Elizabeth rested her cheek in her hand. "Every night I go to bed right after dinner, but I still wake up so late, and then end up sleeping most of the afternoon away too. I'm beginning to think I'll never get my strength back."

Tess put her arm around Elizabeth's shoulders. "Of course you will. You were very ill, and it takes time to recover, that's all. Your father says the infection isn't entirely gone yet, and you'll probably not regain full strength until spring." When Elizabeth let out a frustrated sigh, she added, "Have patience. Each day is a little better."

Elizabeth remained silent for a moment. Finally she said, "Now that we've gotten ourselves into such a dilemma, we simply can't drag Jonathan, completely unsuspecting, into an argument about his actions—his very identity. It would be horribly unfair. Papa will react badly before he learns half the matter, and he'll doubtless make accusations that will sting deeply. And who knows how Jonathan will respond."

She shook her head. "No, I refuse to allow the little time we've left to be spoiled by a row, and with Christmas at hand! We'll simply have to wait to sort all this out until after he returns to his command."

"But that's weeks from now!"

"We'll have to bear it and pray that nothing of this matter comes out before then. I won Papa over to the patriot cause after he vehemently opposed it for so long. I can win him and Mama over to this, too, given enough time—I know I can!"

"This is a very different matter, Beth. It concerns the welfare of their daughter, and that's something a parent doesn't take lightly."

"All the more reason for us to wait. It'll take weeks, if not months, of discussion and reflection for Mama and Papa to even begin to accept this. After all Jonathan's suffered, I won't see him hurt by what should remain a private family discussion. He risked everything he owns—his very life—to rescue me and all those poor men from that wretched ship. That must count for much even in this case."

Tess patted her arm. "I'm just afraid it'll not be enough to overcome the prejudices that I shared myself at first and still struggle with from time to time."

Catching her breath, she sat bolt upright. "But if you were married when they learn of Jon's situation, they could do nothing! There's yet time for banns to be published so you can wed before the end of the year, and it would thrill your parents. Talk to him! I doubt it'll take much persuasion, and then you can make arrangements with the vicar when he comes Sunday afternoon to serve you communion."

Elizabeth clasped her hands. "Oh, I want nothing more dearly, and he does too! That's the perfect answer."

The words were no sooner out of her mouth than euphoria gave way to dismay. Stricken, she said, "What am I saying? That would be terribly unfair to Mama and Papa, and how could they ever forgive either of us when the truth came out? Besides, Jonathan will never agree. Washington threatened to revoke his commission if he weds, and he's sworn to only go against the decision of his clan's council as a last resort if they won't be persuaded to allow us to marry. We can do nothing at least until the war ends—which I've begun to think it never will."

Tess's shoulders sagged. "I'm growing dotty in my old age. You're right, of course. But how will you keep this from Jon? He'll know from your face the instant he walks through the door tonight that's something's gone wrong."

Elizabeth lifted her chin. "No he won't. I'm going to put this matter out of my mind until he's gone back to his brigade, and you will too. Until then, we'll enjoy the time we have together. And in the meantime, we'll pray mightily for the Lord to prepare Mama and Papa's hearts."

Her expression reflecting doubt, Tess rose, with Elizabeth following suit. "Your mother must be wondering why we haven't come down."

A she led the way to the door, she cast a reproachful look over her shoulder at Elizabeth. "I hope the Almighty will hear our petitions. But it concerns me that we've too often asked his blessing on our course before making sure it's his will and not ours."

"Everything's going to work out perfectly in the end, Aunt Tess," Elizabeth said cheerfully, feigning a confidence that at the moment eluded her. "Wait and see."

# Chapter Thirty

H IS MOUTH TIGHTENING, Carleton broke the packet's wax seal and unfolded the heavy outer wrapper. Inside lay two sealed letters.

The thinner was inscribed in Andrews's hand. The thicker bore Washington's unmistakable address. It was not an encouraging omen that the General had written the missive himself instead of dictating it to one of his aides or even leaving it for them to compose.

Carleton had no sooner than entered the house, weary to the bone and with dusk coming on, when Washington's most trusted courier had ridden in, ruddy cheeks and windblown hair and clothing testifying to a swift, unsparing journey. At sight of the man, a sense of foreboding had gripped Carleton's chest. It had been a difficult day, and this was not the conclusion he had hoped for.

He had immediately dismissed the courier to Sarah's care for the night, with orders to present himself at dawn to carry a response back to the General. Now, feeling the others' gazes on him, he slipped Andrews's letter into his coat pocket and retreated to the fireplace to scrutinize the other, sorely tempted to consign it to the flames. Had there been no witnesses, he well might have.

With the distinct sensation that he was about to open Pandora's box, he broke the seal and held it up to the light of the candles on the mantel. Quickly scanning the contents, he found halfway down the third page the summons he had feared, demanding his immediate return.

Dread settled over him at the certainty that more bad news was yet to come. He returned to the letter's beginning and noted the date: 23 November. Considering weather and distance, the courier had wasted no time on the way. Carleton let out his breath, dismissed the room's expectant silence from his consciousness, and read the letter through.

It began with commendation for the blow he had struck against the British, an important coup that was enheartening patriots and plummeting the morale of loyalists and British alike. Washington had received reports that recriminations were flying thick and fast between Howe and Clinton, in itself a great service to their cause. Consequently he had strongly recommended to Congress that Carleton be promoted to major general and Andrews to brigadier. This request had been approved with exceptional speed, and he congratulated Carleton on his new rank.

The news did nothing to improve Carleton's humor. Rank cynicism insisted that this was but the prelude to a coming blow.

Rubbing his now throbbing brow, he plowed through a lengthy update on the army's situation and engagements while he had been absent. And then the letter's tone abruptly turned peremptory.

Although he understood Carleton's situation, Washington wrote tersely, he had no choice but to order him to return to the corps at the earliest instant. Many of the army's top officers were already applying to secure a furlough home as soon as the army settled into winter camp, and a few had simply departed without waiting for official leave. He could not do without Carleton's presence any longer.

What followed, however, was the real reason for the letter, Carleton realized at once: A matter of the utmost urgency had arisen, one that could not be conveyed in a letter and about which they must confer at the earliest instant, in person and privately.

Carleton read the sentence over twice, feeling he had been punched hard in the gut. Only the worst of news could warrant such urgency, and instinct warned him it had to do with the war on the western frontier.

He skimmed the rest of the letter: If unavoidable circumstances made it impossible for Carleton to accompany the courier on his return, his reply must include the reasons and the date of his expected arrival. To this Washington added a caution. He had learned that the already high reward for producing Carleton, alive or dead, had been doubled. Therefore, he was ordered to exercise the utmost caution on his return to the corps and to give a wide berth to British- and loyalist-held areas.

Should the corps no longer be at White Marsh when Carleton arrived, Washington noted, they would have moved to a winter camp somewhere in Philadelphia's vicinity, as Congress insisted—for whatever good that might do. The letter concluded with the repeated command for Carleton to conclude his business in Boston and return to the corps without delay.

"Jonathan? Is anything wrong?"

He looked up to meet Elizabeth's anxious gaze, swiftly calculating how much he could reveal. "I've been promoted to major general and Charles to brigadier," he said, forcing a cheerfulness he was very far from feeling.

"Oh, Jonathan—major general!" Anne cried, frank admiration in her tone. "What wonderful news! Congratulations!"

"Well done, Jon," Dr. Howard agreed heartily, his face wreathed in a broad smile. "Very much deserved. Please communicate our congratulations to Charles as well."

Abby happily echoed their sentiments, as did Tess, without apparent reserve. Yet Carleton did not miss the pointed glance she directed at Elizabeth.

The murmur of conversation filled the room, breaking off when Sarah appeared at the door to announce dinner. Tess led the way, the others following.

Carleton shoved the letter into his pocket and, keeping his expression neutral, held out his arm to Elizabeth. She laid her hand on it lightly, smiling up at him. When she congratulated him on his promotion, however, he noted a tremor in her voice.

ELIZABETH TOOK A SIP of wine to wash down the mouthful of beef pasty that seemed to stick in her throat. She felt on the verge of crying.

Seated beside her, Carleton took part in the conversation with outward good humor, as though nothing concerned him. Had she had not known him so well, she would not have guessed that he concealed very different emotions. But she was certain of it, and of at least part of the reason.

"So, Jon, what news from General Washington?" her father asked, looking up from his plate between bites. "If you can tell us, of course. Is everything going well at Philadelphia—any new developments?"

Carleton leaned back in his chair, downed a last swallow of wine, then held the glass for the servant to refill. It was his third—a worrisome sign as Elizabeth had only seen him drink more than one glass at dinner when something troubled him.

For some moments, as though entirely at ease, he regaled them with details from Washington's report drawing approving smiles with his account of successful skirmishes; disgust at those who professed patriotism, yet persisted in selling goods to the British, while withholding them from the Continentals; and anger at the fall of Fort Mifflin, the burning of the Pennsylvania navy, and the torching of the Germantown estates.

Again he emptied his wineglass.

Elizabeth slipped her hand onto his as the servant refilled it. He avoided her gaze but left the glass on the table.

"Did Washington say anything about your returning to the corps, Jonathan?" her mother asked, while spooning a slice of pudding onto Abby's plate.

Elizabeth glanced quickly at Carleton. As the muscles of his jaw hardened, a painful constriction closed over her breast.

He hesitated before saying gruffly, "He says there's an urgent matter he must discuss with me personally, one that can't be conveyed in a letter. He wants me to accompany the courier back directly."

It felt as though the air had gone out of the room. While astonished exclamations and questions rose from around the table, Elizabeth pushed a forkful of pudding across her plate, appetite entirely gone.

Her mother put down her fork and regarded Carleton with disappointment. "We were hoping you'd not have to leave so soon." She transferred her concerned gaze to Elizabeth, then quickly away.

Abby pushed back her chair and ran to Carleton's arms. "Oh, please don't go! Why can't you stay until Christmas as you promised?"

"I have duties to attend to, Abby. When you're older, you'll understand that you can't always do as you please."

Her father sat back in his chair, watching Carleton with a frown while Abby retreated to her chair, downcast. "I wish you could stay the month, Jon, and I'd encourage you to do so if you'd not open yourself to charges of insubordination or neglecting your duties. From what you've told us, and judging by Charles's promotion, everything appears to be going quite well with him in command of the brigade."

"I've every confidence in Charles's abilities." Carleton pushed back his plate, dessert uneaten, and stared at his wineglass. "But evidently too many officers are applying for furloughs home for the winter, and—"

"What about that urgent matter Washington mentioned? If it's so serious that the two of you must discuss it in person, I don't suppose it wise for you to delay leaving."

Carleton responded with a faint smile. "If I didn't know better, Tess, I'd think I've outstayed my welcome and you're trying to get rid of me."

Dismay registered on her aunt's face. Feeling Carleton's covert glance, Elizabeth concentrated on mashing her pudding with her fork.

Tess responded with a chuckle that sounded forced. "Not at all. I'd be delighted if you'd move in permanently, Jon, but I don't think any of us want you to hazard Washington's censure by disobeying his summons. Did he give any indication of what this urgent matter is?"

Carleton shrugged. "It might be any number of things. At the moment, I'm less concerned about that than I am about my ships—and even more about Beth's health." Turning to her, he said softly, "It's clear I'll not be able to stay as long as I hoped, dearest, but I don't want to rush away either. I do have very good reasons to stay, which will give us at least a little more time together."

Elizabeth lifted an imploring gaze to his. "You know I want you to if possible, but don't worry about me. I'm growing stronger every day. It's just the thought of your leaving so soon—" She broke off and looked down, biting her lip.

The others eagerly pressed Carleton to delay his return, but he brushed their objections away with a weariness that was suddenly quite evident. "In fact it's impossible for me to leave before the end of the week, much less tomorrow. I'll need horses and supplies for such a long journey, and that alone will take several days to arrange."

"Let me take care of that for you, Jon," Dr. Howard volunteered. "I'm a fair judge of horseflesh, and if you tell me what else you need, I'll see to it. That'll give you and Beth more time together."

Carleton gave him a grateful look. "I'll take advantage of your offer. Thank you. The other concern is that my ships sail for the Caribbean before winter sets in. *Destiny* just launched yesterday and work on painting and rigging has just begun. And to make things worse, the shipyard has run out of oakum to finish caulking *Invictus's* hull, and more must be found immediately."

He stopped, then with a frustrated gesture continued, "Eaden can certainly manage all that, but one of my frigates arrived in port this afternoon with word that a couple of weeks ago a squadron of the Royal Navy intercepted two of my merchantmen on the return from India with full holds. Naturally my ships are well armed for protection against pirates, but they're no match for warships. One was sunk and the other would have been if three of my 74s and a couple of French 50s hadn't been close enough to hear cannon fire and arrived in time to drive the attackers off."

Exclamations of outrage and concern resounded from the others.

"Your ships and their cargoes are insured, I assume."

"Of course, Samuel. What concerns me much more is how many of my crew were lost. Only a few could be rescued."

Elizabeth drew in her breath sharply. "I'm so sorry."

Carleton grasped her hand, his fingers closing over hers with painful pressure as he met her gaze with a hard one. "Howe swore to hunt down all my ships and either destroy them or take them prize," he said, his voice tight. "And so it begins."

His eyes had shaded to the cold smoky grey that always set Elizabeth on guard. She could feel fury boiling up in him, held under only tenuous control.

To the others' anxious questions, Carleton explained curtly that he had authorized Eaden to take over official command of his privateers, a role the captain already exercised informally. With *Black Swan's* captain, Guilliam La Coque, as his second in command, Eaden would have full authority to determine strategy and tactics against any hostile force as he saw fit, for which he was more than qualified by training and experience.

Carleton had also arranged for both of them to meet with the commissioners of the Eastern Department Navy Board in Boston on Friday along with Eaden. "That's a meeting I'll not miss under any circumstances. I've been intending to consult with the commissioners about coordinating the operations of my ships with other privateers and with the Continental Navy—such as it is. But I put it off because there's been so much else to attend to and I thought I had plenty of time."

"When will you leave?" Elizabeth said into the silence that fell over the room.

Deliberately he reached for his wineglass and drained it. "Monday," he said as he set the empty glass back on the table. "A week's delay is as long as I can justify."

"I wish we could stay ever thus—with you nestled so sweetly in my arms and your head on my shoulder."

Elizabeth released a sigh and turned her face up to Carleton's kiss. "We knew from the beginning there'd be many such partings. I'd only hoped you could stay longer, but I'll not grieve you with reproaches or tears. We'll take joy in the days we have left. I'm more than grateful we've had as much time as we have."

She drew her bare feet up under her and tucked the blanket over her knees. Carleton shifted on the settee to afford her more room beside him and directed a cautious glance toward the door of his chamber, which he had deliberately left standing open.

Slightly taller than average for a woman, she was the perfect height when she stood beside him, he thought. When he held her like this, in the crook of his arm with the crown of her head under his chin, the sensations that swelled in his heart left him breathless, fighting to keep his actions under control.

She had withdrawn to bed shortly after dinner, as usual. Less than an hour later, he had given in to exhaustion as well. As soon as Tess's maid returned downstairs from preparing the chambers for the night, he made his apologies and retreated upstairs after Abby.

To his surprise and pleasure, as soon as her little sister closed her door, Elizabeth had slipped out into the passage, a blanket wrapped over her floor-length dressing gown. After making sure the soft murmur of conversation from below remained unbroken, he quickly drew her into his chamber, weariness forgotten.

"It's quite scandalous for you to be alone with me in my chamber in such a state of undress," he murmured now. "If we're caught, we'll be accused of being entirely wanton."

She tossed her head and gave him a slow, seductive smile. "If we're going to be thought so, we might as well justify the opinion."

He let his gaze linger on her lips, the sensation of her pressed against him leaving him as heady as though he had drunk too much wine. Which, indeed, he had in this instance though his mind remained clear enough to give him no excuse.

"The door's open."

"You can close it. No one will know."

"Don't tempt me," he whispered into the glorious, silken tendrils curling at her temple.

"As often as you've been at my bedside—"

"Ah, but you've been ill, my love. And since I was the one who rescued you, it would've seemed awkward to raise objections as long as I behaved myself. And someone's . . . generally . . . been nearby to ensure it."

"With a few exceptions." She glanced up again, mischief dancing in her eyes.

He drew in a steadying breath and sat back with regret, loosening his embrace. "I seem to remember promising at our second encounter that I'd never compromise your reputation."

The blush that so prettily suffused her cheeks assured him she remembered the incident as vividly as he did. When he grinned, she suppressed a giggle, pressing her fingers to his lips.

Slowly she sobered. "Truly, I didn't mean to tease you, dearest." She caressed his cheek with a tender touch. "I'd not compromise either of us. I simply meant to ask you . . . that is, I wondered . . . the other letter you received, the one you slipped into your pocket, was it from Charles?"

He pretended to consider. "I forgot all about it."

"You never forget anything," she chided with a reproachful frown. "If you don't want to share it with me—or can't—I do understand, and I won't take offense."

He shrugged. "I'm sure it's only to do with the brigade—nothing of particular interest."

Masking his reluctance, he drew the letter from his pocket. He had intended to read it in private in case Andrews detailed the urgent matter Washington referred to, and as he broke the wax seal and unfolded the page, he held it at an angle to the candlelight that would prevent her from reading what was inscribed inside.

The letter was uncharacteristically terse and formal, leaving Carleton with the distinct impression that it had been submitted to Washington for review before being sent, a suspicion reinforced by its having been included with the General's correspondence. Andrews wrote only that he was sure Washington had shared news of the corps and the salutary effect Carleton's successful raid was having among those who held the patriot cause dear. The rest he needed not repeat other than to say that he was especially delighted to hear of Elizabeth's safety and that her health was on the mend. He asked Carleton to offer her his kindest regards and fervent wishes for her quick and full return to health.

As Carleton had directed, Andrews had had the brigade's clothier, quartermaster, and commissary order needed supplies for the troops. He congratulated Carleton on his new rank and shared his intent to promote several subordinate officers, which he assumed would meet with Carleton approval.

The visit to the Vander Groots had not gone well, Andrews continued, in language couched with obvious care. They had insisted on talking to Carleton, and Andrews had assured them that he would indeed call on them after his return to camp.

Here Andrews's stiffly formal tone abruptly gave way. "Jon, I know you've much to concern you there, but please return as quickly as you can. I'm as anxious to speak to you as is General Washington, and I can't overstate the importance of recent developments that will be of great concern to you. Please come. Only take care on the journey. Your enemies are more determined than ever to stop you."

Carleton glanced at Elizabeth and forced a smile. Deliberately he folded the letter and returned it to his pocket.

"As I said, it's only about boring military matters. Charles also sends you his regards and fervent wishes for your quick return to health."

Although he kept his voice and look even, he could tell she was not deceived. Staring down at her clenched hands, she said, "He's very kind, but . . . he gives no further explanation of this mysterious urgent matter Washington mentioned?"

"He merely says it's of great importance and urges me to return as quickly as possible."

"What do you think it concerns?" she questioned, avoiding his steady gaze.

"There are too many possibilities to indulge in speculation. I'll simply have to wait until I get there."

"There's nothing else?"

"No more than what Washington wrote."

Which he had not shared fully, a fact she could not have missed any more than she did his implied refusal to share Andrews's letter. In unspoken apology, he drew her more closely into his arms and rested his cheek against the top of her head.

He could feel her distress as she clung to him. And something beneath the surface that puzzled him: a strange, conflicting emotion almost akin to . . . relief.

The memory of the meaningful glance that had passed between her and her aunt at the dinner table returned. He had noted too many such secretive glances of late, and the unsettling feeling that both women were concealing something from him returned. Yet when he had questioned Elizabeth a few days earlier, she had denied that anything was wrong so guilelessly he was tempted to believe her.

Had the two of them had not been in the place where they had first met, where they had each concealed their true allegiance from the other, fearing the discovery of their dangerous alliances, perhaps he might have dismissed his suspicions. But the memory of Elizabeth's calmly innocent response when he had tried to shock her into admitting her ties to the rebels before he knew the truth of it would not leave him.

That she was not being honest with him now stung as much as his inability to fully disclose to her the contents of the letters . . . and other things. For on discovering that they both served the patriot cause and more—that they loved each other—both of them had promised to never conceal anything from the other again.

It was a promise neither had kept. He wondered if they ever could, but quickly assured himself that once the war and the harsh necessities that came with it ended, their hearts would lie entirely open to each other. It was what he wanted more than anything and knew she did too.

He glanced down to find her looking up at him, pain darkening her eyes. His heart softened. As always, her fragile beauty entranced him, while the sweetness of her nature, the goodness of her character, and the quickness of her mind and spirit knit his soul inextricably to hers.

What he kept from her was for fear of grieving or worrying her—or placing her in greater danger. If she concealed anything, it must be for the same reasons. Until she felt she could disclose the matter to him, he would let it go and not spoil the little time that remained until he had to leave her once again.

"Beth, I love you so," he said huskily. "I worry about you constantly, more now than ever. I hate the thought of leaving you when you're still so thin and pale."

"Please don't be concerned. I'll be fine. You've no choice but to return to the fight, while I'm left behind to . . . " Sighing, she let the words trail off.

He bent to gaze into her eyes with concern. "Do you worry about what your role will be now, little Oriole?"

In the candlelight, he saw the glisten of her tears, and she pressed into his arms to bury her face against his chest. "Now I've been exposed, the door to my service is closed. Our cause has been my life for so long that I can't even begin to conceive how to go on from here."

"Certainly for you to continue as a spy is impossible, Beth. But that isn't the only service you can do our cause."

Taking him by surprise, she sat up and pushed him away. "I suppose I can sew bandages or knit stockings for the troops." With a groan of frustration, she covered her face with her hands. "I'm miserable at sewing and knitting and other 'womanly' arts! I haven't the patience for them."

Her response was so unexpected that he could not help himself. He began to laugh.

She gave him a fierce look. "You laugh now, but when we're married, you'll be the one to suffer from my incompetence. Perhaps you'll want to reconsider."

He laughed harder, head thrown back, slumped against the settee's back as he fought to keep his mirth in check to avoid attracting attention from belowstairs.

She lightly slapped his arm, unable to suppress her own laughter, finally clasped him by the shoulders and fairly shook him. "Oh, stop it!"

Regaining control with difficulty, he captured her by the wrists, holding her so she could not pull away, and brought his face close to hers. "I do not love you for said womanly arts, but for yourself as you are. I'd not change a thing, nor will I ever reconsider taking you as my wife." Raising an eyebrow, he drawled, "You're exceptionally expert at the only womanly art I care about, and I can afford to hire any other work done that's needed."

Her blush deepened, and she cast him a look that caused his heart to melt. After a moment, however, tears welled up again, and she threw herself into his arms.

"What shall I do now? How will I occupy the days that stretch out empty before me while you're gone doing important service? This separation is harder than any we've ever faced."

He stroked her tumbled curls, and sliding his other hand beneath her blanket, traced the supple curve of her back to her waist as he drew her against him. "Perhaps God means to give you a fallow time for rest and reflection—a Sabbath rest, if you will. I've had such times and chafed mightily at them, but in looking back I see their value. You're still unwell, and it'll be some months until you regain enough strength for any further service. In the meantime, be assured that God still has work for you to do, though it hasn't yet become apparent. My experience has been that it often doesn't until the time comes to act. Dear heart, school yourself to be patient and let God work in you as he pleases."

For some moments she sat very still in his arms. At last, pulling back and touching his cheek, she surprised him again with a wry smile.

"You're a fine one to talk, Jonathan Stuart Carleton."

He conceded a rueful chuckle. "That's a charge I won't contest. I've striven against giving up control of my life as stubbornly as anyone—perhaps more so at times." He cupped her face in his hand. "When I weary of the fight, you lift up my arms. I want to do that for you too."

She slipped her arms around his neck and kissed him. "And you do. I'll take your advice to heart then. I'll let this winter do its work in me and listen earnestly for God's direction."

She brightened. "And I'll pray that before the next campaign begins I'll be well enough to come to you. With Pieter gone, you'll need another doctor, and perhaps I can fill at least a part of that need. Why canna I become wee Dr. Robbie McLeod again, as at Bemis Heights?" she demanded, affecting the broad Scottish brogue McLeod had taught her.

Chuckling, he bent his head until his brow touched hers. "You see—there is work for you still."

His feigned pleasure was rewarded with her sigh of pure happiness. But the thin blade of fear twisted in his heart. Briefly he touched his lips to hers, then pulled back to regard her with grave intensity.

"Promise that you'll go outside only to attend Sunday worship with your family once you're able, but never alone, should you suddenly feel weak or fall ill. Always bundle up warmly, and stay away from strangers—in case you encounter anyone who might be sick."

"You're even worse than Papa!" she grumbled.

"I don't want you to lose all the ground you've gained, or who knows how long it'll be until I see you again. If I must, I'll speak to your father, and I know he'll agree with me."

She gave an exasperated sigh but allowed him to gather her back into his arms. "Well then, if that's the price I must pay to regain my freedom, you have my promise."

Her parents' voices reached them clearly from the base of the stairs. He rose hastily, drawing her to her feet, and shooed her toward the door, commanding in a hoarse whisper, "Haste! Back to your chamber!"

Giggling, she flew to the door ahead of him, her bare feet making no sound on the rug. She was across the passage and over the threshold of her own room before her parents reached the landing.

Turning, she blew him a kiss. He heard the muffled click of her door as he shut his own and leaned back against it.

He did not move until her parents, followed by Tess, passed by and he heard the muffled closing of their chamber doors. It was not his and Elizabeth's near discovery that caused his heart to pound, however.

After quietly exchanging silk suit for worn buckskins, and shoes for moccasins, he crossed to a deep wing chair by the fire and sat, head resting against its back, eyes closed. As had become his habit in the weeks since Elizabeth's fever had broken, he waited until the faint nighttime sounds of the house settled into silence, broken only by the low moan of the wind curling around the eaves.

When the tall case clock on the landing chimed the half hour after eleven, he got to his feet. From the top dresser drawer he took his loaded pistol, checked the priming, then slipped it into his beaded belt.

Easing out the chamber door, he closed it soundlessly behind him and descended the stairs with caution, avoiding several steps that creaked. Below, feeling his way through the shadows, he followed the lower passage to the rear entry at the back of the house.

Faint firelight glowed from the kitchen where Sarah waited. She came to unlock the door and, giving him apprehensive look, drew it open.

He nodded to her, knowing that she would be there to let him in when he returned. Then without a glance back, he slipped outside into the windswept, star-studded night.

## Chapter Thirty-one

*Friday, 5 December*

"**O**NKEL ALEXANDRE! *C'est vous!"* Uncle Alexandre! It *is* you!

The man striding down Long Wharf clad in the uniform of a French admiral and attended by a clutch of naval officers arrested mid stride. The moment he caught sight of Carleton, his face wreathed in a broad smile and he advanced, arms flung wide.

*"Jonathan, quelle heureuse recontre! Justement celui que je cherchais."* What a happy meeting! Just who I was looking for."

Reaching Carleton, he drew him into an embrace and kissed him on each cheek, both of them laughing.

Gazing at his maternal uncle, Admiral Alexandre Bettár, le comte de Caledonne, Carleton reflected, was like seeing his older self in a mirror. The only alteration the years since their last meeting had wrought was to deepen the fine lines across the count's brow and at the corners of eyes the same intense blue-grey as Carleton's.

At the age of sixty Caledonne still maintained a trim figure and military bearing. His neatly curled hair, once as blond as Carleton's, had gone white but was still abundant and thick, its contrast with his ornate cocked hat, dark blue uniform coat and breeches, and crimson waistcoat intensifying a deep tan gained from years at sea.

Carleton knew him to be energetic, kind and generous, warm and witty, and unshakably loyal to his family. He had not risen to his high position by the exercise of these qualities, however, nor by mere chance. A fierce and canny seaman, he was as implacably opposed to the power of his country's great rival, Britain, as Carleton's adoptive father, Sir Harry, had been. But Caledonne was as well a master of intrigue all the more dangerous to his enemies because of his outwardly guileless manner.

"*Mon Dieu,* but it's good to see you again after so long!" he exclaimed now, holding Carleton at arm's length to take him in. "How well you look!"

"I can say the same of you," Carleton returned with a smile, studiously ignoring the looks passers-by directed at them.

Although he was by now a familiar figure in Boston's North End, when in uniform he attracted more interest than he welcomed. And for his and Eaden's meeting with the Eastern Department Navy Board that morning, he had donned one of the new uniforms ordered to replace those worn threadbare during the Saratoga campaign.

Beneath an ankle-length forest green cloak that fluttered in the blustery wind, his hip-length French dragoon-style jacket of grey-brown faced in matching green, supple buckskin breeches, and knee-length boots closely hugged the lean contours of his tall form. A dark grey shoulder belt carried his sheathed sabre with its gilt and silver pommel, and he wore a striking dark green leather helmet adorned with gold chains and a flowing, blond horsehair crest.

His uncle was also receiving a considerable share of attention. Clearly amused, Caledonne enquired, "How long has it been since we last met?"

"Three years. A little more."

"I feared we'd finally lost you to the Indians altogether. I know you consider the Shawnee to be your people, my boy, but never forget that we're your family still."

"I could never forget," Carleton protested. "My love hasn't changed, sir, nor will it."

Caledonne clapped Carleton on the shoulder, his smile reflecting a relief that told Carleton the matter had genuinely concerned him. "But I forget my manners," the count said quickly. "Let me introduce you to my officers." Turning to the men with him, he proceeded to do so.

When they had exchanged bows and pleasantries, Carleton turned back to Caledonne. "You're fortuitously come, Uncle Alexandre. Eaden and I just left a meeting with the commissioners of the Eastern Department Naval Board, and he's gone on to other appointments. It's almost two, and I was on my way to dine at the Bunch of Grapes." He indicated the tavern a short distance away at the corner of State and Kilby streets.

Caledonne's eyes brightened. "I suspected if we didn't find you at your warehouse, you'd be across the street at the best public house in Boston. It is the favorite resort of your high Whigs after all."

Carleton chuckled. "Not to mention yours in this part of the world."

With a broad smile, Caledonne beckoned his officers to follow. They strode across the street to join the boisterous company that gathered opposite the landward end of the wharf under a sign adorned with three gilded clusters of grapes. In moments the door flung open and the bell rang.

With deep bows and a hearty welcome, they were immediately ushered to a large table at the front window. Caledonne's officers ranged themselves around the far end, while the count took the head, with Carleton on his right. A glass of Madeira quickly appeared by Caledonne's plate and a brimming pint of ale by Carleton's. Soup and bread promptly followed.

Carleton relaxed in his chair and nodded toward the imposing French warship, visible from the window, docked at the far end of Long Wharf with her escorts riding at anchor farther out in the bay. "I thought I recognized your flagship, *Néréide,* but I was afraid my eyes deceived me. Does Louis the Sixteenth know his favorite admiral is brazenly consorting with Britain's enemy in this hotbed of rebellion while France remains—at least officially—uninvolved?"

"Since that state of affairs is very soon to change, *le roi* will desire my personal assessment of how things stand in George the Third's former colonies," Caledonne responded in high good humor. He swallowed a spoonful of soup and indicated three large ships lined up at the cranes along at the near end of the wharf. "Actually we were escorting those merchantmen. They're loaded with contraband for your army."

Carleton threw back his head, laughing. "I should have known."

Caledonne regarded him with a smile of satisfaction. "We hailed *Hornet, Eagle,* and *Columbia* just off South Carolina and were informed of the small matter of General Burgoyne's disaster at Saratoga—and your audacious raid on New York Harbor. I assure you, when the news of both successes reaches Paris, a declaration of war will be nipping at its heels."

Carleton made a dismissive gesture. "How long have your ministers been covertly supplying our army? It's high time Louis cast off caution. Your aid to our cause is already provocation enough for Britain to declare war though their diplomats still hesitate to throw down the gauntlet."

"Nor will they. King Louis will be the one to throw it down—but at the moment of his choosing."

They had no sooner than finished the meal's first course when platters loaded with joints of beef, veal, mutton, and ham were delivered to the table, accompanied by an array of succulent squab, a couple of savory vegetable dishes and a lavish hunting pudding. The tavern's proprietor, burly, red-faced Captain John Marston, arrived to carve the meats with a flourish, then offered profuse compliments and moved on to the next table, leaving them to serve themselves.

When they had filled their plates to overflowing, at Caledonne's urging Carleton gave an artfully abridged account of events from his receipt of Howe's letter until the present. He knew his uncle would be under no illusions as to its thoroughness since it was from him that Carleton had learned the skill of appearing to share every detail while not doing so.

*Destiny's* rigging was soon to be finished and a new figurehead had been put in place, he concluded, and caulking had finally been completed on *Invictus*. She had been launched just that morning, and the riggers already swarmed over her, hard at work. Both ships would be provisioned and ready to sail before Christmas. With nothing further to hold him in Boston, he planned to leave for White Marsh on Monday.

After congratulating him on his promotion, Caledonne gave him a searching look. "But you must leave your lady so soon?"

Carleton drained his tankard and set it down. While a waiter refilled it, he stared across the crowded dining room, contemplating whether to mention the urgent matter Washington had cited.

"I'd hoped to stay until after Christmas," he said finally, "but I've staved off my departure as long as I can without incurring my commander's censure."

His uncle gave studious attention to his plate. "How does Mademoiselle Howard?"

Carleton shrugged. "Not as well as I wish. She's over the worst of the illness and growing stronger, but her pallor worries me. And she tires too easily."

"What of her family?" Caledonne transferred his intent gaze to Carleton. "You find them congenial?"

"Very much so. They've been kindness itself." Deciding against elaboration, Carleton added with a meaningful glance at Caledonne's rapidly emptying plate, "I hope you're free to join us for dinner this evening— if you've any room left. The elder Miss Howard's cook is a wonder."

"It would be my pleasure as long as you're sure my visit will be welcome."

"Eaden and Rodrigo have dined with us a number of times, and they've been warmly received. The Howards delight greatly in company. They'll never forgive me if I neglect to invite you."

"Then I'll look forward to meeting them tonight—and especially your lady love." Smiling, Caledonne swallowed a bite of rare beef and washed it down with a draught of wine. "Tell me more of your meeting with this Navy Board."

Carleton pushed away his plate and folded his arms on the table. "If you ask me, our local commissioners are worth a dozen of Congress's Marine Committee. They've taken hold of their responsibilities like a dog worrying a bone. I'm persuaded we'll be able to work effectively with them. I ordered Eaden to coordinate his plans with theirs as far as practicable—and to give no quarter to the Royal Navy or to any British East Indiamen that come his way. I'm quite confident of his abilities in that regard."

"Teissèdre told me about the attack on your ships and that Howe's intention is to ruin you if he fails of executing you."

"Maintaining a mounted brigade is ruinously expensive, and if I don't keep my merchantmen and privateers in service, there'll soon be no money left to fund it. And then I'll be of no more use against the British." More softly Carleton added, "And I'll have nothing to offer Miss Howard for our future."

"Have no fear on that score," Caledonne said, eyeing Carleton as he attacked a generous slice of pudding. "Your ships are under our protection."

Carleton sat forward so abruptly he had to grab his pint to rescue it from falling. Foaming ale slopped across the tablecloth.

"Uncle Alexandre—" he began, his voice a low growl.

Caledonne stopped him with a raised hand. "France looks the other way while privateers flying her flag and manned by her citizens join you Americans in attacking British shipping. It's known your fleet makes use of our flag when prudent, and it's only one of many our navy informally protects."

Carleton mopped up the spilled ale with his napkin. "So that's why your 50s lay near enough to come to my merchantmen's rescue. But—"

"Your ships deliver all manner of goods to our shores and purchase from us products you'll sell elsewhere. You see, it's greatly to our advantage to ensure that your merchantmen as well as our own continue to ply the seas. It's simply a matter of business."

Frowning, Carleton waved his explanation away and said sharply, "I know what you're about, and in case you hadn't noticed, I'm not a child you have to rescue. I'm perfectly capable of managing my own affairs."

"And you do it as easily as you arranged payment of our dinner with a single glance at Captain Marston." With a casual shrug, Caledonne sat back in his chair, wiped his mouth on the napkin, and dropped it on the table. "But you're also my nephew, the only child of my dear angel Julianne, whom I've missed sorely these thirty years. She'd not forgive me—I'd never forgive myself—if I didn't assist her son in every possible way."

The raw emotion in his uncle's voice and his reference to Carleton's mother made it impossible for him to protest further. He cooled his temper by tossing down the remaining contents of his pint.

Caledonne fixed him in a keen gaze. "You know, of course, that one does not tweak the British lion's nose as you have without inviting severe retribution. I'd be surprised if Howe has not doubled the price on your head."

Carleton considered his uncle, unconvinced that he had simply made a lucky guess. But how could he have learned of this when even Teissèdre could not yet know? Or did he?

"He has," he conceded gruffly.

"What of Miss Howard? He's offered a reward for her too?"

"There's been no mention of her. As yet."

"Ah." After a tense silence Caledonne sighed. "That does not bode well."

"No. Although some loyalists still infest the area, considering how difficult it would be to capture her here, where revolutionary fervor abounds, and carry her away without detection . . . " He spread his hands and let the words trail off.

"An assassin then."

"The most logical solution. I relieved Eaden of a detail of his most experienced marines soon after we arrived here. They keep watch on the house twenty-four hours a day, fully provisioned by the new manager of my warehouse—Teissèdre's agent, as I'm sure you're well aware."

"A wise precaution," Caledonne approved, his tone dry.

"I'll never risk her life again, Uncle Alexandre."

"And yours? Howe can get to you as easily. By now your movements around the city are well known."

"As you said, I take precautions. Two of my marines shadow me everywhere I go. For example, there's one over there." Carleton tipped his head toward a table against the far wall occupied by a lone, muscular young man who appeared to take in the crowded room with an indifferent gaze. "The other's on guard outside. They're sharpshooters and keen as hunters after partridge."

Caledonne regarded him through narrowed eyes. "Who knows?"

"Besides me and the men themselves? Eaden. You. The manager of my warehouse who keeps them supplied. And the Howards' housekeeper, who has custody of the house keys and lets me in and out at night. Her husband, one of my majors, was also formerly employed by the Howards. He was most instrumental in bringing Miss Howard to safety."

"They can be depended upon then. But not even Teissèdre and your Monsieur Stowe?"

Carleton shook his head. "They don't need to know. Though I'm sure our mutual agent Teissèdre will learn of it soon enough from the man he employed to be my manager and keep an eye on my affairs."

Caledonne's visage relaxed into a broad smile. "You miss nothing, do you, Jonathan? I trained you well."

Carleton assessed his uncle with a level look. "So did Sir Harry. And from the Shawnee I learned—shall we say—other useful talents."

Caledonne sobered. "I always suspected Sir Harry sent you to Lord Oliver's deathbed to get you away from Black Hawk as much as to force you to pay your respects to the man who gave you away."

Carleton flinched, but let the remark pass. "I was not deceived in that, but I went because I loved Sir Harry and he wanted me to. I never meant to stay ten years, however. Nor to become a man I despised."

"Ah, yet *notre bon Dieu* did not leave you there, either physically or spiritually." His tone laden with regret, Caledonne added, "In spite of our differences, I never doubted Sir Harry to be a man of the highest principles. I wish our relationship had not become so contentious. Both of us were at fault, to be sure, but if I'd been more diplomatic, he might have sent you to me instead."

"My life would have turned quite differently if he had. But he was deeply suspicious of your involvements and feared I'd be drawn into them. So he taught me to despise intrigue and espionage. How ironic that I've become the very thing he feared." Carleton gave a bitter laugh, then slowly sobered. "Yet had I not entered on this course, I'd not have met Miss Howard."

Caledonne clamped his hand over Carleton's. "The Father uses all things for our good after all."

"I've trouble believing that."

"But you will learn it." Caledonne made a dismissive gesture. "When wars cease, Jonathan, then there'll be no more need of these clandestine methods. Until then, what choice have we if we're to prevail?"

"By 'we' whom do you mean? The French? The Americans?"

His uncle regarded him with a faint smile, clearly marking Carleton's caustic tone. "Both of us together, *naturellement.*"

"And the Shawnee?"

"Alas, that will depend on which side they ally with."

Carleton gave a short laugh. "Just as after the last war, both sides will abandon the tribes no matter their allegiance or the outcome of the contest."

"Consider that perhaps God has placed you in a position to make a difference." Caledonne paused before asking, "But what about your journey back to your Rangers. It will be a long and dangerous one. You'll take some of your marines with you?"

"They're needed here. And once I'm in the wilderness, I can take care of myself."

By now the tavern was emptying. Carleton pushed back his chair and rose, Caledonne and his officers following suit.

"With only the weekend left before I have to leave, I promised Miss Howard I'd be home early." Putting on cloak and helmet, Carleton added with a laugh, "And if I don't alert everyone to your visit in time for the ladies to make proper preparations, the consequences will not be to anyone's liking."

# Chapter Thirty-two

"I'M AMAZED AT HOW LIKE you are to each other," Elizabeth murmured, returning Caledonne's warm smile across the dinner table. "If it weren't for the difference in your ages, you could be twins."

"I'm told my mother resembled my uncle closely and that I look like her. Though I suppose not in every respect," Carleton amended, his tone dry.

Elizabeth stifled a giggle. "Of course not, silly. You're quite obviously a man—a fact I'm more than happy about."

"So am I," he drawled, raising one eyebrow. "And I'm glad you're not. A man, I mean."

His lazy glance lingered on her lips, and a delicious tingle bubbled through her veins like champagne. He had dressed for the evening in a formal suit of finest charcoal grey wool with intricately embroidered facings and a silk waistcoat the same deep blue-grey of his eyes. With candlelight burnishing his blond hair, the effect was even more striking than usual. Just to look at him scattered her thoughts.

To keep from scandalizing everyone by melting into his arms in front of them, she bit her lip and hastily transferred her attention to Aunt Tess, who occupied the table's head, with Caledonne on her right. Tonight Elizabeth felt as though she really saw her aunt for the first time. With the anxieties of the past month, she had lost weight, and, wearing a gown of the newest fashion in Carleton's gift of royal blue faille, with her silver-streaked black hair dressed in a most becoming style, she looked younger and more vital.

Caledonne's attentions most certainly played a part, Elizabeth mused. She suppressed a smile as the count leaned his head close to her aunt's to say something in a low tone that caused her to blush and laugh.

Elizabeth had expected to be impressed by Caledonne, but when Carleton returned from fetching the admiral in the chariot and ushered him into the parlor, she had for a moment felt distinctly intimidated. Not quite as tall as Carleton, he nevertheless made an imposing figure, lean and militarily erect. His features differed from Carleton's in a some-what aquiline nose; a slightly thinner, less generously formed mouth; and a jaw and brow of softer modeling—minor characteristics that the two men's striking similarity obscured except to a keen eye. And clad in the dark navy-blue uniform coat of a highly decorated French admiral, with crimson sash and waistcoat, his coat, breeches, and cocked hat richly ornamented with gilded braid and snowy lace, he projected the same commanding force as did his nephew.

Her parents and aunt had also clearly felt it. In fact, Elizabeth had noted with momentary alarm, they had initially been quite taken aback, undoubtedly because they remembered what she did not: the war two decades earlier in which France and England had been mortal enemies.

It had soon become apparent, however, that the count was not one to stand on ceremony or flaunt his high connections at the French court. Like Carleton, Caledonne possessed an instinctive charm and a manner so open and kind that it quickly set them all at ease.

They had spent more than an hour conversing about their respective families. Caledonne confided that he had lost his cherished wife ten years earlier and that he had three living children—two daughters and a son—and five grandchildren, of whom he was unabashedly proud.

Their discussion had continued at dinner with increasing friendli-ness and intimacy. At Caledonne's insistence they were soon addressing one another by their given names as though acquainted for years.

Elizabeth found herself liking the count very much and was delighted to see that her family did as well. Even Abby was as attracted to him as she was to Carleton, a response Caledonne returned with unaffected kindness, remarking that she reminded him very much of one of his granddaughters who was about her age.

Returning her gaze to Carleton, Elizabeth said softly, "What a dear, sweet man your uncle is! It's plain to see where you learned to be so charming."

"He is very good," Carleton agreed.

There was something indefinable in his thoughtful tone that caused Elizabeth to wonder. Although it was clear from their interaction that Carleton loved his uncle dearly and held him in great regard, she also sensed a wariness in him deep beneath the surface. Before she could question him, he took her hand under the table, his fingers tightening over hers, the light in his eyes capturing her heart.

"He's obviously very much taken with you, and I don't blame him. As beautiful as you always are, tonight you're even lovelier."

She bent her head, blushing, and smoothed the gracefully flowing petticoat of her robe de la français with her free hand. "If so, then you're the cause of it."

"Not at all—though that silk does look exceptionally well on you," he said with a pleased smile.

She had never had a gown so elegant as the one Sarah and the seamstress had created from the shrimp-colored silk, and not even the elegant gowns that had been shipped back from Philadelphia with Tess would have done for tonight. They had cut the seams of the tightly laced bodice with extra width to allow for adjustment as she regained weight. Delicate fly fringe trimmed its ruched, elbow-length sleeves and the edges of the stomacher as well as down the open front that revealed the matching petticoat beneath.

Looking around the table at her parents, Aunt Tess, and Abby, Elizabeth reflected with pride that all of them looked exceptionally handsome that evening, clothed in garments made from the fabrics Carleton had generously supplied.

When they finally rose from the table, he gave her a concerned look. "Did you rest this afternoon?"

She shook her head reluctantly. "There was too much to do to prepare for tonight."

In fact, the afternoon had been a whirlwind of preparation from the moment Carleton brought news of his uncle's visit until Caledonne arrived. Excitement had temporarily banished weariness. But to her frustration her limbs now felt heavy, and she was having difficulty keeping her eyes open and restraining a yawn.

She took the arm he offered, struggling to mask her weakness although his worried gaze told her he noted it. They followed the others across the passage into the drawing room. Her father waited for them just inside the door, while the others clustered nearby, still occupied in conversation.

"You'd better make your apologies and go directly to bed, my dear," he told Elizabeth with a stern look.

"Papa, please! I'm not a child—"

"It's nothing to do with being a child," Carleton reproved gently. "You aren't fully recovered yet. I was afraid tonight would be too much of a strain for you."

Her father gave a stern nod. "If you keep wearing yourself out like this, Beth, you'll fall ill with another infection."

"I'm taking you upstairs to bed," Carleton said firmly.

By now the others clustered around them, concern on each face. Caledonne stepped to Elizabeth's side and took her hand between both of his.

"It's clear to see why my nephew has completely lost his heart, Elizabeth. I'm delighted to know we're to be family."

When Elizabeth expressed her distress at having to curtail their visit, he responded, "I cannot stay much longer myself as my squadron must prepare to depart in the morning. We'll have opportunity to share our hearts at greater length another time. For now, I'd not have you do harm to yourself. I also have daughters and understand a father's heart—and a lover's." He directed a meaningful glance at Carleton, and then returned his grave gaze to her. "I pray I'll have the honor of calling upon you again very soon."

Elizabeth curtsied, fighting disappointment but too exhausted to resist any longer. "I pray so as well, Alexandre. Godspeed on your journey back to France."

WHEN ELIZABETH HAD KISSED Abby good night and she had retreated to her own chamber with Jemma, Carleton sat on the side of the bed and brushed the tears from Elizabeth's cheek. "Don't despair, dear heart. Even a week ago, you'd not have been strong enough to bear such a late dinner with company. And you and I have the next two days together before I have to leave."

"You're not going into Boston tomorrow?"

"I made sure everything's in order there. Your father's found a pair of horses and ordered the supplies I'll need. They'll be delivered tomorrow, so I can devote myself to you for the entire weekend."

She returned his smile. "I'm determined to join you as soon after the New Year as possible. Surely I'll be well enough by the end of January—"

"And brave the worst of the winter storms?" he chided. When her tears welled up again, he said firmly, "There's still a shadow in your eyes and not enough color in your cheeks. You've gained hardly any weight. You don't eat nearly as much as you should."

She looked down. "I . . . I can't seem to force down more than a few mouthfuls. I keep thinking of . . . their suffering."

"Is this what's been troubling you?" He tipped her face up, forcing her to meet his earnest gaze. "I know exactly how you feel, dear heart.

The thought of what our prisoners endure makes me sick to my stomach. But making ourselves ill over their fate won't help them. We have to remain strong and win this war so we can free them."

She threw her arms around him and pressed her face against his chest. "I promise I'll do better."

He gently cupped her cheek in one hand and trailed the other down her back. "I don't want to worry about you while I'm gone. Your father said it'll be spring until you're strong enough to travel. For now you must stay here where you're well taken care of and get your strength back."

Nodding, she took a shaky breath and released it. Keeping her head bent, she murmured, "I don't ever want to be a burden to you or interfere with what you need to do."

He held her away from him. "Never think that, Beth. I've no greater joy and peace than when you're by my side. That's why I want you entirely well before you join me. I wouldn't be able to care for you properly were you were to fall ill again. I don't want to risk losing you, not after all we've gone through."

She pressed her hand over his. "I know. Until the morrow then, dearest of my heart. Bid your uncle *adieu* for me."

He gazed deeply into her eyes, entranced as always by the gold flecks in their expressive, warm brown. Then he drew her close and lowered his mouth to hers for a long moment that was yet far too short.

"Until the morrow," he whispered, suddenly feeling an unaccountable stab of fear to release her from his arms.

THE HOUR THAT FOLLOWED Carleton's return downstairs sped quickly in talk of the war and France's imminent entry into it. Slouched in his chair, Carleton watched his uncle, halfway between amused admiration and conviction. There was no denying that Caledonne had taught him much that plainspoken Scots Sir Harry never could have.

Effortlessly Caledonne regaled his hosts with an analysis of the issues involved for France, the personalities who maneuvered for power within the court, and how events would likely unfold when news of Saratoga reached Paris. Dr. Howard was particularly absorbed in the discussion, and he and Caledonne engaged in a lively debate, opposing each other on several matters with good humor and mutual regard, while Tess and Anne chimed in on one side or the other. Each time they turned to him for comment, Carleton merely smiled and shrugged.

At last the clock on the landing tolled ten, and Caledonne started up, exclaiming at the lateness of the hour and apologizing that it was necessary for him to return to his ship. When Tess sent a servant to have the chariot brought around, Carleton marked with interest a subtle reluctance in her manner.

"I can't remember an evening I've enjoyed more," Dr. Howard said heartily as he and Caledonne bade each other farewell, and Anne echoed his sentiments.

"I'm so glad you came," Tess told Caledonne as he bent to kiss her hand. "Please don't forget us. Any time duty or pleasure brings you back to the area, we'd be most delighted to have you call."

Caledonne straightened but did not release her. "It would be impossible to forget you, Theresa," he murmured. "I shall look forward to renewing our acquaintance at the first opportunity."

Carleton had to turn away to hide his smile. The admiring glances his uncle bestowed on Tess had not been lost on him, nor her becoming blushes when they bent their heads together in intimate conversation.

When everyone had bidden his uncle farewell and retired to their seats at the fire so he and his uncle could make their private farewells, Carleton escorted his uncle to the drawing room's open double doors. "I wish you could stay longer, Uncle Alexandre. It seems we meet only to take leave of each other."

Caledonne paused on the threshold. "There'll be further opportunities, I'm sure. I especially hope you'll visit us at Nice again soon. It's been far too long."

"I'll come as soon as I may. I've dearly missed visiting with my cousins—and you—and rambling around the countryside."

"Then until we meet again, please extend to your dear lady my regrets and my very best wishes. I can't tell you what pleasure it gives me to see your felicity in love. There's no greater satisfaction in life, and you've chosen very well."

"I'm blessed beyond my deserving," Carleton allowed.

Caledonne hesitated before saying, "I know how it pains your heart to leave her. But we'll pray that, with our countries formally allied at last, this war will quickly be brought to a successful end, and there'll be no more sad partings."

"I'll join you heartily in that prayer."

Sarah approached along the passageway, bringing Caledonne's cloak and hat. After donning them, Caledonne turned to take Carleton by the shoulders and regarded him earnestly.

"You cannot know how dear you are to me, Jonathan. I see so much of your mother in you—not only in your appearance, but in your spirit. She'd be quite proud of the man you've become, as am I."

Carleton bent his head. "I've not always made the best decisions."

Caledonne chuckled. "I don't know anyone who has, including me. But always *le bon Dieu* sets us back on the right path, *n'est-ce pas vrai?*"

*"Mais, bien sûr,"* Carleton agreed, feeling less than certain of it.

Caledonne released him. "At least now you're back among us . . . though I presume you do mean to return to the Shawnee from time to time."

"As often as I'm able. But until this war ends much will depend on Washington's approval. The few reports I've received from the western frontier indicate that many of our warriors have allied with the British and gone on the warpath again. That concerns me greatly."

"The Shawnee are fierce warriors. They served us well in our last conflict with Britain, and I'd hate to see them fight against us now. Many in the army deeply regretted that our defeat forced us to abandon them and our other native allies. As a result, white settlers now trespass on their lands with impunity and subject them to much ill treatment."

Until now they had spoken in low tones, but without his realizing it, Caledonne's voice began to rise. "I confess I was more than gratified to learn you'd been discovered among them—that, in fact, you're the Shawnee's great war chief who cast both Americans and British out of Ohio Territory last year. My own nephew—White Eagle!"

It filtered into Carleton's consciousness that the murmur of voices behind them had ceased and that a heavy silence suddenly enveloped the room. Sarah hovered in the passage, waiting to escort Caledonne outside, and Carleton read an alarm in her dark eyes that caused his stomach to clench.

Before he could glance around, Caledonne drew him into a warm embrace. "May you be abundantly blessed of God, Jonathan. I pray we'll not again be parted for so long."

Carleton returned his embrace. "Until we meet again, God go with you, Uncle Alexandre."

Every nerve taut, he watched Caledonne follow Sarah down the passage and out the front door. Then, feeling the others' eyes on him, he swung slowly around.

His questioning gaze first found Tess, seated by the fire opposite Elizabeth's parents. Ashen, she bent slightly forward as though about to rise from her chair, one hand pressed to her brow, the other clenched over the chair's arm.

Turning full around, he glanced toward Anne and Dr. Howard. They stared at him, their faces paralyzed with a shock and horror that instantly disclosed the truth.

They had not known.

# Chapter Thirty-three

HIS EXPRESSION CAREFULLY MASKED, Carleton stood at the fireplace, supporting one arm on the mantel. A still coldness possessed him, and he surveyed the room, feeling as though he watched actors upon a stage playing out a scene whose outcome he already knew.

"Last fall and winter the London papers were full of the lurid exploits of this White Eagle—the looting, the scalping, the wholesale slaughter of innocents burned out of their homes! And now I discover I've harbored beneath my roof—"

"In case you've forgotten, Samuel, this happens to be my roof," Tess snapped, "and I'll be the one to determine who's harbored under it."

Dr. Howard's lips compressed and a flush burned on his cheeks. "And as a consequence, I've allowed the addresses to my daughter, under false pretenses, of a savage—a bloody butcher!" He shook his finger at Carleton. "You, sir, you are that man! Have you the gall to defend yourself?"

"As I'm neither savage nor butcher, I've no need to do so."

"What other description fits your actions?"

"You presume to judge me, yet you know nothing of the matter, nor of my actions except what you've read in the papers. And we all know how accurate those are." Carleton gave a harsh laugh. "Beth knows the truth of it—"

Dr. Howard let out a contemptuous snort. "And from whom did she learn this 'truth'? You?"

"Samuel . . ." Tess looked from her brother to Carleton, then back again before saying faintly, "Beth accompanied Charles to find Jon among the Shawnee, and—"

"What?" Elizabeth's parents exclaimed together.

"Charles was convinced she was the only one who could persuade him to return, and she wouldn't have remained behind in any case. Once there, she was adopted into the tribe, and—"

"Adopted?" Anne broke in, her voice rising. "Our daughter doesn't need another family, Tess. She has one." She faced Carleton, eyes narrowed. "I assume this was your doing."

"It was not," he answered stiffly. "She chose it." Even as he spoke, however, fragmented images of that chaotic council meeting when Wolfslayer pressed his right to enslave Elizabeth, only to have Blue Sky put an end to it by adopting her, rose up to accuse him.

"My own sister allowed her to go all the way to Ohio Territory among the Indians, into danger I can't even think of!"

"How was I to stop her, Samuel? As you well know, Beth's her father's daughter. She chooses her own course." Tess waved the subject away. "What matters is that she learned the truth from the Shawnee themselves—that it was a shaman named Wolfslayer who was responsible for these brutalities and who deliberately did everything possible to lay the blame at Jon's feet."

Scowling, Dr. Howard jabbed his finger at Carleton. "At the very least, *he* led the raids and *he* is responsible for unleashing such horrors."

"Samuel, please stop this!" Tess pleaded. "Think of Beth—"

"That's exactly who I am thinking of!"

"How can you not have told us of such a—a critical matter, Tess?" Anne demanded.

Her eyes red, Tess looked down and wadded her handkerchief into a ball in her lap. "It's . . . complicated."

"Well, perhaps you'll do us the courtesy of at least trying to explain it," Dr. Howard said, his tone dripping sarcasm.

Snapping up her head to meet his accusing gaze with narrowed eyes, Tess related her conversation with Elizabeth little over a week earlier. "Since it was impossible to tell you earlier, she quite rightly forbade me to bring the subject up until after Jon left so as not to—"

"In other words, the two of you deliberately conspired to deceive us!"

Arms folded, Tess drew herself up with a hauteur Carleton had never guessed her capable of. "We did not conspire to deceive anyone," she said crisply. "The stars were not in alignment, that's all."

Had Carleton not been so enraged, he would have been hard pressed to not laugh. He met Tess's glance with one that caused her to flush and again drop her gaze.

"I apologize, Jon. It isn't fair to put you through our private family squabbles. Beth intended to explain everything when they might hear it calmly—"

"Calmly!" Throwing up his hands, Dr. Howard rounded on Carleton. "You could have told us yourself, sir."

Carleton kept his level gaze on Tess. "I was under the impression you had been told."

Tess's mouth tightened. "When Stowe and Briggs brought the news, I did tell them I'd explain everything fully. I meant to. I'm sure that's what Stowe told you, Jon."

Carleton slid his gaze to Dr. Howard. "Beth also confided that you told her you knew all of it."

"How could I possibly have known what I didn't know?"

"It's my fault, not his or Beth's. With all that happened, Samuel, there was never a good time to try to explain the rest."

Dr. Howard kept his baleful stare on Carleton. "And so you just assumed that we were completely sanguine to have our daughter marry an Indian war chief who fought against—*against your own people?* You expected that, naturally, we'd welcome you into our family with open arms?"

"As I recall, you didn't exactly welcome me with open arms."

"And I shouldn't have changed my first opinion! I left our daughter in your care, sir, and you've not done well by her. You see her now, health completely broken because of the path you led her on. And I suppose you expect her to live a life of privation among these primitive savages. How long do you think she'd survive?"

Every word struck Carleton like a hammer blow. "I'll never allow her to live a life of privation," he returned when he could speak. "In case you've forgotten it, I have the means to provide her every luxury she could ever desire."

As though fighting to contain himself, Dr. Howard stalked across the room, then swung around and returned to confront Carleton. "Indeed you do. Yet you conceive yourself to be an Indian—"

"Shawnee," Carleton returned, his tone steely. "And I do not conceive myself to be anything other than what I am, sir."

"I stand corrected," Dr. Howard mocked, back stiff, hands propped on his waist. "To be precise, a Shawnee war chief—the great White Eagle, who brutally raided our border settlements, setting homes to the torch and scalping innocent women and children—"

"Those who committed such unpardonable acts did so against my express orders."

"So you say. And to think I once believed the best of you!"

When he began to turn away, Carleton gripped him by the shoulders. "Then believe it of me still! My heart has not changed. I've not always succeeded in what I intended, but I've always meant good and striven for it. If you saw what I've seen, endured what I have, know what I know, you'd not doubt me."

"We want to believe that, Jonathan, and perhaps it's even true. But how can we possibly accept this fantasy that you consider yourself to be one of those uncivilized savages?"

Carleton flinched, feeling as though Anne had struck him. He released Dr. Howard and moved away.

"Madam, barbarity isn't confined to the native peoples. Our culture may be different from yours, but we're no less civilized. And I've done nothing differently while fighting among the Shawnee than I have in battle against the British. All those directly under my command obeyed my orders to spare any who could not or would not fight. Only those who refused to surrender, giving us no choice, died. All the others we captured and drove out of our lands unharmed."

"How can you say they were unharmed?" Anne cried. "By your own admission they suffered the loss of family members and homes, to say nothing of the terror they must have experienced."

"And what have my people experienced? Do not you Whites do exactly the same things you blame the native peoples for doing?"

"What is this talk?" Dr. Howard exploded. "You're as white as any of us!"

"The color of my skin does not define who I am, nor my worth nor that of my kindred. That is for God alone to determine."

"God! And what does the Almighty think of what you've done?"

Carleton looked quickly away to prevent anyone seeing the effect of the doctor's words. All too vividly he remembered the horrors Wolfslayer and his warriors had perpetrated. Indeed, it had been impossible to stop his own warriors from all of it, though he had imposed every possible restraint. Without allowing them to loot and take scalps as was their custom, he could have gathered no force at all to drive out the settlers who, despite repeated warnings, continued to encroach on Ohio Territory and wantonly murder any who stood in their way.

At last he returned a piercing gaze to Elizabeth's parents. "You laud my promotion while decrying the acts that gained my rank. The Lord God of Hosts made me a warrior, and I refuse to be ashamed of it. If there's to be freedom and justice, men like me will have to fight those who oppress the weak. And unfortunately war brings with it death and destruction. Let those who begin the conflict answer for the consequences."

"The issue is on whose side you're fighting!"

"The issue, sir, is the cause I fight for. You Americans claim to fight for liberty but hold human beings in bondage." Carleton struck his chest with his fist and continued fiercely, "I freed the slaves I inherited because I was a slave. I'll never hold men in bondage again nor turn my back on those who cry out for justice."

"That's what this is all about, isn't it, Jonathan?" Anne said, her tone softening. "Elizabeth wrote us how greatly you'd suffered among the Indians. It's to be expected that such trauma would pervert your thinking—"

Stung, he rounded on her. "This is what you believe—that my mind has become twisted because I suffered abuse?"

"I didn't mean—"

"I'd not undo what God allowed me to endure among the Seneca," Carleton cut her off. "It gave me the gift of clarity and purpose. It hardened me physically, but softened my heart to those who suffer."

Dr. Howard snorted. "Well, that's apparent. Do you even believe in the true God any more? Or do you now worship pagan idols as they do?"

Carleton fixed him in a level, calculating look that caused Dr. Howard to flush. Tight-lipped, he returned to his chair and sat, arms folded and gaze averted.

"Lest you forget, it was the Whites who taught the Indians to take scalps for money," Carleton said, his voice thick. "You fight over this continent like dogs over a bone—the British lusting for profit and the Americans for land—and ignore the fact that this land belonged to someone long before you ever came here. Them you kill without mercy, take their scalps, and loot their homes. I've seen it with my own eyes."

"Have you . . . taken scalps?" Anne asked, her hand pressed to her bosom.

"That you can ask me that, madam!"

Dr. Howard made an impatient gesture. "Considering your opinions, why did you return to fight for the very people you once led attacks against?"

"Because I couldn't go on living apart from Beth. Because I hope to earn a reputation that will give me a voice for the Shawnee once you Americans have won the war—as I know you will. For when that day comes, my people will depend upon your good will for their very lives."

The words shook. He brushed past Dr. Howard and strode to the window, pushed aside the draperies and stared into the blackness outside, the impossibility of explaining himself or his actions in a way they could ever understand or accept bearing upon him like a heavy weight.

It struck him forcibly that, following in the wake of the wrenching shock of Elizabeth's capture and the effort to rescue her, staying with her and her family these past weeks had clouded his sense of who he was. He remembered it now with piercing clarity, and he was grateful.

He turned back to them, teeth gritted. "You accuse me and my people of being savages and blame us for taking vengeance for the same injustice that drove you Americans to war with the British. Are your lives worth more than ours? Have we done any more than you've done to us? We are men even as you are. We love our families; revere God; feel pain and love; and seek justice, liberty, peace—just as you do—and for this you despise us!"

In the tense silence that ensued, he sank into the nearest chair and stared into the air, pointedly refusing to meet Tess's sympathetic look.

Anne exchanged a glance with her husband. "But, Jonathan, you can't change what is. You've every advantage of appearance, charm, wealth, connections—yes, and rank—and the prospect of so much more. Will you cast all this aside for—what? A life among the Indians? Do you expect our daughter to do the same for your sake and us to bless it?"

Dr. Howard let it out in a sigh and wearily rubbed his eyes. "I've no doubt you're sincere, but Anne is right. This is quite misguided. Surely you see that there's no future in such a life for Beth. There's certainly no future for the Indians. The settlers will continue to flood into their lands, and they'll finally be driven away. They can't win this battle."

"Do you think I don't know that? My hope is that by joining my voice with those who counsel my people to a prudent course, their destruction might yet be avoided."

"If you insist on tilting at windmills, that's your privilege, but what do you expect us to do?" Dr. Howard sputtered. "We've overlooked a great deal, but we'll not bless your marriage to our daughter unless you abandon this fanciful attachment to the Shawnee and sever all ties with them forever. Return to the life you were born to live, Jon!"

A taut silence reigned, broken at length when the clock on the landing struck the quarter after eleven. The candles guttered, casting ghostly shadows across the room.

"It's growing late and we've a great deal to consider," Dr. Howard said abruptly. "We'll speak privately again tomorrow when Beth's out of the way. Sunday, too, if need be. But we must have your decision before you leave."

"Until we can talk further, please don't discuss this matter with Elizabeth, Jonathan," Anne implored. "We may yet be able to sort this out. We love you and wish to see the two of you wed, but not like this."

"Beth needs to know!" Tess objected. "There've been enough secrets already, and this will have consequences for her life none of us can foresee. It's her right to decide what she'll do, not yours."

"We're her parents, Tess, not you," Anne said tensely. "Please honor our request and keep silent."

She returned her gaze to Carleton. "Elizabeth loves you, and she'll naturally side with you. And that would be unfair, not only to her father and me, but also ultimately to her by forcing her to choose between us and you, between a future that's in her best interests and one that would be disastrous for her. You see that, don't you?"

Carleton bent his head and rubbed his temples, too wrung out to think clearly.

"Please promise us this," Anne repeated. "I don't think it's too much to ask."

"If you can think I'd ever pit Beth against you, then you know me not at all." Rising, he added, "Nor will you ever."

He turned away from them in bitterness of soul and strode out of the room, leaving them to stare after him.

STANDING IN THE DRAFTY PASSAGE outside Elizabeth's closed door, Carleton grasped the jamb on each side and pressed his brow against the solid panel. The murmur of angry voices reached him from downstairs, but no sound came from within her chamber. He was grateful that she slept undisturbed.

For some moments anguish held him immobile. Finally, shoulders slumped, chest painfully constricted, he turned toward his own chamber. As he did so, a faint shaft of light farther down the passage drew his eye.

It lay beneath Abby's door, and on impulse he went to it, his footfalls muffled on the runner. Hearing the angry conversation more clearly from downstairs now, he realized with a sinking heart that Abby's chamber was directly above the drawing room.

He gave the door a light tap and called softly, "It's Jonathan."

"Come in!" came the eager reply.

He edged the door open and looked inside. Only the faint gleam of banked embers on the hearth and the glow of the wavering candle flame on the bedside table lighted the room. Abby sat ensconced in the bed beneath blankets piled to ward off the chill, a woolen cap covering her head and a heavy coverlet wrapped around her shoulders.

At sight of him, a welcoming smile wreathed her face. She laid down the book she held and reached out both arms. Forcing an answering smile, he crossed the dim chamber to gather her into his embrace.

"It's late. What are you doing still up?"

Her smile faded and she looked down. "I heard everyone talking downstairs, and I couldn't sleep."

"I'm sorry we kept you awake."

"I hate when the people I love quarrel. I decided to read so I wouldn't hear."

He pulled a chair beside the bed and sat down. "Does reading keep you from hearing?"

"If it's a good story." Glancing shyly up at him through her lashes, she asked hesitantly, "What's everyone so upset about?"

He shrugged, suspecting that she had overheard a great deal more than she wanted to admit. "Grown-up things. When you're older, you'll understand."

She folded her arms, her lips forming a pout. "Everyone says that. But I understand more than you think."

He leaned toward her, thinking that, except for her dark blonde curls and blue eyes, Elizabeth must have looked very much like her at twelve. "I know you do. You're quite perceptive. But there are burdens only grown-ups should bear."

Tears came into her eyes. Again she looked down, struggling to blink them away.

"Mama and Papa are very angry with you, aren't they?" Her voice quavered.

Her anguish struck him forcibly, and for a moment he was at a loss how to respond. At length he said, "Time will set all things right." He pushed to his feet. "And speaking of that, it's time for you to be asleep."

Not looking at him, she scooted down to lay her head on the pillow. He pulled up the covers and tucked them around her.

"Good night."

She looked up, and the sadness in her eyes stabbed through him. "Good night, Jonathan," she whispered.

He kissed her cheek. Straightening, he turned quickly to keep her from seeing the emotions he could not conceal and strode to the door.

"I don't care what they say. Beth and I love you. Please don't go away."

He arrested, for a long moment stood motionless. Finally he glanced back at her.

"I love both of you, too, Abby. With all my heart. Always remember that."

He turned away then and stepped into the passage. Without looking back, he shut the door behind him.

# Chapter Thirty-four

*Saturday, 6 December*

AWAKENED BY THE MOANING WIND and a spate of rain rattling against the siding, Elizabeth turned her head on the pillow and forced open her eyes. Dawn faintly brightened behind the windows' heavy curtains, softening the shadows that wrapped the chamber.

Had she dreamed? The sensation of Carleton's having bent over her sometime in the night's darkest hours remained so vivid that she could not be certain.

Held motionless in deep slumber, she had been unable to awaken or respond when he lightly kissed her lips. He had whispered something then, his voice too muted for her to make out what he said. Yet somehow she had known that it was a prayer and that he was grieved.

When she sat up, however, the memory of Caledonne's visit immediately flooded back, and she shook off her troubling thoughts. It had only been a dream after all, she assured herself, suddenly eager to find out what everyone had conversed about after she had retreated to bed.

She stretched and rubbed her eyes, then swung her legs over the side of the bed, shivering in the cold as she slipped her feet into her thick woolen slippers. Her dressing gown lay across the foot of the bed along with a heavy coverlet. She drew on the former and wrapped the latter around her before dancing across the icy floorboards to the fireplace.

From beneath the dense covering of ash she raked free a few cherry embers, laid on strips of pine kindling, and with the bellows coaxed a wavering flame to life. To this she added twigs from the woodbox, then small logs, and in minutes a crackling fire brightened and warmed the room.

It was the earliest she had awakened since Carleton had brought her home. Exulting, she determined that she would not allow any weakness to waste a minute of their last two days together. They would enjoy the day without interruption and the morrow as well. She straightened and turned toward the bed.

Startled, she stopped in mid step. Carleton's violin case was propped against the bedside table on the side opposite from the bed, where she had not seen it earlier.

She stood frozen, at first puzzled, then with dread settling into her breast. At last, feeling as though she had been wrenched back into the dream, she went woodenly to it.

It was then that she saw the folded sheet of paper lying on the table next to her Bible.

The page had not been sealed. Her name was written across the outside in his hand.

She snatched it up, tears starting to her eyes even before she unfolded it. Disbelieving, she rapidly scanned the letter's contents, the deep ache that took residence in her breast making it difficult to breathe.

*Dear heart,*

*Forgive me.*

*I swore we'd have the weekend together, but now to my sorrow I find I cannot keep my promise. Please believe that if there were any way I could stay and hold you close for even one more hour, I'd do so without hesitation.*

*Never doubt that my love remains true and unchangeable always. I hope in time you'll come to understand that only concern for your welfare could drive me away. Indeed, it's better for you if I go.*

*Do not grieve, dearest one. May God lead you on your way and may his arms enclose you more securely than can mine. Perhaps some day, if he wills, we'll find our way back to each other again. I pray it will be so, but if not, that peace will ever surround you and joy fill your days.*

*My heart is too full to say more than: I love you.*
*Jonathan*

Clutching the letter, she ran to fling open the door, the coverlet falling to the floor behind her. Wracked by sobs, she crossed the passage to thrust open the door of Carleton's chamber and came to a halt on the threshold.

The fire had burnt to ashes on the hearth. His packs and weapons, all his personal possessions were gone. Crossing to the armoire, she found nothing inside but his elegant suits and shoes, abandoned now. All other trace of him had been removed.

She pressed her hand to her mouth to stifle an outcry, then ran back into the passage and stumbled downstairs, clinging to the banister to keep from falling. Except for faint sounds issuing from the kitchen along with the savory aromas of breakfast cooking, the house was cloaked in silence.

She flew down the lower passage and around the corner. Stepping into the rear entry, she threw open the back door. Cold wind curled inside, cutting through her thin shift, but she paid it no heed.

Dark clouds hung low overhead, and a downpour mingled with sleet had started. She could see no movement anywhere in the misty vista of muddy, forlorn gardens and the sweep of winter-brown lawn past carriage house and stable to the ancient barn at the bluff's precipice.

She pushed the door shut and leaned her back against the cold boards. The mantel clock in the drawing room to her left began to toll seven, echoed seconds later by the tall case clock on the landing. The soft murmur of her parents' voices and tap of footfalls descended the stairs and passed through the dining room. Then chairs scraped across the floor in the morning room.

"There you are. What are you doing up at this hour, Beth?"

She lifted her head dully to see her father emerge from the morning room's rear door, followed by her mother, their expressions reflecting alarm. They hurried to her, and her mother encircled her shoulders with her arm.

"You're freezing! What's the matter?"

She was shaking so hard she could not speak. They supported her between them into the morning room and made her sit down. When Jemma appeared in the doorway, her mother sent her upstairs to fetch a blanket.

"What's wrong, Daughter?" her father asked, his brow creased with worry.

Elizabeth found enough air to gasp, "Where's Jonathan?"

It was not lost on her that her parents exchanged an apprehensive glance. Before either could speak, Jemma returned with the coverlet, which she tucked around Elizabeth. Sitting beside her, she began to gently chafe Elizabeth's icy hands.

Tess entered from the dining room, pale and red-eyed as though she had been crying. "What did you say? Jon's not here?" she said, looking around anxiously.

Elizabeth shook her head and tears spilled. Realizing she still clutched the crumpled letter, she shook it at her parents and cried, "He's gone! What have you done?"

Abby ran into the room and clutched Elizabeth, her face puckered with distress. "He was here last night. He came and kissed me after I went to bed."

"When? What time?"

Abby frowned. "Around eleven-thirty, I think. I was reading." Tears welled into her eyes. "I knew he was going away."

"So the coward's run off instead of staying to answer for himself," Dr. Howard growled. "You heard me tell him we'd try to sort the matter out today. Evidently he'd no intention of changing his mind."

'What are you talking about?"

"Samuel, hush!" Anne transferred a warning glance from Elizabeth to her father.

Sarah appeared in the passage doorway, bearing a covered dish. Tess sprang from her chair and crossed to her.

"Have you seen General Carleton?"

"No, ma'am," Sarah said slowly. "Not since last night." When Tess raised her eyebrows, she explained with resignation, "I be in the kitchen late and I let him out."

"Did he say anything to you?" Elizabeth asked anxiously.

Sarah's face softened. "He don't tell me why or where he be goin'. He just ask me to keep on watchin' over you, Miss 'Lizabeth, make sure you be safe."

"As if we can't watch over our own daughter!" Elizabeth's mother huffed.

Dr. Howard glared at the housekeeper. 'I'm beginnig to believe there are more intrigues in this house than in George the Third's court!"

"Oh, hardly, Samuel!" Tess scoffed. "Your behavior last night is exactly why Beth and I didn't want to bring up this issue in front of Jon."

Sarah abruptly handed Tess the platter she held. "I go talk to Perry and see what he knows." She hurried down the passage toward the kitchen to seek out the estate's old caretaker.

With a clatter, Tess unceremoniously deposited the platter on the sideboard and took a seat. Elbow propped on the table, she leaned her head on her hand.

"I pleaded with you not to do this, Samuel. If you'd only listened to what Jon had to say—"

"*Me* listen? He's the one who refused to listen to calm reasoning."

"Tell me. All of it," Elizabeth said blankly.

Tess proceeded to describe the scene that had played out while Elizabeth slept, including every harsh word spoken. When her parents interrupted now and again to dispute her account or insert their opinions, Elizabeth waved them peremptorily to silence, her anger a palpable force in the room.

When Tess finished, Abby tore out of Elizabeth's arms and faced her parents, pale with fury. "I heard everything you said. How could you speak to him like that? You drove away my sister's only love! He's the only brother I ever had, and I love him as much as Beth does. He saved Beth from a horrible fate, and now he's gone forever because of you!"

Whirling around, she stormed out of the room, sobbing. The sound of her angry footfalls ascending the stairs, followed by the slam of her chamber door, echoed in the room.

Silence reigned. Trembling uncontrollably, Elizabeth pushed to her feet, clutching Jemma to stay erect. Turning a despairing gaze to her aunt, she said, "You were right. I should have told him at once. What must he think of me for keeping this a secret—and lying to him?"

"Elizabeth," her mother pleaded, "surely you can understand our concern that Jonathan could conceive himself one of those savages. Why, for all we know he's given up the true faith for their pagan religion."

"Jonathan told the Shawnee about Jesus when he first came to them," Elizabeth said dully. "They're very resistant to what they conceive to be white man's religion, but a few converted because of his witness, along with some members of other tribes living among them."

She looked away, swallowing with difficulty. "He gathered a little congregation there, and not long before we left, he lead us all in taking communion . . . " She could go no further.

For some moments no one spoke. At length her father said gruffly, "He might have told us."

"Hasn't it become apparent to you yet that Jon doesn't easily bare his soul," Tess broke in, her tone caustic.

"That a man of such wealth, such great prospects that he could accomplish so much would believe himself to be an Indian and even fight against his own people—our people! What would all our connections think if we allowed you to marry him, Elizabeth? What kind of future could he offer you when he's made such a name that there are those who'd gladly hang him? Someday you'll have a daughter of your own, and you'll understand that this is not the life we desire for you."

"I'm not a child, Mama! How can you make decisions for me or believe you know better than I what's in my best interests?"

"If he'll only return to his senses, give up this fantasy, and try to make amends for the evil he's done, we can forgive the past and welcome him back as is our Christian duty."

"Papa, he doesn't believe he needs forgiveness! He has good reasons for what he's done and the way he feels, for who he is. If you can believe his allegiance to his people—his love for them—to be a fantasy, then you'll never understand him."

"And you do? Do you also believe yourself to be one of them?"

"In some ways, yes, Mama. You'll always be my family, but I love my Shawnee sister, Blue Sky, as I do Abby. I love and respect the Shawnee and have come to see that the injustices they suffer—"

"Injustices? What of their injustice to those they slaughtered? Is that of no account?"

At that moment Sarah stepped back into the room, her cloak darkly soaked and dripping onto the rug. "Perry don't find nothin' amiss. A couple tracks in the mud near the back door, that's all. He say they be moccasin prints."

Taken aback, Dr. Howard said, "The horses and supplies I purchased for him are to be delivered today. Did he take horses from the stable?"

Sarah shook her head. The downpour drumming against the windowpanes sounded loud in the small room.

"He's out in this storm without horses or supplies," Elizabeth whispered. She turned to her father. "You reminded me of how God used the evil actions of Joseph's brothers to save many people alive and said that perhaps God used Jonathan, and Pieter, too, for the same purpose. Have you changed your mind?"

"I didn't know everything then," he protested, hands raised.

"And you don't now!" Tears blurring her sight, she looked from him to her mother and back again. "How can I ever forgive you for this?"

"I'M SO SORRY. FOR INCONVENIENCING YOU. I knew you were sailing this morning, and—"

"You could never inconvenience me." Caledonne finished filling her cup with steaming tea and set down the pot to regard her with a concern that caused her to hang her head. "It is I who must ask your forgiveness for causing such great distress to you and your family."

"There's no way you could have known." She forced down a swallow of tea and set the cup back in its saucer on the table, careful to keep the liquid from sloshing over the rim with the ship's sway in the bay's choppy waters.

He laid his hand over hers, frowning. "You're chilled through, Elizabeth. It isn't good for you to be out in this stormy weather when you've been so ill."

"I'll be fine, truly." Gratefully Elizabeth leaned on Jemma's arm as the young maid scooted closer and tugged the blanket he had brought them more closely around both their shoulders.

On returning to her chamber Elizabeth had hastily washed and dressed with Jemma's aid, while Sarah quietly ordered the chariot to be hitched up and brought around the front of the house. It had been impossible to escape without detection, however, and Elizabeth had faced a gauntlet of anxious questions and objections from her parents and aunt as she rushed past them out into the downpour, taking only Jemma with her.

All during the drive into Boston, she had prayed that Caledonne's ships had not yet sailed and hoped against hope that Carleton had gone to him. They had arrived to find Caledonne's flagship still moored at the end of Long Wharf, with her escorts waiting in the bay beyond. At sight of them Caledonne instantly had them admitted and suspended preparations for departure. Carleton had not been there, however, and seeing Elizabeth's distress, the admiral escorted her and Jemma to his cabin, relieved them of their wet cloaks, and ordered his steward to bring tea, while she related briefly what had happened, fighting tears.

She glanced around the admiral's snug sitting room, then back to Caledonne. Looking into his expressive smoky eyes, so like Carleton's, she said, "Please, call me Beth as Jonathan does. You're so like him that I find comfort in just sitting here with you."

His smile warmed her. "I'm glad of it. But you must also call me Uncle Alexandre as he does. It's my confidence that one day you will be my niece indeed."

"I pray you're right . . . Uncle Alexandre," she said hesitantly. "But I greatly doubt it now."

He shook his head. "Beth, do not fear that he will not come to you again or even perhaps cease to love you because of this. When he spoke of you and I observed the two of you together, I could not doubt that his heart is inalterably fixed on you—and yours on him."

"I've ruined everything now," she said tearfully. "I wasn't truthful with him. How can he continue to love me?"

Caledonne let out a regretful sigh. "Ah, it seems we always fear to address truths that may be hurtful, yet the secrets we keep inevitably result in even more pain. But it is love's nature to forgive."

"I don't know whether I can ever forgive my parents for driving Jonathan away," Elizabeth confessed, dabbing the tears from her eyes.

"They said cruel things to him."

Caledonne sat back in his chair, his fingers steepled. "Our blessed Lord came for this very purpose—that we may be forgiven for our sins against him and, in turn, forgive others," he reminded her gently. "Did Jesus not say that if we refuse to forgive, God also cannot forgive us?"

"But they hurt Jonathan so! He's suffering, and I don't know where he's gone." Tears overflowed.

"Yet you must forgive them, even now, before you know any more of the matter, and hope that Jonathan will do the same."

Caledonne's counsel was not at all what she had expected, but she could not deny that he was right. "I didn't want to hear this from you," she confessed painfully. "I looked for your anger to match mine, and yet . . . I know this is what I need to hear. I'll try to forgive. In truth, I'm as much at fault as my parents."

"All that's needed is the sincere will. Give *le bon Dieu* time to do the rest."

When she nodded, mute, Caledonne sat back in his chair, brow furrowed. "When Jonathan left your aunt's home he took nothing?"

"Only his packs and weapons. How far can he walk—and alone? Whether he decides to return to Washington or go back to the Shawnee, the journey will be long and dangerous."

Although Caledonne shrugged, worry darkened his eyes. "He has means to buy horses and all the supplies he needs at any town he passes through. And I doubt he'll go directly back to the Shawnee. He's an officer after all. He understands the duties and responsibilities of command and will never shirk them." He frowned. "But his second in command, Charles Andrews—he has a Shawnee wife, does he not?"

She caught her breath. "I hadn't thought of that. Jonathan told me Blue Sky accompanied the women back to the tribe with a party of the warriors for the winter. I know they must miss each other terribly. If Jonathan does go back, I'm sure he'll take Charles with him."

"Then he will certainly go to his brigade first."

Shivering with a chill, Elizabeth took another sip of tea, welcoming the warmth it radiated through her. "He'll be in even greater danger now. Howe will never let his attack on New York Harbor go unpunished."

Caledonne's eyes assumed the same wintry coldness Carleton's did when he was angry. As though he spoke to himself, he muttered, "One who has made himself the renowned war chief of a tribe as fierce as the Shawnee will not easily be outwitted by these English dogs."

His words held a deadly softness and an arrogance that took her aback. In speaking with him so intimately the previous night and this morning, it had been easy to lose sight of the fact that he had not made the connections and achieved the power and reputation he had through fortune or softness. It struck her forcibly now that Caledonne would be a very dangerous enemy.

When he turned his glance back to her, however, his expression was masked. Very much as Carleton's was when there were matters he did not wish to disclose.

"I must caution you to take great care as well. There will doubtless also be a price on your head."

She felt heat rising to her cheeks. "The British cannot reach me here."

He leaned urgently toward her. "I don't mean to alarm you, Beth, but simply to set you on guard. It may well be that Howe will not go to the trouble of pursuing you since you're no longer a threat to him, while Jonathan is very much so. But I've learned precautions to be always wise. Promise me you'll be especially careful not to expose yourself to any possible danger."

She bit her lip. "That's what Jonathan meant," she murmured. When Caledonne fixed her in a piercing look, she said, "He said much the same thing."

"Then to allay his concerns as well as mine, you'll take every care?"

Forcing a smile, she nodded, a deep uneasiness suddenly clutching her breast.

✳ ✳ ✳

ELIZABETH LEFT THE SHIP, escorted by Jemma and two lieutenants, who sheltered them against the gusting rain beneath an oilskin. Heads down, they almost collided with a couple of fishermen hurrying past them as they ran to the chariot waiting a short distance down the wharf.

They reached the conveyance just as Elizabeth's father dismounted from his horse, the limp brim of his hat shedding a stream of water onto his shoulders, clothing drenched through. He took Elizabeth in with an expression of such pain that she caught her breath.

After helping her and Jemma into the chariot and wrapping them in the blanket he had brought, he thanked the lieutenants and watched them return to the *Néréide,* tight-lipped. He said nothing, however, merely ordered the driver back to Roxbury, then mounted and led the way back.

Elizabeth was shivering uncontrollably by the time they arrived. The women met them at the door and drew them into the parlor to sit before a roaring blaze, exclaiming over their sopping wet clothing. Sarah led her daughter away to help her change out of her wet clothing and to set out dry garments for Elizabeth and her father.

Anne pressed her hand to Elizabeth's brow. "She's flushed, but I don't think she has a fever."

"It'll be a miracle if you don't fall ill again, Beth," Dr. Howard chided. "What were you thinking to go out in such weather—and without a parasol? Is your throat sore?"

Elizabeth shook her head, stretching her icy hands to the fire's heat.

"Where did you go?" Tess demanded anxiously. "We were worried sick."

"To Caledonne, as we suspected. I'm sure he had a great deal to say."

"He did, Papa," Elizabeth said tremulously. "He said I must forgive you, for the Lord requires it. And he bade me show you the respect and honor due you as my parents."

Speechless, Dr. Howard turned to Anne, eyebrows raised.

"Jonathan didn't . . . he wasn't there?" When Elizabeth shook her head, staring into the flames, her mother gently rubbed her back. "I'm sorry. Well . . . we need to get you into dry clothing right away, and then, if you wish, you can tell us what happened with Alexandre."

"I'd like to go to bed now, Mama," Elizabeth whispered. "I'm very tired, and I want to sleep for a while."

"Yes—yes, of course. Let me help you."

Gently her mother helped Elizabeth to her feet, and Tess came to enclose her in her arms.

# Chapter Thirty-five

*Tuesday, 16 December*

"YOU COULD HAVE SENT your aides to deliver the day's returns," Andrews noted dryly as he scanned the regimental returns listing troops fit for duty, in hospital, and absent.

Newly promoted colonels Farris and Moghrab exchanged glances. "We been wondering if somethin's afoot," Farris said. "Our warriors seem particular disgruntled of late."

"When Howe march out against us at White Marsh couple weeks ago, they sit 'round their campfires and do nothin'," Isaiah growled. "And just last week when we skirmish with that British foragin' party on our way here to the Gulph—"

"And what a miserable, godforsaken place this is," Farris broke in, drawing his cloak more closely around his shoulders. He glanced from McLeod and Stowe to the canvas sides of Andrews's marquee, which shivered with gusts of cold, wind-driven rain. "There's scant forage and no place to find shelter. What's Washington thinkin' bringin' us here?"

"Our ammunition depot is here along with the mill that supplies flour for our bread," Andrews reminded him. "But His Excellency is looking for a better place for a winter encampment. We should be moving out within a few days."

Ignoring the interruption, Isaiah continued with a scowl, "—our warriors hang back at the rear like we got the pox."

Andrews shrugged. "We didn't need them. After we refused to take the bait at White Marsh, Howe gave up the attempt to draw us out and marched back to Philadelphia. And we managed to drive off that foraging party without excessive trouble."

"But next time we may need 'em," Farris emphasized gloomily.

Andrews handed the returns to Major McLeod. "I'll make sure you're fully informed of their reasons for discontent as soon as General Carleton returns, Farris—and not before."

"And when might that be?" Farris persisted with a worried look. "Rumors been spreadin' that the gen'l might not come back."

" 'e'll be back any day now," Stowe broke in, his tone fierce. "The gen'l ain't the kind o' man t' abandon 'is command, unlike some as is named Gates, Mifflin, and Conway."

Andrews raised his eyebrows but decided to let the comment stand on its merits. "There's work to be done. That'll be all for now, gentlemen."

When the two colonels had gone, letting in a swirl of fine snow through the marquee's door flap, he strode around the back of his camp desk, wishing mightily for a blazing fire and a hearty meal. His stomach pinched with hunger and his hands and feet felt frozen even through the thick leather of winter gloves and boots.

Concern for Blue Sky and their son sharpened. Were they safe and warm at Grey Cloud's Town by now? Had they enough to eat? What about the rest of the people?

Sighing, he pushed the nagging worries to the back of his mind and focused on the matters closest to hand. "According to his response to Washington's letter, Jon intended to leave Boston last Monday. But I just got this from Miss Howard this morning. It appears he left a couple days earlier."

Stowe grabbed the letter and both men bent their heads over it, the older man's lips moving silently as he read.

McLeod looked up, frowning. "This must ha' come as quite a blow."

"I'm sure it did. I can't imagine what he's feeling. To have rescued her from the vilest conditions at such loss, watch her almost die, then have this happen—"

Motioning McLeod and Stowe to seats, Andrews gathered his cloak around him and dropped into his chair, sighing. "I know Jon well enough to agree with you, Stowe. He'll certainly never abandon his command. Nevertheless, I'm quite concerned that he's not shown up. If he left late Friday night as Miss Howard says, he'd easily have been here a couple of days ago—even taking precautions to avoid Howe's agents."

"I thought as 'ow they was doin' better," Stowe burst out. "Dr. 'Oward was right cold t' the gen'l when we first come, but 'e was beginnin' t' thaw by time Colonel Moghrab and me left."

"I can understand her parents' point o' view on this issue, but it's a shame Jon got caught in the line o' fire."

Andrews took back the letter from McLeod, folded it together with the sealed page addressed to Carleton, and set them back on the desk. "And clearly Miss Howard didn't come out of this very well either, James. She sounds quite distraught."

"So often our sorrows are o' our own makin'," McLeod observed sadly.

"Well, thankfully Caledonne seems to have been of some comfort to her. I met him at Nice when Jon and I stopped on our way from England to Virginia three years ago. He's a fine fellow, very much like Jon. Wouldn't want him for an enemy, though."

McLeod chuckled. "That can be a verra useful trait." He hesitated, then ventured, "I don't suppose ye can tell us what's up with the warriors."

"His Excellency was, shall we say, less than happy when I informed him that, over his objections, I was going to reveal to them a highly sensitive matter he'd related to me in confidence. He made it clear that if I tell anyone else, he'll have my head and my hide on a platter. Now that he has this congressional delegation to deal with as a result of the intrigues to replace him, I've no doubt he'll carry out his threats with a high hand, and I don't relish the prospect of being made an example."

McLeod raised his hands in surrender. "Then we dinna need to know. But that leaves Jon ridin' into a firestorm unawares."

Andrews shook his head, his jaw hardening. "I've set patrols to be on the lookout for him. Hopefully they'll intercept him before Washington's guards do so I can forewarn him before he's dragged into a meeting with the General."

"I knew I should'a gone back t' Boston," Stowe muttered.

"What could you could have done?"

"Ride with 'im 'ere. There's times a man oughtn't be alone."

"And those are just the times he insists on it," Andrews pointed out. "He'll talk when he's ready. If he reaches that point."

He did not add: *And if he isn't waylaid during the journey and never makes it back.*

*Friday, 19 December*

"LOOKS LIKE YOU GOT your wish, Farris," Andrews called as he rode past the colonel.

"The Gen'l's too kind pickin' a glorious day like today to move camp," Farris responded with a grin. He clapped his gloved hands together in an effort to restore circulation. "It's especially nice of you to post my regiment at the column's rear . . . behind the wagons and cattle."

Andrews reined his mount around, hastily grabbing the brim of his hat to keep it from sailing away in the bitter north gale that moaned through the Gulph. "It was your turn, colonel. Since it's wet and we're traveling northwest, you won't have to eat their dust. Be thankful for small favors."

Like the rest of the brigade, he was garbed for the move in heavy buckskins and wrapped in a rawhide robe. Under lowering skies, a fine snow swirled around them, although what remained of the trampled grass, visible between broad slicks of frost-rimed mud, still poked above the thin layer that had accumulated. At a short distance the landscape dissolved into a white mist that Andrews judged would offer some concealment if they encountered any more of Howe's foraging parties.

Well before the first brigade moved out that morning and in advance of the other cavalry units, he had sent out a patrol to scour the area, one that did not include the recalcitrant warriors. In spite of every effort at conciliation and the unchanged friendship and respect they showed him personally, to a man they had again stubbornly refused to take any part in the brigade's duties.

At least they had not gone home. With Spotted Pony at their head, they clustered astride their mounts behind Farris's regiment, resentment in every taut line of face and body. Andrews prayed earnestly that all of them would arrive at the new camp instead of drifting off into the woods and disappearing along the way.

Drawing his rawhide robe higher around his neck to keep out snowy drafts, he motioned to Briggs to follow and spurred his horse, convinced that he would never be warm again. He rode the length of the long column to make certain there were no stragglers. Ahead of the drovers, who had managed to collect their bawling charges into a reasonably compact body, and the line of baggage and supply wagons, Isaiah's dismounted troops stood at attention at the rear of his regiment, which held the column's van.

Andrews pulled his pocket watch from the pouch on his belt and checked the time. Shortly after three. They were well behind schedule. He had hoped the Rangers would be one of the first sent off; instead, they had been assigned to the rear, the next to the last to leave. Already the heavy cloud cover cast the landscape in an early dusk, ensuring that they would arrive at their destination at nightfall. He had to wonder if Washington meant to make a point.

Behind the Rangers the final brigade was only beginning to sluggishly form up. Andrews rode back to check on their progress and studied the soldiers with pity. A dispirited lot who hunched their backs, shivering, against the force of the wind, many of them wore shoes that sported large rents, while others had wrapped their feet in rags or lacked footwear altogether. Most were filthy and unshaven; some lacked weapons; and, with few exceptions, their clothing hung in tatters on spare, wasted bodies. The majority of those who wore some semblance of a uniform were clad in British scarlet, taken from enemy prisoners and dead.

Andrews knew that few of the men had broken their fast that morning, that, in fact, entire regiments had been issued no food for a couple of days. He didn't like the look of the horses and oxen either. Already gaunt and hollow-eyed, they hung their heads and shambled along as though it took their last reserves of strength to drag themselves across the ground.

The corps was beginning to look depressingly similar to its appearance the previous winter at Morristown. It was no secret that most of the army's commissaries and quartermasters were either corrupt or completely incompetent. Whether lazy or simply frustrated by the daunting challenges of their task, many resigned without giving advance notice, often neglecting to inform their superiors even after the fact. And with Congress exercising an iron grip on running the war, while lacking the necessary expertise for the task, it seemed as though every process of the army was broken. The army was already unable to fight, and if the needed clothing, food and forage, weapons and ammunition could not be secured, their cause would soon be altogether lost.

Andrews shook off his dark thoughts, brought his horse around, and went to join Isaiah at the van. At his nod, the colonel raised his hand

and motioned the column forward. With a jingle of spurs and harness, the column began slowly to crawl down Gulph Road's rutted dirt track to the protesting creak of wagon wheels and lowing of cattle. Shoulders hunched against the biting wind, the Rangers put behind them the foreboding chasm that split the rocky hills brooding over them on all sides.

As he drew his horse into line next to Isaiah, Andrews glumly ruminated on Washington's general orders two days earlier. He had thanked the soldiers for their fortitude and patience despite the defeats the army had suffered. Heaven had given them signal success, nevertheless, he insisted, citing France's generous aid and the likelihood that she would soon formally join the war against Britain.

The General had gone on to apologize that he could not provide his men the best winter quarters. To abandon the fertile region around Philadelphia would be to allow the British to despoil it, while towns farther away were overcrowded with refugees from British-occupied Philadelphia and could not accommodate an additional 12,000 men. Consequently he had settled on a nearby location that would be easily fortified, where they could build weather-tight huts for the winter. He concluded by appealing to his soldiers to be of one heart and mind and exhorting them to surmount every difficulty with an endurance and determination becoming their profession and the sacred cause in which they were engaged.

*All well and good,* Andrews thought now. *But even the best of sentiments don't fill empty bellies or put bullets in muskets.*

The previous day the situation had reached what had felt like its lowest point yet. Congress had ordered civilians and soldiers alike to join in a day of Thanksgiving for Gates's victory at Saratoga. Since there had been no corresponding celebration following the victory at Trenton and Princeton the previous winter, it had come as a slap in the face to Washington and his corps as well as a bitter reminder of the defeats they had suffered and their current want of every provision necessary for life.

They had dutifully obeyed, however. Following a meal so Spartan that their stomachs remained oblivious of it, the soldiers marched in the cold to an open field, where they listened to a Thanksgiving sermon. Afterward they straggled back to their ragged tents and that night went to bed, most without even the covering of an ice-cold tent, and with neither food nor rum to warm them.

Although his brigade was much better supplied than the rest of the corps, adequately provisioning the troops was becoming a challenge. Philadelphia's vicinity had been stripped by both armies, and the Rangers' commissaries were being forced to range ever farther afield to find the needed goods. Then the quartermasters had to transport them long distances, running the danger of interception by roving British cavalry.

Just as worrisome, on his return after escorting Carleton to the rendezvous, Farris had reported Howe's intent to hunt down and capture or destroy Carleton's entire fleet, both merchantmen and privateers. Since Carleton kept the brigade supplied at his own expense, if the British were to succeed, even he would very quickly run through all his considerable resources.

At thought of Carleton, Andrews's chest tightened. His arrival was long past due, and Andrews was growing increasingly worried. That there was no practicable way to trace Carleton's movements, no way to discover what had become of him, especially concerned Andrews.

His heart also ached for the misery Elizabeth must be enduring. Several times he had tried to respond to her letter, only to set paper and pen aside. He simply did not know what to tell her. All he could do was continue to pray.

It was nearing twilight with a stinging sleet mingling with the snow, by the time the Rangers turned from the winding, tree-lined road overhung by immense rocks and entered the new camp, a place named for the valley itself and for the iron forge located along the banks of the creek that powered it. The first brigades to arrive had begun to set up orderly rows of tents in their assigned areas. Along the narrow lanes, ragged soldiers without blankets or coats gathered around smoky camp-fires to ward off the cold.

As soon as they reached their campsite near Valley Creek, Andrews put his troops to work setting up their camp. Accompanied by Farris, Isaiah, and Spotted Pony, he rode along the camp's perimeter to assess their surroundings as much as was possible in the declining light. Twenty miles northwest of Philadelphia, the region's brooding hills, heavily forested with huge, ancient trees, ringed a desolate, windswept plateau.

The only sign of local inhabitants was a straggle of small homes and barns set amid bleak fields long divested of crops. There would be no accommodations for the men other than tents until huts could be erected, and officers would find it necessary to share cramped quarters in what few houses might be rented. Andrews took heart, however, to see that the sloping edge of the plateau and the surrounding heights, along with the creek and the Schuylkill River that formed its western and northern boundaries, provided natural defenses, to which the corps' engineers had already begun to add redoubts and trenches.

But as he studied his surroundings in the gathering darkness, a peculiar gloominess settled in his bones. He struggled to reassure himself that their new situation was an improvement over the Gulph even while instinct warned him that the army's plight that winter might well turn out worse than what they had endured at Morristown.

## Chapter Thirty-six

LATE THAT SNOWY AFTERNOON Carleton led his horses across a rime-edged, pebble-strewn stream, keeping a tight hold on the reins and a cautious eye on the footing. By the time he climbed onto the opposite bank, he was thoroughly chilled, his already sodden boots and breeches darkly slicked and liberally smeared with mud.

He waited stoically while the horses drank their fill. Finally he mounted and rode up the watercourse's rocky draw, leading the pack-horse and keeping the Indian trail he had been shadowing at a distance in view between the towering trees that cloaked the ridge.

When he reached the broad outcrop halfway to the top, he dismounted and made a cursory inspection of the shallow cave he had spied from below. Reassured that there was no sign of recent habitation, with dusk gathering he settled behind a screen of pines and firs near the precipice to watch and listen for several moments.

There was no movement along the trail, no sound beyond the creak of the trees' limbs overhead, the dry rustle of withered leaves in the wind, the skitter of small creatures through the brush. At last he rose and removed weapons and ammunition from his mount, unsaddled it, and unloaded the packhorse, stowing everything inside the cave.

He hobbled both animals by the stream, where a long, narrow clearing bordering the bluff's upward swell afforded a swath of drying grasses with green still showing beneath a thin layer of snow. Working with practiced ease in the failing light, he gathered firewood and built a small, smokeless fire.

Warmed by the flames and his exertions, he substituted dry leggings and moccasins for wet breeches and boots. These he washed free of mud at the creek and laid before the blaze to dry. He spent a few more minutes cutting armloads of springy boughs from the surrounding pines, strewed them at the cave's mouth, and spread his buffalo hide over them to serve as a mattress.

He collected a handful of nuts from beneath an immense chestnut nearby, broke them free of their spiny outer shells, scored their tops with his knife, and set them to roast on a rock at the edge of the fire's coals. A few miles back he had stopped to hunt for small game, gutting and skinning the fat hare he took. Now he washed the carcass in the stream, spitted it over the fire, and while it roasted, cooked a measure of parched corn in a small iron kettle hung on a tripod over the flames. When the food was ready, he forced down what he could. The rest he set aside for the morning.

It was by now full dark, and snow and wind had diminished. The moon had not yet risen, and high above the leafless treetops, a glittering sweep of stars bejeweled the black heavens. After adding more logs to the fire, he wrapped his bearskin around him and sat cross-legged on the strewn boughs, staring into the leaping flames without seeing them.

On retreating to his chamber after the confrontation with Elizabeth's parents, he had realized that he could not stay. To endure further recriminations was past bearing. Anger spent, he discarded his first impulse to seek counsel from his uncle while the *Néréide* was yet at Boston. Caledonne could delay no longer in sailing for France, and Carleton had no desire to attempt hasty explanations that, in any case, could change nothing.

His heart called him to return to his people, but to simply walk away from his command and the men who depended on him was impossible. Remembering Washington's summons, he determined first to return to his brigade, learn what matter was so urgent, and then decide on the most prudent course for the future. Thus he had barricaded pain behind immediate purpose.

Mindful that the British had doubled the reward for his capture or death, he donned his weathered buckskins before slipping silently downstairs, packs and weapons slung over his shoulders. As usual, Sarah had appeared to unlock the door. She did not meet his gaze, her sorrow and his silence a barrier between them thicker than a wall. Gruffly he thanked her for all she had done and asked her to continue watching over Elizabeth and to do everything necessary to keep her safe.

He had walked away then, feeling the click of the lock behind him like a knife thrust beneath his ribs.

Dark clouds portending rain had scudded across the sky that night, cloaking him. The high garden hedges blocked any view from Pierpoint Mill across Stony Brook to the west, and a rank growth of shrubbery and trees along the carriageway to the east provided a dense boundary from the clustered houses beyond them. Alert to intruders nevertheless, he moved silently through the shadows to the barn, where he found the captain of his marines at watch.

After relaying his orders, he left there to cross Stony Creek above the mill. He kept the road in sight while easing soundlessly through the woods on the far side. At that hour no other traffic moved along the rutted road.

A steady drizzle descended as he emerged from cover to cross the bridge over Muddy River. Wrapped in his buffalo robe, he walked all the way to Cambridge, agony at leaving Elizabeth sharpening with every mile that passed behind him and blotting out the discomforts of rain and cold.

He spent the remainder of the night sheltering from the strengthening downpour in an abandoned redoubt above the bank of the Charles River, a lingering reminder of the siege of Boston. With dawn faintly brigtening the shrouded sky, he walked down to the dock on the river below, where several farmers loaded wooden boxes of cheeses, meats, and root vegetables onto a small sloop for delivery to the Boston markets, while taking no account of the unabated rain.

They agreed to carry letters across the bay for a small sum: one to be delivered to Eaden's lodgings, explaining that Carleton found it necessary to return immediately to his brigade and repeating his orders for *Destiny* and *Invictus* to sail south as soon as possible and for Eaden to take command of his privateers; the other to Caledonne aboard *Néréide*, with the same cursory explanation along with instructions for Teissèdre.

Day was breaking when he entered the awakening town. In the rain and garbed as a longhunter, with the drooping brim of his weather-beaten hat covering his fair hair and shading his features, he reckoned he would attract little attention. It had been easy enough to acquire horses and tack at a local stable. He then secured the supplies and equipment he would need at a mercantile and loaded everything onto one of the animals along with his packs.

He was chary in doling out coins from the concealed store he carried, replying tersely when questioned that he had sold a number of furs, that his horse had gone lame, that he was in need of ammunition and other supplies for his journey west. He wrapped most of his weapons in a length of rawhide secured behind his newly purchased saddle. In case anyone showed too much interest, he kept one pistol holstered in full view on his belt along with his keenly honed tomahawk. These he backed up with the sheathed knife dangling from a rawhide thong around his neck and his grim, forbidding look.

From there he had traveled across the mountains to Albany, where he traded the horses for fresh ones before continuing to the upper reaches of the Delaware, then south. Driven by the black despair that haunted him too often, he was in no hurry to reach his destination. He shunned all human habitation, staying within sight of, but not on, one or another of the ancient Indian paths that crisscrossed the wilderness and seeking concealment each time other travelers passed.

He had no appetite, and during daylight hours an occasional handful of parched corn and dried berries sweetened with maple sugar sufficed for energy. In the evenings when his stomach gnawed with hunger, he made a solitary camp and took solace in hunting small game or netting fish from a stream. Growing increasingly haggard and gaunt, he lost track of time's passing.

During the day the rigors of the journey afforded enough distraction to keep at bay the demons that hounded him. It was when light faded from the sky and darkness swallowed up the world that dread and despair attacked like a relentless, unseen army.

He tried to console himself with having succeeded in wresting Elizabeth from Howe's grasp and restoring her to her family against impossible odds. That she was safe and would be well again was all that mattered. The loss to him personally was nothing.

Except for the loss of *her.*

He berated with bitter scorn his delusion that they could ever make a life together. In spite of his angry words, he could not blame her parents. They had their daughter's welfare at heart and had not been prepared for revelations that shocked them deeply, that were beyond their experience and comprehension. And they were right in saying he had no acceptable future to offer Elizabeth.

Nor could he blame Tess. Certainly not Elizabeth. She had only meant to protect him after all. How could he chastise her for keeping secrets when he was burdened with so many that he could never tell her?

Once again he faced the same intractable dilemma that had tormented him among the Shawnee long before Elizabeth finally found him: A Shawnee warrior could never find peace or acceptance among the Whites; he could not sever his heart from hers any more than he could break the ties of love and loyalty that bound him to his Shawnee kindred; apart from either he could not live with any sense of peace or wholeness. Nor could he ask her to sacrifice the ties of family and home and comfort for a harsh life among his people that offered only privation and wandering and hardship because of the merciless attacks of her people, who were bent on driving the native peoples from the ancient lands of their ancestors.

It was fully apparent to him now that in spite of all hope, in spite of his most desperate efforts to find a bridge between the two worlds that claimed him, there was none. There was only an unfathomable abyss.

At last, in the unbroken solitude of that desolate wood, he raged at the heavens. "Why do you torment me? How have I offended that I'm to be forever a man of no country and no home?"

His despairing cry resounded through the forest aisles and back from the hills, only to fade slowly away. Gusts of wind rattled the bare branches of the trees and swirled a shower of sparks upward from the fire as though the stars immeasurably distant in the night sky had drifted from their moorings. As he had from his.

The still voice that a year earlier had commanded him to return with Elizabeth to his former life and, more recently, to set the prisoners free, now remained stubbornly silent.

"Lord God, if it's your purpose to leave me always alone, then release me from these bonds," he whispered finally. "Take away this longing— this ache in my heart. I cannot bear it!"

Silence stretched long, but at last the reply sighed on the wind: *You have not yet learned.*

"Learned what?"

But his plea brought no further response.

Hunched by the fire while the heaven's diamond lights gradually shifted on their inexorable circuit and the waning moon climbed into the sky, he finally gave in to exhaustion. Drawing his bearskin over him, he sagged onto his bed of pine boughs, too weary to remain upright.

Yet for some time longer he suffered, anguish holding sleep at bay, until by slow degrees consciousness mercifully faded.

❋ ❋ ❋

*Saturday, 20 December*

HE ROSE RELUCTANTLY to a clouded, windy dawn. As far as he could reckon, his destination lay less than a day's ride south.

After eating what he could of the previous night's leavings, he threw the rest to the fire. He loaded the horses, then carefully scattered the fire's embers, stamping out the dying coals on the damp ground, and sweeping away the traces of his presence. Finished, he led the animals back down the draw before mounting.

Still shaken by doubt, he spurred his horse deeper into the forest's fastness, driven by the certainty that there was yet suffering to come. But blindly he grasped the hope that the One who had always gone before would not leave him to endure alone.

AS THE SUN APPROACHED its zenith, he stopped at a tavern on the outskirts of the nondescript village of Bennett, nestled in the folds of low hills, and over a measure of rum enquired casually if anyone knew where Washington's corps might be camped. When questioned with narrowed glances directed at his tomahawk and sheathed knife, he allowed that he had been wounded at Bemis Heights and, having recovered, was returning to his regiment.

The admission gained him respectful looks from the bartender and the few men at the scattered tables. He volunteered nothing further, and at last, with noticeable relish, one man shared rumors that an effort was being mounted in Congress to replace Washington as commander in chief with Saratoga's victor.

Carleton downed his drink, accepted a refill, and waited out a leisurely discussion of the two generals' merits. At length one man ruminated that he had heard the army had recently moved from White Marsh to Gulph Mills. Another insisted that the corps had moved again the previous day into what was to be their winter camp.

A place called Valley Forge, he told Carleton. And accompanying him outside, he pointed out the road.

## Chapter Thirty-seven

CARLETON STOOD IN WASHINGTON'S MARQUEE, staring at the letter he held, signed by Virginia's governor, Patrick Henry. A sickening dismay washed over him.

Could the day possibly get any worse?

Weary, cold, and dispirited, he had hoped to find his brigade unnoticed, change into uniform, and discover if Andrews could tell him anything about the reason he had been summoned before he sought a meeting with Washington. Instead, with the worst of luck, he had ridden out onto Gulph Road at the same moment Washington's advance guard, escorting their commander to the new camp a day late, had rounded a curve a quarter mile below.

Carleton had immediately tried to pull back into the trees, but his packhorse baulked, his mount reared, and the riders charged forward to surround him. His gruff explanation that he was merely passing through the area had been to no avail. One of the guards, whom he recognized too late, leaned forward in his saddle to look beneath the drooping brim of Carleton's hat and exclaimed, "General Carleton! We've been on the lookout for you."

By then Washington was approaching down the road astride his white stallion, surrounded by the rest of his guard, and any hope of escape had disappeared.

"Jon, I don't know what to say," Washington said, his voice gruff.

Carleton slumped into a camp chair. Propping his elbows on his knees, he supported his brow in one hand, the letter drooping slack from the other.

Over him flooded the wrenching memory of Black Hawk's motionless body arrayed for the journey to the wigewas of Moneto, the haunting death chant sung by his people as he slowly circled his adoptive father's grave, sifting the sacred tobacco through his fingers onto the bark slabs covering the still form below. And only hours later the tumultuous council meeting where Cornstalk, bearing regal, face carved in weary lines by the long, vain struggle against the Long Knives, stood with him against the warriors' cries for vengeance and their demand that White Eagle become their war chief.

The great sachem had warned of the destruction such a course would unleash. But at the council's angry refusal to listen, he had at last gripped White Eagle's shoulder, his dark eyes full of understanding and urgency, and said, "You must follow the counsel of your heart." And so White Eagle had gone to war against his former kindred.

Now Cornstalk also lay dead at the hands of white men. Denied even the rites befitting so great a sachem.

Washington's voice filtered into his consciousness. "Be assured that I am disgusted and appalled that such a thing could be done to our most loyal native ally and his son and companions. I am equally confident that Patrick will do everything possible to make sure this vile act will not go unpunished."

Carleton rose abruptly and strode toward the marquee's door flap, detouring around the welter of folded camp cots and packs belonging to the General and his aides that had been cast inside at random.

"Jon, stop!" Washington commanded. "I understand how you must feel—"

Carleton rounded on him. "How could you? Cornstalk was my brother, Black Hawk my father. Both were betrayed and murdered by the Long Knives—to say nothing of Red Hawk, Ellinipisco, and Petalla.

Four good men dead for no reason!" He again turned away. "There's nothing left for me here."

"What of your brigade? What of the woman you love?"

Flinching, Carleton glanced back to give Washington a hard look. To his relief, the General had appeared to accept his explanation that his tardy arrival was due to the weather, the time taken to exchange horses and resupply, the longer northern route he had chosen in order to avoid those who might lie in wait for him. He had no intention of explaining anything further.

"Please sit down."

Carleton hesitated, teeth gritted, finally returned unwillingly to the chair and sat, fighting to curb his emotions long enough to hear Washington out. "I should have been there. I knew I shouldn't leave them. Perhaps they might have listened to my counsel."

"If you had stayed, the British would likely have taken you captive. By then they knew that White Eagle and Jonathan Carleton are one and the same."

When Carleton made no answer, Washington continued, "Surely you cannot imagine that I approve of what happened, Jon. My heart is sick over this. Cornstalk was our friend, and for it he was shamelessly murdered by our militia. I abhor what those men did."

"I don't believe that you approve it. Nor do I believe that there'll be justice for Cornstalk's murder."

Washington let out a sigh. "Unfortunately, you are most likely right. But my greatest concern is to win this war. I simply ask you to be patient and counsel your warriors to do so. Allow Patrick to fully investigate the matter."

Carleton gave him a smoldering look. "That's always the case. When it concerns the native peoples, it's never a matter of importance. The truth is that nothing will be done, and you know it. Nothing has ever been done when an injustice is perpetrated against the Shawnee and our brothers and uncles and grandfathers. Why should this time be any different? Black Hawk's murder was not avenged by you Long Knives. But if one of my people does what you judge wrong, all of us pay the price."

With visible effort, Washington controlled his temper and walked around to the other side of the camp table. "I cannot deny that there has been injustice enough—on both sides. The Shawnee have massacred too. You, in fact, led them in war against us." Cutting off Carleton's furious response, he waved his words away. "Be that as it may, you know Patrick will do all he can to—"

"I know he means well," Carleton broke in, his voice heavy with scorn. "But what can he do? Do you truly believe any witness will come forward to testify against those who carried out this slaughter? The blood of Cornstalk and those murdered with him cries to the heavens, and no Long Knife hears it or pays attention!"

"I hear it, and so does Patrick! We have long been friends, Jon, and all I ask is that you see reason. Whatever you may think now, starting another Indian war will not help the Shawnee. Or you."

Rising, Carleton answered thickly, "I also count you a friend, sir. But if the day comes when I must choose between our friendship and the welfare of my people, that day I will return to the Shawnee and take up the tomahawk against all Long Knives."

Washington fixed him in a shrewd look. "Will you indeed? If the British succeed in persuading the Shawnee to ally with them, they will demand that you be turned over as a gesture of good will. And they will offer an even greater reward than they do now. You faced this once and prevailed, but the danger has not diminished, especially not since you successfully carried out an attack at their very heart."

Carleton regarded him with bitterness, knowing that he was right. Vivid images of the council meeting at which his fate had been coldly debated, and the desperate fight for his life against the shaman Wolfslayer that followed, tumbled like sharp shards through his mind.

He had come perilously close to death that night. With Elizabeth as witness. And if he had died, she would have been enslaved. Only by God's grace had they been spared.

"No," he conceded at last in angry frustration. "As much as I wish it, my hand is stayed. Not because of the British, but because I know that if I take up arms for my people again, it will be a fight to the death. And that day will mark their destruction."

"You may count yourself Shawnee, Jon, but you are also inescapably American. Was it not that tool of the British, Lord Dunmore, who caused Sir Harry's death? Was that not the reason you chose to join our cause—because of that injustice?"

Hands clenched, Carleton drew in his breath, let it slowly out. "I've not forgotten it."

Of a sudden it struck him forcibly that if one could pile up all the evil deeds each side committed, it would be impossible to count them all or to determine which one had the right to exact final vengeance against the other. God alone, who knew the depths of every individual heart, could judge with true justice and held the power to enforce it.

He became aware that Washington was saying, "You must find a bridge between the worlds you belong to—and I do not deny the difficulty you face in doing that."

Thinking of Elizabeth, Carleton gave a scathing laugh. "That's been my longing from the beginning, and I comforted myself that one must exist somewhere. But now I know it for a vain hope. Our worlds are too different. Neither side will listen, and I'm forever condemned to inhabit a no-man's-land between the two."

Washington came to take him by the arm, his grip painful. "Do not quit striving now. You have gained influence in both worlds that no one else has. Who knows but that you may be called to a greater task."

When Carleton considered him with a guarded look, he continued, "You wish to go back to your people. Well, I am sending you there as my envoy—not only for our sake, but also for the Shawnee. If they cannot be persuaded to ally with us, at least they might be persuaded to resist the British lure and remain neutral in this contest."

Taken by complete surprise, Carleton said slowly, "Coming on the heels of Cornstalk's death, that'll be a tall order indeed. Black Fish's party wields great influence over the tribe, and they advocate allying with the British."

"Black Fish did exactly that last winter. The British armed his warriors, and during the winter and summer he led raids against the Kentucky settlements."

Carleton stifled a groan. "If there are reprisals—"

"The situation will quickly get out of control. That is why it is imperative that you negotiate with the tribe to prevent that. It is in your own interests if you are ever to live at peace among them. The question is whether you can safely go back to them now and also whether they will allow you to return to report to me." Washington stopped, then added, "And whether you will choose to return."

A bone-deep weariness engulfed Carleton, making it hard to think. "It's unlikely the British will send any force into Ohio Territory this winter, but in case they do, I have strong allies among the people as well. If I undertake this charge, however, I'll take Andrews and all my remaining warriors with me." His tone made clear that his terms were not negotiable.

The General repeated softly, "You will return?"

Carleton met his probing gaze with a masked one. "That remains to be seen."

Washington's mouth tightened. "I will trust your better sense. Make arrangements then. And take gifts if you're able. Sadly enough, I have no money to spare. I cannot even feed and clothe my own troops."

Carleton gave a slight bow. "It'll soon be my people's hunger time, and they'll need all manner of supplies—food and clothing and such."

"Whatever you deem necessary."

Carleton could hardly take in how completely the cry of his soul in this matter had been answered. He could come to no other conclusion but that the Lord had prepared the way, and gratitude washed over him.

At the same instant, both of them became aware of a murmur of voices outside the marquee, rapidly rising to a din, and of bobbing light and shadow moving along its canvas sides. Before either of them could move to investigate, Andrews burst inside with Laurens and Tilghman pressing in behind, their expressions reflecting alarm.

Andrews glanced from Washington to Carleton and back. Sketching a salute, he said breathlessly, "Forgive us for intruding, Your Excellency, but the news about General Carleton's return passed through the camp in a flash, and the men have gathered to offer their regards."

He was interrupted by swelling shouts of "Huzzah, General Carleton! Huzzah, General Carleton!"

Exchanging concerned glances with the two aides, Andrews spread his hands helplessly. "They've endured much and appear to be looking for a hero, sir."

Frowning, Carleton brushed by them and strode outside, the others hurrying after him. He could hardly find space outside the marquee to stand because of the throng that milled around it. At his appearance the tumult became deafening.

It was full dark, but in the flickering light of rude torches, he recognized members of his brigade among the men. With the others they shouted his name and extolled the success of his raid on New York Harbor.

As he glanced around, he saw his warriors clustered off to one side, their expressions wavering between pride and anger. He started to see Spotted Pony at their head and directed a sharp glance at Andrews, who pressed into the crowd beside him.

"Later," Andrews muttered.

Turning back, Carleton raised his hands to silence the jostling men. "I thank you heartily for your good wishes," he called in a loud voice when the noise had diminished, "but this victory could not have been accomplished without the support and guidance of our commander, His Excellency General Washington. It's at his feet that your laurels should be laid, not mine."

"Huzzah, General Washington!" Andrews cried out, echoed enthusiastically by Tilghman and Laurens.

The crowd quickly took up the chant, intermingling it with their huzzahs to Carleton. The tumult continued for some minutes. Finally the officers managed to impose enough order to march the men back to their tents. As he thoughtfully watched them file off, Carleton noted that several officers directed guarded and even hostile glances at him and Washington.

"That was not needed, Jon. This victory was yours alone."

Remembering the conversation in the tavern a few hours earlier, Carleton answered, "I'll allow no man to elevate me above my commander . . . and my friend."

Washington returned Carleton's bow, his mouth briefly twitching in a faint smile.

"When did you return, Spotted Pony—and why?"

"Red Fox sent me back," the warrior said, clearly noting Carleton's cool tone. He gave a terse account of all that had happened, concluding, "Black Fish calls you to stop fighting on the side of our enemies and come help us to fight against them, White Eagle."

Carleton slid his gaze to Andrews. "But you did not think it important to advise me of this—not even of Cornstalk's murder?"

Andrews flushed but did not drop his eyes as he explained the circumstances. When he finished, Carleton relaxed and gave him a wry glance.

"I understand."

"We also were commanded to speak to no one of the murder of Cornstalk and those with him, nor to return to our people," cried Brown Bear from the tent's rear. "Perhaps they hold us hostage too so they may kill us when it is convenient."

"It's nothing of the sort—" Andrews's protest was quickly cut off.

"Why should we stay and listen to more of the Long Knives' promises? Crooked Oak, one of the Shawnee scouts. "They are possessed by *Matchemenetoo*. Their words are as barren as the winter fields."

His countenance dark as a thunder cloud, Sinking Ground said, "There must be vengeance for this evil deed."

Carleton lifted his hand to quiet the warriors who packed the marquee. Beyond weary and with a growling stomach, he had already spent more than an hour reviewing the brigade and patiently receiving the men's enthusiastic approval of his victory at New York. He had commended Andrews for his conduct while in command and congratulated him and the officers he had raised in rank on their promotions. Finally, before withdrawing to his marquee with Andrews and Stowe, he had spent several minutes taking the measure of the new surgeon Andrews had appointed.

All the while, Carleton had been uncomfortably aware of Andrews's covert scrutiny. He gained the distinct impression his friend knew more of what had happened at Boston than Carleton wished he did.

At his orders, the warriors had gathered to wait for him. Indeed, they could not have been prevented from doing so. Carleton was not in the mood for a confrontation, but from what little Andrews had time to tell him of the past month, he knew that if he did not take control of the situation immediately, a firestorm would likely erupt.

"I share your grief and outrage," he told them. "A man could have no better friend than Cornstalk was to me. My heart bleeds because of his death and that of his companions." He looked around at the warriors, meeting each angry gaze with an earnest one. "Most deeply am I grieved that they did not receive the rites due to renowned warriors and leaders of our people and that their bodies are not buried among us. It is my desire that before we talk more of this matter we sing the death chant and bring to mind their heroic deeds."

The charged atmosphere in the marquee instantly muted from rage to sorrow. With many tears they sang the drawn out, mournful notes of the chant together. Gradually their voices dwindled away, and Carleton moved among them, embracing each one and offering what comfort he could.

At last they squeezed between the folded camp cots, packs, and weapons stacked in the corners to sit cross-legged on the marquee's hide floor, wrapped in bear or buffalo robes against the frigid air. For some time they all remained silent and motionless.

"Does it surprise us that the *Shemanese* never keep their word?" Spotted Pony said finally, his voice heavy. "Is it not better for us to fight to the death than to live like dogs they kick out of their way whenever it pleases them?"

"The British are eager to ally with us," Brown Bear began.

"Have you forgotten that Howe doubled the price on White Eagle's head," Andrews broke in.

When the others protested that Wolfslayer was dead and that they would never sell White Eagle to the British, Carleton said grimly, "Be assured that the British will require my scalp as the price of an alliance with them. Can you swear that no one among our people will ever betray me for a price or because of a grudge or that the British might not overcome me by stealth when I'm among you?"

None spoke and and all eyes remained downcast, while he surveyed them, teeth clenched. "I have sworn undying enmity to the British because of what they did to Healer Woman. But that is the least that concerns our people. The British speak with the poisonous tongue of vipers. Are we now to follow the course that Cornstalk warned against so that we may suffer the ruin he foretold? For when the Long Knives win this war, which they surely will, they will lay waste to our towns like

a hungry man empties a bowl, devouring all it contains and wiping it clean.

"No, my brothers. There is another path, and we must find it. Does not Blue Jacket counsel wisely that we join hands with our uncles and grandfathers? Only by standing together have we any hope of prevailing."

"Even if that can be accomplished," Brown Bear objected, "such alliances will take years to conclude, and these murderers will walk free."

"We have greater matters to consider than vengeance for this one act, evil as it was," Carleton countered. "If we allow ourselves to be distracted by seeking to avenge every outrage, we only justify the Long Knives in coming against us with ever greater force, and we will never live in peace. We must act more wisely."

Again his gaze swept the assembly. "Washington is also angry at the deaths of Cornstalk and the others, and he assured me that Governor Henry of Virginia is seeking justice—"

He raised his hands to quiet the scornful outcries that arose. "Hear me, my brothers. Governor Henry is my friend, and I will write plain words to him to unstop his ears that he may understand our grievances and do what is right. But whether he takes heed or not, Washington has appointed Golden Elk and me as emissaries to our people to call a great council and find a path we can walk together if that is possible."

He noted that Andrews and Stowe exchanged surprised glances that quickly reflected delight.

"And what did he want from you in return?" Spotted Pony demanded.

"That I persuade our people to either join with the Long Knives against the British or stay out of their war," Carleton said frankly. "I held my tongue and promised him nothing, only that we would return to our people and call together the council. I told him I must take all of you with me and that we will carry with us food and other supplies so our families will not starve or go naked this winter. He agreed freely to this."

"What about weapons, bullets, powder?"

Carleton shrugged. "Are these not supplies our people need, Brown Bear?"

The mood of the assembly immediately brightened.

"How soon shall we go?"

"The brigade cannot stay in this place, Golden Elk. There's not enough forage for our animals, nor food for all of us. I will consider where we can move our camp, and when that is done, then we must gather the supplies to take with us." Carleton included the others in his gaze. "It will likely be the beginning of *Ha'kwi kiishthwa,* the Severe Moon, before we can get away, and then we'll face the worst of the *pepoonwi* winds. So prepare well."

He looked from one expectant face to another, his heart lifting in spite of the ache that refused to relinquish its painful hold on his chest. "We're going home."

WHEN CARLETON DUCKED back into the marquee after bidding the warriors good night, he found Andrews waiting for him. From his expression, Carleton immediately sensed what was coming.

Before he could retreat outside, Andrews extended a sealed letter to him. Carleton stared at it dumbly, unable to move.

"Beth wrote me and sent this along for you. Jon, I'm more than sorry—"

"Let it be, Charles," Carleton said brusquely.

When he made no move to take the letter, Andrews stared at him in disbelief. "Aren't you going to at least read this?"

"To what purpose?"

"To what purpose?" Andrews exclaimed. "To know what she says!"

"There's nothing anyone can say," Carleton returned in a steely voice.

"Don't you care? Judging from her letter to me, she was distraught and—"

"Do you think I feel nothing?"

"It's as clear as day that you do! I know the pain I felt when I sent Blue Sky and our son away—what I've felt every day since then. If I believed I'd never see them again—"

Carleton turned abruptly away. "What I feel is none of your affair."

"This from you, who embraced me when it felt as though my heart had been ripped out of my chest, who comforted me and assured me that I'd see them again!"

Carleton rounded on him. "I've said all I mean to say on this matter."

Andrews regarded him for a long moment, deep sadness shadowing his eyes. "If you refuse to confide in anyone, it'll eat you up inside. Believe me, I know. If you won't talk to me, please talk to James—"

Carleton raked his fingers through his hair. "Enough!"

"At least take her letter and consider reading it."

His hand shaking, Carleton snatched the letter from him and without looking at it shoved it into the pouch on his belt. He strode to the welter of camp furniture along one wall of the marquee, pushed the stacked packs aside, and pulled out a cot, unfolding it with a jerk.

"She went to Caledonne. His ships hadn't sailed yet. She said he comforted her."

Carleton dragged the other cot free and shoved it toward Andrews. "The morrow will come too soon. I'm going to get some sleep. I suggest you do the same."

"You'll just leave, then, and never let her know where you've gone or whether you're ever coming back?"

Carleton drew in a ragged breath as a bolt of anguish seared through him. Forcing himself to steady, he said in a hard voice, "Don't bring this up again, Charles."

He became aware that his limbs were stiff with cold. Hastily he stripped off belt and boots, found his bearskin among the scattered packs and wrapped himself in it. Stretching out on the narrow cot, he threw his buffalo robe over the top and turned his back, eyes closed.

For some moments the only sound was the wind rattling the sides of the marquee. At length he heard Andrews sigh and unfold his cot. After some rustling, the guttering candles extinguished and the creak of wood and canvas told Carleton that his friend also sought sleep.

But, weary in body and soul as he was, oblivion remained a stranger. Carleton stared into the darkness, feeling like a storm-tossed vessel adrift on a relentless, battering sea.

At length, hearing Andrews's slow, steady breaths, he reached over the side of the cot into the freezing air and caught up his belt from beside his boots. Drawing off the pouch, he pulled it under the bearskin, slipped the letter free, and dropped the pouch back onto the ground.

She had gone to Caledonne in her grief. Teissèdre would not fail to follow the instructions Carleton had sent him, and now that his uncle knew what had happened, he also would keep watch over her. As would God. The assurance eased in some measure the agony that tormented him without ceasing.

He ached to read what she had written yet feared it with a dread that shook him. He could not. Not yet. Perhaps never. If he yielded and returned to her, he would only do irreparable harm.

He slid the folded page into his shirt and pressed it hard against his breast as though the thin paper could stanch the flow of desire and grief. He found it impossible to turn loose of it though its mute witness of love rent him as nothing else could.

And he knew he would never be free of it.

## Chapter Thirty-eight

*Friday, 2 January, 1778*

HEAVY-EYED, ELIZABETH RETURNED her family's greetings as she settled into her place at the morning room table.

"It's good to see you up and about again," her father said with a heartiness that felt affected. "I believe you're finally over the worst of it."

"There's a little more color in your cheeks this morning," her mother observed, smiling.

Tess chimed in her agreement and Abby put down her spoon and beamed at Elizabeth.

She forced a smile. "Thank you. I'm feeling much better."

It was the first time in a month that she had felt well enough to come downstairs. Christmas had come and gone almost unnoticed in the concern for her health. As her parents had feared, she had caught a bad chill on her visit to Caledonne's flagship and had lain ill for weeks with a lingering fever, wracking cough, raw throat, aching limbs, and streaming nose.

Jemma set a bowl of thin porridge and a creamer in front of her and poured a cup of coffee. Elizabeth laced the coffee with cream and took a sip, staring at the porridge with no appetite.

"I want to see you eat all of that, my girl. If you're ever to regain your strength, you must put on some weight."

Elizabeth summoned a cheerful tone. "Yes, Papa"

An unfamiliar voice reached them from the front door, then Sarah's muted reply and the sound of the door's closing. They all glanced through into the passage, and after a moment the housekeeper rustled into the room.

"A courier just bring this for you, Miss 'Lizabeth." She laid a sealed letter at Elizabeth's place before withdrawing quietly with Jemma.

Elizabeth reached for the letter, her heart leaping. As she scrutinized the address, however, disappointment deflated her spirits.

"Is it from Jonathan, dear?"

Noting the hesitation in her mother's voice, Elizabeth shook her head. "It appears to be in Charles's hand."

When she made no attempt to open it, Tess prompted softly, "Would you rather be alone to read it?"

Elizabeth looked up to find everyone watching her with worried looks. Abby ran around the table and slipped onto the chair beside her.

Carleton's place during his stay with them.

She bit her lip and drew Abby against her in a quick hug. Deciding there would probably be no reason not to share at least parts of the letter with them, she composed her features and broke the wax seal. At the top of the first page was inscribed *26 December, 1777, Valley Forge.* Wondering where the town was, she focused on the rest of the letter.

Carleton had returned to the brigade safely, Andrews wrote, and described the warm reception he had received. A detailed account of Cornstalk's murder followed, with the furor it unleashed among the warriors. He went on to say that Washington was sending him and Carleton to the Shawnee as his emissaries to assure them that justice was being sought against the murderers, to persuade them not to start a new border war, and to negotiate for either their neutrality or support in the war against England.

They would leave the first full week of January and planned to return as soon as possible. If Carleton had not yet written, it was because he was heavily engaged in meetings with Washington, preparations to move the brigade across the Delaware to a winter camp in New Jersey, and gathering supplies for the journey to Ohio Territory. He would undoubtedly write soon.

Saying nothing of Carleton's response to her letter, Andrews closed with his warmest regards and prayers for her welfare, sentiments he assured her that Carleton would extend as well.

All hope that a letter would yet arrive from Carleton fled, and the neatly inscribed words blurred before Elizabeth's eyes. If he wished to write, he would already have done so. And now within days he and his party would head west to Ohio Territory.

"Is everything all right?"

Elizabeth forced herself to look up and meet her mother's anxious gaze. *How can you ask that?* she wanted to scream. *Everything is the worst it could possibly be!*

Instead she bit the back the angry words and, as she had often since her visit to the *Néréide*. She reminded herself of Caledonne's admonition to be patient, to love and forgive her parents, to trust God to work all things for good.

She had no idea how even the Almighty could ever bring any good whatever out of Carleton's leaving or Cornstalk's death.

"Cornstalk, the Shawnee's great sachem who opposed waging war against us, has been murdered," she said dully. She read Andrews's description aloud, voice shaking, unable to take satisfaction in the dismay plainly written on every face around the table.

Tess sagged back in her chair. "Well. Coming after our discussion with Jon that night, I can imagine what he must be feeling."

Into the silence that followed, Elizabeth said, "Washington is sending him and Charles as his emissaries to the Shawnee in the hope that Jonathan can calm things and keep the tribe from allying with the British and attacking our western settlements again."

"General Washington must place a great deal of trust in Jonathan to send him on such an important mission." Anne cast a meaningful glance at her husband.

"You shared my opinion of the situation, my dear," he responded. Frowning at Elizabeth, he said, "As much as he claimed to love you, I never conceived that he'd simply walk away if we voiced our concerns."

"Samuel, will you hush?" Anne snapped.

Tess drummed her fingers on the table. "You did considerably more than voice your concerns, brother mine."

"Don't you see that Beth's heart is broken?" Abby pressed protectively against Elizabeth. "You're making it worse and worse!"

"Abby, that's enough," Dr. Howard ordered. "Someday you'll be a mother, and then you'll understand a great many things you don't now."

"I'll never understand how you can be so mean!"

Unable to bear more, Elizabeth squeezed her eyes shut and pressed her hands over her ears. "Stop it!"

"Please, Abby, back to your seat." Although her mother spoke softly, it was plain she was on the verge of tears.

As Elizabeth was. Gently she steered her little sister toward her chair. Face flushed and mouth set in rebellion, Abby obeyed with dragging steps and flounced onto the seat, arms crossed.

Elizabeth bent her head and surreptitiously blotted away her tears with her napkin, hoping no one noticed. She heard her father sigh, then he pushed back his chair and came to crouch beside her.

"I'm sorry. I shouldn't have spoken so harshly."

"Not to me or to Jonathan," Elizabeth reproached. "But you always speak what you think—"

"—without considering the effect," Tess finished for her, glaring at her brother.

"Curse my too-ready tongue," he said, crestfallen. "Truly I didn't mean to hurt you more, Daughter. Will you forgive me?"

"Of course, Papa. But don't you think a better question is whether Jonathan will do so?" She gave a weary shrug. "But now it's too late to ask him."

✸ ✸ ✸

EARLY THAT EVENING, after a strained day spent fighting to contain anger and grief, Elizabeth sought the solitude of her chamber. To have Carleton with her for so long, believing that everything was finally resolved, only to have hope completely dashed, had left her with a bone-deep loneliness, an unsettledness too painful to bear.

She had read through Andrews's letter several times during the day while alone. But now, with Carleton's violin and his letter cradled on her lap for the sense of his nearness they offered, she read it again.

It seemed more noticeable to her that Andrews had worded the letter with care. One sentence especially drew her attention: "We leave the first full week of January and plan to return as soon as possible."

It struck her that he did not say that they would return. Or if they did, when. They *planned* to, but plans could change. *As soon as possible* could as well mean never.

The only certainty she had left was questions: Once Carleton was back among his people, would he cast his lot entirely with them and never come back again? Would he be drawn into another savage war? If so, would he fall on some far-away battlefield where she would never learn his fate?

As nothing else could have, this missive, along with the absence of one from Carleton, brought the finality of their separation into stark reality. Since his leaving, she had struggled to put on a brave front, but now courage entirely failed. Fear engulfed her and on its heels despair and something akin to panic.

She knew surely that if she were to endure, she dared not yield to the emotions that bore over her in a crushing wave. With desperation she fought back to a measure of calm.

She took up Carleton's letter. Even though, from Tess's account, he had been very angry at their deception, he still pledged his unchangeable love.

That night he had said to her parents that he would never pit her against them. And it occurred to her that his life had been so fractured by being torn from his own parents without explanation at such a young age and the subsequent loss of his mother, then of every man who had been a father to him, that he could never allow himself to become the cause of a rift between her and her family. Particularly not her father.

She felt certain suddenly that the reason he had not responded to her letter was because he had not read it, fearing that to do so would shake his resolve to stay apart from her.

*Father, strengthen my faith,* she pleaded. *Help me to trust you even in this. I know your will for us is good, and I'll not give way to doubt and be robbed of your peace.*

Blinking back tears, with her finger she traced a line at the letter's close: *Perhaps some day, if he wills, we'll find our way back to each other again.*

The assurance that he also still held on to a ray of hope warmed her.

"Lord, you carried us safely through the worst man can do," she whispered, "and you saved many others in doing so. Nothing is impossible for you. If it's your will to bring us together again, I know you'll accomplish this somehow. You are my God, and I'll cling to you through this storm, too, knowing that, whatever happens, you'll bring us joy at the end of it."

## Chapter Thirty-nine

*Sunday, 4 January*

FOLLOWING THE BRIGADE'S WORSHIP service that morning, during which McLeod had blessed him, Carleton, and their warriors for their journey, Andrews spent an hour going over his final orders with Colonels Moghrab and Farris. It was early afternoon by the time Andrews ushered the two colonels and Major McLeod out of the longhouse he and Carleton shared with their servants.

He returned the colonels' salutes, and they moved off, leaning into the blustery north wind, while McLeod lingered. Bitter cold had settled in a week earlier as the Rangers, along with the other cavalry units, had removed from Valley Forge at Washington's orders to establish camps across the Delaware in New Jersey. With food in such short supply that a mutiny had been only narrowly averted, and with men and horses daily succumbing to exposure, starvation, and sickness, the General had been forced to disperse mounted units to areas where food and forage could be more easily supplied.

In fact, the situation had deteriorated to the point that, had Washington not ordered it, Carleton determined to move the brigade on his own authority. He had chosen a location directly north of Trenton and a short distance southwest of Baptist Meeting House. The site lay near a ford across the Delaware and within a day's ride of Valley

Forge. Offering easily fortified meadowland that lay amid wooded hills, it was bordered by a tributary of the Delaware. Several companies of New Jersey militia had joined them at Carleton's offer to keep them supplied.

McLeod drew at his clay pipe and sent a stream of fragrant tobacco smoke into the crisp air. "The men are makin' good progress buildin' their shelters, considerin' it's been only a week since we moved camp."

From the slight rise the longhouse occupied, Andrews surveyed the camp with satisfaction. "This weather's certainly motivated them."

Although the sun hung low in the southwestern sky, the troops and many of the women still moved purposefully along the lanes at their tasks, heavily bundled against the weather. In spite of the cold, weather-tight longhouses, snug wigewas, and a scattering of log cabins already housed the majority of the brigade, with columns of smoke from multiplied campfires swirling overhead in the wind.

Still more habitations were rapidly going up along the orderly arrangement of lanes that radiated from a central parade ground. Corrals for each regiment's horses, furnished with south-facing lean-tos for shelter, ranged along the camp's perimeter inside steadily expanding fortifications, and a number of log barns were being framed for storing forage, tack, and other supplies.

"I see Jon's returned."

Andrews turned his gaze in the direction McLeod indicated. A large party approached along the main road through the camp. As they drew closer Andrews could see Carleton in full uniform at the van, flanked by Spotted Pony and Stowe, with a strong guard composed of the brigade's warriors ranged behind.

They drew to a halt by a detail of Rangers occupied in completing a roof on one of the half-finished log cabins. Carleton dismounted and handed the reins of his bay stallion, Devil, to Stowe, then Spotted Pony led the party off. For some minutes, Carleton lingered in good-humored conversation with the men that soon set them all laughing.

"If I'd not seen it with my own eyes, I'd never ha' believed any man could mold such a motley crew as this into a disciplined force. I believe our troops'd follow Jon afore they'd follow e'en Washington."

"He's always had a way of securing others' loyalty. He's fair and just and amply rewards discipline and courage, while brooking no nonsense. Our men—and women too—respect that and love him for it."

"It doesna hurt that we're the best supplied brigade in the army."

Andrews returned McLeod's grin. "That too."

As they spoke, several women joined the men at the cabin, and the conversation appeared to sober. Carleton bent his head as though listening closely to what they said, then responded with a nod and a smile.

"You'd never suspect there's anything wrong, would you? Did he ever mention anything to you about what happened at Boston? Or about Cornstalk?"

McLeod shook his head. "Nae. Not a word. He's buried it deep."

"I've known Jon a long time. The more he's troubled, the less he talks about it."

"He's said nothin' about the visit to the Vander Groots either, though that surely must ha' been wrenchin' to him."

"I'm glad you came with us again, James. You did much good on both occasions." Andrews pulled off his hat, shoved his fingers through his hair, and settled it back on his head. "It's a good thing Jon wasn't with us when we called on them the first time. I expected a harsh reaction, but it was hard enough for me to bear, and I know it affected you greatly too. Thankfully their grief and anger has had time to moderate."

"His visit was clearly a comfort to them, but with the burdens he's already carryin', he's payin' a price for it. If he doesna find relief soon, it'll fester and grow worse. A man can only endure so much pain afore it tears him apart."

"Well, I tried to draw him out when he first returned, but you know how well that went."

McLeod shrugged. "It's my business to counsel those who are hurtin'. And since ye're leavin' o' the mornin', I'd better feel him out tonight."

"Tread too far, James, and you'll have your head handed to you."

McLeod gave Andrews a wry look. *"Praemonitus, praemunitus,"* he said with a chuckle. "Forewarned, forearmed. You'll join us at my mess tonight?"

"I'll get him there," Andrews assured him. "The rest is up to you, my friend. And for Jon's sake I wish you luck."

"It'll nae be luck," McLeod responded.

"MOST OF THE MEN are still in tents, and food, clothing, and forage are in as scarce supply as when we left."

Carleton downed his measure of rum and set the cup back on the rude puncheon table where they sat along one side of the main chamber in the 3rd Troop's longhouse. Looking up, he returned the hearty greetings of a group of men who edged past in the smoky, crowded space before pushing away his half-eaten bowl of mutton, cabbage, and potatoes with distaste.

"Speaking of food, have a conversation with our commissary," he said, eyeing the two colonels.

"Yes, sir, gen'l," Farris drawled. "I'd say our cooks need serious admonishment too."

Isaiah mopped gravy from his bowl with a piece of dry bread, took a bite and chewed thoughtfully before swallowing. "Leastwise our bellies ain't empty like some."

"We can be grateful for that, at least," Carleton allowed with a grimace. He returned to the subject at hand. "The corps' in no condition to oppose Howe's foraging parties,much less counter an attack. If the army's commissary, clothier, and quartermaster departments aren't reorganized quickly, it'll be a miracle if Washington has any force left by the end of the winter. As one would expect, Congress has relegated his suggestions for reform to yet another committee, where they'll doubtless die a lingering death."

"To think it's only been a year since our victories at Trenton and Princeton—and barely more than two months since Saratoga." Andrews blew out a breath in frustration. "The army's in worse case now than when this rebellion started three years ago."

"They've endured. And they've only to stand fast to place victory out of Britain's reach. Whether that'll be possible or not—" Carleton spread his hands.

"What o' the intrigues against the General?"

Carleton gave a short laugh. "Worse and worse, James. He made no reference to it, but his anger lies close beneath the surface." He absently noted that Andrews and McLeod exchanged glances. "Laurens confided that General Conway offered such an affront that had his situation allowed it, His Excellency would have answered the insult by challenging him to a duel. Since Congress promoted Conway to major general over numerous senior brigadiers and appointed him inspector general of the army, his condescension has become so outrageous that Washington refuses to conduct any business with him and is barely capable of being civil to the man. If this continues, Congress will be forced to choose between them."

"If I wasn't so eager to see my wife and son, I'd love to stay to see the outcome of this contretemps," Andrews said with glee.

Carleton's mouth twitched. "His enemies severely underestimate Washington if they think they'll so easily overthrow him."

When they finished their meal, Andrews made excuses and left hastily with Farris and Isaiah. As Carleton moved to follow, McLeod stepped casually into his path.

"I've lately acquired a bottle o' exceptional Scots whiskey and thought we might share a dram afore ye take yer leave on the morrow."

"Lead on, kindly parson," Carleton said with a laugh.

Cloaked against the chill, they stamped through the snow the short distance to the major's wigewa in companionable silence and settled cross-legged at the fire circle. Through half-closed eyes, Carleton watched McLeod build a warm blaze, then deliberately uncork the bottle of amber fluid and tip a generous measure into two earthenware cups.

Carleton took the cup the major extended and, lifting it toward him in salute, emptied it in one swallow. He released a slow breath, savoring the trickle of the whiskey's fiery trail through his veins. By degrees the constant tension that denied him rest eased.

"Ye've been lookin' weary o' late, sir. Perhaps this'll help." McLeod poured another dram.

Aware that McLeod fixed him in a keen gaze, Carleton eyed him warily. "There's been much to do the past few weeks." This time he took only a sip of the whiskey, allowing the fluid to linger on his tongue.

McLeod took a draught of his own drink. "It was good o' ye to take time to call on the Vander Groots and hear them out. Ye were a great comfort to them, ye know."

Surprised, Carleton said, "I'm grateful you went along. You did much more than I ever could."

"Ye were his commander, and just that ye came made all the difference. There are no words to give succor for such loss. That ye sat and listened and grieved with them eased their sorrow."

Frowning, Carleton finished his drink. When McLeod again refilled his cup, a vague suspicion mingled with the warmth the liquor spread through his limbs, setting him on guard.

"Comin' atop o' Cornstalk's murder and yer leavin' Miss Howard as ye did, ye're bearin' a heavy burden. And now ye're also carryin' concern for the welfare o' the Shawnee and how ye're to counsel them."

Carleton regarded McLeod stonily. "You've been talking to Charles, I take it."

The major returned a mild look. "I'm chaplain of the brigade, and also o' its commander. Charles believes rightly that I ought to know what concerns ye. He loves ye greatly, did ye not know it, as do I, and—"

"I know your love well and return it. But these matters are my affair and no one else's."

McLeod studied him intently for a long moment before saying softly, "Ye know I lost my wife and children a few years ago durin' Lord Dunmore's War."

Taken aback, Carleton nodded. "I marvel that you show no bitterness or anger toward our warriors."

"Believe me, I was a different man then," McLeod returned, his voice turning ragged. "I suffered, as ye do now. I still do. Ye see, I brought my young wife all this way across the sea from Scotland, leavin' our families behind. It was my decision to settle along the frontier where we'd have our own land and the freedom and opportunity that afforded. And a few years later, with our farm and two children thrivin', I returned from huntin' to find my life in ruins. I was overcome by such grief and guilt that I thought it'd crush me. I couldna talk to anyone, and I railed against God and swore revenge on the murderin' savages."

Carleton rubbed his hand over his face. "James, I'm truly sorry."

"I know what ye're feelin', Jon. Charles told me a bit about the losses ye've suffered in yer life. They're more'n most men have to deal with. And as I did, ye think you're stronger than other men, that ye can bear yer pain alone. But no one can. God put us on this earth to bear one another's burdens, and ye're less than half a man if ye hold back yer trust, not only from those closest to ye, but from God as well."

"Trust!" Carleton sprang to his feet and paced across the wigewa. "How am I to trust when from my earliest memory those I've loved most dearly have been stripped from me one by one? I think of it constantly: Who'll be taken from me next? Caledonne? Charles? Stowe?" His voice breaking, he added softly, "Or Beth. Howe could still get to her."

McLeod let out a sigh. "Were he determined enough, there'd be nothin' ye could do to stop it, even were ye standin' right beside her."

Staring into the shadows, Carleton clenched his hands. "Trust results in nothing but heartache—as you should well know, James."

Silence fell between them, broken only by the hollow sough of the wind around the wigewa. At last McLeod said dryly, "Oh, I know how hard it is to give up control o' yer life to the Creator of the Universe when ye've made such a fine job o' directin' yer affairs yerself."

Carleton blew out a breath and cast him a rueful glance. "I've certainly done that."

"Yer trouble is ye've held command o'er others most o' yer adult life, Jon. Ye're used to bein' in control. But ye still canna see what the Almighty sees nor understand what he does."

He pushed slowly to his feet and came to Carleton's side. Standing beside him, his hand on Carleton's shoulder, he said, "Ye've yet to learn the hardest lesson o' all—one I had to learn through much grief, one all o' us who follow the Savior must come to understand: Our life's meanin' and purpose is not to be found in any person or place or possession or power, but in Christ alone."

Taking a shaky breath, Carleton bent his head. *The hardest lesson,* he mused, pierced again by the whisper that had accused him that night in the forest: *You have not yet learned.*

His voice muffled, he said, "Black Hawk told me that I'd wander all my life, that I'd never find a home either among my people or among the Long Knives."

McLeod nodded. "He understood the truth o' it. God calls his children to live as strangers and aliens on this earth."

Carleton looked up, his chest painfully constricted. "But others have homes and families, James. Why am I condemned to live forever so when this longing for the peace of my people and for the comfort of a wife and children torments me without ceasing? How have you? You've never remarried. Have you no hope that one day you'll again find the sweet love you once found comfort in?"

McLeod's countenance reflected his own pain. "Nae, I've not given up the hope. But God requires more o' some than o' others for his own inscrutable purposes, and so I had to learn to want his will afore my own. When he broke my pride, he called me to minister to others, whether in joy or in sorrow, and to trust him in the doin' o' it. We dinna seek an earthly home, Jon, but a heavenly country that we receive by faith and a city that hath foundations, whose builder and maker is God."

Drawing him gently around, McLeod placed both hands on Carleton's shoulders. "Give him your whole trust for the days ahead. E'en when ye dinna understand. E'en when ye canna see the end o' it. That's what he's been waitin' for. The Father who gives good gifts to his children has a good future in store for ye, but ye must trust him! Seek first his kingdom and his righteousness, and though it may yet take a while, though he may test ye sorely, if ye'll endure, he'll surely give ye the deepest desires o' yer heart."

CARLETON RODE SLOWLY down the line of troops standing at attention in the freezing dawn light. Spotted Pony and Andrews flanked him, with Stowe and Briggs and the entire party of the brigade's remaining warriors following close behind, each resplendent in his finest dress. At the rear trailed the long pack train loaded with goods.

This morning Carleton also had donned his most richly beaded and quilled buckskins and heavy winter gloves and moccasins. His *opa-wa-ka,* three snowy eagle feathers, was affixed to the crown of his head. Although he took little notice of the bitter cold, by habit he had wrapped his bearskin around him against the icy wind.

He returned the men's salute and nodded to colonels Moghrab and Farris at the head of their regiments. As he passed McLeod, he met the chaplain's piercing look with a firm one.

The invisible sun lifted above the horizon behind dark, scudding clouds as he rode from the camp at the van of his party and headed toward the Delaware's ford. Every nerve thrilled to the familiar lure of the wild, of the forest and of his people, and he recognized something ruthless, even cruel in his soul: the mysterious power of the beautiful, brutal, savagery of untamed nature. Since his first encounter with the Shawnee as a youth, it had called him back to the wilderness again and again. Even the great passion that bound him to Elizabeth could not subdue it.

Yet she exerted an equal magnetic sway over his soul as constant as that of the moon on the restless sea. At times he felt as though these two opposing forces tore so powerfully at his spirit that they would rend him in twain. Again, as on that first journey back to the Shawnee after Pathfinder rescued him from the Seneca, he was back in that same place, riding farther and farther from her, not knowing what the future held for them—if anything at all.

His conversation with McLeod the previous night nagged unceasingly at him. Unable to sleep, he had turned the chaplain's words over in his mind with increasing conviction: trust or doubt? Steadfast faith or a falling away?

*What power has faith without trust?* he questioned.

He felt as though, like the patriarch Jacob, he wrestled with God at the crossing of the Jabbock River. He saw clearly now that for his entire life he had swung one way, and then the other, like a ship without a rudder.

It was not that he did not believe. He did, to the very core of his soul. But that more was needed than simple belief now impressed itself deeply on his heart. He had reached a point at which he had to decide, and then live out that choice without turning back.

Teissèdre had been right in saying that Carleton was afraid that if he trusted God—truly trusted—the Almighty would disappoint him.

Would capriciously refuse to give him what he most longed for. Would reject him as unworthy of his love.

As though a blinding light shone over him, he knew the truth of it suddenly: That God had accepted him at the cross, that nothing else was wanting, but that he had remained willfully blind. Yes, and proud.

Disappointment, he saw now, arose from a lack of understanding of what was most important, not from the Father's failure to freely provide it. He must choose to trust that the gifts God gave him were the very best for him. For only the One who had made him could know that.

For some minutes, he rode ahead in silence, pondering what *was* most important to him. At last, as they approached the ford, feeling as though his hip, like Jacob's, had also been put out of joint, he cried silently, *Lord, I want to trust you with an undivided heart. Will you give me that great faith? Truly, it's the only gift I desire from you.*

Abruptly he turned Devil out of the line of warriors, and drew to a halt at the side of the road, watching them pass by him with questioning looks. He nodded assurance to Andrews and Spotted Pony, and with an exchange of puzzled glances, they led the column on to the ford.

Wheeling his stallion, for a long moment Carleton gazed hard to the east, the bleak landscape blurring before his eyes. He drew in a deep breath and let it out, feeling at last the certainty of his decision even as he quailed at its import.

*From hence I will trust you, my Lord and my God. Yea, even though I never see her dear face again, this day and always I will put my trust in you alone.*

He could no longer put off what fear had kept him from. Hand shaking, he pulled off his gloves, drew Elizabeth's letter from the pouch on his belt, and broke the seal.

*Dearest of my heart,*

*There are no words to tell you how deeply grieved I am that I cannot look into your eyes and beg your forgiveness. I meant to spare you the very thing that resulted in your being hurt even more deeply. Yet your sweet letter assures me that you've forgiven me even so, and I cling to that.*

*How great a void your absence has left! Everywhere I turn, I miss your presence and ache to see you. Yet though the miles may separate us in body for a time, they can never divide our hearts.*

*Do you remember that night when, after such a long absence, I found you again? I promised then that if you chose to stay with your people, I'd stay with you. My mind has not changed, my love. It's my decision to make—not my parents' nor yours. I choose it freely, but only if you are willing. I swore never to be a burden to you, and that resolution will not change.*

*Please don't think you do me harm by any division between my parents and me. I know someday they'll come to understand. But even should they not, you are the one I choose as my husband, for God brought you to me, and I'll never regret any price that allows us to be one.*

*Jonathan, no matter where you go, my soul will cleave to you and to you alone until my last breath. I pray with you that God in his mercy will keep us both safe and bring us back to each other again. May it be soon, beloved! Until then—*

*All my heart and my prayers go with you.*
*Beth*

He folded the page and pressed it to his heart, fighting for breath against the agony that cleft him. There was not time nor were there words to answer her. And a deep sense that he was not to, that God was working in her life as well as his, and that anything he might say or do would interfere in that working, stayed him.

Only God could bridge the chasm that lay between them. If it was his will. Carleton had to trust her also into his Lord's keeping, not knowing where the future would lead them.

Wiping the tears from his eyes, he whispered brokenly, "Farewell, heart of my heart. Fare thee well! May the Almighty keep you safe in the shadow of his wings all the days of your life."

Blindly he thrust the letter back into his pouch, pulled on his gloves, and reined Devil hard around. Then turning his face to the west, he spurred forward toward the ford and the path that lay before him.

## Chapter Forty

*Late February*

ELIZABETH SLIPPED OUT OF BED and, shivering, pushed aside the
heavy draperies at the window overlooking the side yard. Drawing
a blanket around her shoulders and legs and letting the curtains fall
closed behind her, she settled on the draft-chilled window seat, breath
pluming in the frigid air, arms clasped around her knees. A longing for
spring to arrive, for sunshine to beam from a blue sky, for green grass
and budding trees and birdsong gripped her with piercing intensity.

The scene outside did nothing to lighten her melancholy. At a little
distance, dense mist shrouded the landscape. Nearer at hand, the visible
expanse of yard and garden lay covered in crusted drifts of icy snow,
except where the servants had cleared the carriageway to the stables.
Along the estate's eastern perimeter, the fog-blurred branches of the
denuded trees and shrubbery intertwined amid the snowy pines gave the
scene an even more ghostly look in the early morning hush.

It was the next to last week of February. No letter had ever arrived
from Carleton. She had spent much time in prayer, but although her
heart continued to soften toward her parents, the great emptiness that
Carleton once filled had only grown deeper and more painful.

At the end of January a beautiful new pianoforte had been delivered
to the house. When her parents first led her into the library to see it,

fury had surged through her. It had taken all her willpower to restrain the angry charge that they thought they could buy her affections from Carleton very cheaply if they believed any object could ever replace his love.

But seeing their delight in giving her this gift, she had quickly been overcome by shame. They knew she was grieving, and because they loved her and felt deeply their powerlessness to repair what had been broken, simply wanted to find some way to comfort her. So she swallowed her pride and thanked them with a humble spirit.

Unwillingly she had forced herself to begin playing again, tutored by an excellent teacher her mother engaged from the village. Abby had joined her in taking lessons, and this had become a particular joy as she turned often to Elizabeth for help when she practiced.

In fact, music had not only become as great a solace to Elizabeth as before, but also served to bring Carleton closer to her heart. She kept his violin at her bedside along with his miniature portrait to hold when she prayed for him. She had found courage to take out his sheet music and a hymn book he had brought with him from England and left behind at her parents' Boston town house when the British arrested him for treason.

In the latter the text of a hymn by Charles Wesley titled "Temptation" brought a measure of encouragement and steadiness each time she read it. Now as she stared out the window into the foggy dawn, the hymn's words crept into her thoughts. It comforted her to think that they had been precious to Carleton as well.

*Jesus, lover of my soul,*
*let me to thy bosom fly,*
*while the nearer waters roll,*
*while the tempest still is high;*
*hide me, O my Savior, hide,*
*till the storm of life is past;*

*safe into the haven guide,*
*O receive my soul at last!*

*Other refuge have I none;*
*hangs my helpless soul on thee;*
*leave, ah! leave me not alone,*
*still support and comfort me.*
*All my trust on thee is stayed,*
*all my help from thee I bring;*
*cover my defenseless head*
*with the shadow of thy wing. . . .*

She had once found him after many months of uncertainty and despair, she reminded herself. Surely she could do so again. Hope rose in her breast at the thought.

All that wearisome winter she had been careful to follow her father's and Carleton's instructions exactly. The physical strain she had endured and the specter of the American prisoners' suffering, coupled with the pain of Carleton's absence, had robbed her entirely of appetite. Yet she forced down as much food as she could and had regained some weight and strength.

She had also kept to the house until the previous Sunday morning, when with her father's permission she had ridden in the chariot, warmly bundled, the short distance to First Church. To attend worship with all her family after more than two years had been another sweet solace for her aching heart.

Spring was not far off now, and if Carleton did not come or write by the time warm weather returned, she decided she would go to Valley Forge. If Isaiah's duties kept him from accompanying her, she was certain he would help her find someone trustworthy to conduct her to Grey Cloud's Town. And if Carleton refused to return, she would stay with him as she had promised.

With a sigh, she reined in her runaway thoughts. She had earnestly pledged to submit to God's will instead of willfully pursuing her own path as she had far too often, with disastrous results. She could not foresee the consequences this time either.

"Not my will, Lord Jesus," she whispered. "Let thine be done, and I will praise you no matter what comes."

Unconsciously she rested her brow against the cold glass. After a moment her gaze sharpened, caught by movement among the trees below. She sat up, startled.

A swirl of mist wrapped the trees, obscuring her sight. When the movement was not repeated, she concluded that she must have been mistaken.

She began to turn away, but arrested when the shadowy form of a man materialized suddenly out of the shifting fog below and directly across from her window, moving stealthily through the withered, close-grown vegetation. She saw him for only an instant before he vanished from sight again: Tall and broad-shouldered, he was covered from head to foot in a grey cloak with the hood drawn over his head, which rendered him almost invisible.

Although he had turned slightly to glance toward the house, she had not been able to make out his features, shaded by his hood. Yet something in his stance and movements resembled Carleton's so strongly that she stared, stunned, at the place where he had disappeared.

Heart pounding so hard her hand shook, she hastily scrubbed the fog of her breath from the pane and craned her neck in an effort to get a clearer glimpse. Farther along the overgrown border toward the stables, she saw snow drop from a branch as it sprang back into place.

Was it an apparition? Traveling such a distance through winter storms, Carleton could not have reached Grey Cloud's Town much before now, at the earliest. To return so quickly was impossible.

Had something happened to keep him from going after all? Who else would have reason to lurk beneath her window?

Suddenly certain that it had to be Carleton, she threw off the blanket and ran to the armoire, pulled out her cloak, and swept it around her shoulders, clumsily tying the ribbons at the neck. The floor was icy, and she hastily caught up a pair of shoes and carried them with her into the passage. Hearing the murmur of her parents' voices from their chamber down the hall, she eased the door shut behind her.

She flew down the stairs and to the back door without making a sound. Her father's riding boots, newly polished, stood on the rug just inside the entry. She discarded her shoes and, leaning against the wall, jerked the boots on, every nerve urging her to greater haste before Carleton could vanish again, perhaps forever.

Behind her in the kitchen, blocked from view by the angle of the wall, she could hear the cook and maids walking back and forth, talking softly, and the crackle of the fire. The outer door was unlocked, and pulling her hood over her head, she stepped outside.

She was instantly engulfed in dense fog. Damp cold seeped through shift and cloak as though she wore nothing. Colors muted and objects near at hand blurred into indistinct shapes, while everything beyond a few yards lay concealed from view. The world seemed to hang suspended in a breathless, expectant hush as though it awaited something she could not fathom.

She found it difficult to breathe, trembled so hard that stamping through the icy drifts in the oversized boots proved difficult. She wanted to call Carleton's name but feared that if she did, he might go away and she would never find him.

"Jonathan—oh, Jonathan, please don't go," she whispered, stumbling on uneven ground along the hedge bordering the garden.

Just then a light breeze wafted in from the bay, shifting the streamers of mist enough that she could see through them all the way down to the barn and stables. A man stood at the back corner of the barn on the edge of the bluff, darkly outlined against the white mist rising behind him.

It was not the same one she had seen, she was certain, for he did not wear a cloak. And before the mist again swathed him from her view, she saw him raise a gun to his shoulder.

Instinctively she stepped back, her foot catching on the exposed roots of the giant, spreading oak behind her at the garden's end. From the corner of her eye she caught a bright flash among the trees along the carriageway to her right, and at the same instant the almost simultaneous crack of two rifle shots reverberated through the air. Her ankle twisted beneath her, and as she fell, she heard and felt a missile whine by, stinging her cheek and ripping the hood from her head.

She sat down hard in a snowdrift, the breath gone out of her. Before she could move, a man ran up from behind her, carrying a rifle, and bent to look into her face, his own as ashen as the snow.

"You all right, miss?" he panted.

She nodded, staring at him wide eyed. Taking her in with a quick, keen glance, he straightened and darted off, vanishing into the fog. If not for the muted sound of scuffling that reached her from the dark blur of the trees, she would have thought him a figment of her imagination.

"Beth! Where are you?" Her father's frantic shout echoed through the preternatural stillness.

She struggled to her feet, favoring her sore ankle, and grasped at the hedge to keep from falling again.

"Elizabeth!" her mother screamed from the direction of the back door. "Samuel, where is she? That sounded like gunshots!"

Elizabeth heard Abby's and Tess's fainter voices calling her name. Then her father was suddenly beside her, hair disheveled, clothed only in shirt, breeches, and shoes. Roughly he clasped her to his bosom.

"She's here! I have her!"

Holding her away from him, he ran his hands over her form as though to assure himself that she was not hurt. He touched her cheek, and when he drew back his hand, she saw that blood streaked his fingers. Clearly shaken, he stared at her as though too appalled to speak.

"I'm all right," she gasped.

Her mother, Tess, Abby, Sarah, and Jemma surrounded them, with the rest of the servants trailing behind. The clamor of exclamations and questions made Elizabeth's head ache.

"Let her talk!" her father cut them off. "Beth, what happened?"

When everyone quieted, she tipped her head and listened intently but heard no sound from the direction of the trees. It took several moments more for her to find her tongue.

"I . . . I saw someone . . . in the trees . . . over there. From upstairs, he looked like . . . like Jonathan." She gulped in air. "I came down to find him and . . . I saw someone with a rifle down by the barn. There was a flash from the trees, and then I was sitting on the ground. And another man—a stranger—bent over me and asked if I was all right. Then he ran off that way, and I heard . . . what sounded like people . . . fighting."

She glanced down, her mouth going dry. "See. There are his foot-prints."

Looking where she pointed, the others stared, open mouthed. Abby uttered a soft cry and threw her arms around Elizabeth's waist, while Sarah pressed in to lightly touch her cheek.

"Looks like you had a real close call, Miss 'Lizabeth. I'm sorry I wasn't there to stop you goin' out." She lifted the hood of Elizabeth's cloak and, shaking her head, pushed her finger through a hole in the fabric. "That there's where the bullet pass through."

Elizabeth started back as Sarah drew a pistol from beneath her apron. The others saw it, too, and her mother and Tess clapped their hands over their mouths.

"You can tell me later where you got that," her father said curtly, holding out his hand, "but for now give it to me. I'm going over there to see what I can find."

When Sarah reluctantly handed him the pistol, Anne protested, "Samuel, no! If someone's still there—"

Waving her to silence, he quickly checked the priming and cocked the weapon. "Take Beth and Abby back inside."

"No, Papa! I'm staying right here until you've safely returned."

"So am I," her mother insisted. She ordered the servants back into the house, then, with Tess supporting Elizabeth on her other side, Sarah and Jemma leading the way and Abby following, she helped Elizabeth to limp beneath the oak's spreading limbs, where they sheltered behind its thick trunk.

Dr. Howard gave them an anxious look but after a brief hesitation ran off, following the footprints in the snow. He quickly disappeared into the fog.

Elizabeth stared at Sarah, feeling numb. A number of times since Carleton had gone, Elizabeth had gained the impression that the housekeeper hovered over her. She had assumed it was because of her illness, but now she wondered.

"Sarah, what did you mean about stopping me from going out?"

Sarah glanced at her, then away. "Never mind," she said, compressing her lips in a firm line.

Caledonne's warning that she was in danger echoed suddenly in Elizabeth's mind, along with Carleton's more veiled charge to be very careful while he was gone. The suspicion that Sarah knew much more than she feigned seized Elizabeth.

With the others, she listened tensely to the sound of her father scuffing through the undergrowth beneath the trees. After several minutes, he came running back.

"Someone's walked along there. One set of tracks comes from the direction of the road, one set from here." He gestured toward the tracks along the garden. "Several more come up from the stables, and it looks like they dragged something—or someone—away with them. There's a trail of blood."

At the women's horrified exclamations, he urged them toward the house. "Go back inside and stay away from the windows."

He handed the pistol to Sarah. "Where'd you get this?"

"Gen'l Carleton give it to me."

Elizabeth bit her lip as the others stiffened.

Although her father's mouth tightened, he let the matter lie. "Keep this with you, and if any strangers try to break in, don't waste time asking questions. I'm going to get my pistols and go down to the stables and barn to see if anyone's still there."

"Bah! Do not trouble yourself, monsieur. I assure you that will be entirely unnecessary."

Elizabeth whirled around with the others. She stared hard at the darkly shadowed figure who strolled toward them from around the corner of the garden.

"Who are you?" her father demanded, reaching to take back Sarah's pistol.

As the man emerged fully from the shifting mists, Elizabeth's mouth fell open. "Monsieur Teissèdre! What are you doing here?"

Dr. Howard scowled. "You know this man?"

"It's all right, Papa. He's Jonathan's agent. He trusts him with everything."

"You've naught to fear," the Frenchman broke in. "General Carleton set his marines on guard to protect you. This man and his accomplices who came this morning—"

Tess pressed her hand to her bosom. "Accomplices!"

"Jonathan told us nothing of this!" Elizabeth's mother exclaimed.

Teissèdre doffed his hat and bent his rotund form in a slight bow. "He did not wish to distress you and your daughter or for you to live in fear."

Dr. Howard rounded on Sarah. "You knew all about it!"

Narrow-eyed, she nodded. "He don't want to tell you. He don't know what you do if you learn Miss 'Lizabeth be in danger 'cause o' him."

"Why doesn't that surprise me?" Tess questioned dryly.

"It isn't his fault if I'm in danger," Elizabeth protested. "Howe alone is responsible—"

"Ah, but you're mistaken, mademoiselle. General Howe is being recalled to England, and General Clinton will take command. These men who've been sent to attack you are his agents."

"How could you possibly know that?" Dr. Howard demanded.

Teissèdre turned an enigmatic glance on him, but before he could respond, Elizabeth asked quickly, "You've heard from Jonathan?"

"Alas, no . . . not since he left here. You are aware General Washington sent him to the Shawnee?"

Elizabeth's heart constricted. "Yes. He's gone then?"

Teissèdre inclined his head. "When I am assured of your safety, I'll go to find him." He came to take Elizabeth's hand. Fixing her in a piercing gaze, he said, "This is not the first attempt on your life, mademoiselle. The general's marines have stopped all the others, but no one can anticipate every device of the enemy. This one has come too close."

She drew in her breath sharply and glanced toward the others. The color had drained from their faces. She felt Abby's arms tighten around her.

"You cannot safely stay here any longer," Teissèdre continued quietly. "Caledonne has come to take you to France."

IF YOU ENJOYED this story and would like to offer feedback, we invite you to email the editor, Joan M. Shoup, at jmshoup@gmail.com. We'd love to receive your comments.

We always appreciate thoughtful reviews posted on the book's detail page on Amazon, Barnes and Noble, Christianbook.com, and other  online sites. Thank you for telling other readers about this series!

# Glossary

*74:* a common warship of the eighteenth century originally designed by the French to carry 74 guns and later adopted by all major navies.

*50:* an eighteenth-century warship that carried 50 guns.

*banyan:* a calf-length, Persian-inspired, silk or flannel men's robe equivalent to a dressing gown, worn at home during the day over the clothing as an alternative to a coat or jacket, or at night over a nightshirt before retiring to bed.

*Baptist Meeting House:* present-day Hopewell, New Jersey.

*berth deck or lower gun deck:* the deck below the main deck.

*bulwark:* the side of a ship above the upper deck.

*close-hauled:* with sails set for sailing as nearly against the wind as the ship will go.

*courses:* lowest sails on a square-rigged ship.

*cutter:* a small, single-masted vessel, fore-and-aft rigged with two or more headsails, a bowsprit, and a mast set farther back than that of a sloop.

*Erebus:* the personification of darkness in Greek mythology; a place of darkness in the underworld on the way to Hades.

*futtock:* the rib of a ship.

*gun deck or main deck:* the deck immediately below the upper deck.

*macaroni:* dandy, fop.

*night dress:* a woman's casual dress worn at home at night.

*quartering:* sailing nearly before the wind.

*ratlines:* the small traverse ropes attached to the shrouds of a ship in order to form the steps of a rope ladder.

*reef:* to reduce the area of a sail by rolling or folding a portion of it.

*shrouds:* ropes supporting a ship's mast.

*yards:* a spar tapered on both ends and attached to a mast to spread the head of a square sail.

*York Island:* The original Dutch name of Manhattan Island

## Appendix

### Shawnee Characters

*Black Fish:* the Chillicothe sept's primary sachem, who favored war with the Americans.

*Blue Jacket:* a sachem of the Piqua sept who attempted to form an alliance with other Native American tribes to stop the Americans from forcing them out of Ohio Territory.

*Cornstalk:* the principal sachem of the Maquachake, one of the five sub-nations of the Shawnee, and of the Shawnee tribe as a whole. After defeat in Lord Dunmore's War in 1774, he refused to fight the Whites and counseled the tribe to honor the peace treaty. Murdered at Fort Randolph on November 10, 1777.

*Elinipscico:* a son of Cornstalk murdered at Fort Randolph.

*Petalla:* a Shawnee warrior murdered at Fort Randolph.

*Red Hawk:* a Shawnee sachem murdered at Fort Randolph.

# Shawnee Terms

*Ha'kwi kiishthwa:* the Severe Moon; January.

*longhouse:* a long, bark-covered dwelling that usually housed several families of a clan.

*Long Knives:* the Americans, whose soldiers carried swords.

*Kini kiishthwa:* the Long Moon; November.

*Matchemenetoo:* the Bad Spirit, the devil

*Melo'kami:* spring.

*Miyamithiipi:* Miami River

*Moneto:* the Shawnee's Supreme Being of the universe.

*motchitteheckie:* evil-minded people.

*Pelewathiipi:* Ohio River.

*Pepoonwi:* winter.

*Pooshkwiitha:* the Half Moon; April.

*Shemanese:* white men.

*Shkipiye kwiitha:* the Sap Moon; March.

*Washilatha kiishthwa:* the Eccentric Moon; December.

*wannine:* crazy, insane.

*wigewa:* a large rectangular or square dwelling for one family framed with poles and overlaid with bark, woven mats, or animal hides.